Many Hands

an anthology of polyamorous erotica

Duck Prints Press, LLC
Schenectady, NY

Edited by boneturtle, E. Conway, Rhosyn Goodfellow, Catherine E. Green, and Nina Waters.
Significant contributions also made by Aceriee, E. V. Dean, Lacey Hays, A. L. Heard, Alec J. Marsh, Pallas Perilous, Rachael L. Young, Alessa Riel, and others.

Print manuscript formatting by Hermit Writes.
E-book formatting by Nina Waters.

Published by Duck Prints Press, LLC
Schenectady, New York
duckprintspress.com

ISBN (ePub): 978-1-962488-17-4
ISBN (PDF): 978-1-962488-16-7
ISBN (Trade Paperback): 978-1-962488-15-0

Contents

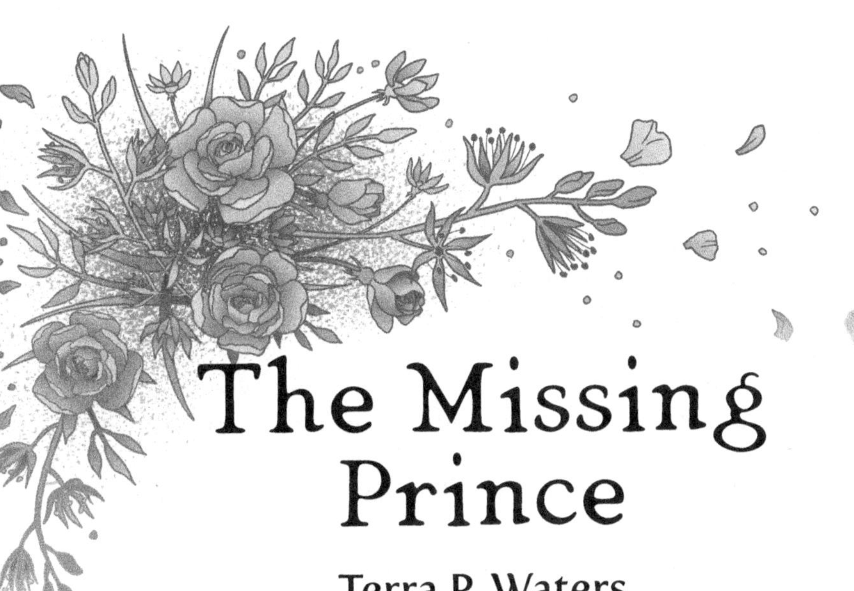

The Missing Prince

Terra P. Waters

action and adventure, arranged marriage, bisexual, blow job, cunnilingus, established relationship, f/f/m/m, f/m, f/m/m, fantasy, fuck or die, hand job, kidnapping, past tense, penis in anus sex, penis in vagina sex, pirate, royalty, soulmate tattoos, soulmates, telepathic communication, third person limited point of view, twosome + twosome = foursome

The afternoon sun warmed everything it touched, though the biting wind undid most of the sun's magnificent effort. A young woman stood on the steps of her mother's palace, shivering in her sleeveless pink silk gown and cursing herself for leaving her fur shawl behind. Her curly black hair would have sheltered her neck and shoulders, but this event required it be up in an intricate style. The gems on her hairpins sparkled in the sunlight like stars shining amid an inky sky.

"Ala," said the man beside her, placing a hand at the small of her back, "I'll get your shawl."

With a decisive shake of her head, Ala said, "I need you with me when he gets here." She turned and grasped Kormac's hand tightly. When he smiled, a fan of creases appeared at the outer edges of his eyes. Though he was only seven years her senior, time had been less kind to his skin than hers. "Please?"

"Your mother doesn't want me here," Kormac said.

"What she wants doesn't change our matching soul marks." Ala brushed her thumb against the rose-shaped mark on the underside of Kormac's forearm. Nodding toward the grand avenue that approached the palace, she said, "There's a rumor Prince Théophile also has a commoner soulmate."

"Do you think it's true?"

Ala nodded. "Otherwise, why would he agree to marry an *impure* princess?"

Kormac chuckled. "Should we let him know just how impure you are?"

Though her eyes rolled, Ala leaned against her consort. "I'm sure *that* would be the perfect topic to bring up at tonight's state dinner with the prince and his ambassador." She kissed his neck. "Just how many times we've ravished each other."

The rumble of his laughter was the distant thunder that promised a summer storm. Five years living together as soulmates, and Ala still shuddered at the thought of getting him alone. She turned toward his solid chest, grasped the lapel of his black silk jacket, and rose onto her toes—

—only to be thwarted by the fanfare heralding Prince Théophile's arrival. His procession turned onto the boulevard, a phalanx of cavalry proceeding a gilded carriage drawn by four ebony-black horses. Several simpler carriages followed the prince's, each drawn by matching sets of steeds.

"Beautiful," Ala breathed, standing straighter.

"I hope you mean the horses."

"You know I mean the horses, love."

A hiss drew Ala's attention to her mother's admonishing look. "Please don't ruin this. Without royal heirs, you might as well hand your throne to your Bellsbourgh cousins. I've worked long years since your ruined engagement to—"

"I know, mother," Ala murmured, keeping a perfect smile on her face despite her annoyance. "You've made me well aware of the stakes."

A curt nod was her mother's only reply before she turned toward the prince's arrival. His coach stopped at the foot of the stairs. A footman opened the door and held up his hand to help the occupant out, but the man who stepped from the coach didn't take it. His light skin contrasted with the brown curls atop his head and a gold-and-ruby circlet perched there like it floated on a cloud. His face was rather square, with a thin nose and thick, pale lips. Dark eyes looked up and met Ala's before the woman beside him—Ambassador Freeman—stole his attention. Ala felt a pang of envy toward the ambassador for the theft of the prince's gaze.

Ala made herself take the slow breaths she'd forgotten to inhale while enraptured. She murmured to Kormac, "He's handsomer than I expected."

"I…agree?" Kormac's tone caught her attention; she would have to ask him about it later.

Two guards escorted Prince Théophile and Ambassador Freeman up the palace stairs. The thick red carpet rolled out for the occasion muffled their footfalls, and they arrived at the top quickly. Théophile looked younger than his purported age of twenty-eight, his body thin under his silks and furs.

When the ambassador introduced him, Théophile greeted them. "Your Highness, Queen Sedrina of the mighty nation of Traulor"—his voice was deeper than Ala expected, his vowels slightly accented as his lips moved around them gracefully—"I bring humble greetings from my mother, Queen Brunhilde of Athium. I thank you for your gracious hospitality and look forward to making your acquaintance."

The queen gave him her hand, and he took it, bowing to press his forehead against their clasped hands.

"Welcome, Prince Théophile. I would like you to meet my daughter, Crown Princess Ala'amour of Traulor."

He reached to take Ala's outstretched hand but stepped on his robe and stumbled. Kormac shot forward, catching him by the hand and elbow before he could trip down the stairs. "My apologies, Your Grace," Kormac murmured as he steadied the prince. He gave the prince's guards an apologetic nod, let go, and stepped back with his hands up.

Ala turned to give her hand to the prince once more, but his eyes lingered on Kormac. Was the interest she saw there the reason Queen Brunhilde had agreed to the political marriage? But the prince had a commoner soulmate. Was it a man? Was he among the personnel in the carriages below?

When Ala's mother cleared her throat, Théophile tore his eyes away from Kormac and set them on Ala.

Their fingers met. His skin touched hers, and a jolt of electricity shot through her. Her gasp tasted like a storm as Prince Théophile's eyes widened. Ala gripped his hand, pulling it closer and twisting so she could watch the rose blossoms unfurl on his arm, two of them, left- and right-leaning, joining the upright one he must've already had.

"How?" she asked, meeting his eyes again, falling into the honey brown of them.

"I thought you already…"

Showing him her arm and her soulmate mark revealed it now transformed to include a right-leaning blossom that mirrored the one she shared with Kormac. "I do." She dragged her fingers across his mark again; he shuddered. "With this third flower, *you* must already…"

He answered her with slight hysteria in his voice. "I *do*!"

Beside them, the queen spoke through clenched teeth. "The nation is watching. Turn and wave to the people."

Théophile let go of Ala's hand, sweeping his cape up and facing the crowd gathered at the base of the stairs. He waved, and when Ala did as well, the onlookers cheered.

"Come," said the queen, turning away from the crowd and taking her guard's outstretched elbow. "We have much to discuss."

Ala thought to reach for Kormac, but Théophile offered her his arm. Ala took it, and they followed the queen into the palace. She felt Kormac's eyes on her back as the Athiumite ambassador and her guards trailed their prince, followed by Traulor's ambassador to Athium, Lord Cormier, then the closest of the Bellsbourgh cousins: her late father's brother and his sons.

As they walked, Ala leaned toward Théophile and said, "Having more than one soulmate is supposed to be a myth."

"I've never heard of it before." he said, his accent thicker and his voice less certain than it had been during his greeting.

"I'd ask if that mark of yours was some sort of trick"—she shook her head—"but I felt the connection form."

"That man," he said, looking over his shoulder. "Your man who caught me, he is…?"

"My soulmate, and my consort, Kormac Montgomery."

Théophile looked back again and said, "I—I think he is mine, as well."

Ala caught Kormac's eye. "You touched both of us today. That means…" His bushy eyebrows rose, then understanding crossed his face. With a small, shy smile, he said, "It will not be a hardship, Your Grace. Not for me, anyway."

Ala chuckled at the compliment and tried not to think of the ways Théophile could fit into her and Kormac's lovemaking. Then she took a sharp breath as she stole another glance at his mark. "You have another soulmate." He nodded. "Who are they? What are they like?

Théophile cleared his throat and nodded toward the queen. "Perhaps a question better left for another time."

Regretfully, she agreed, "Another time."

Once they were ensconced in the south drawing room, the queen asked their guards to leave. The only people in the room were Ala, Kormac, Prince Théophile, Lord Cormier, and Ambassador Freeman. Queen Sedrina addressed them. "We need to appear in the ballroom shortly, or there will be talk." She approached Théophile and held out her hand. "Give me your arm, please."

Théophile obeyed.

Inspecting his new soulmark, Sedrina frowned, deep creases framing her mouth. "How did you arrange this? This trick is unnecessary. The arrangements for the wedding have been made. You knew coming here that Ala was already marked, as you were purported to be. Is that why you adjusted the design? To augment the deception with this preposterous multiple soulmate *farce*?"

Théophile gave his ambassador a wide-eyed look, then turned toward Ala. "Y-your Highness, it is no trick. I'm as surprised as you."

"I felt it, Mother," Ala said, stepping between the queen and her betrothed. "The bond is real. We have to…" Her cheeks flushed, and she couldn't make her tongue work. Sidestepping the exact words, Ala said, "Théophile should stay with us tonight."

"Before the wedding?" asked Ambassador Freeman. "How do we know this isn't some trick of *yours*? There's been resistance among your people to the match. A soulmark would do wonders for quieting that talk." She shook her head. "The wedding must come first."

Sedrina held the ambassador's eyes for a long moment before saying, "Fine. The wedding is tomorrow, in any case."

A sharp pain stabbed Ala in the heart. "But we have to—" She took Théophile's hand, marveling at the sense of calm that suffused her. She opened her mouth to continue her argument, but between her mother's glare and that of the ambassador, she gave in. Slipping her hand from Théophile's, she said, "Tomorrow."

Théophile's nod showed disappointment, but he acquiesced. "Perhaps there will be some time to get to know each other?"

The queen laughed. "The noble families are waiting for us so the banquet can begin. All of this"—she raised an eyebrow at Ala—"can wait."

Ala nodded. There was nothing she wanted less than to parade her fiancé around the aristocracy so they could judge him, but given the circumstances, it was the least bad option. She shared a glance with Kormac, who had made an art of keeping out of the queen's way. The wry turn of his lips promised a litany of held-back thoughts would come Ala's way when they were alone.

Théophile held out his arm, and Ala took it, letting him lead her from the drawing room. They walked in the queen's wake, the ambassadors behind them; Kormac fell in line with the guards farther back. Théophile murmured, "I know what the ambassador has told me about you and why my father agreed to this match, but not much else. I'd like to learn more."

"I..." Her face on fire, Ala said, "You really should learn more about Kormac. Before he was my consort, he was an officer of the royal guard."

"Did he guard you?" Théophile asked, his voice warm and breathless, as if he thought the idea cute.

"Not really." She patted his arm, then leaned closer, whispering, "He was a spy. He spent several years in Carth, gathering information."

Théophile looked over his shoulder at Kormac, like he sought spy craft on his face or in the manner of his walk. "Our spies, the few that we have, are also assassins. Is he...?"

"Trained to kill?"

Théophile gave her a wide-eyed nod.

"Oh, yes. He won't tell me the details because I'm not yet the queen, but he's killed before."

Théophile shuddered. "Oh, my."

Ala worried she'd put too much enthusiasm into her voice, but the prince didn't seem scared so much as turned on. Well, he *was* their soulmate, after all.

The scent of skin blossomed under Ala's nose; the sweat-salt tang danced across her tongue. Lips as soft as rose petals teased her mouth. A hard length moved inside her, the perfect ache of pleasure rolling with her hips. Hands held hers against a smooth chest, the reverberations of a moan tickling her fingertips.

Kormac's presence was steady against her back; it wasn't him below her. Théophile lay there, his back arched, neck long. He took one hand from the tangle with hers and used it to brace himself against the headboard. "Please…" he murmured, gasping when she rolled her hips again.

"He sounds so pretty when he begs," Kormac rumbled, his lips hot against her shoulder.

"You want more, my lovely prince?" Ala said, watching Théophile shudder.

"Yes!"

Behind her, Kormac lifted Théophile's knees, tilting Ala forward onto his chest. When Kormac thrust in, Ala felt Théophile's cock twitch inside her.

"I think he likes that, love," she said over her shoulder.

Kormac rumbled and thrust again, his belly hitting the small of her back.

Théo threw his head back and moaned.

Ala woke unsatisfied but eager for the wedding to take place, if only so they could get to the wedding night that much quicker. Kormac's hand was on her waist; she laced her fingers with his. He stretched, his groan a low rumble against her back.

"We're dreaming about him," she said, burying her face against his chest and throwing her leg over his hip.

"Mm-hm." Kormac grasped her leg behind the knee and shifted her closer.

She had just tilted her face up to meet him in a kiss when there was a loud knock on their bedchamber door. "Your Grace? Captain Montgomery? It's an emergency!"

"It better be," Ala muttered, rolling away from Kormac and toward the armoire. She took out a dressing gown and pulled it on while Kormac put on a pair of pants and a loose shirt.

He met her eyes and waited for her nod before opening the door. "The princess needs to prepare for the wedding."

The page on the other side of the door was a young man. He held out a card with a trembling hand. "The Athiumite embassy sent word. They were attacked before dawn, and Prince Théophile is missing."

"*Missing*?" Ala's stomach dropped as she stalked forward. Kormac took the card from the page and glanced at it, then handed it to Ala as she joined him at the door. "Has the queen been informed? Do we know who's behind the attack?"

The page shook his head. "I'm sorry, Your Grace. I just have the note."

Ala told the boy, "Inform the queen immediately!"

"Yes, Your Highness."

The boy took off. Kormac closed the door and began gathering his things. "Love, if we don't find him in the next two and a half days…"

"I know." She set the card on a table and went to her closet. The gown from last evening hung there beside her wedding gown. Ala reached past them for a pair of plain brown riding trousers. "We have to find him, or we're dead."

The queen and several generals were in the war room when Ala and Kormac arrived. When she saw Ala, she asked, "What are you wearing?"

"We're going—"

"You're not going anywhere," her mother insisted before gesturing to Kormac. "Your consort can join the effort, but you're my heir. You can't risk your life."

"My life is already at risk. If we don't find him in time…"

The queen scoffed. "Don't be stupid. You've already bonded with your soulmate. Whatever magic we saw yesterday won't kill you. It can't."

Ala opened her mouth to argue, but a look from her mother promised serious consequences to continuing. She pursed her lips and fumed but kept silent.

Filling the vacuum left by Ala's silence, Kormac asked, "What do we know? Were there any witnesses? Any clues who could have done this?"

"Not yet," said General Martisk. "I've sent guards to investigate."

General Blanchet said, "If this was done with ransom in mind, we should hear from the kidnappers soon."

"We have several enemies in common with the Athiumites." The queen sighed and set a hand on the map spread over the table. "It could've been any of them."

"How do we find out?" Ala asked. "The longer we stand here speculating, the farther his kidnappers will have taken him."

"You're right," Kormac said, squeezing her arm. "I'll take this to Petikan."

"When you see the spymaster," the queen said with a nod of approval, "tell him to report to me as soon as he's dispatched his agents."

"I'll go with you," Ala said to Kormac. At her mother's glare, she explained, "I can help Petikan organize whatever information comes in. I'm fully briefed on Athium's current affairs. After all, I was supposed to marry into the royal family today."

With another nod, the queen said, "The wedding will have to be postponed."

"Yes, Mother." Ala gave a perfunctory bow, then took Kormac's hand and led him from the room. Once they were out of earshot, Ala told him, "Have Liam prepare you travel rations so you can go after Théophile as soon as we learn who's behind this."

Kormac stopped, meeting Ala's eyes as he whispered, "You have to come with me."

Ala frowned. "You heard Mother. She wants me to stay here."

"But what happens if I find him without enough time to get him to you?"

"We die." Ala's mind slipped away from the thought of disobeying her mother like her hand would avoid a hot stove. "I can't just…run away. I'm the heir."

"You'll be a dead heir if we don't find Prince Théophile quickly."

"What if it is a trick? What if he's not really our soulmate?"

"We shared a dream with him last night."

"If it's possible to fake this mark"—she uncovered the recent additions to the soulmark on her skin—"it would be possible to fake a shared dream."

Kormac frowned, licked his lips, then said, "It's not just your life, love. If I don't get Théo back to you in time…even if he and I were together before—"

"You might lose two soulmates."

He grasped Ala's hand and brought it to his lips. "Losing a soulmate can drive wise men mad. Losing two? I wouldn't survive."

The thought of Kormac dying when she could've saved him by disobeying her mother strangled her heart. She put a hand to her aching chest and nodded. "I'm going with you. "

The scent of brine and rotting seaweed invaded Ala's nose. She pressed her face to Kormac's back and set her hand on his hip. His breath sounded too ragged for sleep. She moved her hand farther around him and found the skin covering Théophile's ribs. Kormac's wide fist engulfed his cock.

Wait.

This was a dream. In the waking world, they needed to *find* Théophile first. *Then* bed him.

Ala scrambled off the mattress and circled it until she could see Théophile's face. He was bound, blindfolded, and had a dirty gag in his mouth. The urge to play with him was strong, but she resisted, pulling out the gag and removing the blindfold. "Hello, love."

"Kiss me," he groaned. "Please, Princess…"

"Théophile," she said, grasping Kormac's wrist so he would stop moving his hand. "We're coming to get you, but we need your help. Where are you?"

"The port city. Channois. They say we'll sail with the noon tide." He turned his head toward the mattress, letting Kormac kiss his neck. "Oh, gods!"

She grasped his bound hands and squeezed them. "Is there anything else? Anything you want to tell us?" She looked past Kormac's shoulder and saw a shadow standing in the doorway.

"Hester," Théophile groaned, nodding toward the shadow. "Find Captain Hester, here in Channois. Her boat is The Blue Macaw. She'll help you find me."

Ala woke with a start, hissing with pain as her neck gave a twinge that radiated down her spine. As she got her bearings, she realized she still wore her traveler's disguise, and that she and Kormac had fallen asleep in the coach they'd commandeered for the trip south, following a tip from one of Petikan's spies. There was something important about the dream, something—

Ala gasped and shook her consort. "Wake up!"

"I know," he muttered drearily. "I'm here. I'm awake."

"We must go to Channois. That's where we need to find—" Her mind drew a blank. "I can't remember! How am I supposed to find her if I can't remember her name?"

"Hester," Kormac said, smiling when Ala threw herself into his arms. "Captain Hester. I remembered that much. And her ship, The Blue Macaw."

"Do you know how we find a specific ship in Channois?"

Kormac shrugged. "We go to the harbor and ask, I would imagine."

"If he's on a ship, we have to know what direction they're heading. We can't search the entire ocean."

"Whoever has him will have registered their destination with the harbormaster." He sat up, stretched his arms, and twisted, releasing a series of quiet pops from his spine. "Even if they paid the harbormaster to register a false destination, he'll know the real one."

She put her hands on his chest and leaned in, kissing him. "I'm glad you're with me. I'd be useless on this endeavor without you."

He gave her a sly smile and said, "I very much doubt that. In fact, I'm looking forward to letting you at the Channois harbormaster. I'd bet my last silver you'll be able to get that destination from him in less than a minute."

He grew quiet, smile falling away.

Ala laced her fingers with his. "What's troubling you?"

"Hester," he said, shaking his head. "She was with us last night. Watching."

Ala shivered as she remembered the shadow she'd seen. She looked at the mark on her arm. The rose she shared with Kormac was mirrored by the one they shared with Théophile.

When they met Hester, the pattern would be complete.

Kormac stood and opened the carriage door, calling their new destination to the driver.

Ala pulled back the curtain over the window and watched the passing forest. Her mark itched, and desperation built in her throat. There was so little time!

They changed horses mid-morning, leaving the carriage to ensure an earlier arrival in Channois. Too soon, the sun had passed the halfway mark in its journey across the sky. The tide was heading out, and Théophile's ship with it.

The city gates stood on the ridge above the water. It had been some time since she'd been to Channois, but the road down the hill was wide and unmistakable. At the end sat the docks, and beyond, the glittering ocean.

A half mile short of the docks, their horses could no longer speed through the dense traffic. They gave their horses to the city watchmen—Kormac's royal guard badge held off questions—and they continued to the harbor on foot. Kormac seemed to have a preternatural ability to arrive at a space between people just as it appeared. The desperation to find her new soulmate and cement the bond was a tight band around Ala's heart; it beat so hard she could practically hear it above the din of the crowd.

When the crowds parted, Kormac loosened his hold on Ala's hand, then dropped it when he approached the window of a building that faced the docks: the harbormaster's office. As he spoke to the comely young clerk, Ala took in their surroundings.

A dozen docked ships were visible.

There was a strange tickle at the back of her neck, and Ala swatted at it, thinking it a fly. As she turned to shoo it, her eyes lit on a woman passing from the street onto the docks. She wore a long sleeveless red coat that accentuated her curves and prominently displayed her thick arms. Her black hair fell in waves around her shoulders, and she wore a tri-point hat with a bright-yellow feather in the brim. When Ala glimpsed her face, it seemed familiar, like someone she should know.

A sudden urge to shout came over her. "Hester!"

The woman stopped and turned. The ground swayed under Ala's feet, and she couldn't see anything but the woman striding toward her. Hester's eyes were narrow, and her cheeks flushed pink as she approached. Did she remember sharing their dream the night before? Did she feel the same flutter in her chest at the sight of Ala, the same craving to reach out and—

The woman took Ala's hand, a spark of recognition coursing between them. "Who are you?" She narrowed her eyes. "How do I know you?"

Ala gently turned Hester's arm, baring the underside of her forearm to the sun. Her mark showed two flowers, one tilting right, one standing straight in the middle. She placed it next to Hester's, showing that she had three flowers now—the same two as Hester, plus the left-leaning flower she shared with Kormac. She kept her voice low as she said, "Théophile needs our help."

Hester's hazel eyes widened, then her jaw clenched. She nodded down to their arms. "This is a trick. They don't match."

"But there was only one rose until I touched you." Ala held her gaze. "Soulmate magic can't be replicated."

"I already have a soulmate."

"I did too."

Ala turned to Kormac, who seemed to sense her eyes on him as he turned away from the clerk and met her eye.

Hester gave a low whistle. "I'll entertain this farce for a few moments more." A chuckle slipped through Ala's lips. "What sort of trouble has my prince found himself in?"

While waiting for Kormac to finish with the harbormaster, Ala quickly explained their situation. "...and the worst part is, our bond hasn't been consummated."

Hester hissed, turning away from Ala. "I told Théo something bad was going to happen."

"It's not his fault."

She pursed her lips. "Two days?" Ala nodded. "We have less than a day to find him."

"He's on a ship. He told us last night they were sailing from this harbor at noon today."

Hester nodded as Kormac joined them. "They would've left with the tide."

"So we're not that far behind him." Ala pulled Kormac closer and told him, "This is Captain Hester."

Kormac gave Ala a lopsided grin. "Great job, love. I thought we'd be looking for hours." He held his hand out.

Hester gave Ala one last look before taking Kormac's hand. They both hissed, then sighed as Kormac pushed up his sleeve. It now matched

Ala's, with three flowers in a bunch. Hester's was the same.

"It should be impossible," Hester said. She shook her head. "In any case, we have a soulmate to save. Any idea in which direction the ship headed?"

Kormac said, "A little pressure on the harbormaster and he gave them up. They're heading north, toward Lomberg."

"The pirate city," Hester said with a chuckle, starting off at a brisk walk, forcing Ala and Kormac to follow on her heels. "I know the fastest way to get there."

"Can we go?" Ala asked. "Which is your ship?"

"The Blue Macaw," Hester said, pointing down the harbor the same direction they were walking. "Come on! They're hours ahead of us, and we'll need to dump weight to have a chance of catching up with them."

Ala reached between her legs, finding a head of soft, curly hair as its owner lapped along her folds and worried at her clit. At first, she sank into the pleasure, her breaths harsh, her hips twitching when the sensation became intense. She opened her eyes to search for Kormac, but he wasn't there. Neither was Hester.

She and Théophile were alone.

Ala fought the urge to give in into him; she pulled away.

"Please," he murmured, following her. "We don't have much time left. Let me spend my last few hours in your arms. Let me forget where my body is."

Ala pulled him into a tight embrace, tears rolling hot from her cheeks and onto his shirt. "You sound like you've given up."

"I've tried to reason with them," he said, cupping her face in his hands and meeting her eyes. "They think I'm lying. They think it's impossible that I'm about to die."

"Just…" Ala sighed and tried to think, fighting against the haziness of the dream. "We're on The Blue Macaw and chasing you as fast as we can. If you can get them to slow down or stop, it would help."

"How? I'm not a sailor."

Ala kissed him and said, "But your soulmate is. Haven't you learned anything about sailing from her?"

"I see her so infrequently," he said. "She tells me grand stories, never the boring bits about how a ship works."

"Then pretend you're in one of her stories," Ala said. "I want to rescue you, Théo. I want to pull you into my arms, but we aren't catching up fast enough. I need you to be your own hero."

He stepped back enough to look down at her, his eyes wide. "What if I try and they kill me?"

"Soulmate sickness is going to kill you anyway."

"Unless The Blue Macaw reaches me first."

"Théo." She gave him a hard look. "Were you taught, as I was, that we must be honorable? We must be a beacon of morality for our people? We must be polite?"

"Of course."

"Throw that out the window." Ala ignored Théophile's gasp. "I need you to be meaner than you think you can be. I need you to do whatever it takes to get free, to help us find you."

She watched emotions play out across his face until he made a decisive nod. Then he kissed Ala and said, "I think I'll enjoy having you be one of my soulmates."

"We've got to live that long first."

Théophile gave a hesitant smile, then kissed her again. "I'll see you soon."

When Ala woke, she noted the angle of the sun, cursed, and pulled on her jacket. Moments later, she joined Hester and Kormac at the helm. They looked like twin pillars of stoicism, both with grim frowns and tense shoulders.

"I spoke with Théophile."

"What word?" Hester asked, squinting at the horizon.

"It's time for plans of last resort." When Kormac raised an eyebrow, she explained, "He's going to do whatever he can to slow down that boat."

"May the gods be merciful," he replied, a dash of skepticism in his voice.

"Hey," she said, grasping his hand and holding it to her cheek. "The gods chose *us* as his soulmates." Meeting Hester's eyes, she added, "The three of us. I'd wager he's tougher than he looks."

Hester said with a wink, "I've yet to break him."

Ala blushed at the insinuation, her soulmate sickness making her body exquisitely responsive. Her connection with Hester remained unconsummated. Any ecstasy they might find would be short-lived and muddied by Théophile's absence. She tucked herself under Kormac's arm and kept her eyes on the horizon.

The man in the crow's nest called, "Smoke! Smoke ahead!"

Ala and Kormac raced to the rail of the ship. "There!" Ala cried, pointing when she saw the faint smoke wisp on the horizon.

"Could this be the trouble you asked our prince to make?" Kormac had a tentative smile on his lips.

"It must be." The soulmate sickness curled tightly in Ala's gut.

Slowly, a small schooner came into view. Flames licked up from its deck, and its sail hung in blackened tatters. What if Théo hadn't survived the fire? What if he'd left the burning wreckage and drowned? The possibilities tumbled over each other in Ala's mind, chipping away at the sliver of hope in her heart.

Hester pulled her vessel next to the schooner, and Ala leaned over the railing, searching for any sign of her soulmate. Instead, she watched as the wake stirred up by The Blue Macaw lapped over the deck, hastening its sinking.

"Captain, there!" called the sailor in the crow's nest. Ala glanced up, then followed the direction he pointed. The coast of Lomberg stood in the distance, but just a mile out, there sat a speck of brown on a sandbar. "Is that him?"

Hester joined her at the rail, raising a spyglass to her eye. "It's a lifeboat."

Kormac called from the opposite rail, "There's no one alive on this schooner, no one swimming."

Ala said, "If he's still alive—"

"*He's still alive*," Hester roughly emphasized each word. "I'd know if my soulmate were dead. I'd feel it."

Gently, Ala said, "Not everyone does."

"I would." Hester's eyes blazed as she returned to the helm, taking the wheel from the first mate and turning it. The ship moved in a wide arc toward the coast.

Ala scrambled to the bow, standing with Kormac's arm around her as they watched the sandbar creep closer. Then, the figure on the sandbar pushed his lifeboat back into the ocean; as they watched, he boarded it and rowed toward them.

"That's him," Ala said, clutching Kormac's hand tightly. "That has to be him."

Kormac took a labored breath, then wheezed sickly.

Ala turned to him, her stomach knotting up at the gray tint to his face, the blue pallor of his lips. "Love, we've almost got him back. Fight it! Hang on!"

Hester joined them, saying brusquely, "The 'mate sickness is killing him. Bring him to my quarters." She took one of Kormac's arms across her broad shoulders, and Ala took the other, inadequately small for the task.

To make up for her lack of size and strength, she said, "Kormac Montgomery, don't you dare die on me!"

His reply was a pained groan.

The three of them staggered toward the stern and through the open door to Hester's quarters. The room was small and worn, with drying clothes on lines crossed this way and that. A wooden desk held a stack of books and a plain clay plate with the remains of a meal. They headed for the bed, which was large enough for two, but only just. As she dumped Kormac onto her bed, Hester pulled a knife from her belt and held the handle out to Ala as she said, "Get his clothes off—get close to him. Maybe your bond will keep him going for a few more minutes."

Ala took the knife and grabbed Hester's arm before she could leave again. "I touched Théo just after Kormac did. It'll be my turn next."

Hester cupped Ala's face in her hands, placed a firm kiss on her lips, and said, "No one's dying here today, Princess. As captain of this ship, I forbid it." Then she left Ala reeling and stepped out of the room.

Making quick work of their clothes, Ala lay down next to Kormac, pressing as much of her skin to his as she could.

"Love," he said, grasping Ala's hand in his own, weaker than he'd been even a moment ago. "I'm sorry I wasn't fast enough. I'm sorry I didn't guard him that first night. I should never have trusted our lives to the embassy guards."

"Don't." Ala scooted up so she could make him meet her eyes. "I refuse to let you go. I refuse to let you lose hope. He's almost here. You must hold on a few more minutes."

"Kiss me."

Ala pressed her mouth to Kormac's, pouring as much of their soulbond into the kiss as she could. It had to help, right? Was he breathing easier? Maybe slightly. She ran her hand up and down his side, hooked her leg over his thigh, pressed her chest to his. It had to be working, right?

A clatter announced the lifeboat knocking into the side of the ship.

"He's here," Ala told Kormac. "Théo and Hester will be right with us. They'll make you feel better, love." His eyes remained closed, and his breath shuddered. "Hurry!" Ala's lungs felt tight. "Hester! Théo, hurry!" Her voice gave out.

After an eternity, the door crashed open. Théo staggered toward them, blue marks around his wrists, his skin dreadfully pale. Ala welcomed him into the bed, weakly climbing over Kormac so Théo could touch him as well. Just placing her hand on the side of Théo's neck relieved the tightness in her chest. Kissing him was a balm to her sickened soul. She wanted to be selfish and keep all his kisses, but she would never do so at Kormac's expense.

As Hester joined them, she picked up the knife from where Ala had dropped it and tore at Théo's clothes. Despite her enthusiasm, she was careful not to pull him away from where he placed careful kisses on the unconscious Kormac's face.

Ala allowed herself to skate her hand over Théo's skin, marveling at how velvety it felt compared to Kormac's rougher complexion. As Hester joined them—also stripped bare—Ala caught her hand, squeezing it with wordless thanks.

Hester winked, then said, "I know how to wake up a man," and kneeled between Kormac's legs. She ducked down and took Kormac's soft length into her mouth.

Ala shivered with desire.

Kormac shuddered under them, taking a sharp breath.

"That's it," Théo crooned, kissing his lips again. "Wake up for us, Kormac. There's a good man."

Kormac grumbled, squeezing Ala against him and returning Théo's kisses.

That was an improvement.

The desperation driving Ala, driving all of them, remained. She gave Hester's hair a caress, moved to Théo's side of the bed, then pressed herself against his back and snaked her hand between his stomach and Kormac's side. Just a little lower, and she cupped the head of his cock in her hand. He took a sharp breath and thrust against her. When his hips tilted back, she got her fingers wrapped around him and began stroking. The faster he reached orgasm, the safer all of them would be.

Théo squirmed amusingly in Ala's arms, and she barely noticed when Kormac made the grunt that meant he was getting close. Looking over Théo's shoulder, Ala called, "Hester! Théo's hand!"

She must have understood, because she didn't hesitate to take her mouth from Kormac's cock. Taking Théo's hand, she wrapped his fingers around Kormac's length, then surrounded them both with her own hand. Ala wasn't sure she'd met a woman with hands as big as Hester's, and the thought made her shiver again. She pressed close to Kormac and watched as their soulmates stroked him.

"Please," he said in a hoarse whisper, holding Ala tighter. "Almost..."

Ala took what felt like the last shred of her energy and let go of Théo's cock to move close enough to seal her mouth over Kormac's and kiss him deeply. His groan against her lips was long and loud, so different from the sounds she usually coaxed out of him during their nights in the palace. His skin flushed hotter, and Ala looked down to see the last few jerks of his cock as he came, Théo's and Hester's hands still around him.

When Ala took her next breath, it didn't feel as though she'd inhaled any air at all. Her arm gave out and she fell back, looking up at the wooden ceiling of Hester's quarters. She tried again to gasp, but the air wouldn't come.

Soulmate sickness was killing her. She couldn't go! She couldn't leave Kormac. In a panic, she grasped Kormac's hand, squeezing it tightly.

"Ala?" he asked, his voice thick and confused. "Are you—?"

Unable to answer, Ala tried to breathe. Her body felt horribly icy.

"Shit!" Hester snapped as she slid off the bed and onto her feet. She gathered Ala's limp form into her thick arms and said, "On your back, Prince." Ala pressed her temple against Hester's shoulder, taking comfort in the warmth of her skin.

A terrible calmness fell over Ala; she felt disconnected from herself as she let the last of her breath go and whispered, "I'm going to die."

"Not on our watch," Hester said, leaning down and placing Ala onto a great surface made of warmth and happiness. Ala's lungs loosened, and she gasped, the stretch of her lungs ecstatic around that rush of air. She distantly realized she was laying with her back against Théo's chest; at some point Kormac had taken her left hand and put his lips against her ear.

"Please, love. We're almost there!"

The next breath didn't come, her lungs too weak. Her eyes slipped closed, and as hard as she tried to open them again, they wouldn't cooperate. Hands gripped her thighs, spreading them and tugging her so her back slid against Théo's chest. "Come on, Ala," he murmured into her ear with his accented voice. She shivered. "Stay with us a moment."

White-hot pleasure bloomed between her legs as a tongue slipped through her folds. Who—? Oh, that was Hester's wild tangle of hair.

One more lick left enough saliva for a cock to slip up and into her.

Another sweet rush of air shuddered into her lungs. Ala inhaled a second, then a third, panting as Théo murmured into her ear, "You feel wonderful, darling." His right hand caught hers while Kormac still clung to her left. Théo's hips tilted, rocking forward and back in little motions that lit her up. Blood rushed through her ears, her heart pounding against the cage of her chest.

"Théo," she groaned, a desperate, broken shudder of a sound.

"I've got you," he whispered back, his free arm tight around her waist, holding her as he thrust deeper, making her breath catch—with pleasure, now. The head of his cock dragged against the front wall of her pussy, lighting her up from head to toe.

"Oh, gods!"

And then Hester's mouth settled over her clit, hot and wet, with skillful flicks that made Ala circle her hips, though whether from a need to get away from the intensity of the sensation or to press deeper into it, she couldn't have said. The way Hester drove her mad was comparable to the skills Kormac had developed over the years, and Ala pictured Hester doing this for other women, indulging when her travels took her away from Théo. Jealousy roared through her, like it did when Ala thought of the people Kormac had been with before they found each other. No more. Never again. They were Ala's soulmates. They belonged to each other now.

Théo's mouth found the sensitive skin of her neck, suckling on it as he thrust deep, filling her, stretching her out. He moaned against her skin, the magic of their impending soulbond flowing through them; she thought he must be close to the edge again. Or perhaps that was…Ala opened her eyes, watching the way Théo brought up and spread his knees, planting his feet and pushing Ala's thighs farther apart.

Kormac shifted beside them. He skimmed his fingers across the skin of her chest, then cupped her right breast and gave it a gentle squeeze. His lips closed around one nipple, his clever fingers gently pinching the other. Pleasure screamed through Ala's body. She trembled, caught between the three of them as they worked her up, up, up.

One last thrust of Théo's cock and Ala came, clenching around him, crying out, pushing Hester away as the pleasure became overwhelming. Théo held onto her tightly, thrusting into her just a few more times—each riding the line between pleasure and pain—before he followed her. He gasped and shuddered as he came, his cock pulsing inside her.

Their soulmate bond locked into place, a heavy blanket of warmth that settled around them.

Ala sighed, pulling Théo's arms tighter around her middle.

Wait.

There was one loose thread still hanging.

Ala opened her eyes and found Hester rising from her position between Ala's legs. Ala reached for her, and she obeyed as though Ala's gesture was a summons, holding herself up on her knees and one powerful arm. She let herself be pulled into a kiss, and Ala tasted herself on Hester's lips. A shiver of renewed interest flooded her, but Hester pulled away.

At Ala's whine of complaint, Hester said, "Rest up, 'mates," and climbed out of bed. She pulled on clothes at random until she was decent, then turned back to Ala, Théo, and Kormac and winked. "Once I give my crew orders for returning to Traulor, I've got plans for you all."

Théo chuckled in Ala's ear and Kormac squeezed her hand. Shifting to lie between her prince and her consort, Ala said, "Something tells me we're going to like those plans."

Hippie Ipsum

YF Ollwell

anal fingering, bipoc, blood drinking, blow job, bondage, clitoral fingering, cock ring, cunnilingus, drug use (casual), dubious consent, established relationship, f/f/m/m/nb, f/m/m, hand job, historical with magic, interspecies relationship, jealousy, kissing, m/m, m/m/m, master/servant, non-binary, open relationship, orgy, partner sharing, past tense, penis in anus sex, penis in vagina sex, pining, the 1960s, third person (alternating) point of view, thrall/vampire, trans male, united states of america, vaginal fingering, vampire, voyeurism

"Christ," announced Aster, parting the tangled blond curtain of his hair and staring a foot and a half upward at Edmund. "Who brought Goliath?"

Heathcliff stepped forward, the ill-fitting hems of his bell-bottom jeans scraping the dirty floor, and beckoned for Edmund to follow. Abernathy recognized the peculiar grin stretched across Heathcliff's round face—hiding fangs.

His beloved master was on the hunt.

"Heath," he introduced, an appropriate surfer twang hiding his real accent. He offered a shake Aster didn't return. "This is Eddie…" The same hand settled around Edmund's waist, pale fingers splaying downward to stroke his upper thigh. "My lover."

"Charmed," Edmund said in the voice that surprised Abernathy every time: shockingly soft for a man of his stature.

Heathcliff turned to Abernathy, eyes bright in the shared joke of their deception. "And Abby here is our—"

"—traveling companion," Abernathy finished for him. For how well Heathcliff imitated humans, how much he adored them, he had yet to learn that "thrall" raised too many questions. Besides, it was a shoddy title compared to "lover." "Pleased to meet you, as well," he stammered after a token sweep of eye contact to the other hippies.

"I'm Aster." He stood from the throne of his overstuffed loveseat, evacuated an androgynous redhead from his lap, and returned that overdue shake. "I get the feeling you already knew that."

"I suspected," Heathcliff murmured.

"I'm pretty much the boss around Firefly Village," Aster barreled on. "Well, not *really*, but I picked out this spot and built this house. This group here"—he stepped back slightly, made a sweeping gesture to them where they stayed sitting or otherwise lounging—"are *my* lovers:"

"Haskell."

The evacuated redhead, who raised one hand in stoned greeting.

"Poppy."

A sweet girl who couldn't have been taller than five-foot, black hair long enough to sit on. She pushed it to the side for a shy smile.

"Taryn."

A lapsed scholar, muscles lean and powerful under his warm brown skin, clean-cut hair beginning to shag.

"That's Chae-won."

She grinned under her shock of messy, startlingly green hair—grinned at all of them, Abernathy included. If he were alive, he might have blushed then.

"Finally, Bruce and Cassidy."

The last two, a long-haired man and short-haired woman more occupied with each other than with Aster, briefly parted to nod to the three vamps.

It didn't frazzle Abernathy nearly as much as he'd expected. He was a decent actor when he needed to be…when Heathcliff asked him to be. He deferred to his master, who tracked each greeting without a hitch.

"Pleasure to meet you all," Heathcliff announced broadly, stepping forward and integrating himself further into the group. Edmund immediately followed, guided by his partner's coaxing arm, and Abernathy followed with his intentional, unaccompanied stagger. The grin remained: what Aster might have read as charismatic, magnanimous, seductive. Abernathy knew better; it was hunger. "I think this will turn out to be a fruitful arrangement. For *all* of us."

"Depends," Aster cautioned. "You guys smoke?"

What I do for a meal, Abernathy thought, hacking wildly as they shared one emaciated joint after another.

"It's no worse than an opium den," Heathcliff whispered close into his ear.

Abernathy nodded; he'd have nodded at anything Heathcliff whispered to him. He tried to smoke, and he listened to the varying commune woes—Poppy's concern about which crops took and which didn't, Taryn's parents pursuing legal action to force him home, Haskell and Chae-won's endless catfights with "those Spahn Ranch bitches and their creep-o boyfriend"—background noise to the object of his desire.

In the haze of smoke, Heathcliff looked gorgeous as ever. Abernathy hadn't known him in life, only this strange afterward, but he imagined the living Heathcliff in perfect detail. There was an exuberance in him that in Abernathy was long dead. When he looked sidelong at Abernathy, flashed fangs to him and him only…

It wasn't fair. When he wasn't considering the object of his desire, he considered the evil, opposite-of-object—Edmund, silent as ever. He knew nothing about his master's husband, an odd shadow over his afterlife. The two had exchanged perhaps fifty words in the last century. This was for the best, as Abernathy thought Edmund might like to kill him if he knew the way he felt about Heathcliff. He also thought, in his more pathetic jags, that Edmund would be perfectly justified in said killing. It was sick. It was wrong. Heathcliff and Edmund were committed to each other.

Abernathy turned from Edmund—who was taller than him, who was much bigger and stronger, who was Heathcliff's Dark Intended and not merely his thrall—and settled on the fiery curls framing Heathcliff's ear.

Fat white worms of want writhed in his stomach.

"Listen," Aster began, breaking Abernathy's attention. He shook his head to get hair out of his face, a gesture Abernathy had seen horses make, and pinched off the roach as Bruce-or-Cassidy passed it. "You're a laugh riot, Heath, and I feel like the world's biggest asshole having to do this. But it must be done. What do you three plan on contributing to our community?"

Heathcliff paused, lowering his grin for the practiced illusion of a stifled good mood. "Good question."

"You know, the model we run here," Aster continued, not hearing, "everyone gives, and they get in return. That's how we're able to be self-sustaining. Like, Chae-won has a driver's license, Taryn can lift the truck, Haskell's an ace about crops… You get the idea. What have you got?"

Heathcliff pursed his lips, rested his head in his palm, and pretended to think. After a moment he squeezed Edmund's thigh and grinned.

"How about this," he said. "You can have Eddie."

Aster raised an eyebrow.

"I know something about free love," Heathcliff murmured. "And I know you've been feeling him up with your eyes all night. You're not particularly subtle."

"Guilty as charged."

"Oh, don't be. He's a total hunk," Heathcliff gushed, the strangeness of this decade's word disrupting his and Edmund's cloying intimacy. This became only more in Abernathy's face when Edmund bent down, tilted Heathcliff's chin upward with one large hand, and kissed him softly. "Besides, I don't mind if he strays. So long as he gets my permission." If this was true, it was news to Abernathy. He struggled to imagine a more monogamous couple, save for Romeo and Juliet.

"How progressive," Aster joked.

"Mm-hmm. I'm biased, of course, but I believe he's more than good enough for our share." Heathcliff's stroking of Edmund's thigh grew more drawn-out, and Abernathy thought he should look away. He curbed that instinct when it put him in the minority; the hippies eyed Edmund, their hushed conversations growing more hushed. Abernathy glanced up at Edmund: *what's his stance on all of this?*

"He's a novelty, I suppose," Heathcliff continued. "Given he's so big."

"That so?" Aster purred, stretching and scratching the back of his neck in a gesture too casual not to be calculated. "How big?"

"Seven-two," Heathcliff shared proudly, fielding the innuendo. "Is that right, babe?"

"Seven-one-and-a-half," Edmund answered.

"Seven-one-and-a-half. He's funny, too."

"Sure," muttered Aster. He spent another sweet moment with his neck craned back, chewing over the possibility Abernathy himself squirmed in place considering. "You make a good case," he continued, "but I wanna be sure I'm getting my money's worth, hypothetically speaking."

Heathcliff stretched up to whisper in Edmund's ear—"Stand up, love"—and Edmund followed, standing across from Aster at his full, towering height. Heathcliff got onto his knees beside him, clinging to one leg.

"Okay—"

Before Aster could finish, Heathcliff snaked one hand up, undid Edmund's fly, and freed his cock.

Aster's eyes promptly left Edmund's face. Somebody whistled. Abernathy couldn't tell who, looking away with such mortified force his lower jaw clicked.

He looked again immediately.

He'd never seen Edmund this way—of *course* not—but, a man of his stature. He could make an educated guess. Edmund was already half hard: enjoying the attention? Enjoying Heathcliff's, at least.

"Didn't I say?" Heathcliff cooed sweetly, wrapping a small hand around the base of Edmund's cock and squeezing. "He's quite the specimen."

"No kidding," Aster coughed. His voice pitched low now, taking on the breathy quality Abernathy clocked as arousal. "Christ, what a fuckin' monster."

"I know." Heathcliff packed each word with lurid exaggeration. "I'm a lucky boy." He slowly stroked upward, forcing Edmund's legs apart, coaxing his arousal. Edmund's cock twitched obediently in Heathcliff's hand; when he swiped his thumb over the tip, Edmund shivered, and a drip of pre-come drooled down his shaft.

Abernathy realized how wet he was.

"Look," Heathcliff huffed. "He's very well-behaved. He doesn't buck his hips when I tease him, though I'm sure he'd like to. Wouldn't you?"

"Yes," Edmund answered instantly.

"Maybe soon," Heathcliff said.

Aster licked his lips.

"Is this enough of a demonstration?" Heathcliff followed up the silence, sounding impatient. He paused, spit crudely into his hand, then treated Edmund to one more luxurious stroke.

"Hell no," Aster answered, a debauched grin stretching across his face. "Show me more."

Heathcliff paused, expression murky… He looked over his shoulder at Abernathy, whose eyes practically bulged from his skull. "Sure. Only, I might need help. Care to join us, Abby?"

Abernathy balked. "I. What?"

"Oh, come on. When in Rome, hm? It's all in good fun. Edmund won't mind at all, will you, dear?"

"Not at all," Edmund answered. "If—if you feel so inclined, Abernathy." This was becoming the most words Edmund had ever spoken to him.

The proposition shocked him, to say the least. He ran it over in his mind, wearing down its edges—a joke? The hunt? Demented teasing on Heathcliff's part?—but nothing emerged. His gaze drifted back in Edmund's direction. The direction of his cock, specifically; could Abernathy say he'd never considered this? No, he could not. Part of the want for Heathcliff that reared its head when he was at his most desperate and confused. Abernathy shifted where he sat, feeling his thighs stick and rub together.

When in Rome. Sure. He crawled forward.

"Good," Heathcliff murmured, which would have sent Abernathy crawling itself. It wasn't that he'd *never*—long nights in the anatomist's lab, when it was noon over the British Empire—but not in a lifespan. From this angle, Edmund's cock looked downright intimidating.

"What do I"—Abernathy hesitated—"*do*?"

"What you like," Heathcliff answered, and took the tip of Edmund's cock between his lips.

Abernathy squeaked, louder than any response from Edmund himself, who gasped, lost in the room's soup of heavy breathing. One hand hovered to the back of Heathcliff's head, thick fingers lodging in his curls. Abernathy watched Heathcliff, not moving, until Edmund glanced down in his direction expectantly.

Abernathy peeled his slick thighs apart as he reached up and wrapped his hand around the part of Edmund's cock that wasn't currently in Heathcliff's mouth.

The weight of it alone made him throb with unexpected want, and he fell into an experimental rhythm, stroking Edmund up and down. His actions were received well; Edmund's shoulders relaxed and his head tipped back on his neck, sending his curtain of black hair a fraction farther down. Abernathy considered spitting into his own hand, but his master had done an admirable job. In his secret heart, it was that intimacy, fingers gliding over Heathcliff's saliva, turning him on most.

The massive cock he'd been presented with didn't *hurt*, though.

Stroking Edmund, marveling at how his fingers barely managed to touch around it, he considered Heathcliff—who now took considerably more of his husband, his lips brushing Abernathy's hand with each upward motion—and followed his lead. Removing his hand, setting it at Edmund's hip, Abernathy leaned in and pressed his lips to where he'd last touched. In the span of that one kiss, he worked out his niche and sank farther to suck on one of Edmund's low-hanging balls. Pulling closer to Edmund, clinging for dear life as his wobbling knees threatened to unbalance him, he began to mindlessly hump Edmund's leg with a litany of muffled, involuntary whines.

Heathcliff took notice of this with clear intrigue.

"Look at you." He freed his mouth to murmur down to Abernathy. One hand went to the top of his head and patted him condescendingly. "Dirty boy."

"Jesus, okay," shot Aster's breathless voice, interrupting the realization of Abernathy's ultimate fantasy.

Opening the eyes he didn't remember closing, Abernathy saw the leering circle had closed tighter around them. Chae-won pressed to his back.

"You've convinced the hell outta me. Let's go upstairs." Aster stretched and stood, his erection pressing shamelessly into his tight jeans. "Poppy, Haz, Taryn, come with me."

"Don't have to tell me twice," rang a sharp, clear voice—Haskell, standing alongside their lovers to join Aster. With one last glance down at Heathcliff and Abernathy, Edmund followed Aster and the rest as they marched up the rickety staircase. He motioned to re-do his fly before Aster grabbed his wrist, swatted his hand away, and wrapped his own hand around the base of Edmund's cock.

"Don't bother," Aster muttered.

With one lurid glance back, they were gone.

Teams split up pretty quick. Heathcliff wound up in one corner with Bruce and Cassidy, Chae-won ended up in another with a battered copy of *Flowers for Algernon*, and Abernathy ended up in another still, alone.

Abernathy took up his usual role and observed them—observed Heathcliff. His master spoke amiably to the two humans, enough so that they split from each other to listen, but at too low a volume for Abernathy to eavesdrop. All he caught were occasional barks of laughter that made his dead heart cramp with jealousy.

More whispers, more laughter...they got on well. One leaned in from behind Heathcliff and whispered intently, and moments later two spindly hands made quick work of Heathcliff's shirt. Abernathy swallowed hard. Getting on *well.*

He stood right as the three became a tangle of bare limbs. His skin crawled, and his jealousy radiated off him in ugly waves. Edmund was inevitable, *that* he could accept, but anyone else was downright intolerable.

Chae-won read, unbothered, and an actionable idea rose from the muck. Abernathy grabbed the first reading material he found, a crumpled *Life With Archie*. He settled back into his corner and opened the comic to the middle with the intense study he would have given *The Sorrows of Young Werther*. An advertisement, all the order-by-mail human treasures. 50 Bike Decals... 250 Magic Tricks... 500 Krazy Stamps, a bargain at a dollar... Underneath it all, the growing wet sound of *sex*, from that foreign corner, from everywhere.

Bruce and Cassidy—matching bell-bottoms pooled around matching ankles—stood, pulling Heathcliff to his knees. As they met over his head in a sloppy kiss, they tugged him between their bodies in casual competition: on one side to have his tongue wrap lazily around the tip of an eager cock, on the other to coax it between the lips of a slick, swollen pussy. Breathy moans mixed with rushed whispers and laughter.

When Abernathy came back to his senses, the comic lay discarded and his hand cradled his inner thigh, rubbing skin too sensitive through his clothes.

Immediately, he pulled it away, embarrassed with himself. When he turned to the left, he found Chae-won leaning in toward his face with a hard-to-decipher smile.

"You like watching, huh?" she said. When she didn't get an answer, she crawled a fraction forward, arms looping around Abernathy's narrow shoulders.

"You were great," she continued—close enough in his ear that he shivered. "I never woulda guessed looking at you."

"Guessed—" Abernathy furrowed his brow. "What?"

Chae-won grinned, and Abernathy noticed there were two gold studs flanking the bridge of her nose. "You being such a slut."

She took advantage of his embarrassment to crawl into his lap with a quick kiss on the cheek.

"What do you think your friend's up to?" she asked.

"All right, big guy," Aster murmured, leading Edmund to a tidy bedroom taken up by the largest bed he'd ever seen. "Strip 'n lay down."

Edmund complied without a word. He thought he would be more nervous, the least on board with free love. But, that group of humans leering as he made silent work of his clothes…the arousal he smelled through heightened senses…he might come around. His cock pulsed remembering his thrall's mouth and stiffened further as he lay across the massive bed.

"Arms up," Aster commanded, and Edmund followed before he spotted Haskell rummaging in the nightstand. He understood when they stood, a length of cloth rope clutched in their hands. "Legs spread, too, far as you can get 'em."

Haskell tied Edmund's right wrist to the headboard, and Edmund tugged at it experimentally—tight, but not uncomfortable. Keeping his muscular arm at such an angle produced enough of a strain to keep him on edge. Soon, Haskell crossed to get the other side situated, leaving Edmund spread and exposed across the mattress. He hadn't been in such a position since the night he and Heathcliff had met.

"Looking good," Aster praised Haskell's handiwork, palming himself over his jeans before unzipping his fly. "Jesus. Heath's one lucky bastard."

"What—?" Edmund coughed. "What do you intend to do?"

"What do I *intend* to *do*?" Aster repeated, imitating Edmund's accent. "Good question. What do we think?" He turned back abruptly, sending a wave of blond into Haskell's freckled face with a flat *thwack*. "Poppy? Any ideas?"

"Oh—" She detached from Taryn as he pulled her out of her shapeless tie-dye shirt, pushing her black mass of hair behind her ears. Her smile went funny at the corners when Taryn groped at her breasts, and she hid her face behind two manicured hands. "Oh, I can't say," she giggled. Taryn pushed away another thick swath of hair to attach to her neck.

"Sure you can," Aster countered.

"You *know* what I wanna do."

"I wanna suck his cock," Haskell interjected, their gaze not leaving Edmund for a second as they scrabbled to get out of their coveralls.

Aster swallowed a mean laugh. "Haz wants to suck your cock," he informed Edmund. "I've—got half a mind—" Aster punctuated his words with buttons undone, revealing a soft chest and stomach dusted with hair remarkably darker than that on his head. He kicked his jeans off as he crawled onto the bed up Edmund's left side; a moment later he was nude. "—to join them. Maybe after I play with your tits a little." This last line whispered human-hot into Edmund's ear as Aster threw one leg over his broad chest. His cock pressed into Edmund's side.

He braced himself for an unfamiliar hand, and as it came—Aster's warm fingers brushing over him, teasing at one stiff nipple before greedily squeezing his chest—he gasped. Any shame behind that gasp dissipated as Aster's hand kept at it, soon joined by his searching mouth.

Edmund thrashed in his restraints. Only in practice, he discovered, could he feel their delicious power.

"What are you three waiting for?" Aster called over his shoulder. Poppy and Taryn kept pawing at each other, his hand parting her legs as one of hers wrapped around to squeeze his ass; Haskell kicked their coveralls off one leg and crawled between Edmund's legs, going straight for their target. Their mouth wrapped around the tip of his cock as his head fell back, a strangled moan falling from Edmund's lips—as much from remembering Abernathy's mouth on him as from the equally new sensation of Haskell's. They had Edmund halfway down their throat, audibly struggling with his size, by the time the mattress shifted with two more bodies.

Hands… *everywhere.*

On his hips, over his defined abs, squeezing his thighs, on his cock:

stroking what Haskell wasn't sucking, rubbing with the tip of a shy finger (surely Poppy's), dipping down to fondle his aching balls. And on top of all of that, Aster continued pinching and pulling his nipples, pleasure bordering on pain. Edmund meant to open his eyes, watch himself helpless to their human curiosity, but every time he tried, a new sensation washed him away and they fluttered shut, accompanied by his stifled sounds.

Soon, another mouth joined Haskell's, and he curled his fingers into the sheets, hearing fabric rip. He *had* to look when a *third* joined.

Haskell took his cock nearly to the base, their painted lips leaving heavy blue-black smears on his length as they bobbed their head. Each upward motion gave Poppy and Taryn room to kiss and suck at it, lips barely able to meet around the girth as they battled to take Haskell's place. Poppy broke ground as Haskell's enthusiasm caused his cock to slide from their mouth and smack their cheek with a sinfully wet sound. Pre-come smeared across their freckles, gushing from Edmund's overworked cockhead and mixing with their spit.

Any reprieve from this relentless pleasure disappeared as Poppy immediately swallowed him. A high-pitched whine forced its way out of him as he got suddenly close—tight in his stomach, any second. Taryn kissed up his length to join Poppy, and he was somehow between *both* their lips as Haskell mouthed at his balls like Abernathy had—

He came with a scream of a moan as Aster knelt next to his head and expectantly pressed the tip of his cock to Edmund's parted lips.

"Oh," he muttered, and sat back as Edmund writhed to the best of his ability. He opened his eyes to the three hippies gathered between his legs, idly sucking at his softening cock. When Poppy sat up, he saw, embarrassingly, that her face dripped with come—same as Taryn's, he discovered a second later. Only Haskell escaped, much to their obvious distaste.

"You're not done, are you?" Aster asked, and Edmund feebly nodded. Aster pouted. "No, that won't do." He smacked the head of his cock teasingly against Edmund's lips. "Can't you get it up again?"

Edmund waited for his head to stop spinning before he answered. "...maybe."

"Maybe's fine." Aster glanced over his shoulder. "Bottom drawer, Haz."

"Sure." They stood with a mischievous face that Edmund wasn't sure he liked. "If it'll fit him."

They ducked down and returned with an inconspicuous steel ring pinched between two spindly fingers.

"You know what this is?" Aster asked, swinging forward and straddling Edmund's chest. Edmund considered it; he had enough of an idea. His cock stirred weakly, drawing Aster's attention.

"Yeah, he does." He rocked his hips forward to prod into Edmund's mouth. "Let's keep this party going. Open up."

"You're so *weird*," Chae-won giggled into Abernathy's ear. Her mouth traveled easily from his temple to his mouth, kissing him with a startling fervor. She gripped him at the waist as she did it, pulling him in. "Like, what's your problem?"

"Well—" Abernathy's chest rose and fell in heavy jags, pressed to her breasts. "I'm not sure." His eyes darted conspicuously in Heathcliff's direction.

"That's what I mean. You're, like, tripped out." She leaned in ever closer. "I dig that."

Her tongue traced a wet arc across his bloodless cheek, capturing his mouth.

They began kissing in earnest.

Abernathy remembered the boy-girl thing: flirtation cards, invitations to come see the new parlor lamp. Chae-won jogged his memory by pulling down the neckline of her peasant blouse and exposing her breasts. In between kisses, Abernathy realized he should touch them, and when his hands blindly groped upward, she gave an encouraging gasp that spurred him on further. *That's nice.* Nicer when she pitched forward, hips to his own, and knocked him to the shag carpet.

Sensation steadily overwhelmed him. The choppy wisps of her hair on his cheeks... Her lips on his, showering him in kisses... He tucked his face into the crook of her neck and kept it there, sucking a bruise into the skin, savoring her warm life. The sweet smell of her blood—

He'd be a fool to do that; he'd wreck the plan. But his mouth was there, now the focal point of all eroticism. The vein he'd need pulsed in the rhythm of her arousal, and he hadn't eaten, *really* eaten, in months.

His lips met her neck over the growing bruise he'd put there, and he thought, *I won't do this stupid thing.* More of a fleeting, half-heard suggestion. *What would Heathcliff do?* he tried, which made it worse. Thinking of Heathcliff ached, and Abernathy knew he would have drained her dry.

What *would* his master do? He nipped at Chae-won's neck, and she squealed in response. Another nip, and her hands moved from playing with his hair to trail electricity down his skinny body. The old arousal and the new desire for her blood folded in on each other, the former jolting the latter jolting the former, until—

"Hey—" Her lilting confusion—

Heathcliff cried out from across the room at the same moment Abernathy sank his fangs into Chae-won.

Chae-won shrieked and pushed away from him, and Abernathy winced as his head hit the floor with bruising force. It took a full second to realize the sweet iron of her blood barely coated his tongue, already fading, whetting his appetite. Failure on all counts.

"What the *fuck*!" she spat, a hand to her leaking neck. Abernathy crawled backward away from her—she stared at him, eyes racing, coming to invisible conclusions—as though he'd been the one attacked.

"I don't know," he managed, whinging as he wiped his lips with the back of his hand.

"You're too much, man," Chae-won whispered.

He barely heard her.

He stood, hopelessly gesturing apologies.

She wouldn't have it—one hand struck forward, cobra-like, while the other rubbed her neck. "No way," she hissed. "Whatever the *fuck* you are, stay *away* from me!"

"Chae-won," he attempted, but when he took a step forward, she bolted, feet thudding across the carpet.

Poppy clutched Edmund's shoulders as she came, nails digging into his skin, rocking erratically on his cock—she pulled off, collapsing onto the mattress, replaced a second later by Haskell. In short, the general state of the last hour.

So Edmund thought—chest heaving, mouth hanging open in a

helplessly debauched expression, he had no mind left for time passing. That damned ring; seven hundred years ago, it would have been called witchcraft. The pit of his stomach pulled taught with the verge of inevitable, impossible orgasm. His swollen cock ached, throbbing constantly, a mess of spit and arousal and his own dripping pre-come. He gave himself up to their pleasure.

Haskell rode rougher than Poppy, face contorted into a grimace of pleasure as the bed frame creaked. Edmund's back arched with a ruined whimper; he weakly pulled at the restraints before his head hit the pillow. He turned to one side, writhing in horrible, directionless pleasure, and turning to meet Aster's patient expression.

"Hanging in there, big guy?" Aster asked, idly fingering Taryn, who was up next. "Had enough? Or do you not like it?"

He liked it, all right—that was the problem. Aster understood this, his free hand stroking Edmund's cheek in a condescending gesture.

"All right." He patted Edmund's cheek firmly. "You've paid your way. With interest accrued." He crawled down the bed to tap Haskell's shoulder. "Give him a rest, honey."

Haskell muttered their annoyance but complied, raising off Edmund's cock and landing by Poppy's side to finish what they'd started with her help.

Edmund took heavy, gasping breaths, his toned chest shuddering in the moment's relief. His cock throbbed, twitching madly without touch, but slowly he reoriented himself in the room. Poppy and Haskell to his left, idly messing around, Taryn to his right, observing with a lecherous look…and Aster between his legs, untying them, hiking one over his shoulder.

"You wanna come, yeah?" Aster asked.

Edmund nodded, and Aster gave a reedy laugh.

"Use your words, big guy."

"*Yes,*" Edmund gasped out.

"That's what I thought." Aster's expression took on a fond tilt. His hand gripped Edmund's thigh, fingers prodding into pale skin. "You ever been fucked in the ass before, Ed?"

Edmund shook his head. "No."

"Makes sense," Aster replied, considering it. "I bet Heath took one look at you and bent over." The hand at Edmund's thigh shifted, hiked farther up Aster's shoulder. "Ever thought about it?"

Edmund nodded.

Aster cut in before he spoke. "I bet. Why don't we give it a try, huh? That's a fine note to end on."

Edmund turned to either side, where the other three leaned in to watch this newest development play out. He opened his mouth to answer as Aster slid his free hand up the length of his cock, prompting a sharp moan that answered for him.

Poppy giggled over Haskell's shoulder.

"This should do," Aster muttered, briefly observing the mess on his fingers from Edmund's dripping cock. With little fanfare, his hand slipped between Edmund's spread legs, two fingers jabbing at the ring of muscle there. Edmund's breath faltered as they pushed their way inside, drawing an empathetic gasp from Aster.

"God*damn*," he whispered, pushing another fraction in—Edmund seized in pleasure, rattling the bed frame. "This is gonna be good."

Edmund became aware of hands and body weight—the others leaned in, idly stroking his chest or laying across it as if he were furniture in the room. The touch of fingers *inside*, so unlike Heathcliff's, cemented the sense of being owned. By somebody other than Heathcliff, that was.

Aster's fingers retreated, and Edmund whimpered at the emptiness. Aster grinned and rested his hand at Edmund's cock, gently twisting the ring and making Edmund's vision blur.

"You've been a good sport," Aster sighed, pulling the ring off to toss it aside. He hiked Edmund's other leg over the other shoulder, the head of his cock replacing his fingers. "Try not to spill when I do this, all right?"

Edmund managed *yes* before Aster's hips snapped forward, curling the sound into a broken cry of pleasure.

His eyes fluttered shut as Aster fucked him, the sound of sex deafening murmurs and laughs, and he came to an unknown set of hands cradling his head and pulling him into a kiss. He whimpered from that release of pressure alone, hips stuttering up as he painted his chest and stomach with come.

"Aw," Aster cooed, pace never faltering. "That's okay, big guy. You needed it."

Edmund moaned helplessly, tension leaving him in a crashing wave, letting Aster use his body. Aster did so with a few low grunts of pleasure, in contrast to the endless flow of whines and whimpers he pulled from the otherwise solemn vampire. He ultimately came with as little sound, nails digging into Edmund's thighs as his cock spasmed deep inside of him. Edmund took it, the burn of overstimulation offset by the new sensation of Aster filling him up.

Time ceased to move.

Edmund's restraints loosened—he opened his eyes to find Taryn, the one who'd kissed him—and he collapsed, awash in affection. Hands roamed his body. Mouths kissed and cleared away his pleasure.

"Eddie," Aster murmured, crawling up his body and wrapping his arms around his shoulders. "I believe this is the start of a beautiful friendship. What do you think?"

Edmund thought this was going to be the best meal of his afterlife.

Abernathy flung open the first door he found and shut it behind him, rattling the frame. A bedroom, lived in but not currently occupied. Ideal.

Pushing aside a few more Archies and a well-worn issue of *Drum*, Abernathy sat on the mattress, placed his hands over his face, and wept. Of course it would turn out this way. Swimmingly for everybody except poor, wretched Abernathy, whom life-after-death continually handed the short end of the stick.

Worse, he'd now been wound up and left dry twice.

He lay down, comics wrinkling under him, and attempted to flush out the bad feeling. A few passing strokes of a finger over his soaked underwear set his heart stuttering.

He fished for *Drum* to outsource the fantasy. The Kris Studio hunks were appealing, but they weren't Heathcliff. Other times, he might have rationed the want, doled it out, but now he didn't bother. He let it live as it lived.

He could only get so far along, worrying his clit and sliding his fingers in and out of his slick hole. He applied more pressure, and the jolts of pleasure took on a burning edge to no result. He needed someone else's hand.

He hiked his legs up, exposing himself to no one, and sunk three fingers deep as they would go. Sending his mind down a river of free-association: Heathcliff's slender hands between his legs, that wicked tongue of his in the same place—or hot by his ear, holding his hand and kissing his cheek as he coaxed Edmund's huge cock inside—

"Occupied?"

What was that? Not the voice, but the thought? It vanished. Not the knocking, though—

"Helloooo…? Oh, *Abby*!"

Abernathy jumped, head swiveling.

Standing in the doorframe was Heathcliff. He looked inordinately pleased. "Fancy seeing you here," he cooed.

Abernathy opened his mouth to speak and failed. Instead, he drew his fingers from himself as he would have withdrawn from a hot iron. Not that it mattered—he'd been caught.

This did little to dull his arousal.

Heathcliff stepped into the room, and his hips sauntered like a human drunk. *Drunk on his own debauchery*, spoke the internal Victorian. When the room's bare bulb caught him, Heathcliff's lips shone slick.

"Don't stop on my account," Heathcliff continued, eyeing Abernathy's frozen body with an avidity Abernathy had never experienced, only imagined. "But I'm surprised, Abby. I thought you'd hit it off with…that green-haired girl whose name eludes me."

"I'm sorry," Abernathy coughed.

"What for?"

Abernathy'd trapped himself—no way out or forward without fessing up. Heathcliff came closer, leaning over the bed; Abernathy began to sweat.

"It's lewd."

His voice disappeared in Heathcliff's *cackle*.

"That's rich," Heathcliff started, crawling into bed alongside Abernathy. Abernathy curled into the mattress, back to his master. "Considering you earlier. You're not feeling *shy*, are you?" Heathcliff's hand landed on Abernathy's hip with an electric shock. "Turn," he said, and Abernathy obeyed instantly. His master's face loomed closer than ever. "You know, I like all this free-love business. I haven't had this much fun since the Souls."

"That's." Here were all the once-human details, the smattering of freckles, the scar over Heathcliff's upper lip…the warm lust in his eyes. They nearly stunned Abernathy into silence. "That's good to hear, sir."

"Don't do that," Heathcliff insisted—sharp enough to make Abernathy jump. "Not *now.*" Close, in Abernathy's ear: "You think I haven't seen you looking at me?" Closer: "That me and Edmund can't *hear* you?"

Abernathy's mouth dried out; his thighs clenched tight together.

"I'm sorry," he repeated dully. "I'll take my leave at first dark tomorrow."

"Now what would you do a *stupid* thing like that for?"

Abernathy blinked. He blamed his confusion on the hand, drawing all thought to his hip. "It's hardly befitting of my station," he attempted, hearing the bitterness seep in, "and I don't suppose Edmund would be too pleased."

"He likes you," Heathcliff insisted.

Abernathy kept back a harsh laugh. "He has a strange way of showing it."

"I'm serious." Heathcliff paused. His hand rubbed maddening circles on Abernathy's skin. "We discussed, ah, inviting you in for a night. If you were so inclined."

Abernathy considered this, stunned. "You wanted to?"

"It was Edmund's idea," Heathcliff corrected. "He's grown quite fond of you. It's adorable. Makes this"—he made an oblique, circular gesture with one hand—"a case of good timing. Didn't you see how thrilled he was to have your mouth earlier?"

"I couldn't say," Abernathy answered honestly.

"Well, he was." Shockingly—agonizingly—Heathcliff's hand curved around Abernathy's waist, threatening at where he needed it. An embarrassing sound ripped from Abernathy's throat, and Heathcliff took the opportunity to sneak his hand farther. Abernathy's clothes went with it, jeans pushed to mid-thigh. "And I'm sure he'd love more."

One slender finger met Abernathy's clit, and he whimpered. "Sir," he gasped desperately, hiding his face in the crook of his elbow. Heathcliff didn't relent, rubbing small circles into his sensitive skin. "I wish you wouldn't do that."

"You don't like it?" Heathcliff asked.

"It's not right."

"Oh, stop that." Heathcliff's hand wandered down, teased at Abernathy's entrance. "You can't convince me. My God, you're wet… Is that from thinking about *my husband* fucking you?"

Abernathy whined and jerked his head. He was of two minds on the subject as that damned finger worked its slow way inside. If only it was about sex, he thought miserably. It had to be more complicated…wrapped up in a hundred years' marinated longing.

Each twinge of pleasure, compelled by Heathcliff's skilled hand, made his heart sink inward. Heathcliff's voice, near-hidden by the blood rushing in Abernathy's ears, stung more. He snapped when Heathcliff's finger crooked inside, cold lips at his neck.

"*Heathcliff*—!" His voice broke as he reluctantly writhed free from the embrace. He sat up, shaking. "I *can't*."

Heathcliff blinked at him, the frown crawling slowly across his face.

"I think that, well." The words dried up. He chased them to little success. "It's hardly fair. Considering the way I feel. I don't care about circumstances, or going along for the hunt, or—or any of that. I can't accept it if tomorrow will be the same as before." Abernathy slumped, skull hitting the headboard with a flat *thwap*. He turned his head and met Heathcliff's yellow eyes, intent and inscrutable. Abernathy wilted back into himself. "You know," he said—asked.

Heathcliff sighed. "I *suspected*," he began, emphasizing with an arch of his eyebrows. "You're not exactly *subtle*, Abby."

Abernathy bristled. "I'm sorry."

"There you are with that again," he said, sharp enough to sand another sorry off of Abernathy's tongue. "I suppose I've been rather cruel to you these past decades."

"In a sense."

"I apologize. For not being considerate, as you said." Something dripped into Heathcliff's voice that Abernathy wasn't sure he'd heard: sincerity.

"Thank you," he murmured, posture relaxing—though not into Heathcliff's waiting arms, as much as he ached to. "You've treated me with such kindness. You and Edmund both."

"Why are you talking as if I'm going to toss you out on the street?" Heathcliff picked up the intimation and leaned in, wrapping his arms loosely around Abernathy's chest. "I don't think of you any different."

"That's the problem," Abernathy muttered. "Edmund—"

"Stop." Heathcliff's hand gripped Abernathy's shoulder. "He *likes* you, Abby, really he does."

"But do *you* like me?" Abernathy asked. He expected hesitation; it didn't come.

"Abby," Heathcliff started—condescension in his tone that made Abernathy shiver. "If I didn't like you, I wouldn't keep you around." Slowly…steadily…he curled Abernathy back onto his side. He met no pushback. "And I meant what I said about free love. I want to give it a try if you do."

"And if Edmund does," Abernathy cautioned.

Heathcliff giggled, pulled Abernathy only closer. "Oh, he will," Heathcliff whispered, back in Abernathy's ear, making him the closest to hot all over he could be. "I walked by the door earlier. He sure *sounded* like he was coming around. And I don't have to remind you we're a package deal."

Abernathy picked up the implied question and nodded, considering it only afterward. If there was more to learn about Edmund—and, if what Heathcliff suggested was right, there was—he felt open to learning. Compelled, even. As for *physically*… He clenched his thighs in a gesture that made Heathcliff laugh.

"Poor thing," he crooned, his hand wandering back to its place and coaxing Abernathy's legs apart. It didn't take much. "You haven't gotten any relief, have you?"

"No," Abernathy answered— whined as Heathcliff teased his sensitive clit.

"That's our first order of business. We'll talk about the rest tomorrow, after we're all well-fed. What do you say?"

Abernathy's answer vanished when two fingers shoved into his aching hole. He cried out in sheer pleasure, muffled immediately by Heathcliff's lips crashing into his. They kissed with abandon, jigsawed together, Abernathy stretched out and utterly vulnerable. *If anyone saw* rang half a thought, and he imagined Edmund in the room with them, silently aroused.

Touches, hands, the afterimage of Heathcliff's fanged grin behind eyes squeezed shut—Abernathy finished moments later, tears spilling down his pallid cheeks as he shook in Heathcliff's arms.

Heathcliff kept pushing his fingers in and out of him, not letting up until Abernathy's pleasure withered away. Panting heavily, they paused their kissing for Abernathy to turn on his side to face Heathcliff.

"Thank you," Abernathy gasped.

"Don't thank me yet," Heathcliff murmured, pushing at Abernathy's chest and gesturing for him to sit back.

Heathcliff pulled his shirt over his head, exposing his pale chest, and made similar work of his jeans—Abernathy watching all the while. He couldn't have asked for a more enraptured audience. Slowly...deliberately...he spread his legs for Abernathy. Heathcliff was wet—swollen lips slick with his arousal—and his clit throbbed as he brushed it with his thumb, the sight alone making Abernathy follow. His mouth watered.

"My loyal servant," Heathcliff sighed, gazing down at Abernathy—who, on instinct, knelt between Heathcliff's legs. "Show me how much you love to *serve* me."

Abernathy closed his eyes and worshipped his master.

By morning, maybe—blackout curtains, a boon to the vampires, obscured the passage of time—the hippies called it quits. They fell asleep where they were.

Heathcliff observed this scene with a fang-heavy grin, one arm around Edmund's waist and one arm around Abernathy's.

"Well," he announced, "this *has* been a fruitful arrangement. What do you two think?"

"Agreed," Edmund said.

"Agreed, as well." Abernathy stumbled through. He'd gotten the rhythm with time. Time he had in spades—more time than ever. A grin matching Heathcliff's spread over his face, beyond conscious control. "...what happens now?"

Heathcliff sauntered over to Aster's prone frame, crouched beside him. He pushed his hair to the side, exposing a pale neck.

"Breakfast," Heathcliff murmured, and sank his fangs in.

Love, With Bloodstained Jaws

(Or: Five Times Levente's Omegas "Seduce" Him, And One Time He Seduces Them.)

Lyonel Loy

5 + 1 things fic, alpha/beta/omega dynamics (non-traditional), alpha/omega, alpha/omega/omega, anal fingering, blow job, established relationship, fantasy, fighting to fucking, flirting, heat sex, humor, knotting, m/m, m/m/m, marriage before love, omega/omega, penis in anus sex, present tense, public sex, rimming, rough sex, royalty, semi-public sex, sloppy seconds, soldier, third person limited point of view, veteran, victor/war prize, voyeurism

I: Wet

"let's get you out of those wet clothes"

A month ago, Levente was a conqueror at the head of a victorious army. Shiny, new crown resting light upon his brow, resplendent at the altar as he took for brides the beautiful omega princes of the kingdoms he had vanquished to win his throne.

I'll never force you into my bed, he'd taken great pains to assure them. *You'll have all the time you need.* And if the time they needed was forever, Levente would have learnt to make do. He's no monster, after all.

But Levente has always known his own worth. His omegas *would* come to desire him, he'd been sure.

And how right he'd been! Now they do.

They desire him greatly. They had needed no time at all.

Their desire might kill him.

"Oh, alpha," Raihan coos, just as wide-eyed and innocent as the virgin he had not been on their wedding day. "You poor thing! You're soaked through."

Beside Raihan, Melchor, too, is trying for doe-eyed and sweet. Unlike Raihan, he misses the mark by a mile. "Best get these off, alpha," he says, fluttering his eyelashes in a spectacularly awful attempt at coquettishness as he reaches to paw at Levente's sodden clothes, "or you'll catch your death."

Levente nobly resists the urge to drag Melchor into the water with him. He bats his omega's hands away instead, hauling himself out of the courtyard's central fountain with all the dignity a king can muster after being flung in headfirst by his own omega brides. "And I'm soaked through," he snarls, spitting tepid water with every word, "because I fell into this fountain, because you *pushed me*."

"Technically speaking, he picked you up and threw you," Raihan points out. And technically speaking, Melchor only got the drop on Levente's sorry arse because Levente was busy pivoting away from Raihan's attempt to trip him into that same fountain. But who's keeping score? Certainly not Raihan.

"It was terrible of me." Melchor almost manages to sound sincere. "You should punish me, alpha."

"With my cock, I expect," Levente mutters, more sour than a basketful of still-green mangoes. His sodden clothing clings like seaweed to his legs as he splatters his way across the courtyard, his omegas trailing in his watery wake, and throws himself down on the nearest bench to wring himself out.

"With your cock," Melchor agrees, entirely undeterred by Levente's best imitation of unripe fruit as he sinks down onto his knees to bully his way between Levente's. "Your knot too, if it pleases you. And maybe your hands?"

He nuzzles at the bulge between Levente's legs, mouthing with shameless greed over the sodden cloth. Levente had not been hard, but that is rapidly changing; he shoves Melchor's head back with swift alarm nonetheless.

Levente remembers those sinful lips wickedly curled, those dark eyes shining with fell light. Melchor captive, chained, still laughing and half mad, painted in the blood of his enemies. His host had been the last to break in the final battle that won Levente his kingdom; instead of routing with the rest of his forces, Melchor had charged forward alone, carving a brutal swath towards Levente until he was finally pulled down by sheer weight of numbers.

Levente did not become a king by obeying every stray impulse of his loins. This man's teeth are going nowhere near his cock.

"Your punishment should be to go *without*," he grumbles, only half serious.

But Raihan gasps in theatrical shock as he materializes behind Melchor like a wraith, something wicked and silent passing between Levente's omegas. It is Melchor who is on his knees, caged between Levente and Raihan. Why is it Levente who feels like prey?

"Oh, Melchor, how *dreadful*," Raihan mourns, and slips his unfastened robes—*when* did he unfasten his robes?—off his shoulders. The cascade of silks drags Levente's gaze down Raihan's body, scarred skin and hard brown nipples and strong thighs already wet with his slick—

"Raihan," Levente manages to squeak, "everyone is watching."

Like Alphonse. Poor, shy Alphonse: the omega commander of Levente's cavalry, ferocious on the battlefield but timid in love. He might have been rushing to Levente's aid; now he stands frozen, starry-eyed and quivering, held in thrall by Raihan's perfection.

"They can well depart if the sight offends their eyes," Melchor says. "Raihan is beautiful, and beauty should be shared. Would you deny the world his allure, or Raihan their adulation? Surely our king is not so cruel."

Raihan beams, radiant as he steps past Melchor to drape himself over Levente's unresisting lap. "You are beautiful also," he says to Melchor. "Don't you agree, alpha of ours? Share your beauty too, Melchor. Such a terrible punishment, my darling, to be displayed nude and yet denied. Forced to look on as another is taken."

"Terrible indeed," Melchor agrees, and all Levente can do is sit choking as Melchor's robes share the fate of Raihan's.

"I shall prepare you," Melchor declares, "to take the cock I cannot have," and that is all the warning Levente gets before Raihan seizes in his lap, crying out sharply. Back arched, clinging desperately to Levente's shoulders.

In the distance, Alphonse moves at last. With a soft "*Oh*!" of muddled confusion, he claps his hands over his adorably flushed cheeks and rushes away, his king's plight forgotten.

Levente cannot flee. He can only clutch Raihan to his chest, transfixed by the filthy noise of an eager tongue working within a tight, dripping hole. Until Raihan cries out, incoherent, reaching down with shaking fingers to fumble for Levente's cock, and Melchor pulls back.

"Allow me," he says, and rises to help; his face glistens with the wetness of Raihan's pleasure. Between the three of them, they free Levente's achingly hard cock from the sodden confines of his trousers and guide the tip to Raihan's eager hole. Levente grips his omega by the hips, tries for a single futile moment to temper the speed of Raihan's descent—he might as well have tried to block a raging river with his bare hands.

He will not last. He *cannot* last.

He is gasping, slumped back against the bench with pleasure knifing white-hot up his spine. Helpless as Raihan fucks himself down brutally, chasing his own release, and Levente wants so desperately to last. But the heat and the sharp, shocking pleasure of his omega using his cock drives him unstoppably, uncontrollably, to his climax.

He squeezes Raihan's hips in warning, beyond words, and Raihan's warmth clenches down the length of him, milking him of every drop—

And pulls up and away before the knot catches.

Raihan rises, ethereally graceful even with Levente's spend leaking between his thighs. It's all too easy to notice only Raihan's delicate beauty, to forget that he was Melchor's equal and mortal foe long before Levente was a speck of dust in the eye of the warring lands that would become his kingdom. Levente is forcibly reminded when Raihan turns to scoop a laughing Melchor up with easy strength and deposits him neatly in Levente's lap: bare back to soaked-and-heaving chest, trapping Levente's pulsing cock and swollen knot between their bodies.

Melchor slippery-slick and squirming. His scent is sweet with desperation.

Levente reaches between them. Melchor's hole twitches so eagerly when Levente strokes it—despite his earlier words, he would never leave his omega wanting—but Melchor pushes his hand away.

"You mustn't, my king," he says. His eyes, pleasure-blown, shine wicked and wild. "I'm being punished."

"He'll have to go without his alpha's knot," Raihan agrees, guiding Levente's hands to lift Melchor's legs, "until he learns his lesson."

Levente sits, struck dumb, holding Melchor as Raihan moves them—splayed wide over Levente with his eager hole displayed. Levente is shaking almost as much as the naked omega in his lap, his swollen knot forgotten as Raihan grinds the head of his own smaller cock over Melchor's dripping entrance.

"Our alpha will forgive you soon, I know." A single brutal thrust, as hard as Raihan had fucked himself on Levente, and Melchor is speared open and writhing, screaming Raihan's name. "Until he does, my darling, I'm here to sate you."

2: Warm

"huddling for warmth"

Levente's omegas are battle-scarred, all inflicted by the other: *there is none other mighty enough to mark us,* Raihan had declared with pride. On their wedding night, Levente had urged his bristling brides to put old quarrels aside for the good of their newly joined realm.

To Levente's immense regret, they've taken his words very much to heart.

A hyperactive royal sex life is *probably* good for the unity of the realm.

"Alpha," Raihan whispers by his side, "we're so cold," and Melchor shivers exaggeratedly.

Levente is groggily impressed. The roaring hearth-fire has been put out, the creaky, old window flung open to let the cool autumn air in. Levente's omegas are huddled against him, one on either side—and he had not awoken until they spoke.

"If it's sex you want, you could have just *asked,*" Levente groans, running a hand down each of their backs. Hard-muscled, enchanting patterns of softness and rough scars—this isn't the worst way to be woken.

"Oh, we fucked each other already tonight," Raihan assures him, and wriggles; his plush rump pushes into Levente's hand. "Now we're both so terribly sore. Won't you comfort us?"

And yes, his hole is dripping wet at Levente's fingertips, the rim puffy and flushed blood-warm from hard use. Melchor's too, when Levente's questing fingers find his quivering entrance, and Levente is suddenly very awake.

What a gift! A firm, round ass in each hand, two freshly fucked holes dripping come and slick at his fingertips, his omegas shuddering against him as he trails feather-light touches over their sensitized rims. Levente dips his fingers into their clenching heat and the noise of it is so wet, so slick, so loud in the quiet of the night.

If only he could see their holes now, swollen fat and tight around his fingers.

He pushes his fingers in deeper, harder, testing the give. Melchor's hole yields more readily—their cocks are near equal in size, but Raihan uses his more eagerly; Melchor takes a cock well but is hesitant with his own. Levente generously fills him with a third finger so that both channels are more fairly stuffed and runs his sword-roughened fingertips over their rippling inner walls. Stroking, teasing, glorying in their trembling and gasping.

Until one of them whimpers, or maybe they both do, and Levente offers mercy. Holds his fingers still.

Just for a moment.

Just long enough for a single shuddering breath, and Levente spreads his fingers. Stretches their well-used rims wide.

They squeal as one, clinging to his chest, reaching across him to clutch at each other. Melchor pushes back, trying to fuck himself harder onto Levente's fingers; Raihan thrusts forward to rut his leaking cock against Levente's bare thigh. Levente clicks his tongue chidingly, and to his amazement, they obey and still, shaking with the effort of holding back their desire.

"Lie still, my darlings," Levente says, and grins unseen in the dark. "The hour grows late. Rest. Let your alpha keep you warm and comfort your poor sore holes."

Levente too is desperately hard, but he will endure. For the first time in all the months of their marriage, he has won—or has been granted—the upper hand in the strange game his omegas play. He will milk this opportunity for all it is worth. He will milk his omegas too, of every drop of slick and spend he can wring from their twitching cocks and dripping holes.

He wants to know which of them will be the first to find release; he wants to know how many times he can coax them to climax with their aching cocks untouched, shuddering and desperate in the cool autumn air.

He wants to know which of them will be the first to beg.

3: Throne

"obligatory heat scene"

"Please, Prince Melchor, let us announce y—"

Levente's royal guards, personally handpicked for their courage and strength, tumble back with terrified "meep"s as Melchor storms into the throne room like an entire rampaging army—apparently, a six-to-one numerical superiority is too much of a disadvantage. Even though Melchor is clearly unarmed, dressed in a sheer slip that hides nothing of his body, and very much in heat.

Raihan trots in behind him as Levente gathers enough of his wits to scramble to his feet. "Your mate is in need, alpha," Raihan calls, grinning ear to ear. "*Such* a shame. He built a fine nest, but there was no alpha in it to sate him."

"Yes, yes," Levente stutters, trying to adjust his robes to hide his achingly hard cock—he does not know why he tries, when all the alphas and half the omegas present are very clearly also hard. "We'll go right away." Must he dismiss the court? "Ah, begging pardon—"

"What? Go? I've waited long enough." Melchor stalks towards him, fearsome eyes glinting with the fever of his heat. "Court is closed for the day," he imperiously announces, shoving Levente back onto the throne. "Your king will be attending to his mate. Leave now, or stay and watch; I don't give a shit."

Not a single one of their damnable court moves, but Levente finds to his own shock that he does not mind. There is a scandalous part of him that preens—*see what is mine*.

Levente will contemplate this later, when he doesn't have an angry omega in heat on his lap.

Melchor's slip is already rumpled and torn; he must have been clawing at it, too heat-addled to pull it all the way off. Levente grips the flimsy material and rips, baring Melchor's flushed skin to be admired and stroked. Running his hands down his omega's heaving sides, cupping over firm buttocks.

Melchor snarls his satisfaction and pushes harder into Levente's arms, nipping almost affectionately at his face and neck. His breath rasping hot and sweet as Levente fondles him, thrusting his hips back eagerly as Levente spreads his arse and strokes his exposed hole, heedless of the longing eyes of the watching court.

Melchor's thighs are already drenched. Yet more slick escapes his twitching hole as Levente dips his fingers in past the swollen rim, dripping down Levente's hand to soak them both. Melchor whines, rutting down desperately at the bulge of Levente's cock as Levente kneads at his opening. Testing the supple stretch of his hole.

He is warm and wet and ready.

Levente will not torment Melchor or himself. He works his own cock swiftly free—he's gotten quite practiced in the months of his marriage. Taking an indulgent moment to slide its leaking head up the cleft of Melchor's buttocks, he lets the full, hard length of it press hot and heavy between Melchor's cheeks and spread them wide.

The noise that tears from Melchor's throat is halfway between snarl and whimper. His fingers dig into the sturdy linen of Levente's jerkin, clawing until Levente hears the thick cloth rip; Melchor might also be tearing into skin, but Levente has never been bothered by blood. He runs a soothing hand down his omega's back, working the thick head of his cock into position—pressing hard at Melchor's strong, swollen rim, grinding and teasing, demanding entrance.

Melchor gasps in his arms, shuddering, thrusting eagerly back. His greedy, wet hole strains to open around Levente's girth, the rim stretched out thin and helpless and still yielding farther. Farther, farther yet, until all at once the slow push becomes a rush of heat and slick pressure, and every glorious moment of that slide is a homecoming.

They curl close around each other, trembling and struggling for breath. Melchor's head rests on Levente's shoulder as he shivers and gasps, and Levente holds him close and strokes his back and tries to calm his own racing heart.

They are woken from their reverie as a small commotion breaks out amongst the watching crowd. Levente looks up and is astonished; *Alphonse*, of all omegas, blushing furiously under a chorus of catcalls as he drags a widely grinning alpha out of the room by the hand—even Melchor turns to whistle encouragement.

Raihan shouts for the alpha to *take good care of him*, and yes, Levente remembers now. That alpha was one of Raihan's warriors.

This has wonderful implications for the future of their new kingdom.

But right now, Levente can barely think of the realm. Melchor's wet heat is heaven and hell at once, and pride and duty demand that Levente bring the omega in heat release before finding his own.

He rocks up into Melchor's warmth, slow and seeking. His hands cup again over Melchor's buttocks, kneading and squeezing roughly in the way Melchor loves, and the answering clench of Melchor's channel around him is almost his undoing. Levente bites down on his own lip, pushing back the rising tide of climax. He thrusts up, hard and purposeful, and is rewarded with a pleasure-soaked cry that echoes through the cavernous room. Melchor writhes in his lap, cock dripping. His shaking hands scrabble frantically at Levente's chest and shoulders, searching and scratching even as Levente tries to sooth him.

To no avail—Melchor settles only when Raihan steps forward, plastering himself to Melchor's back and caging him in between them. Melchor hums his happiness, rocking back affectionately against Raihan's chest, head tilted up for a sloppy kiss. Wet and messy and eager, until Melchor screams suddenly into Raihan's mouth, and the powerful spasm of his channel as he does shocks an answering yelp out of Levente.

Raihan's arms are wrapped around Melchor's chest, pinning him in place. Clever fingers tormenting his nipples—scratching over the sensitive buds, flicking, squeezing, dragging Melchor inexorably to his release, and the heat and the wet, clenching pleasure sends Levente hurtling to his own climax.

Melchor is still shaking when Levente forces himself past the white-hot waves of his pleasure. Still whining high and desperate and pleading, Raihan's fingers still on his nipples, rubbing mercilessly over the over-stimulated buds.

Levente forces his nerveless hands back to Melchor's quivering hips, grinding him down hard on Levente's growing knot. He leans in close so his tongue can free one of Raihan's hands from the teasing—licking, suckling, the small pink nipple hard and peaked in his mouth. Melchor trembles hardest when Levente swirls the tip of his tongue around the little, stiff bud, whining high and sweet. From the corner of his eye, Levente can see Raihan tugging and flicking at Melchor's other nipple, and he times his own softer torture to that motion. Melchor cries out, head thrown back, but his cock still spurts weakly against Levente's belly. His channel still ripples around Levente's cock.

Also at the base of Levente's cock—Raihan's fingers again, prodding at Melchor's helplessly stretched rim. Melchor thrashes in their arms, his scream sharp and overwhelmed, and Levente would feel terrible if he didn't know just how much Melchor loves being taken apart like this.

But Levente does know, and so he nips punishingly at the soft skin of Melchor's chest. Grips his omega bruising-hard by the hips to drive him down harder on the fat knot splitting his abused hole wide. Raihan strokes sweet violation over Melchor's straining rim, Melchor's nipples surely driven to tingling oversensitivity by tongue and fingers, and together they force Melchor ruthlessly from one climax to the next.

Or maybe his first climax never stopped at all.

Melchor's nipples are peaked, his chest flushed red; his cock, wrung dry, is still twitching and hard. He is drenched in his own spend and slick, and already, warm lines of Levente's release escape his hole past the barrier of the knot, coating them all.

If Levente could have Melchor every day like this, he would; the hunger in Raihan's eyes says he would as well. This heat is a gift Levente intends to treasure. Later, much later, he will carry Melchor to their bed; together, he and Raihan will hold Melchor down and lick him clean everywhere.

But for now: Melchor came to Levente to be sated.

Levente will sate him in full.

4: Watcher

"walking in on sex..."

"*There* you are," Raihan purrs as Levente stands choking on his own tongue. "We've been waiting so long, alpha."

"Hrkl!" says Levente.

After close to a year of marriage, Levente had let his guard down. He was not prepared to walk in on Raihan and Melchor curled together on his bed, each with a mouthful of the other's cock, fingers stuffed in dripping holes, the air thick and sweet with their desperation.

"Begging pardon," Levente says, and backs hastily out of the room. "I intrude."

Levente wants nothing more than to be on the bed between them. His swollen cock wants him between them, as do his omegas...but Levente has been on the back foot too long. Raihan and Melchor plot not against Levente's reign but his dignity; Levente must seize this brief opportunity while his omegas are undone by each other's suckling and stroking.

He must regain the upper hand.

He has one chief advantage: this is his palace, and he is her king; he is privy to her secrets. Levente keeps the only entrance to the hidden tunnel behind the royal chambers locked and trapped. He is a warrior, not a spy, and never intended to use it. But for the sake of the last tatters of his dignity, Levente will set honor aside and wriggle through this dusty disgrace of a tunnel built for shoulders far slenderer—a task made far more difficult by his treacherous cock's eager interest in the proceedings of the amorous omegas on the other side of the tunnel wall.

Melchor's eager growls and the wet slide of his channel as he fucks himself down on a sweetly whimpering Raihan are so loud through the wall separating Levente from them. "So tight." Raihan's breaths are rasping gasps, his words punctuated by the sharp slap of skin on skin. "You're so warm around me, Melchor, make use of me, *oh*—"

The sound of Raihan's helpless orgasm washes through Levente like a release of his own. He turns his head, sinking his teeth into the meat of his upper arm to keep from crying out; his fingers press desperately into the dusty stone under him. His cock battles the confines of his trousers, leaking in its eagerness. The memories flood through him: Raihan spread wide and begging, the warm wetness of Melchor's channel around his fingers and cock.

Levente wants, so desperately, and he could have it all; he only has to turn around.

But he is not crawling through this filthy disgrace of a tunnel to indulge his libido or his disobedient cock; he is here to listen in on Raihan and Melchor's plotting while their tongues are loosened by pleasure. Surely now, languid from orgasm, they will speak freely, and he will learn what fresh madness they have planned.

"Do you remember the night you first bested me?" Raihan asks. His voice still quivers, and Levente is overcome by a flood of lustful memories: how Raihan's hole quivers too, when it is stuffed full and dripping; how Raihan's chest heaves; how he blushes. "It has dogged my memories for years. Did you regret not killing me while you had the chance?"

A soft sigh, a kiss. "I remember," Melchor says between the languorous, wet slide of skin on skin. "I don't regret sparing you, my Raihan. I only regret that I did not throw you down that night and make use of you."

Raihan's breath catches.

Levente too is holding his breath. He has one hand clapped tightly over his mouth, holding in his moans. The other hand, as traitorous as his cock, kneads against his will at the hard bulge of his desire.

"You should have," Raihan whispers. His words echo strangely in the tunnel's narrow confines, *youshouldhaveshouldhavehave.* "I wanted you too, that night, when you had me helpless. Tell me now, Melchor. How would you have used me?"

Usemeusemeuseme, the tunnel walls whisper, and Levente barely bites back a squeak. He must not make a sound; his omegas will hear. Melchor especially, wild and sharp and canny—will he be wrathful, if Levente is caught now? Levente has not yet tested his blade against Melchor's—why does the thought quicken his blood? Why does his cock pulse under his hand?

"Like this." A slick swift glide, a gasp. "Ah, my Raihan, how swiftly your cock rouses. I would have pinned you under me, used your cock to fill me. Left you writhing and dripping with your own hole untouched."

Raihan moans; Levente presses his face into the crook of his arm and moans with him. His hips jerk, thrusting his traitorous cock into the tight grip of his disobedient hand in time with the rhythmic slapping of Melchor fucking himself down. Levente must stop himself—he cannot come like this, a voyeur in a filthy tunnel—but he cannot. His climax is rising as warmth in his belly and tightness in his spine, just as Raihan's cries tremble with the closeness of his own release. The sound of his hand around his cock is so slick and loud in the confines of the tunnel—surely they must hear him?

On the other side of the tunnel wall, Raihan climaxes, screaming, and Levente shatters with him.

"Ah," Raihan gasps. Levente is gasping too, his face turned into his sleeve to guard himself from the dusty air; his trousers are soaked with his shame. "Ah, Melchor. So many years we've spent at war. We could have had this long ago."

"We could have," Melchor agrees, softer and sweeter than Levente has ever known him. "But I find that I do not regret it. We would have slain Levente on the field had we fought together from the start, and then we would not have our alpha."

"Aye, he has been worth the wait." Raihan sighs. "Perhaps he'll prove himself worth *this* wait also, and join us in his own soft bed instead of pawing at his cock alone, hidden and watching."

On the other side of the tunnel wall, Melchor yelps. Levente lies frozen, mortified unto death. He will never leave the confines of this tunnel; he will perish here, drowned in his own shame. Let his omegas board up the door; let this serve as his grave.

On the other side of the tunnel wall, Melchor starts to laugh. "Bless your ears," he says. "I didn't notice a thing."

"...and failing to follow through."

5: Warrior

"more fighting than fucking"

"You don't have to," Melchor is saying hurriedly, still glancing back towards his enormous and enormously enraged family gathered in the middle of the throne room. "It really doesn't matter that much, I—"

Raihan cuts him off with a quick kiss. "Go soothe them, my darling," he says, already dragging Levente out the side door, away from the mob. "I'll explain."

The look Melchor shoots them is half frazzled and half grateful as he storms towards his family, shouting quite unsoothingly. Raihan slams the door shut behind them, plunging them into the side passage's musty darkness.

Levente slumps against the cold stone wall and sinks slowly down into a heap. "His mother," he says, lightheaded, "wants me to—" He cannot find the words. "*Melchor* wants—he—he wants that?"

Raihan wrinkles his nose at the whiffling. "Aye, they think it long past time you bested Melchor and claimed him," he says, settling himself primly down before Levente. "The first to prove your strength, the second that you can please him."

"We've been married an entire year." Levente protests, but Raihan only scoffs.

"Any fool can stand by an altar and speak some pretty words," he says. "You bested me with your own hand, and so by our ways I am yours. But it was your troops who captured Melchor. Why should he call you his mate, and not them? If it took twenty strong warriors to best him, surely twenty also are needed to please him. Your Alphonse, who led them: he is such a sweet little thing. It would be lovely to see him under Melchor, spread wide and undone."

"Oh gods," Levente says, strangled and faint. He *can* imagine it; it is indeed a lovely picture, and he does not think Alphonse would be at all opposed. And with a sudden horror: "Oh gods, *Alphonse*. Will *he* have to…?"

Alphonse has been spending time—a great deal of time—with Raihan's warrior Hailuan.

Until Levente learnt of this fresh madness, he had been delighted.

"No one expects this of an omega not born to our ways," Raihan assures him. "Or perhaps your Alphonse could do the claiming; he is more than strong enough, and Hailuan is not too rigid to yield to his own mate."

Levente drops his head into his hands and groans. May the gods have mercy on his cock and on his soul—he can imagine that too. "I did not fuck *you* on the battlefield," he points out. It is a feeble protest; it is the last he has. His resistance is slipping away, yielding before his heating blood. To test himself against a warrior like Melchor, truly test himself—Levente did not become a conqueror by shying from battle.

"No, but you could have." Raihan sighs, his dark eyes soft and dreamy. "Ah, I was terrified when you threw me down. But then you helped me back to my feet so gently—I knew then that I wanted you. I would have given myself to you then and there, if only you'd asked."

"That's good to know." Levente's throat is suddenly tight. "I did not wish to force you two into this marriage, but I saw no other way to unite this new realm."

"Force? We wanted you, you lout." Raihan laughs, and his smile is fond. "Did you think our families would have yielded to this match if it were not so? This is a warlike land. It is not our way to sell one for the safety of the rest."

"I did not know." Levente lets his head fall back, thumping lightly against the stone wall behind him. Relief washes through him, but it does not quite wash away the distant worry. "Are you sure Melchor wants this? He seemed uncertain, and I have never seen him shy from asking for what he wants."

"He does not shy from asking for sex, but sex is only sex." Raihan's fingers stroke over Levente's face, his lips, his cheek; Levente turns his head just enough to press a kiss to his omega's fingertips. "We first crossed blades as children, Melchor and I." His dark eyes are hazed with the memory. "I remember well that day: I was small then, but he! Just a slip of a thing with a blade too big for his hands. 'That one has his father's blood-thirst,' my own mothers told me, 'and his mother's wrath. One day you must kill him or claim him, our Raihan. Let that day come swiftly.' "

"But you did neither," Levente murmurs, as though the spell of the tale might be broken by noise. "Nor did he."

"Melchor had his own reasons, I'm sure," Raihan says, and kisses him—it might be Melchor's lips that he seeks. "For me: I could never bear the loss. The taste of battle is far less sweet in his absence." Another kiss, this one meant for Levente. "We two were the mightiest of our peoples; we have always been bound by fate. Now you are our alpha. But Melchor is also my mate, as I am his. I know this of him: he wants the claiming. Will you have him?"

Everybody in Levente's new kingdom is utterly insane.

Levente must have grown just as mad; he will.

The taste of blood is iron-sharp.

All his world is wrath and ruin, torn earth and churned mud. Pain as clear and clean and crisp as the first cold rains of spring, and a fury as sweet as death.

The air around him sings of war.

Before him, Melchor snarls and paces. Half a swagger, half a stagger;

his face too is a mask of blood. Levente matches him threat for threat, step for bloodstained step. The hilt of his sword is blood-slick in his hand, every breath an exquisite agony; he must end this fight soon, or fall.

Levente lunges, much too quick; his shaking legs buckle, his knees hit the trampled ground. Melchor springs for his throat like a wolf, sharp teeth and sharper sword and all-consuming hunger.

But Levente has never in his life been prey.

He is a conqueror, a king with a stolen crown; he has won himself an army, a kingdom, a throne. No weariness sinks deep enough to bow him while there is a fight yet unfinished, and Melchor is as bruised and battered and bloodied as he.

He sweeps his blade up to meet his mate's, all his strength behind the counter-stroke. Steel against steel, their blades clash and lock; the scrape of metal rings out like a scream. Levente pays the noise no mind—let all the world go deaf! They shattered the quiet of the night long ago.

There is no trickery left in either of them, no cunning, no artifice: only sharp, bared teeth, the strain of overtaxed bodies, and strength.

Levente plants a foot into the broken earth, digging through the mire to solid ground. And all the way he pushes, pushes, his shoulders screaming against the terrible power that is Melchor's blade driving down against his own. Melchor is strong—brutally strong, gloriously, gorgeously strong.

But Levente is stronger.

His foot finds purchase; he anchors himself with it. Locks his arms and shoulders, puts all the strength of his back and hips into the press. *Do you see this, my Melchor?* Up, up, and forward. *Do you see my strength? Will you take me for yours?*

Inexorable, unstoppable, Levente stands.

Will you have me for your own?

Melchor's bloodshot eyes are wide, alive with terror and exultation intertwined. Still he fights on, pushing grimly back into the blade-lock, his bared teeth glinting sharp and white in the moonlight. But Levente bears down, forcing his omega one step back, another—not an inch yielded without a fight. Melchor snarls even as he shakes against the strain—until his arms weaken for just a single, precious moment that Levente feels as a tremor through their interlocked swords. A moment that Levente does not waste.

A final push, a vicious twist, and Melchor's sword goes flying.

For several long, gasping breaths, they both stand frozen. Mud-stained, blood-stained, shocked and staring.

Then finally, *finally*, Melchor yields.

Kneels.

Levente throws his sword aside and sinks down also to his knees—it is not right to stand over Melchor, not after the magnificence of their fight. Leans in close and kisses him, and the kiss tastes of blood and of victory.

"You can be rough with me if you wish," Melchor tells him, soft, his words half swallowed between them. "I don't mind."

Violence is the language Melchor speaks most fluently; he does not know what to do with tenderness.

Levente gentles his touch further yet. "If it pleases you," says he, "any other time you wish, we can hunt each other through the night, and fight and fuck to our hearts' content." He wants to kiss the blood off his omega's bruised and bloodied lips, but blood flows too from his split lips and bitten tongue, from jagged cuts over his cheekbones and brow—their blood smears and mingles. "But tonight—tonight is your claiming, my Melchor, and you fought like a king."

Already, mottled bruises are forming over the sharp edges of his omega's cheekbones and jaw, vividly beautiful in the moonlight. Levente strokes over them, slow and soft. "Tonight you have yielded yourself to me. So I beg you now—let me be gentle. Let me prove to you my worth."

This time, it is Melchor who leans forward, to kiss and be kissed. "You may." His words are soft, close to shy; his eyes are unbroken and wild. "May I—?" He reaches almost hesitantly towards the ties of his own breeches. "Levente, please, I want to be unclad before you."

"*Of course*," Levente says at once. But it takes the two of them together to free Melchor from his clothes and armor, fumbling with hands grown stiff and sore from their fight. Melchor himself tears through the ties of his breeches after their fingers fail them both; now he lies back, splayed out and beautiful and bare, Levente's for the taking.

Levente hoists Melchor's legs up, lifts his hips, spreads him. It is well worth the pull in his aching shoulders; Melchor quivers, and the little exposed hole clenches and drips. The smooth, strong lines of Melchor's parted thighs beg to be kissed, and so Levente does. One thigh to the other and back to the first, all the way down to lick a broad wet stripe over his omega's hole and weakly twitching cock.

Melchor jolts against him and moans. His hole spasms against Levente's tongue; Levente licks it again, trails kisses over the rim, plunges his tongue in deep and plunders it. His jaw is a single bruising ache; blood drips from his cuts.

But the desperate, shocked sounds of his omega's pleasure are worth any pain.

Melchor cries out with every wet thrust. His hole is eager and warm; his hips push desperately back upon Levente's tongue. His quivering legs are tight around Levente's shoulders, pulling him in close. One hand is fisted in Levente's hair, but the other—

The other clenches against the torn earth. Empty, fitful, seeking.

A final, soft kiss to Melchor's little desperate hole. Another to the head of his leaking cock, his belly, both nipples, the hollow of his throat. Upward until Levente can kiss his omega gently over the lips and ask, "Do you want Raihan here?"

Melchor nods, almost frantic. His legs slip down to Levente's waist, still clinging tight. "I want you," he says in a rush. "I want you so much. It is only—"

"I know," Levente murmurs, and kisses him again. "We are three." They don't have to call out; already Raihan has melted out of the darkness, folding down to his knees to tenderly rest Melchor's head in his lap and nuzzle them both.

"Raihan and I," Melchor says, soft and halting, "we were incomplete also, until you came."

Raihan watches them with dark, solemn eyes, nodding his agreement. "We had been too long at war," he says. One hand rests over Melchor's chest, his heart; the other reaches for Levente. "We could not become each other's without first becoming yours."

And Levente, tongue-tied, can only curl forward into the arms of the omegas he has won and been won by.

They are his, and he is theirs.

+I: Tender

"didn't we already have a heat scene?"

Raihan's eyes are fever-bright. The air is thick and warm with the sweetness of his heat; his thighs are drenched with the slick of his desire. His hips jerk in staccato rhythm: forward to rut his hard, leaking cock into the silk sheets under him, backward to push himself harder onto Melchor's fingers in his desperate dripping hole.

His eyes watch Levente, and they are worried and hungry and wild.

"Are you *sure*?" he asks, yet again. "You don't have to. I love your knot."

"I'm sure," Levente says, his voice hoarse with nerves. He is trembling, clutching the small glass vial of oil in his clasped hands like a lifeline—he is still more sure than he's ever been in his life. "I want this. I want to share this with you."

Deep in his belly, that aching want wages brutal war against his fears. Against vicious whispers that he should be already knot-deep inside the omega in heat, not on his back with his legs spread wide. Not offering up his own hole that can take nothing without oil.

Levente pushes the whispers aside. This is Raihan's heat, Raihan's desire, and Levente wants to give this of himself. There is no need for shame or fear; he is safe between his mates.

"It'll be good," Melchor promises. He never stops licking and kissing over Raihan's nape and shoulders; his fingers pump unceasingly in Raihan's hole. But his fearsome gaze is locked on Levente, ravenous, and is this how it feels to be taken? Hunted, yet desired? "Show him, darling. Show our alpha how good your fingers and cock will feel inside him."

Levente shudders; a whimper breaks from his throat. Yet his legs part, his knees draw up, and he lies spread and on display. The inescapable scent of Raihan's heat has his cock hard against his belly. He wants to sink into Raihan's waiting hole, wants to fuck in deep—but he wants also to be fucked. He has taken his mates so many times like this, looming over them as they offered themselves; now he wants to be taken in turn.

He wants to be devoured by the hunger that always consumes Raihan, every time their mate fucks deep into Melchor.

And *there*! That hunger is already in Raihan's eyes and in the sharp glint of his teeth, fanned high by the fires of heat as he eases the vial of oil from Levente's slack and yielding hands.

"It'll be good," Raihan says. The stopper of the glass vial releases with a *pop* that seems louder than its size should allow. "You give yourself so wonderfully, our alpha. We'll make you feel so good."

The first touch of an oil-slick finger, and Levente is lost.

He had never before been touched there. He had never thought to be opened there. He was a fool. Raihan teases and touches him as skillfully as he uses a blade, wielding that trembling, twitching hole as the instrument of Levente's own demise. Levente has never feared pain—he had readied himself for pain. But Raihan pets over his rim, rubs oil in deep, slips one finger and then another into him with aching slowness, strokes him where he has never been touched, spreads him where he has never been opened—and there is no pain.

There is only a yielding, a terrible, delicious vulnerability, and pleasure.

"Please," Levente gasps at last when Raihan has worked three fingers into him and pleasure is sizzling up his spine. It is the only word he can still find. "*Please.*"

"Of course," Raihan says, "my darling." For a horrible moment, Levente is empty and bereft, his hole twitching and open and cool with oil; then the head of Raihan's wonderful cock kisses the desperate rim, breaches it, and Levente is again filled. Stuffed full. Raihan's cock is so much smaller than his own; how do his omegas take the stretch? But the stretch is wonderful also, overwhelming and all-consuming. Levente is quivering from the fullness, unable to hide his whimpers and his moans. Melchor reaches out to soothe him with the hand not working to sate the need of Raihan's heat; Levente clings to it. Raihan too is trembling, and Levente knows well the pleasure of a cock sheathed in softness and warmth—he pulls his omega down, kisses him with all the intermingled heat of their shared desperation.

Raihan sobs into the kiss.

Levente's heart seizes; he holds his omega closer, strokes him and croons, and Melchor hovers close and worried.

But when Raihan looks up, he is smiling through his tears.

"I'm so lucky," he whispers, half choked, and his eyes shine with his happiness. He clutches at Levente, reaching back to pull Melchor close to them both. "How did I get so lucky? I love you both. I love you both so much."

Levente kisses him again, kisses Melchor; he holds them both to his chest where his heart is swollen with love. “I love you,” he tells them between the kisses, pressing all his truth into each word. “I love you,” and Raihan returns the kisses and words with ardor.

But Melchor whimpers, opens his mouth and shuts it again, hides in the kisses and against them. “We know your heart, darling,” Raihan tells him, and Levente murmurs agreement and peppers him with yet more kisses, until he smiles again. “Be at ease. It is well.”

They can give him all the time he needs to find the words; they have all the time in the world.

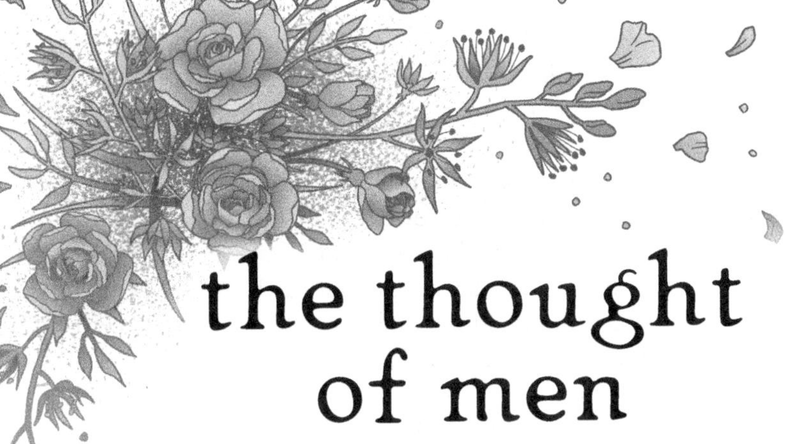

the thought of men

ilgaksu

anal fingering, anal sex, attraction at first sight, bipoc, egypt, established relationship, historical, m/m, m/m/m, present tense, sex pollen, third person limited point of view, trans male, trapped together, twosome to threesome, vaginal sex

I shudder at the thought of men. …I'm due to fall in love again.
(from *Enough Rope* by Dorothy Parker, 1926)

Cairo, Egypt. 1925.

Allan Lau Fei-Yu isn't sure when exactly he lost all control over his life. He has a deepening, gnawing suspicion it might have been somewhere between four to six minutes after his birth. He has an even stronger suspicion that any hope of reclaiming it fled screaming about twenty seconds after he walked into the same room as Karl von Betzenstein and his husband.

When he enters The New Cairo hotel, it is winter in Egypt. In the last few years, he's become unaccustomed to this kind of warmth. But for much of his childhood, he'd been well-adjusted to the sweltering heat of a Hong Kong summer, where the water in the bay glinted like sweat, and the air felt as swallowable as the bay, and the body—in rebellion against starch and iron—still leaked. He has settled, for the first time in years, for what is most comfortable: a secondhand linen suit. He is painfully aware that his heat-strained face, framed by the slow remove of his hat, picks him out as New Here.

It is never, Allan knows, safe nor sensible to be New Here, and if you must be, you cannot, cannot be noticeable as such. But it is hard to be unnoticeable when you are Chinese in faux-European gilt. Since subtlety is rendered beyond him, he lets himself gawk like it's his first day on Earth. It is a beautiful building, in fairness. Jaw-dropping, even. He expects the building garners this reaction often. It soars, in lake-cool colours of marble and shining steps and airy dimness, as if a cathedral architect was brought, hands bound, to build a shrine to—

"Excuse me, sir," a bellboy says without much sincerity, pushing a suitcase-laden trolley past the second Allan leaps out of the way. He nods at Allan's startled, automatic "Sorry" as if Allan's apology is mere lint.

Anyway, the sweat is managing to dry on Allan's face. A little miracle from that architect. He barely has time to consider it before he must continue on. He has an important meeting regarding future employment.

Allan has only been in Cairo a few days, enough that he's barely recovered from travel, but even he's managed to hear of Karl von Betzenstein. For all the expanse of wealth below, the world of those above-ground here is small. A goldfish bowl: mundane to those standing outside it, but the whole world for those within.

And oh, come on. It's the kind of story that brings everyone together around the bar table, rich and poor and poorer, gossip truer than family, blood, loyalty, or money, for those few hissed minutes: the sole von Betzenstein child, heir and spinster both by twenty-eight, and not ugly, you know, but somehow the suitors had stopped coming. And the father hadn't cared much, had he, given his desire for a devoted little secretary who performed with perfect aplomb, like a lamb might, only—

Allan startles. The waiter by the door of the garden room has apparently asked him whom he's here to see at least once, by the confused look on his face.

"I'm here for," Allan says, corrects, corrects again, swallows, speaks up: "I'm here as the guest of Karl von Betzenstein."

The waiter, whose face had been posed in a mask of exquisitely polite boredom, transforms. He looks borderline gleeful.

"Of course!" he says, the elasticity of his smile devouring the subdued, brittle Bakelite of his previous expression. "Mr. von Betzenstein! This way, sir."

Allan follows the rapidly escalating gait of the waiter through the weave of European-style wicker chairs and white cloth, afraid of knocking into carefully set crystal. It reminds him, unpleasantly, of dancing. He's spun out into stilling and catches himself just before he crashes into one of the flimsy chairs, just in time to hear a heavily accented "Oh, you're the specialist Malik suggested."

Allan looks up and immediately wants, very badly, to sit down.

The problem is—and it is a very immediate problem—this: Karl von Betzenstein, for all he is towering above Allan, has the kind of face last seen on a Renaissance painting of a young martyr. A St. Sebastian hung at life-size, all so other men can justify staring too long at him, at an image of something boyish and beautiful, bearing up under multiple penetrations, hands tied above his head and mouth half open in what could, conceivably, be argued as agony.

Then, he smiles. He leans forward slightly and reaches out towards Allan, who does not shrink back as he usually might because he cannot move, paralysed as he is by the smile. The dark sweep of eyelashes over darker eyes. The ash of the irises against the faint wave of golden hair around his face. It is cut so brutally short in places Allan imagines the rasp of it against his own fingertips, how it would lengthen into the curls that fall forward as Karl von Betzenstein—as he moves, touches Allan's arm over his shirt, and—

pulls up said limp arm, fits his hand into Allan's clammy one, and shakes it.

Ah. Fuck.

"There," Karl von Betzenstein says. "Now I can sit down again."

"Oh," Allan replies. "Yes. I'm terribly sorry," and sits opposite him. At noticeable speed.

Von Betzenstein clearly notices. He raises his eyebrows and sips from a half-empty cup of coffee, brewed so black it seems to leave a shadow of itself against the emptying china.

"Which specialist are you again?" he asks. "Do you drink coffee?"

"Yes, Mr. von Betzenstein," Allan lies, and is sighed at.

"No," Karl replies. "That's my father. I only kept that name because it would've caused even more of a scene, and these sorts of people are very boring and hate scenes. You, however, are too nervous to be boring, so don't bother."

"Thank you," Allan manages. He thinks there was a compliment in there somewhere. He would like there to have been.

"Welcome to Egypt. You can call me Karl." Karl pauses. "Do you have a reason you should be nervous? You seem in a hurry."

Allan looks behind Karl, to where the selection of seated patrons all seem turned towards them, eyeing Allan first before being dragged back to Karl in his fine-knit jumper that appears, to Allan, to be sans a shirt. He hasn't seen the fashion for that in person yet. It must be new. The effect is striking. The cloth sits against his skin like water.

"No," Allan replies, wanting to sink into Karl for all his tone is scalding. "No, I don't have anywhere else to be."

Before Karl can reply, he seems to spot someone out of Allan's sight. His whole expression morphs. He lights up from the inside, transforming his previous disaffected boredom. "Malik!" he says. "Finally. You're here. This is the—" He looks back at Allan. "You didn't say what you did yet, did you?"

And then—

Allan had been sure he'd just met one of the most beautiful men in the world in Karl von Betzenstein. Surely the most beautiful in Cairo. Now, he is reassessing, because Malik ibn Sumayya, his actual main point of contact in the city, is standing before him.

"Good morning," Malik ibn Sumayya says to Allan in a voice so deeply and instantly soothing that Allan has to fight not to simply melt into the sound of it. "Doctor Lau, I presume? Did you have a safe journey? I am so sorry about him."

Somehow, he is nothing like Allan had pictured from the gossip: Malik ibn Sumayya, up-and-coming translator of some reputation, significantly dented after he'd seduced the von Betzenstein daughter five years prior while working as her language tutor. Although it's never been clear at what state in the proceedings virginity entered the past tense, they'd married secretly. By the time the father von Betzenstein tracked them down in Marsa Alam, said marriage had clearly been consummated to such an extent, and with Karl—who, back then, was still called by the name written on a Bavarian birth certificate—so clearly willing, annulment was out of the question. The old man had disowned Karl on the apoplectic spot, Karl had renounced the von Betzenstein fortune in the same self-righteous breath, and now father and son were a punchline through the whole archaeological community.

It's a strange situation. Allan had been warned on the boat over how half the city won't have dealings with Karl von Betzenstein, and the other half are waiting, all bated, for the day his father dies, in case Karl contests the inheritance.

"It's a pity," Allan remembers being told, "Anything he ever does, that translator of his, they'll say it was because of the von Betzensteins. He'll never be his own man."

Malik certainly carries himself as though he is, regardless of the court of public opinion. He sits opposite Allan and next to Karl, and smiles directly at Allan, gaze clear and dark. Though Allan's brain had kept rambling on to itself looking at Karl, when looking at Malik, it goes blissfully empty. Quiet in a dreamy, peaceful way Allan can't remember feeling in a long, long time. Maybe not ever. Allan is not a naturally tranquil person. But he looks at the calm intensity of Malik ibn Sumayya's eyes—the lenses of his gold-rimmed glasses no kind of shield against them—and at the sharp definition of his nose and mouth, the breadth of his shoulders in the crisp grey of his suit jacket, and Allan realises, as though shoved underwater, the exact depth of what could become a problem. It is bottomless.

Malik smiles at him.

Allan, helplessly infected by it, smiles back.

This job is going to be, Allan realises, complete and unrelenting hell.

Allan is right, moreso than he could have ever known. It is hell because, as it turns out, Malik ibn Sumayya and Karl von Betzenstein are very competent, very kind—in their own ways—and very, very in love with each other. When they are sitting in front of tables covered in maps, Malik hands Karl his tiny cups of black coffee in an established schedule, and Karl smiles at him like Malik was the first, even only, man on Earth. When they are standing in the market bartering for supplies, Karl is greeted by Malik's contacts with the long-running familiarity of an established, if slightly odd, spouse. When the pair surround Allan, the weight of their attention is overwhelming.

There is a particularly painful dinner in a gentleman's club with investors. Allan can only take so much of the bachelor humour before he has to take a break else bang his head against the wall until he passes out. He claims some excuse and hides in a balcony enclave, three doors down from the privately rented dining room, and contemplates once again how much his career means to him.

Karl finds him within minutes.

"They are all bastards," Karl says of the men Allan is now avoiding, smoking one of his little, bitter cigarettes. "Don't take it personally. If you do, I think this will be a very long month for you." He offers Allan one.

Allan shakes his head. "They make it difficult not to."

"Of course they do. If it was easy, more of us would stay."

"More of us?"

"Men like us. The strange ones."

Allan goes very, very still.

"Ah. I'm sorry." It's so clearly uncharacteristic, an apology from Karl, that he looks surprised at himself as much as Allan is. "Malik is always telling me I should be more sensitive about it. Some people carry a lot of shame about inversion."

"And you?"

"It is a social anomaly," Karl replies, "and anomalies are data. There is no morality to data." He inhales, exhales bitter smoke. "We looked you up, of course, before Malik suggested you. It sounds like the situation in London became unpleasant."

"Yes," Allan says, blinking away memories of whispers in crowded conference halls and the rapid sink of opportunities in the wake of rumours. "Yes, very unpleasant."

Allan looks at the shape of Karl's mouth around the cigarette, and he wishes he could learn to want less. He's always wished it. Wanting less might have saved him from so much. It could save him still.

The first night of the dig proper, Allan is returning to his own bedroll when he hears it: a low and unmistakable moan.

Outside the door to his own tent, Allan stops dead. He turns back and retraces his steps. It's only a few. That's how he heard it, with them so close. Allan pauses outside Karl and Malik's. He's heard wrong, he tells himself. He's inventing things. He should just—

Allan's gut twists. He reaches towards the tent.

His fingers almost brush the canvas, but then he hears it—

"Get on your knees."

In the small, wet space between inhale and exhale, Allan's whole face flares up, torchlit with embarrassment. He does understand the concept of conjugal enjoyment. It seems to be, as it happens, being very much enjoyed. From inside the tent, Karl lets out a whine that pulls up and through Allan like fire even as it tapers off into a shaky laugh.

"Fuck," Karl says, a little hoarse, then: "Make me."

Another moan, in a low echo. It throbs through Allan's whole body. Want sears through him.

He flees. What else can he do, given the circumstances?

The next day, Allan can barely meet their eyes. It helps that he can busy himself with the minutiae of his own pack, head bent low over his supplies. He looks up once to see Malik kneeling in front of Karl to fix a loose bootlace in the open doorway of their tent. It's unclear if they're relying on the shadows or simply don't care. It's brazen in a way that makes Allan feel borderline nauseous. He remembers last night, and in between blinks, he swears Karl's head snaps up in his direction, because suddenly Allan is being stared at—direct and unblinking, eyes glimmering within the half-dark of the tent.

Sensibly, Allan bolts.

They catch up with him inside the tomb.

"Morning," Karl says cheerfully. "You look tired."

Fuck. Do they know? No, they can't know. Still— "Do I?" Allan says, in no mood for Karl's antics.

"Karl," Malik mutters in warning, and Karl drops it in favour of keeping pace with the rest of the group.

The air has a strange, grainy quality, dust stirred up from the dark as down into the maw they go. Within minutes, Malik stumbles, almost slamming into Allan. Catching himself with a hand to the carved wall just in time, Allan turns to find Malik looming over him—and close.

"Uh," Allan says.

"Malik?" Karl pauses, turning to face them. His brows are drawn down, mouth tense. "What's wrong?"

"Nothing," Malik says, "I tripped." Then to Allan, as though an afterthought, "Sorry." Allan swallows. This close, Malik looks strangely flushed.

This close, Allan swears he can see the beat of Malik's pulse in his throat, when the bob of it settles from him swallowing. His breath seems almost erratic. Behind the outstretched palm of Malik's hand, the painted wall glimmers in the half-light, speckled with mica and dust. Allan looks at the parted lips of dancing girls and feels, absurdly, as if he's being mocked by the memory of long-dead artisans.

"It's fine," Allan says, remembering how to breathe and turning away. "He's fine. We should carry on."

"I see," Karl says. Allan waits for some added witticism, but it never arrives. Karl seems oddly subdued. He has been for some time now. "Let's keep going. Don't fall behind."

"We won't," Allan promises.

Malik doesn't reply, but when Allan starts walking again, Malik follows him, almost in sync with his steps. Above them, the ceiling presses in, and around them, Allan swears he can feel the weight of each and every painted eye.

They get lost.

Allan, quite honestly, has no clue how it's happened. One moment, they're with the rest of the group, voices echoing through the dark, and then…

The voices get quieter, distant, then gone, like stars being snuffed out in the dark. Behind Allan, Malik's breath has ratcheted up louder, higher, every few minutes, but every time Allan has asked if he's fine, Malik has said, "Yes," clipped and tight, and Allan has become almost—

Well, almost afraid to ask. And so he's stopped asking, and kept walking, and gotten turned around in some dizzying loop.

There's another stumble, Malik losing his balance, all grace gone as though a colt rising from the ground for the first time. Malik crashes into Karl, who ricochets off Allan, who is forced forward by mass and gravity and all the laws of the world that still reign, despite this being a place, ultimately, for the dead. But they are not dead. This means that when Allan trips over his own feet, urging him on still farther, he steps forward blindly.

In the end, they hear the mechanism activating only seconds before they fall through the floor.

Allan has a sense of his stomach lurching, something glittering in the air as his own body slices through it, like the gold shimmer that had been on the painted walls above, like the paint that had once adorned the dancing girls for powerful men, and still does now, in all the best clubs—

Time suspends, reanimates itself, and when Allan hits the ground, he does so hard. All the breath punches out of him in that one blow, and it takes him a few beats to recover.

"What just happened?" Karl snaps, struggling to his feet. But for a faint bout of breathlessness in his voice, almost a wheeze, he behaves as if immune to the impact. Allan can only look up as Karl stomps over to him, swaying slightly. "What did you do?"

"Sorry," Allan manages.

Karl looks at him, down there on the floor, and visibly deflates. "Oh, no," Karl says, "Don't look at me like that. Now I have to feel even more bad."

"You're feeling bad about something else?" Allan asks.

"Don't you?" Karl retorts. "I feel terrible. I have done since we arrived. Malik also clearly feels terrible, for all he's being a martyr about it, as per fucking usual."

"It's nothing," Malik insists, gingerly rising to his feet and brushing off dust and debris. The faint metallic glint of it seems to stick, ever more insistently, to his skin.

"Don't pretend. We're lost. How the fuck are we lost?"

"I don't know, Karl," Malik replies. There's something strange under his usual melodic calm. "That's how being lost works. Please don't go marching off again. It'll make it worse."

"I can't just"—Karl throws up his hands—"stand still."

"Are you—?" Allan's throat sticks. He swallows, hard, around it. The air has gone from grain to syrup in his mouth. "Karl, are you feeling quite all right?"

"Fine," Karl says, clearly attempting to sound irritable—and failing.

His voice is fading into something slower, drawn out. "I'm…fine. Why…wouldn't I be?"

"Habibi," Malik interrupts, stern in a way that Allan has never heard. No, well, he has. His own stomach tightens in response. "Don't pretend."

"It's the heat."

"I don't think it's the heat. We are underground."

"I know we're underground. Allan knows we're underground. Everyone knows we're underground!"

"Please don't bring me into this," Allan says, to no avail.

"Hase," Karl says, and then says it again. There are other words between. They escape, sharp and foreign, from his throat.

Allan blinks at him.

Malik frowns. "Karl," he says, his voice like the slow strain of honey before it breaks from a jar's lip. "You know I don't understand German."

Karl blinks. He frowns, sounds out the words, mouth moving silently, and then scowls deeper. Allan can barely grasp onto whatever small internal crisis Karl is occupied with. His own thoughts are caught on the swell of Karl's mouth.

"You're fretting," Karl hisses. His breath has audible weight now, rasping through the air in taut ribbons. "Like a little bunny. Both of you." He leans against the tomb wall, swaying into it. "Aren't you men, not rabbits?" He leans heavier against the wall, then shakes his head, ferocious like a dog, and pushes himself away. "No, let's be men and stay on our feet."

"I think," Malik says slowly, "that you've been drugged."

"Oh, do you? Do you think that?" Karl mocks. "I couldn't tell at all."

"Is it poisonous?" Allan thinks to ask.

"Oh, if it's only poisonous!" Karl throws up his hands. "Let's die on our feet then!"

"Karl, stop being dramatic." The exasperation in Malik's voice fades as he turns to Allan, says to him, "Allan, stop panicking."

"I'm not panicking," Allan denies, but he's finding it increasingly hard to breathe. He can feel it now, whatever is inside him, rising and pulsating in a languorous, rhythmic heartbeat. For all it's artificially induced, he knows this feeling. He felt it standing outside the tent last night.

Arousal.

The timing of Allan's life really, really fucking sucks sometimes.

"Yes, you are."

"No," Allan grits out. "I am not panicking." He sighs. "Think about it. How are you both feeling?"

"Oh," Karl says after a moment, audibly surprised.

"Oh," Malik says a breath later, an emotion Allan cannot name percolating through his voice.

"Yes," Allan says, to conclude, aware of the flush rising up through his whole body. "That's not panic."

Or at least, not just panic. Because there is, he can admit in the privacy of his own mind, a degree of panic there. Of course there would be. In fairness, Allan ought to be grateful that this is happening around two men of his own inclination. It's an easier way to avoid his face getting beaten in. He thinks of the other men they've collaborated with on this dig and shudders. But somehow—surrounded by the two most beautiful men he's ever met, and neither of them with any reason to look twice at him—it's still cold comfort.

Malik looks down at his glimmering hands.

"We're absorbing it through our skin."

"Oh, for fuck's sake," Karl sighs. "You think it's on the walls. And now it's inside us."

"I know it is. It's the only sensible explanation."

"Oh, yes," Karl snipes. "Because being poisoned by a tomb aphrodisiac is so very sensible."

"You don't have to like it for it to be a fact," Allan hears himself saying. He didn't plan to say that. In fact, even as he'd thought it, he'd consigned it, very securely, to the vault of thoughts he cannot voice. Like the memory of Karl's moans through canvas the night before, the strange longing challenge in his eyes through the doors of the tent this morning. So how has Allan voiced it anyway?

Karl is staring at him, mouth slightly ajar. "Are we all saying every little thought now?" he asks. "Can I go next?"

"What did I just say?" Allan becomes very, very aware of his own breathing—the almost reedy ratchet of it—and of the weight of being watched. He should like it a lot, lot less. He should still be panicking. Maybe he would be, in a better situation. But right now, the hold of whatever his body has taken into itself seems to be tearing him open and asunder, and they still haven't told him what he—

"You were talking," Malik says, very evenly, "about his eyes."

"And moaning," Karl adds, because of course he does. "There was elaboration on moaning."

Was he? Ah. Shit. That's unfortunate. Allan's whole body flushes a notch hotter at the humiliation. He swallows, audibly, around a mouth that feels full of dust.

"I'm so sorry," Allan says, and Malik frowns.

"No," Karl says. "I think Malik wanted you to elaborate more, actually."

"Stop it," Malik says. "This is pressuring him, Karl. We talked about it."

"Talked," Allan echoes, the word settling oddly in the pit of his stomach. "About me?"

"About the fact Malik wants to fuck you senseless?" Karl rolls eyes. "Yes. I'm ignoring how you're looking at me, Malik, because it's true." He tilts his chin up, and stares at Allan. "But I told him he had to be second."

"I don't understand," Allan says.

Malik makes some small noise.

Allan turns to him. "Is it?" he asks. "Is it true?"

Malik's mouth twists, and then it evens. His shoulders straighten. He faces Allan, and Allan realises he's never wanted Malik more, and it might not fully be because of the drugs.

"Yes," Malik admits, sending a bolt of heat soaring through Allan. "We thought you'd come to us, eventually."

"What?"

"You were taking your time! Were you not taking your time?" Karl sighs. "This is what I get for being ordered to be polite. A waste of time, but Malik insisted—"

"Sorry, what?" Allan is still not following.

"You're British, aren't you?" Karl says. "Aren't you all repressed? We were trying to be respectful of your culture."

Allan blinks.

Karl makes an irritated little gesture back, all sheer pique.

"I'm not British," Allan says, slowly. "I'm from Hong Kong. My name is Allan Lau Fei-Yu. That's not an English—"

He stops talking. The look on Karl's face is priceless. The look on

Malik's is, somehow, even more so.

"I am beginning to think, habibi," Malik says, in his usual calm, clear voice, "that we've fucked this up."

Allan can't help it; he begins to laugh.

"I cannot be expected to fucking tolerate this," Karl snarls.

He closes the distance between Allan and himself in two strides and drops to his knees in front of Allan. Allan has a brief, blinking moment of taking in the closeness, the warmth of breath and the small whitened scar at the corner of Karl's nose, only visible, it turns out, at this distance and angle, and then—

Karl kisses him, hard, and Allan stops thinking. Karl's mouth is fever-hot, breath strained where he exhales against Allan's lips. Malik is silent, or seems to be. Allan can barely hear anything beyond him and Karl. Allan is afraid to pull away first, afraid for when this ends, afraid the end is coming because Malik will surely tear him off Karl any moment, so he takes what he can while he can have it. He kisses Karl back. And, it turns out, Allan isn't sure if he can be expected to fucking tolerate this either.

"Tell him," Malik says, steadier than either of them but only by a bare few degrees, "if you want to stop."

"I don't," Allan replies. The drug is gliding through his veins, sure, but this is the truth. The taste of it just seems to have loosened the fact free. "I don't want to stop."

Allan has no sense of where to touch, or how. It doesn't seem to matter. His body surges on without him. Karl's clothes tangle around his hands. Karl, meanwhile, seems to loosen instead, comes undone as easily as if he's been fully unwrapped. Under the drag of linen, his bare skin feels obscene, as warm silk might feel in summer air. Allan's head is spinning; the whirl of it seems grounding. Familiar. And Allan has no experience of anything but a specific sort of man, and limited experience at that. And the thing is, the more you prevaricate around the technicalities of what classes as virginity, the more outright pitying the reactions become. Allan avoids pity like the plague for this reason alone. He thinks that if he'd been able to explain this to Karl beforehand (though he can't bring himself to imagine the excruciating circumstances), perhaps Karl, of all people, would have understood. But Karl doesn't know to ask, and Allan doesn't know how to say it, and for all his own fumbling experiments, and though he is an avid reader, Allan still isn't sure he could have been prepared for this.

He looks over Karl's shoulder, at Malik, and the plea must be clear in his eyes: help me.

Malik understands, and Malik does. When he slides to his knees beside Allan with practised grace despite the flush along his cheeks, Allan almost thanks him out loud. But he can't form words; his mouth is robbed dry of them.

From this vantage point, Allan finds he can only stare as Malik lets Karl pull him in, their mouths opening against each other wet and familiar. Behind his glasses, Malik's eyes fall shut, lids fringed by eyelashes so full they ought to be obscene. Then, Karl leans away slightly, enough to turn Malik's face, eyes still lidded, back towards Allan.

"Your turn," he says, and Allan doesn't have to be told twice. The moment feels eggshell and ephemeral, for all the desperation drawn taut through Allan, and then Malik's hand reaches out, caresses Allan's hair, slides through it and down to the nape of his neck. A beat. A breath. And then Malik's hand, inexorable, tightens, holds Allan in unrelenting place.

Allan has sensed, from Malik's whipcord arms, that he might be stronger, much stronger, than his mild manner betrays. Now, Allan knows it. A different sort of man might force the point. Malik is not that sort of man. He gentles Allan, as firm as a master with a spooked horse who needs breaking, as resolute as years of water against stone. Allan is neither of these things. He dissolves into the hold; he unravels. He exhales, opens his mouth wider. Melts in closer. Loses time.

"Come here," Karl says, breath hot against Allan's mouth. "Stay."

With that order hanging in the air, he wraps his hand around Allan's cock through his trousers, and Allan is too busy gasping, inhaling over and over without exhale, to say anything at all. Allan does what he's told: Allan stays. Feeling swells, hot and buoyant, at the boundaries of his own skin, which feels permeable, expansive, rapidly eroding. All he can taste is salt. All he reaches for is Karl. The rest of the world has ceased; the rest of the world has never been here at all. When Karl begins to unbutton Allan's trousers, Allan fumbles to help him, Karl's fingers against his own, and then—

The gasp Allan lets out seems not so much to echo as to hang, crystallised and heavy, in the air. It takes Allan a beat to register the fingers of Karl's unoccupied hand wrapped around Allan's wrist, the grip harsh and tight, the pull towards Karl. It takes another to register Karl pressing Allan's hand against the front of his own trousers for what it is. Allan is caught up in the differences, the smooth curve of Karl's body over the clothes, but then Karl's hand on Allan's dick for the first time sends pleasure running through him like a livewire. Allan shudders; Karl makes a low, biting sound, and Allan catches up to the command. He tears into Karl's clothes like a starving man served a banquet, hauls Karl towards himself with a hunger that has finally been unleashed.

Now in Allan's lap, Karl settles, presses in between them with a practised hand, and spreads himself open. This time, when he rocks down against Allan, the grind is slick and hot and sends Allan bucking up against Karl on instinct, a low sound he's not sure he's ever made before falling from his mouth.

"Better?" Karl smirks.

"Better," Malik confirms, as though Allan wasn't even the one being asked. "Look at his face."

Malik loops both arms over Allan's shoulders now, strung loose. He mouths at the back of Allan's neck, licks up sweat. Allan shivers under the heat of his tongue.

"I didn't ask you," Karl retorts, piqued, rolls his hips down again, and harder. "I want him to beg. Don't you think he'll look pretty when—"

When, Allan notices, with a strange, faraway feeling. He said "when," not "if."

"Don't worry," Malik soothes. "We'll get him there. Your problem, amira, is you've always been too impatient. These kinds of things take—"

"Fuck that," Karl says, and snatches Allan up again. This next kiss is vicious in its gut-punch intensity, dizzying with impatience. He licks up from Allan's parted lips to his ear and says, "I'd rather fuck you."

"Oh," Allan chokes out. "Yes. Yes, please."

"You can't share to save your life," Malik chastises. When he turns Allan's face towards him, his hands are gentle but firm. He leans forward and fits his mouth against Allan's just like that, just as simply, and without moving Allan from beneath Karl. They press hard into each other, Allan straining to reach from where he's seated. Malik's hands shake as they slide under Allan's shirt, and in that one single, telling tremble, Allan understands how it might feel to be a god. For all Karl is mesmerising, brattish and mercurial and demanding, Malik's attention feels as it might to have a painting of a past king turn in its frame to regard you. To be the focus of desire to the point it becomes undoing.

Allan has always been ambitious. But this feels like touching power, real power, for the very first time.

"I'm ready," Karl says, thready and desperate against Allan's throat, long before Allan can say he feels the same. But then Karl bites him, just lightly, teeth barely sinking in but enough that Allan's cock jumps with it, and then everything is a scramble.

There's a phrase in French that Allan learned once: l'appel du vide. The impulse—on having snuck onto the roof of the tong-lau tenements in Mong Kok, miles and time away from right now, when Allan was young and yearned to live forever—on gazing down at the spread of the city he was born into as surely as a cradle, and the great yearning expanse of the drop—

The impulse to reach out, step forward, and fall.

In the end, he sinks into Karl without a single sound.

The feeling is indescribable, but Allan's brain, so wired towards categorisation, still tries, flatlines around sensation. He thrusts once, twice, pressed in on all sides by slick, unrelenting heat, body stuttering. And then, Allan comes harder than he has in a long, long time. It is less orgasm and more obliteration. He shudders in the wake of it, curling inwards and around the man above him, hips pushing up and up and farther in like yearning, even in the moment of relief.

Then, the shame hits, and does so in a flood. Allan flushes under the weight of it. He has always felt on the tightrope of ruining what he touches, and now…

"Oh," Karl says, all his breath leaving him at once, and Allan flushes harder, trembles with the anticipation of disappointment, only— "Oh, look at you. You're beautiful." He cups Allan's face in his hands, running both thumbs underneath Allan's eyes. Allan opens his mouth, overwhelmed, but finds himself struggling to make sound. "Malik, look at him."

"I'm looking, Karl," Malik says, voice warm. He leans in, kisses behind Karl's ear, dips down farther and kisses Allan's cheek. "Did that feel good?" Allan makes some dumb sound of agreement. "Good," Malik says, endorsement hitting as praise. "That's what we want, isn't it?"

He pushes Allan's hair off his face, all the strands of it that had been sticking loosely to his forehead, and smiles at him. A vague, insistent part of Allan's brain reminds him of how insane this all is, of how drug-addled they are, about how lots of men say lots of things they don't mean, especially at times like this, but the thoughts are tinny, fragile, rapidly drowned out.

Allan manages to bite down against voicing any of this, teeth in his own lip. Then he realises, with a resolute, throbbing ache, that he's still hard.

He's confused

Karl looks delighted.

"Looks like this bastard drug is worth something," he crows, and clenches around Allan to drive the point home. The noise Allan lets out is low, and pained, and seems to bounce off the enclosed walls. Malik laughs, reminding Allan of how close he is, crowded up against Allan's side. When Allan turns to face him, drawn in by the loop of sound, the warmth of it and of Malik's body, and the look in his eyes to match. Malik smiles at him with all of his teeth.

"I want a turn," Malik says, voice low. He presses a kiss just behind Allan's ear. The heat of it seems to radiate outwards, a lingering, singular spot. Then, breathing against the curve of it, Malik asks, "Will you let me?"

It takes Allan a beat to realise what he's being asked for, a breath to inhale and try not to choke on air and the euphoria of it. When he says, without thinking, "Are you fucking kidding me?"

Karl laughs so hard that Alan chokes on the new feeling of Karl shaking and tightening around him.

Allan loses time; it doesn't so much fragment as simply dissolve. The press of Malik's fingers inside him. The push of his own cock, still hard, buried inside Karl. The bite of teeth at his neck, from Malik at his nape, from Karl under his jaw. The point at which they meet over Allan's shoulder and kiss, open-mouthed, is the same in which Malik finally pushes inside him. He hears the sound leave Malik's mouth as breath, so much so that his own chest echoes in sympathy.

With Malik pressed hard against his back, there's nowhere else to go but here. This. Now. When Malik thrusts forward, Allan moves with him in concert; under them, Karl makes a sound so sharp it tears at rather than moves through the air. Allan and Malik still as though frozen in the same caught breath, shiver together in a silent question as if formed in one mouth.

"No," Karl says, eyes wild, reaching up towards them both. "No, it's good, it's all good, don't stop, why are you stopping? I don't break easily."

It must be the influence of the drug in Allan's brain, that he hears that—sees the fearless glint in Karl's eyes despite the bruised corners of his rough-kissed mouth—and takes it as a challenge. This time, he is the first to move, in a drag of forward-back-forward that settles in a slow, filthy thrust inside Karl, inside Allan himself. The boundaries of Allan's own body simmer, feeling malleable. Like something he wants to push against.

"Hurry up," Karl says, and when Malik laughs, it shudders all through the three of them.

Everything they are is gold. And, even writhing in the dust, Allan knows he will later remember feeling immortal.

Karl comes first. This makes sense when Allan will later remember, albeit a bit guiltily, that Karl hadn't come the first time Allan had fucked him. It had been too quickly over. But this time, the tightening of Karl's body serves as a hot, slick undertow. Karl's orgasm seems to pull him under in degrees, like a slowly tightening thread, until Karl arcs under Allan, lips parting wider and wider with every gasp, each one heavier, harder, heady with sound.

It pulls Allan under, in turn, without any warning at all. This second orgasm shocks him with how close to a shattering it feels. Because, for all Karl might not break easily, Allan is beginning to suspect that he himself might. He doesn't have time to worry as much as he might later. He comes back to himself, body centering itself around the new sting at his hipbone. It seems like Karl accidentally scratched him. Allan wonders how to ask him to do it again. His thought is yanked off-kilter by the sensation of Malik still moving inside him; Malik, who presses his face against Allan's shoulder, hard, the hint of Malik's teeth a sharp counterpoint to the slick burn of his cock moving inside Allan, all sweet intensity. And Allan swears that his world narrows down: the wet press of Malik's mouth against Alan's skin, the heat of his breath distinct from the heat of their mingled sweat, all of it moisture in the aridity of the tomb, all of it evidence of their being living things. Allan wonders at it, at them. Malik sounds like he might if he was hit. His breath rasps out as a struggle. Allan senses a rising frustration in how he thrusts, faster and deeper, like someone trying to claw their way over a finish on will alone.

"Malik," Karl says, under Allan still, voice low.

Allan is very aware of still being inside him.

Karl looks up at Allan then, reaches up towards him with both hands. He holds Allan's face between them, and Allan allows it, stares down into the dark, lash-fringed well of them.

"Kiss him," Karl orders him, and turns Allan's head to the side, at an angle that Malik can lunge forward and reach. He does it, with a desperation that frightens Allan a little, something all too human bursting through the varnish of a painted screen.

Allan does the only thing possible in this moment, the only thing that could possibly make sense to do, which is to kiss him back, ignoring the strain in his own neck as he presses forward into the feeling. Forgetting himself, he reaches out, twists his fingers in dark hair, hauls Malik in closer, tighter: bites his lip for him.

Just like that, Malik comes.

Time seems to lose them, after. It catches up, eventually, to where they've slipped the leash, the three of them tangled on the floor. The stone is warmed from their bodies. Allan lets himself be ensnared by reality again, but slowly. He blinks, licks his lips, tastes shared salt.

His head is on Malik's chest. He can feel the steady ocean shift of each breath as it moves through Malik's body. Under his ear, he can hear the anchor of Malik's beating heat.

"Are we trapped here forever?" Karl asks, sounding not even a little bit maudlin about it. "Is this death?"

"Don't be ridiculous, Karl," Malik answers.

"You're right. I was never this good." Karl yawns.

"I don't see why we can't just climb back out," Allan offers, hating himself for it. He quite likes the sound of being trapped. He quite likes the sound of forever. "The trapdoor broke in half as we fell. Can't you see?"

For the first time in a long time, the three of them contemplate something that is not each other, staring instead at the shaft of light falling through from the hole in the ceiling.

"I am not climbing," Karl sniffs, "until this drug is done with me. Are you right in the head?"

"I am beginning to suspect," Malik says, very mildly, "we might be here for some time."

"I'm—" Allan starts, swallows, spits it out. "I'm fine with that. I don't—" He has to sit up, dislodging the arm Karl has flung with casual entitlement over his torso. And he looks at them both now, beautiful and sweat-slick and shining in the half-dark, displeased only, it seems, at his having moved away at all—and his throat fills with everything he wants to say. "I don't have anywhere else to be."

"I want to schedule him in for forever," Karl says from where he's catching his breath still, head pillowed against Malik's discarded knapsack. "Let's make him stay forever, Malik."

"Karl," Malik says. "Habibi. You can't just decide that for him. He's his own—"

"I don't think I am," Allan interrupts. "My own creature, that is. I think I was yours from that first day in the hotel. The very first time I saw you both looking at me."

There's a pause, during which Allan swallows but does not swallow down what he has said. The two of them look at him, Malik stricken, Karl gleeful.

"See!" Karl says. "Well, it's sorted then. We can fuck until this gets better, and then once it gets better. We can fuck in the tent, too. And then we can—"

"Yes," Malik interrupts, deadpan, "I think we get the picture. Schedule in space for him to breathe, will you?"

Allan finds, staring at them both now—Karl alight with the thrill of the future, and Malik looking at Allan with the steady, amused look of a shared secret—that he doesn't mind if he ends up suffocating. Not even a little.

"I can hold my breath," he says, and reaches out, sore and smiling, towards them.

Lifeline

K. Martin

character injury (permanent), clitoral fingering, cunnilingus, didn't know they were dating, dildo (strap-on), dom/sub, established relationship, f/f/nb, f/nb, face sitting, has a disability, hurt/comfort, misunderstandings, modern, non-binary, present tense, self-esteem issues, tattooed, third person limited point of view, vaginal fingering, vaginal sex, voyeurism

Beep-beep-beep! Charlotte groans and gropes for her phone. It's not where she expects it to be. She peels her eyelids open and lifts her head on a stiff, unhappy neck to look in the general direction of the infuriatingly cheerful beeping.

Beep-beep-beep!

"I'm gonna smash it with a hammer," she mumbles. The damn thing's on the far side of the nightstand, and shutting it up will require actual moving. She grunts as she starts half-shuffling, half-crawling across the bed, dragging her bad leg. "I don't need a cell phone. I can go back to the days of landlines."

(She can't, actually—she *knows* she can't—but she likes to pretend, sometimes.)

When she finally reaches the thing and hits the button to snooze the alarm, Charlotte closes her eyes and tries to reassess. She set the alarm knowing she'd need to get up and eat, hydrate, maybe take more pain meds. Now that she's awake, she doesn't want to do any of those things—she would much rather immediately return to unconsciousness, thank you. If she's unconscious, she doesn't have to figure out how to cope with this without screaming or throwing things.

Her phone buzzing with a notification in her hand startles her eyes back open. She has to turn the brightness of her screen down so she can handle looking at it before unlocking it to see who or what needs her extremely substandard attention just now.

Seeing the text from Lane makes her breath rush out of her lungs.

After a moment of frantic scrolling, she realizes that she…hasn't actually talked to Lane or Theresa this week. Not since the incoming low-pressure system made everything harder. She's responded with emojis in the groupchat, but not an actual update. And she missed her weekly get-together with Theresa. Neither of them know what's happening, so they don't know to stay away and leave her be.

It's why the *ETA 5min, doll* almost feels like a punishment. Especially when Lane's anxiety makes them more punctual than the average digital clock. Charlotte literally only has five minutes.

Or, well. Four, now. Not enough time, in any case.

She squints at her cane, and carefully flexes her left leg—hissing when the muscles scream. Cane's out then. Only way she's making it to the front door to explain is with the crutches. Which—are on the other side of the bed. Helpful.

Charlotte grabs her cane, rolls across the bed, and uses it to hook her crutches and drag them closer. Once she's got them, she pulls her hair out of the loose braid it was in and tries to finger-comb her blonde locks into something that doesn't look like bedhead, twisting them into a low ponytail. Then she starts slowly crutching her way towards the front door of her apartment—she's not moving quickly, but Lane is.

She gets there just in time to unlock and open it before either Lane or Theresa can knock. The hallway fluorescents feel like taking needles to the eyeballs, and she squints at the couple whose bed she's been gracing. "Sorry," she rasps. "Not a good time."

Lane's eyes go huge, almost like an anime character's, but it's Theresa who speaks. "Sweetheart, can we come in?"

Charlotte tries to shake her head, remembers why that's a bad idea, and leans heavily on her right crutch until the vertigo passes. "Bad time," she repeats. "Haven't—bad week." She gestures vaguely over her shoulder at her uncleaned apartment full of dirty dishes and dirty laundry that is absolutely not fit for guests to see. Especially not guests she wants to think well of her.

Lane just gives her the biggest, saddest green eyes Charlotte's ever seen as their hands hover near her, but don't touch. "Can I just—can I hold you? Will that make this worse?"

She can't help but smile at that. "Pretty sure I smell, but. Yeah, if you don't mind keeping me upright."

Lane is nodding before Charlotte has finished answering the question. "I absolutely can do that, thank you, gym days." They try to manoeuvre a little closer, but the crutches present an obvious problem. "Hey, Ree? Can you—?"

"On it," Theresa murmurs, tilting her body sideways to step through the open door and across the apartment threshold, sliding around Charlotte to carefully grip her hips. "Take a step forward into Lane, and let go of the crutches—I'll catch them."

Charlotte doesn't understand any of what's happening right now, but hugs sound great, so she goes with it—lets Theresa guide her weight as she lets go of the crutches and mostly falls into Lane, trusting them to catch her. They do, of course. They don't look it, with their lanky frame, but Lane is easily strong enough to hold her up, and Charlotte sighs, nuzzling her cheek against their flat chest, tension going out of her at the comfort of their familiar smell.

Lane squeezes gently, arms bracing her, and murmurs, "What needs supporting so we can get you back inside and away from the hallway lights?"

Charlotte realizes, belatedly, that this may have been a ruse. "You tryna trick me?" she mumbles, voice muffled against Lane's shirt. "Get inside and see my mess?"

Lane's laugh is more felt than heard. "You caught me. Now, what do you need? There any chance I could get my hands under your thighs, carry you in?"

Charlotte hisses at the thought. "No, leg won't let you. Not today."

"Okay," Lane says easily, sounding confused.

"You need your crutches back?" Theresa asks.

"Probably," Charlotte sighs, unhappy about the prospect of having to disentangle from Lane, and about having to get her crutches resituated—but before she can figure out the logistics, Lane's hands are sliding up her ribs to steady her as they step away, and Theresa is there against her back, fitting her crutches into place under her arms. It's done so smoothly it's like they've practised it.

Charlotte crutches back inside, where it's dark and she's safe from fluorescents, relieved—and also anxious, somewhere underneath the exhaustion. She can feel little flutters of it, but it's not as strong as it usually is. They were, after all, bound to find out eventually about her bad days. She settles at her kitchen table with a sigh, leaning her crutches next to her. At least she's in the kitchen now—closer proximity to food is some kinda progress, right?

"Go on and ask," she sighs, bracing her elbows on the table and her face on her hands as Lane settles next to her tentatively. Theresa stays standing in the middle of the kitchen.

There's a beat of silence before Theresa breaks it. "What do you need right now?"

It's none of the questions she was expecting. "What?"

"You're obviously unwell," Theresa gestures at all of Charlotte with one manicured hand, short nails glimmering in the low light. It's pretty, and Charlotte wishes she'd been well enough to go with Theresa for the appointment. "So what do you need? What will help you right now?"

Charlotte closes her eyes and thinks about all the ways she could answer that, but settles on the truth—they're past the point where she can bluff. "Alarm woke me to eat, hydrate, see about pain meds." She shrugs one shoulder, and tilts her head towards the mess inhabiting her countertops and sink. "More broadly, I need to clean up in here, run the dishwasher. Do a load of laundry or two." She pauses, then reluctantly adds, "Give up on waiting to be stable enough to shower, and just have a fucking bath so I can wash my hair, if nothing else." She keeps meaning to get a shower chair, but.

Theresa nods like all of this is reasonable. "Okay. Do you have anything to eat here that's easy, or already prepared? Do you need groceries, or a takeout order?"

"I don't understand," Charlotte admits.

Lane's hand settles gently on her upper back. "Sweetheart, we want to help. But we need to know what you need before we can."

Nothing about this encounter makes sense. None of her other

datemates have checked up on her since she's gone silent. No one she's ever been with—romantically or casually—has ever done this. But, despite the hit to her pride, the simple fact is Charlotte could use the help. So she takes a breath and admits, "I'm not really sure what's here. Head's pounding too hard to think."

Lane makes a wounded noise before their slender, callused hand lands on the back of her neck and starts kneading gently. Charlotte sighs and leans into it.

"Okay," Theresa murmurs. "First order of business is getting some dinner for the three of us. I can order your favourite?"

Charlotte blinks slowly. Chinese takeout sounds fantastic, and one of the upsides is that rice will be easy on her stomach. "Yeah, I think so."

"I'm on it." Theresa pulls her phone out and starts tapping. "I'll put in for our usual order when it's the three of us—there any extras you want to get? Leftovers for later?"

Charlotte almost says "no" reflexively before she thinks about it. "Extra pork lo mein?"

"You've got it, sweetheart." Theresa taps at her phone some more, and having the food problem solved, at least for the moment, is a relief. She can eat food when it gets here, and then have leftovers for later tonight, or tomorrow for lunch. "Right—Lane? Can you help get Charlotte to the couch?"

Charlotte looks up at her name, confused. "On it," Lane replies, volume low but voice intense, and oh—they're anxious. Whoops.

"Sorry about all this," she mutters as they follow behind her carefully, hands hovering near her waist.

It gets her a scoff. "I was worried anyway, doll—at least this way, I can do something and help make it better. Here, pass me your crutches."

They've reached the couch, so she does, sprawling awkwardly. She'd love to lie down properly, but getting her leg up onto the couch right now is going to hurt, so it can just. Dangle. The floor's there to catch her foot, it's fine.

Except that Lane props the crutches on the coffee table, and then they're crouching down to cup their hands under her leg carefully. "I can lift this onto the couch for you, if you want?" Charlotte nods, too confused and tired to argue about it. She tries to help as best she can, and they get it settled on the couch cushion with minimal additional agony, so she considers it a win. Lane pats carefully at her hip. "Okay, you stay right there, Ree and I got this."

"This" turns out to be taking care of her apartment—the trash collected, bagged, and run out to the dumpster by Lane while Theresa pokes through her cupboards and refrigerator, tapping at her phone to put together a grocery list. Charlotte can only watch, a cocktail of emotions bubbling through her gut as they move easily around each other without words, taking care of various items on Charlotte's to-do list like it's no big deal to just show up and start dealing with her mess.

Luckily, before she can bubble over and erupt into tears, food arrives. Theresa and Lane get it inside and set up on the coffee table before Charlotte can do more than sit a little more upright. She'd expected they'd eat in the kitchen, at the table, but—

"Here?"

Lane gives her a flat look. "We can eat on the couch if it means not having to watch you wince as you hobble around some more."

She doesn't know if it's the unnaturally even tone, the implied disapproval, or just how topsy-turvy everything feels right now, but Charlotte has to bite back on the automatic "yes, Sir," that wants to come out. She focusses on eating instead. Nothing potentially inappropriate can come out of her mouth if it's full of Chinese food. Alas, she doesn't get the reprieve she's hoping for.

"Where are your pain meds, and which ones should you be taking?" Theresa asks.

And oh right, the plan was to have more of those. "Nightstand," she mumbles.

Theresa nods, brown waves of hair falling forward to obscure her face, and then she's up and moving. A moment after she disappears into Charlotte's bedroom, she reappears in the doorway to the living room. "Charlotte, honey, there are four bottles here. Which ones do you need?"

This is not a conversation she's ready for. "Bring them all out, please."

Theresa frowns, but nods once, stepping back to fetch the bottles. When she returns, she sits on the other end of the couch and gently lines up the bottles on the table in front of Charlotte. "Sweetheart, I know you're not feeling well, but—"

"—we need some answers, doll," Lane finishes, voice soft. They gesture towards the bottles with their chopsticks. "I know you don't much like to talk about what you've got going on, health-wise, but this is feeling serious enough that it's something we"—they gesture between Theresa and themselves—"need to know about."

Charlotte stares into her container of chicken-fried rice. "I don't talk about it much because, well. It's hard enough to convince someone to agree to a casual arrangement with me, given the disabilities and limitations. Usually, the less I make it a thing, the more likely I am to be given consideration as a datemate."

"Ableist assholes," Theresa mutters, and Lane hums in agreement.

Charlotte smiles, but doesn't look up from her food. "The short version of the story is that, well. Back in high school, when I was seventeen, I was in the drama club. And one day, I was up on a ladder trying to help with—something, I can't even remember what, now. But I fell." She nods at her left leg. "Fucked up my knee because I fell into the auditorium seats—dislocated it, torn tendons, the works. Needed a lot of surgery and rehab. It's been a mess ever since."

"Jesus," Lane hisses. Theresa reaches out and carefully rests her hand on Charlotte's thigh—the right one, which is closest to her and doesn't hurt.

Charlotte looks up and nods. "Also broke my arm and got a concussion, hence the migraine right now."

"I'm not sure I understand the connection between those parts," Theresa admits.

Before she can answer, Lane turns their head towards their wife. "Migraines can be a post-concussion symptom, especially if you've already got a family history and are prone, or have had more than one, because concussion damage is exponential, not sequential." Charlotte sees Theresa's face scrunch, her mouth opening, and Lane clarifies, "Each new concussion multiplies the previous ones, not adds to them."

Theresa's face smooths out in understanding, and she nods. "Got it." She glances at Charlotte, then reaches out to gather up the medication bottles. "Explain it to me?" she asks quietly, and Charlotte sighs, nods, and puts down her food.

She plucks a clear, yellow-brown prescription bottle and a red-and-white bottle of over-the-counter pain meds out of Theresa's hands. "These two are for the migraines. I probably don't need the prescription-strength one right now—I'm feeling better after eating." She pulls out the blue-and-white bottle next. "This one is for the inflammation, and I do need that one right now, along with this." She transfers the fourth and final bottle from Theresa's lap to her own, another prescription. "Which is a muscle relaxant, because the muscles in my left leg are spasming from overuse, trying to compensate for the instability in the joint."

Lane makes a sad little noise. "I didn't realize it was this bad—I knew you had a bad knee, I've seen you with the soft brace on it, and I've seen you use your cane. We've talked about how bondage on that leg was out, but this?" They shake their head. "Doll, why didn't you tell me it was this bad?"

Charlotte shifts uncomfortably, ducking her head despite the pull in the muscles. "It's not always this bad. Not even *usually* this bad, it's just." She gestures helplessly towards the window. "My physiotherapist is off on vacation, and the weather decided that was the perfect moment to attack me."

Theresa shakes her head, shifting on the couch so she's seated sideways, fully facing Charlotte rather than sitting beside her. "No, that's not quite what Lane means," they murmur, voice pitched soft and soothing in a way that makes Charlotte's back muscles loosen. "We knew you had a bad knee—you've been clear about that. But we had no idea about the rest of it, that it was possible for you to have days like this, that your knee was bad enough to require ongoing physical therapy."

Charlotte doesn't know how to say *well, usually when I mention that bit, the other person/rest of the polycule decides I'm not a good fit, and I didn't want to risk losing what I have of the two of you*, so she doesn't. Instead, she says, "Like I said, it doesn't happen often, so. Never really came up."

"Until now," Lane grumbles, and well, they have a point. And then their features sharpen, giving Charlotte a look she's learned means she's in trouble. "Were you going to tell us, if we hadn't barged in to see it? Like, let's assume you forgot bad days could ambush you like this." They gesture with their chopsticks towards her knee. "Were you planning to tell us about it afterwards?"

There's no good answer to that, and Charlotte rolls her bottom lip into her mouth, gnawing on it. "I don't know," she finally says, slowly. "I don't— It sucks, having you two see me like this."

Theresa slides closer until her taller body is pressed next to Charlotte's on the couch, one arm drawing her close so she can rest her head on Theresa's shoulder. "Sweetheart, nobody likes being unwell. When Lane's sick, they get unbelievably crabby. But when you're dating someone, that's part of the deal—you don't only get them at their best, you see them when they're tired, sad, or sick, and choose to be there anyway."

"Dating?" Charlotte parrots, because apparently she missed a memo at some point? "As in—a relationship?"

Theresa stares, her deep brown eyes going wide as they dart across Charlotte's face. She can't see it, but she can feel Lane staring from the other side of her. "Yes," Theresa says, dragging it out slowly until it sounds like it's half-statement, half-question.

"Oh."

Lane moves in her periphery, shuffling around the coffee table until they can crouch near her and Theresa's legs. "Doll, this is a relationship. Has been for months now."

"Nearly a year," Theresa adds.

"Okay, and when you say that, what—what does that mean, exactly, with how you two do poly?" Charlotte's suddenly desperate to know, because she's getting the feeling that she's had this all wrong, and what she thought she knew about her place in the polycule is going to get turned on its head.

"I— What? It means a relationship, doll. You're our partner, our third." Lane huffs, leaning in and shaking their head, clearly confused. "What did you think you were to us?"

Charlotte glances between them, taking in Lane's big, earnest eyes and the subtle freckles on Theresa's golden skin, at the way there's nothing but care and concern on both of them for all that they wear it differently. "I know that you're married," she says slowly, starting with the facts. "I know that, for a lot of married couples that are poly, their spouse is their primary partner, and then they have a secondary partner, maybe a tertiary." She pauses, but Theresa is nodding in understanding, and Lane reaches out to take her hands, still crouched near her feet. "Usually I'm just a casual partner, or a friend-with-benefits." Charlotte shrugs, at something of a loss about how to explain it. "Whenever I've expected or asked for more, I've been disappointed, so. I figured that's what I was to you two, because neither of you ever said otherwise."

Lane's face, always the more expressive of the pair, crumples, and they turn their head away but don't let go of her hands—if anything, they hold on tighter. Charlotte thinks they're trying not to cry. She doesn't expect Theresa's gentle fingers to carefully tuck under her jaw, coaxing Charlotte to face her.

"Charlotte," she says, her soft voice full of an emotion Charlotte's never heard from her before. "You're not lesser to either of us just because we met and married before we found you. I need you to understand that."

Charlotte doesn't mean to make a protesting noise, it's just that it sounds too good to be true.

The brush of Theresa's fingers turns into her palm cradling Charlotte's jaw, the touch affectionate but firm. "Lane is, hands down, the most loving and attentive partner I've ever had—and probably will ever have. I get up every day knowing that I am loved, that they cherish and value me as a person and their wife. But I don't need as much time and attention as Lane has to give." She pauses to smile down at Lane, who releases one of Charlotte's hands to grip Theresa's knee. "As much as they want and need to give, if we're honest. That's why poly works for us, and why you work for us—because having someone else for them to love, someone to see and appreciate how big Lane's heart is? That's a gift, sweetheart. To both of us, and to our marriage."

"*You're* a gift," Lane murmurs, so soft it's nearly a whisper.

Charlotte's heart overflows through her tear ducts. She lets go of Lane's hand to cup both of her own over her face, and a moment later, Lane's worming their slim body between Charlotte and the arm of the couch so that they and Theresa both can press her between them. She's held until the tears and shaking stop, which doesn't take long, thankfully.

Once her hands drop from her face, Theresa pets her hair. "You need to take meds, now that you've eaten, and then go with Lane to fill the bath. They'll help you in there while I deal with everything out here, okay?"

Charlotte's "Okay" is shaky, but she means it, and neither of them question it, which is the important part. It's hard to want to untangle from—"datemates" doesn't feel right anymore, not when it's the word she's used for the casual, no-strings attachments she's used to—the two of them, but she *does* need to take meds, and to get clean. So she struggles her way up from the couch, reclaims her crutches, and heads to the bathroom, Lane following with soft footsteps behind her.

They slip past her and get to the bathroom first, moving the shower curtain and plugging the tub. "How hot, doll?"

"The hotter the better, honestly—heat'll help my leg," Charlotte says, sitting on the closed toilet lid. Lane nods, adjusts the tap, and then strips off before gesturing for her to do the same, and—

Charlotte's fair skin goes cooktop-hot as she realizes Lane's getting in with her. Still, she needs the bath and probably also the help, so she starts carefully peeling out of her pajamas without standing up. Lane crouches down to help, and Charlotte is struck breathless yet again at how unself-conscious they are nude, and how stunningly attractive they are.

It's hard not to be aware when that lean, strong body is pressed skin-to-skin to hers, her milk-pale skin bisected by the dark ink of their sleeve tattoos as they wrap their arms around her, steadying her as she steps into the tub. Charlotte's never done this with anyone else—having nurses help her teenage self when she was in the hospital doesn't count—and she didn't realize how intimate it would be, to lean back against Lane's flat chest and let them cradle her curvier body.

But the real surprise comes when they start washing her hair—their fingers catch in a tangle, tugging, and the unexpected pull makes Charlotte moan as her scalp prickles, tingles skipping down her spine.

"Yeah?" Lane husks. "That a thing I get to do for you, when you're like this?"

"Sir?" Charlotte whimpers, unsure.

"Slide on down and let me rinse this out," they order, soft and easy, and Charlotte obeys without thinking. Once her hair is clean, Lane soaps up a washcloth and runs it over her body, slow and deliberate. Her skin buzzes at the touch, and desire starts building in her bloodstream—something she would've thought was impossible before it happened.

It has her squirming—until Lane's free hand wraps around her chest, their fingers curling delicately around her throat as they gently pin her against them. "Do I get to make you feel good, sweet thing? Balance out all that pain with some pleasure?"

Charlotte shakes under the hand at her throat and the force of that question. "I—I don't know," she admits. "Never tried, like this."

Lane hums, and the hand around her throat uncurls to stroke down the centre of her chest. "Will you let me try?"

She doesn't have to think about it. "Yes, Sir."

Lane hums again as they pull the plug and let the water drain. "You'll keep me updated, understand? If something aggravates your bad leg or your head, you tell me and we stop."

It's not a request, and this time her "Yes, Sir," is quieter. Less eager, but no less honest.

"Good girl. Here, let me up—I'm gonna rinse us off, and then get us out, okay?"

Charlotte nods and lets Lane do most of the work of getting her upright and both of them under the shower spray to rinse off post-bath. Getting out is harder, because Charlotte has to trust Lane implicitly in a way she didn't when they got in—they're both naked and wet, now, and slipping is so much easier. But Sir holds her steady, going so far as to half lift her injured side over the lip of the tub. By the time she's dry and being tipped onto clean sheets—Theresa must have changed them while they were in the bath—she's gone weak in the joints, and not just with the exertion.

Lane notices. "Anything else that'll help your leg? I'm very eager to wreck you, doll, but only in good ways."

Charlotte flaps a hand towards the bathroom. "TENS unit. Under the sink."

Lane nods and comes back with the unit, a mischievous look on their face. "You know, this isn't exactly how I thought we might play with electrostim, but I can roll with this."

Charlotte bursts into giggles. She's giggling too hard to talk Lane through where and how to place the electrodes, so she has to do it herself with fumbling hands. Lane, meanwhile, arranges pillows under her knee to prop up her bad leg. It leaves her legs splayed, which means Sir will notice she's wet. Not with water.

Lane's fingertips pet gently through her folds, and Charlotte whimpers, hips twisting into the contact. "Yeah, doll? You ready to let me make you feel good?"

Before Charlotte can answer, Theresa bustles in. "—got a load of laundry in, and the dishwasher's loaded, but—*oh*." She pauses, dark eyes going wide. "I didn't realize you'd be out of the bath so soon. I can go," she offers, gesturing over her shoulder.

"You don't have to," Charlotte blurts. At the looks on both faces, she flushes. "I know you and I aren't, well. We don't have sex, really, but." She reaches out a hand, and Theresa moves forward to take it without hesitation. "You can stay? If you want?"

She's not sure why Theresa looks to Lane. "I know she's yours, love. Up to you if you want to share her this way."

Hearing herself talked about that way—belonging to Lane, and as if she's not here—should be infuriating. Instead, it makes the neediness humming under her skin worse.

Lane hums thoughtfully. "You know why you've mostly been with me and just me in bed?" they ask, and it takes a moment for Charlotte to understand that the question is directed at her. She shakes her head. "Ree isn't kinky."

"Guessing it's easier to keep it vanilla between you two if you've got somewhere else to put it?"

Lane nods, and Theresa hums in agreement. "So, for right now, if you want her here, and she wants to be here…" Lane looks at their wife, who smiles and nods. "Then she can sit next to us on the bed and watch."

Charlotte whimpers, because being watched is a rarely-indulged kink of hers—a fact Lane knows.

Theresa settles on the bed, and her gaze feels like a touch as it sweeps over Charlotte and Lane. "Go on, then," she husks. "Show me."

Lane's smile is slow and hungry as their fingers tease between Charlotte's legs again, sweeping lightly up and down as their other hand skates slowly up her ribs to dance across her chest and back down again, causing tingles of anticipatory pleasure to ripple across Charlotte's skin. She can't take the teasing for long, not when she's been alone and in pain for days, when she knows that this is more than a convenience for them, that she *matters*. "Please, Sir? Need you."

"Good girl," Lane says, deep and a little rough, as they sink two fingers straight into her cunt like a hot knife through butter.

Charlotte makes a rough noise, arching up into the pleasure-relief of being full, only to hiss as doing so makes her left leg throb painfully.

Lane pauses, brow furrowing, before turning to Theresa. "Sweetheart, can you come lie on Charlotte's left side and hold her down for me? Don't want her hurting herself."

The smile Theresa gives isn't one Charlotte's seen before. "Of course." And then she's settling on Charlotte's left, one of her legs draping carefully across Charlotte's thigh, the rest of her weight settling heavily against Charlotte's side. Her left arm is under Theresa's torso, and Charlotte can hold onto her waist but not do much else with it.

Lane curls their fingertips up and into her G-spot, and Charlotte whines, tries to jerk, and can't, with Theresa's careful weight against her. "Excellent," Lane murmurs. And then they start torturing her for real, their clever fingers pushing in deep and slow, rubbing at her G-spot but not at her clit as Theresa makes appreciative noises in her ear.

It's on purpose, because Lane knows she can't come like this.

"Can I touch? Please? Wanna come," Charlotte pants.

Sir's eyes are big and dark, pupils blown when they look at her. "No. Not yet. You're *mine*, and I want you to remember that."

Knowing that they mean it—that she's not just Sir's in this moment, or in bed—makes Charlotte tremble and whimper brokenly as she gushes over Lane's fingers.

"You're so responsive," Theresa whispers, kissing along her jawline.

"So pretty when you're desperate," Lane agrees, curling their fingers again.

Charlotte turns and kisses Theresa clumsily, trying to focus on that and not how needy and wide-open she feels, how badly she wants to come when an hour ago she wouldn't have thought having an orgasm was *possible* with how she's felt the last few days.

Theresa catches her moans and whines, nipping them right out of her mouth. She doesn't know how long they've been kissing when Sir says, "Ree? Get my purple cock out of the nightstand for me?"

As Theresa rolls away to do that, Charlotte blinks up at them. "You knew that was there?"

Sir raises an eyebrow at her as they pull their fingers free with an obscene sound. "I'm sorry, do you think I leave my dicks lying around just anywhere? That one's here because it's your favourite, and it's thicker than Ree usually likes."

Charlotte's breath catches, emotion filling her chest so swiftly it feels like her ribs might crack open with the force of it—because that being left here, with her, isn't an accident or a forgetful moment. That's a sign of trust, of permanence—it's Lane recognizing what she wants, and trying to make sure she gets it. She reaches out to grip their arms, all of her shaking—in emotional overwhelm, yes, but also in the frantic need to have them as close as possible.

Sir obliges, pressing her into the bed to kiss her with the usual lazy sort of hunger that's always made Charlotte ache for more of them than she thought she could have—and made her shy away from too many kisses so she wouldn't cry. Now, she pushes into them, understanding she can't only have more if she asks, she already *has* it. She chases their lips when they break away.

Sir chuckles as they plant one hand on her chest to push her down and themselves up at the same time. "Patience, doll. Can't dick you down like you need 'til I get my dick in."

It makes Theresa—holding out the dick in question—laugh, but Charlotte lets out some garbled cross between a laugh and a whimper. "Do need it, Sir," she mewls, dropping her hands from their shoulders for that reason and no other.

Sir looks between the two of them, a sly expression curling across their face. "Ree, you wanna do the honours?"

Theresa makes a surprised little noise, but nods and scrambles around to kneel behind Lane, dropping soft kisses across their shoulders as her hands drop down between their legs to hold them open and carefully push the shorter, bean-shaped end of the strapless strap-on inside. Lane makes a rough, hungry sound as it settles into place before being pushed forward into Charlotte by Theresa's body as she leans towards the nightstand. When she straightens, she's got Charlotte's bottle of lube in her hand.

"I want to see it," Theresa whispers, clicking the cap and drizzling lube onto the purple silicone jutting out from Lane's body. "Wanna watch you take Lane's thickest cock." Charlotte's breath hitches watching Theresa's hand slowly stroke up and down to spread the lube. "Wanna watch you enjoy it."

Sir turns their head to kiss their wife. "Oh, she does, Ree. Just wait—babydoll looks *so* good when she's out of her mind and writhing on it."

Charlotte whines and tries to spread her legs wider, her hips rolling in a desperate attempt to ease the needy ache, but she realizes too late that doing so uses her bad leg. Sir's hands move to still her, and Theresa makes a thoughtful sound. "Would it help—or even work—to have your leg over Lane's shoulder so you can't move it?"

Charlotte tries to clear the horny haze long enough to think that through. "Maybe," she says slowly. "As long as it's held tight, and Sir doesn't lean forward to brace."

Sir nods. "Let's scooch this to the end of the bed, then. I can brace against the edge and the floor, and my lovely wife can help you sit up and stay in place." The first half, directed at her, is an order. The last bit, for Theresa, is half-statement, half-question, and Charlotte feels like a puzzle piece that's slotted into place to complete a picture as Theresa agrees and moves to help Charlotte get into position.

Theresa also carefully detaches the TENS cords from the electrodes, but doesn't remove the sticky pads from her skin. "In case you need more after," she murmurs, and Charlotte presses a soft kiss to her mouth in thanks.

Once they've resituated so Charlotte's reclining in Theresa's lap, Sir crouches. "Tell me if anything hurts," they remind her before gently lifting her bad knee onto their shoulder and standing up slowly, one hand pressing her leg firmly against their chest. Once they've fully stood, Sir looks at her for a long moment, waiting, and Charlotte nods. They drop a kiss across the gnarls of scar tissue from years-old surgeries, and before Charlotte can process the wave of feelings that provokes, Sir's rolling their hips smoothly to sink their cock inside her, and coherency vanishes.

Charlotte moans, head tipping back at the pleasure-relief of being full and the rhythm of Lane's thrusts. It's good. It always is, with Lane, with this cock, with their dynamic. But it's never been quite this good before—never felt like Theresa's arms around her are the only thing keeping her from falling apart, like every twitch of Sir's hips is threatening to tip her over into an orgasm that won't stop building.

Charlotte doesn't know if it's a side effect of the physical hypersensitivity brought on by days in pain, or if it's because she doesn't have to hold anything back anymore. Whatever the reason, she's straining against them both, begging between breaths gone ragged. "Sir, *please*, please say I can—yours, 'm yours, please let me—"

Sir makes a noise almost like a snarl. "Yeah, doll, come on my cock for me."

Charlotte doesn't waste a second once she has permission—her fingers untwist from the bedding to start rubbing frantic little circles around and over her clit. It's a wild race to the finish line—she feels too good after too long spent in agony, is being fucked just right by someone who cares enough to not only learn how to make it good for her, but also to accommodate her leg being a bastard. Of course she won't last.

The touch of her fingers helps, but mostly it's Sir's murmurs giving her permission that tip her over into the orgasm she's been aching for. It drags out like still-warm taffy, and she can feel the way her cunt clenching around Sir's cock has made it harder for them to thrust, so they're grinding instead. And then, as she shudders her way through the last spine-tingling waves of pleasure, she realizes Sir isn't continuing to rock their hips for her benefit—they're stutterfucking between her thighs, chasing their own orgasm.

It's a sweet sort of torture to lie there caught between aftershocks and afterglow as Sir grinds so deep and dirty it almost hurts. Their face scrunches in the almost-there look that's echoed in the frantic judder of their hips, but safewording is the last thing on her mind. Instead, Charlotte squirms at the overstimulation that's starting to shift back around into neediness. But, more importantly— "Please, Sir? Come in me?"

Sir grunts like they've taken a hit to the stomach. "Fuck, you're good to me," they rasp, and then they're moving faster, pressing so deep that Charlotte whimpers as they shudder out their orgasm.

For a moment, they're all still and breathing hard, and then Sir moves, dropping to their knees to hover their mouth over Charlotte's swollen clit. "What d'you say, doll?"

Charlotte's breath isn't the only one that hitches at that, and Lane's head snaps up to look at their wife, eyes scanning over Theresa's face. "Yeah? You need something, love?" At Theresa's breathy noise of assent, they ask, "You wanna give my babydoll a go? Sit on her pretty face, maybe?"

Theresa moans softly. "Can I?"

Sir looks at Charlotte—who nods—and then smirks. "Yeah, love, go on—get her flat and let her give you some proper thanks for taking care of the apartment, hm?"

As soon as it's said, Charlotte wants it so bad she can't breathe. Luckily for her, Theresa moves quickly, getting up to let Charlotte lie flat and strip out of her jeans and underwear before she's carefully setting her knees on either side of Charlotte's head. Charlotte grips her hips, pulling Theresa down towards her mouth—only to moan directly into her folds when Sir chooses that moment to flick their tongue over Charlotte's clit in tiny, rapid strokes.

The moan seems to spur Theresa into moving—she starts rolling her hips, rocking her cunt over Charlotte's open mouth. From the pitch of her breathy moans, it's good for her, which is a blessing when Charlotte can't concentrate to do better—not when her focus and breath keeps getting stolen away by Sir—but she does her best. Theresa deserves that.

And then Sir lifts their head long enough to say, "Come on, doll, be good to my wife—not gonna let you come again until she does," and Charlotte hums her assent without pulling away, redoubling her efforts.

It's harder, because she doesn't know what Theresa likes, but between the fingers sliding into her hair, tugging her gently in the right direction, and Sir's hands steady and bracing on her bad leg, she's not worried about it. She'll get it right.

When Charlotte wakes, she can tell right away that today will be better—easier—than the previous days have been. Her head is heavy, and she feels vaguely hungover, but there's no sick pounding when she opens her eyes or sits up. She's warm and a little stiff after sleeping between Theresa and Lane, and when she flexes her left leg, it's not *great*, but one crutch should be more than enough support to get her to the kitchen to start coffee for the three of them. She's not recovered enough to put her full weight on it with the cane, but today, both crutches aren't necessary.

Of course, once the coffee is made and she's got cups fixed for everyone, she realizes she has a problem—with the crutch, she can't carry more than one mug at a time. She sighs and gets Lane's mug, but when she turns, she sees them lounging in the doorway of her bedroom, bare-chested and with bedhead reminiscent of a cockatiel.

Charlotte makes a soft cooing noise and extends the coffee cup in her hand. "For you."

Lane putters forward and sips gratefully. "Thanks, doll. You have one for Ree?" Charlotte tips her head towards the purple mug on the counter, and Lane smiles. "I'll grab that, you get yours, and then it's back to bed with you, young lady. You are absolutely required to indulge us in morning hedonism."

Charlotte does as she's told, giggling quietly as she follows Lane back to her bedroom, where Theresa has spread one arm across the empty space of the bed, her forehead furrowed in sleep. Lane sets their mugs down on the nightstand and slides into bed first, stroking gentle fingers through Theresa's hair. "Wake up, my love," they lilt softly, almost singing. "The sun is rising, and so must we."

Theresa makes a grumbly noise, curling in closer to Lane's hip before stretching slowly and sitting up. She takes the mug Lane hands her and starts drinking on autopilot—but less than a minute later, the light behind her eyes seems to blink on, because she's smiling and looking at Charlotte. "So, when is your lease on this place up?"

Charlotte experiences a brief mental blue-screen and sits hard on the bed, her coffee sloshing in her mug and nearly slopping over the rim. "Uh. In May, I think?"

Theresa nods. "So a couple months, then." Lane makes an agreeing sound. "Between now and then, I want you to consider moving in with us instead of renewing."

Charlotte's hands tremble with the force of the emotion swelling in her chest, and she sets her mug on the floor next to the bed. "I— Are you sure? You'd really want that?"

Lane reaches out to cup one hand around the back of her neck. "Yeah, doll, we do. We'd talked about it before, a little, but didn't want to move too fast. After this last week, though? I don't think it's too fast anymore—not when living with us means you don't have to struggle through alone if this happens again."

Charlotte leans in to wrap one arm around Lane's waist, draping the other across Theresa. "I'll have to think about it, but—I think I'd like that."

"Good," Theresa murmurs, turning to kiss her cheek.

Athanor

Dei Walker

alchemist, anxiety, bipoc, breast play, character death (past), character injury (graphic descriptions), cunnilingus, employee/employer, established relationship, f/f/m/m, f/f/m/m/m (past), f/m, f/m/m, fantasy, fat, kissing, magic use, mercenary, past tense, penis in anus sex, penis in vagina sex, soldier, third person limited (alternating) point of view, threesome to foursome, tribbing, vaginal fingering

"You"—Balduin's voice cut through the birdsong and chirping insects—"need to give that poor woman a break."

Zosima turned from her partner to stare at the woman meandering several lengths behind them. Alchemist, employer, and current thorn in Zosima's side, Serra Tichelaar belonged behind four walls and a counter—not in the middle of a mountain range. Her auburn curls gleamed in the sunlight, bracelets at her wrists clinking a counterpoint to the birdsong on the path. She and Mattin, the lanky mage who usually balanced Zo's heat and Balduin's earthy steadiness, were so far back that they almost formed a separate traveling party.

She turned back to Balduin as the breeze picked up, carrying the scent of rain from beyond one of the mountain peaks. Zosima scowled, looking at the sky and the dark clouds that loomed on the horizon. "What brought this on?"

"Sun's dropping and we need to make camp, and you've been glowering every night. She's paying us, Zo. Money we need." The swordsman stressed the final word, hazel eyes full of reproach. “You’re the one who told us to get off the usual routes. The one who insisted we head north. With the way you’re behaving, she’s going to take her coin, turn around, and head straight back to Oriscay.”

“I’d like to see her try. In the past three days, she’s slowed us from any kind of reasonable pace, nearly burnt dinner, and fallen asleep five minutes into her watch. No way she’d manage the trek back to town on her own.” Zosima watched as Balduin reached a hand to his jaw, rubbing at the red-gold gleam of stubble. She pressed her advantage. “If it weren’t for that pretty hair of hers, I’d’ve left her to be eaten by the wyvern skulking around camp yesterday morning. Didn’t she say she’d never gone past the first bend in the road before?”

He met her look with equanimity. “You were fine when she hired us. You even smiled. And now you can’t see her without getting that look in your eyes.” Balduin didn’t slow his pace, focused on the road snaking its way through the mountains. Zosima had traveled with him long enough to know what he was thinking: anything could leap out of the brush, from snakes to boars; there had even been reports of manticore in the area. Neither of them had believed the nervous alchemist when she’d hired them, but the farther they’d ventured, the harder it had become to disbelieve.

She raised an eyebrow, her tone icy. “‘That’ look?” Tension rippled across Zosima’s skin, filling her up like a bubble. Her leathers abruptly felt tight.

“The look you give Mattin that means ‘I either want to fuck you or murder you and I can’t decide which one.’”

Zosima scowled. She did not have a fuck-or-murder look. Yes, their employer was attractive—trews and tunic cut in a way that highlighted her broad thighs and the ample curves of her breasts and stomach. Zosima spent far more time wondering what was beneath them than she should, considering that she was leading this group to collect rare magical flowers a week’s journey into the mountains.

Balduin chuckled, eyes sparkling with humor. “That’s the one right there.”

“We’d’ve been faster with Pas—” She snapped her mouth shut on the name. Pain shot through her heart.

“Everything was faster with Pasqual.” Balduin could say the name without flinching, a feat she envied. Or maybe hated: it had been almost a year, and the grief from his death still stung. "He—and Miquela—had been on the road even longer than we have." Balduin glanced down at her, resting one of his large hands over her shoulder. "I miss them too, Zo."

Zosima squeezed her eyes closed. "Miquela could have stayed," she said, "but she left."

Balduin's sigh was audible over the breeze. "We all coped in different ways. But a trek like this, when we've been hired to collect alchemical specimens?" He shook his head. "Neither of us are mages."

"Mattin is, and he's comfortable on the road," Zosima retorted. Her fingers itched to touch the bandolier of daggers across her chest, a reassurance of her competence. She glanced toward the mountains. "We should make camp, I agree. It looks like rain, and the last thing I want is to be caught wrong-footed and wet on the road, trying to get camp up while we're soaked to the bone."

"We can set up camp, get a fire going, and then go…take a walk." Balduin gave her another look, this one far more weighted. "The two of them can take first watch."

"Is that a good idea?"

"I'll tell Mattin you said that." Balduin chuckled. "He has more patience than you, and he won't mind." His hand strayed across the space between them, skimmed down her arm.

The tension inside her coiled tighter, heat sliding through her to burn just beneath her skin. She caught herself from stumbling on a rock and let out a small "*oh*." Balduin's second chuckle told her it wasn't as quiet as she'd hoped.

"You'll feel better for it, Zo." He squeezed her shoulder, then his hand fell away. "I know I will."

"And you think it's wise to leave Mattin and…" Zosima's mouth puckered. "…our employer to themselves?"

Balduin's smile flickered like a candle flame. "Stop disparaging Mattin. He's a luck-mage. And she's getting better. I think once you've worked some of this tension off, you'll see that. Actually, a better idea: start camp, then head off. I'll tell Mattin, and we'll leave our packs, and then…" His mouth curved in a slow, dangerous smile that made her muscles tighten. "Find somewhere else to lie down and work off some of your tension."

Zosima turned to watch as Balduin dropped back to relate their plans. Their employer tucked one of her curls behind her ear, a frown creasing her face as she listened. The bracelets on her thick wrists shone in the sunlight. Mattin's response made her laugh, of all things, her chest rising and falling distractingly. Balduin and Mattin's laughter joined hers, and Zosima's stomach went leaden.

This woman was nothing like Pasqual or Miquela. Too loud. Too nervous. Too unfamiliar with the way of the traveler.

It wasn't long before Balduin returned to her side. They picked up their pace, ranging down the road. It was wide enough for four to walk abreast, an old trade route that had faded without regular use. The remains of campsites reclaimed by the wilderness were not infrequent; it was easy to find one, a ragged semicircle free of tall trees around a clearing dotted with neatly made stone firepits.

Balduin dropped his pack on the ground, unpacking and spreading out the tent he carried. A short time later, as Mattin and the alchemist entered the clearing, Balduin and Zosima slipped away into the woods under the excuse of going to collect firewood and look for a water source.

For a time, Zosima could abandon the shades of Pasqual and Miquela and a lifetime of would-have-beens.

Balduin caught her by the shoulders and kissed her, tongue sliding across the seam of her mouth. She let him in happily, twining her arms around him.

Stupid and risky, part of her mind whispered.

Zosima shoved the thought away in favor of opening her mouth to Balduin, sliding her hands under his tunic and dragging her fingers along the hard muscle of his chest. Gods, it felt good to have him in her arms again.

His tongue swept through her mouth like wildfire. It matched the heat racing across her skin and burning low in her gut. His hands skimmed her body, pulling off her tunic and the breast band beneath it with the ease of practice. Balduin dipped his head down, drawing a nipple into his mouth. She groaned, rocking her body against him at the jolt of pleasure. One of his broad hands rested against her shoulders, holding her in place as he teased one dusky nipple to a taut peak, then turning his attention to the second. Her body went liquid against him.

Balduin dropped down slowly, his fingers working at the laces of her breeches, then he swore, looking up at her with his eyes gone dark with lust. Her fingers caught in the burnished sunshine of his hair and held him there just long enough to steal another kiss. She shouldn't torment herself, and yet something in her wanted to delay the moment.

Cool evening air washed across her ass and thighs as Balduin tugged down her breeches and smallclothes, baring her to the world. He hummed with pleasure and pressed kisses up the inside of her thighs, into the thatch of coarse curls on her mound, everywhere but where she really wanted him. Every touch made the pulse in her cunt pound harder and faster. Her fingers still curled in his hair, she nudged her hips insistently toward him, tried to bring his mouth to the folds of her cunt, the nub of her clit.

He tsked, then finally swept his tongue along her folds. Zosima shuddered and tipped back against the tree, rocking her hips toward him. Frustrated and aching, even this was almost enough to send her over the edge. She reined herself in, tried to focus on the rough bark against her shoulders, the bite of the air against the heat of her skin.

"Come for me, Zo," he rasped against her thigh.

She shook her head. He slid one finger inside her, circling her inner walls. Her body fluttered and rippled around his touch. Her fingers tightened in his hair as she tried desperately to keep from losing the last of her control. Her heart hammered in her chest when he dropped his mouth to her again, circling her clit with greater force. She was close, so close—

She was in command of herself. She closed her eyes so tight she saw stars and steeled herself. "I want you inside me," she said roughly. "I want to fuck you."

He laughed against her cunt.

Zosima forced her fingers free from his hair, allowing him to stand. He rose and backed away; she took a breath of air heavy with the promise of rain, but it did nothing to clear her thoughts.

Balduin stripped off his tunic. His muscled chest was marked with scars like the one that had nearly taken his eye; she remembered many of them when they were fresh and new. Life—especially in their trade—was often far too short.

Nudging several rocks out of the way, Balduin dropped his tunic to the ground.

Approaching him, Zosima kicked off her boots and shed her trousers. The aching pulse of her cunt hadn't eased, the tightness inside her coiled like a serpent ready to strike. Balduin's trousers and boots joined hers on the clearing floor. His erection pointed nearly skyward, twitching as she approached.

"What are you waiting for, Zo?"

"Nothing, now." Zosima knelt over him, dragged a hand between her thighs to coat it with her own arousal, stroked the hard cock before her. She savored how the big man trembled, stretched out and waiting for her. And then, before anything could interrupt them, she wrapped her hand around him and positioned the head of his cock at her entrance.

With a shared groan, she slid down Balduin's cock, sheathing him inside her. His fingers settled on her hips, encouraging her to rise and fall. The last sounds of the world around them fell away, replaced by the sound of flesh on flesh, her groans and his panting mingling. He'd been right—he always was. As she sank down on him again, the walls of her cunt fluttered around him. Her skin felt tight, muscles trembling as she rode him, chasing shared pleasure. He rose to meet her, filling her up and wiping every other thought from her mind.

"Now," he said, his hips snapping into hers. "Zo—"

He came hard, his body taut as he emptied himself into her. She dropped down on him one last time to grind her clit against him, pushing herself over the peak and into her own climax. The world exploded around her, a wash of heat and stars heaving behind her eyes. The bubble of tension within her burst as pleasure raced along her nerves. Zosima dropped her head to Balduin's chest, the sound of his ragged breathing filling her ears, every inhale drawing the scent of sex and sweat deep into her lungs.

A moment later, the sex and sweat was joined by the smell of smoke, the faint patter of raindrops, and the low *boom* of thunder rolling so close that her bones trembled with it.

They exchanged a look, Balduin not yet gone soft inside her.

And then, not nearly distant enough to suit her, the screams began.

Smoke wreathed the clearing, filled Serra's lungs, and stung her eyes.

"I swear," Mattin choked out as he lay on the ground, "it's never happened to me before."

"Right, right." She swallowed and squinted against the smoke. It hurt, but nothing compared to what Mattin must be enduring. He'd been right next to the lightning when it struck. Panic rose in her chest, beating its wings against her ribs. She drew in a breath to calm herself but failed as she coughed and choked on the ashy air. Serra wiped a hand across her eyes. "That's what all the mages say. 'I'll just light a fire,' and then half the clearing's burning. I know your type." She met his pale blue eyes, already reddened by smoke. "Can you feel your fingers?"

His eyes closed for a moment. "My entire arm is in pain, so—yes?"

"It's a start." She looked frantically around the clearing they'd selected for camp. Balduin and Zosima had gone to collect firewood and to check the perimeter or some such; she and Mattin had been putting the camp up as rainclouds rolled in. Her own tent was only half erected; the poles and canvas refused to obey all good sense no matter what she tried. The tent Balduin and Zosima and Mattin shared was already up, the awning out.

"Can you stand up? Make it to the tent?"

"Should." His voice was tight with restrained pain. He reached toward her with one hand and abruptly stopped, skin going pale. "Might need help."

Help. Serra pressed her eyes closed for a moment. Where had the other two gone? How was she supposed to handle this on her own? This was why she'd hired people, why she'd wanted to stay safe and sound inside the walls of her shop in town. The wilderness tried to kill you, that's what the books and journals and stories said. It tried to kill you, and it was trying to kill Mattin, and then Balduin and Zosima would blame her and leave her on the side of the road, and she'd be eaten by whatever monster found her first.

"I've got you," she said, keeping a stranglehold on her panic. *Pretend it's a particularly finicky compound that requires complete attention lest it explode.* "I've salves, potions, in my pack. You're not getting out of this trip to the middle of nowhere so easily." She tried for a smile and received a weak one in exchange. "I'm going to get them. I will be right back, Mattin. I promise." She stepped away, reeling with the combined stimulus of his injuries and the pressure and everything was so much, too much—

But she had to do it.

Serra rushed to her supplies, heedless of the rain now sluicing down. *Focus, alchemist. You can deal with this.* She dragged her bag of medicines back to Mattin's slumped form and took in his injuries for the first time.

It has been a horror of terrible timing. Mattin had finished setting up the mercenaries' tent and left her fumbling to manage her own while he started the campfire. They had seen the clouds coming in, the air growing thick and heavy with the incipient rain. She had fought with her tent while he cleared a space for the fire and gathered wood.

Then he'd called on his magic, and they'd both expected a flicker of flame to answer. It had not.

Lightning had.

It snapped from the sky and struck the wood, a blinding light and heat worse than any of her failed alchemical experiments. When she could see again, Mattin was sprawled on the ground, the sleeves of his tunic and robes gone, the skin beneath a sight she would not soon forget.

She fumbled through her bag, pulling out a small pot of healing salve and a bundle of carefully packed vials. She selected a dark purple one and uncorked it with her teeth, pressing it to Mattin's lips.

"What is this?" His voice was thready, eyes pressed closed against the agony.

"Sleeping potion," Serra said. "It will put you out while I take care of the rest of this. It will stop the pain," she added, biting down on her lip. "You need to take it."

His eyes were glassy with shock and pain, but he swallowed everything without a fight. She was grateful that, if anyone was going to be injured, it was him; she probably would have had to knock Zosima out to get the potion into her. Stubborn woman.

Serra eased Mattin to the ground, grimacing at the burns sheathing his arms and the charred fabric decorating them. She winced at his groan and cupped his face with a hand. "You'll feel better when you wake up. I know this."

"Glad one of us has some faith," he replied, each word forced through gritted teeth.

She watched his eyelids flutter and fall shut, listened to his ragged breathing ease. Serra counted his breaths; once she was certain the draught had taken full hold, she turned to the critical work ahead. Detaching her mind from her fingers, she focused on the task at hand with the same diligence she applied to her alchemical efforts.

"What are you doing?" Zosima's voice pealed across the clearing, louder than the thunder that still rumbled in the skies. "What happened?"

Serra didn't turn from her patient as she kept plucking pieces of burned robe from Mattin's arms and slathering salve over the places where they had been. "Lightning." She was proud she kept her voice from shaking. This was something she could do, and confidence steeled her spine. She might not be able to pitch a tent or split wood for a fire, but she knew her potions and her poultices.

She could save a life.

"Where's Mattin?" Balduin shouted, voice cracking through the rain and Serra's rote motions.

"Hurt," Zosima called back, and for the first time Serra heard something in it other than anger or the cold cut of disapproval.

She knew what worry sounded like all too well, even—especially—when it was usually hidden beneath layers of projected confidence, when those layers came loose to reveal the vulnerability beneath.

"He'll be all right as long as the salve stays on. And we can't leave tomorrow." Serra wiped the back of her hand across her forehead. "I gave him a sleeping draught and the salve; the more time it has to work without interruption, the better off he'll be."

"We need—"

Serra twisted awkwardly to glare upward. "He needs rest if you want him healed. And I won't be responsible for someone moving him."

Something shifted in the air between them. Zosima slid a hand under Serra's elbow and helped her rise. The woman's inner fire radiated, a heat that licked through Serra's sleeve and along her skin. She smelled of rain and sweat and spice and something thicker, muskier, obvious only when Serra stood so close to her. Worry bit at Zosima's face, dragging a furrow into her forehead and her mouth into a frown.

"He'll be fine," Serra murmured as she met Zosima's eyes. The hard, dark gleam she was used to had been replaced by something warmer and more vulnerable. "It's painful, but by the time the salve kicks in and the sleeping potion wears off, he should be mostly set to rights."

"So that's what you've been hauling around," Zosima said, wetting her lips with the tip of her tongue. "I thought it was just…" She waved a hand dismissively.

Serra drew in a breath, nose filling with rain and that musky scent. She recognized it: sex. Something twinged low in her body, a pulse of lust and envy. This was not the time to think about Zosima and Balduin in the woods, hot and sweaty, skin on skin—

And it was *definitely* not the time to think about how much she'd have liked to be part of that. She exhaled again and steeled herself. "I may not be used to this, or have even wanted to be here, but I packed what I thought was necessary."

Zosima looked at Mattin and then over Serra's shoulder. Her eyes darted back, the tension in her sharp features easing. "Thank you," she said, the words coming slow and awkward. "I've—lost a lot of people," she continued doggedly, "and if you hadn't been here…"

"I may not be able to pull a bow or nip a bird off a branch with a dagger, but I'm good at what I do." Serra offered a flicker of a smile, achingly conscious of the hand still under her arm, the wiry strength of the woman holding her up. "You won't lose him—or anyone else—while I'm here."

The worry eased; a tooth dragging at Zosima's lip. She nodded curtly. "You're a good person, Serra Tichelaar. Let me know what you need, and I'll see it done."

Serra chewed on the inside of her cheek. "Can you help me with my tent?"

The next morning, Serra woke to the smell of food and the sound of birds and soft conversation. No rain—and she hadn't been shaken from sleep, shouted at to get out of bed and on the road. Her muscles ached from the events of the night before, tension burrowed deep into her shoulders and back and neck. Most of her ached from walking anyway—only regular application of healing salves had kept her from blisters and agony as they made their way toward the valley and the late-autumn blooms she had requested.

Life would have been so much easier if she'd been able to stay in her workshop. If they'd allowed her to pour coins in their hands, hand them the page with the botanical illustration, and rely on them to bring the samples back.

But no—Balduin had demanded she accompany them, politely and warmly but in no uncertain terms. Zosima, all copper skin and predatory grace, had barely contained her fury but acceded with hissed imprecations. And the tall man, a southerner like Serra, had just patted Zosima on the shoulder and told her it would be fine.

How wrong Mattin had been. Everything Serra did seemed to frustrate Zosima; Serra was too slow, too jumpy, too loud—or too quiet.

Until last night, when her competency hadn't been called into question.

Serra slipped out of her tent, a small cloth packet of herbs tucked into a pocket of her long tunic. Balduin and Mattin sprawled by the campfire, raising hands in greetings as she approached.

"Hail my savior," Mattin quipped.

Serra rolled her eyes. "That's a stretch."

"Not after last night. I owe you my life," Mattin replied earnestly. He lifted his hands, the loose fabric of his shirt falling away to show fresh, unblemished skin. "I'm in your debt."

Crouching near the fire, Serra plucked two mugs from the jumble of drinking vessels beside it and poured hot water into both of them. "We're traveling together. That's what you do, isn't it?" She pulled the packet of herbs out and put pinches into each mug. "Besides—that's what I do. Potions and salves and oils and…all of it." She gestured with one hand, her bracelets jingling against one another. "I may not be a mage, or be able to swing a sword or throw a dagger, but these things, I can do."

"That is more impressive than my own art. My magic is small," Mattin said, accepting the cup. "It shifts probabilities. Weighting a scale with your thumb. Enough to make a guard sneeze at the right moment or make someone's armor deflect arrows better."

With feline grace, Zosima settled beside Serra. Her hands were full of dense, dark bread and hard cheese. She passed a chunk of each across, generosity that warmed Serra's heart. "Until he decides to do something big and showy."

"And end up on my ass for hours afterward. Last night I tried to convince probability that those twigs would easily catch fire. The lightning answered instead." Mattin glanced at the fresh pink skin over his arms and hands. "There was something about that storm…"

Serra rested the bread and cheese on the spread of her thigh, cradling her mug as she waited for the healing tisane to cool. "The tomes say the magic is thick here. What Balduin said about the wyvern? This matches."

"No more magic, Mat—not unless you have to," Balduin cautioned. "No more risks. One near-death experience per contract is more than enough."

"On that, we agree." Serra shifted, knee brushing against Zosima. She expected the other woman to jerk away and was surprised when she didn't. Had something that fundamental changed last night? There was one way to be sure. Serra blew on the tisane again, then ventured, "I'm nearly out of salve. If anything like that happens again—gods forbid!—we'll be out of luck. I need to forage today."

Zosima hummed as she split her end of bread into halves, lodging a piece of cheese between the pieces. "We're not going anywhere until Mattin is healed. If you need to forage, I will accompany you."

Serra's insides fluttered. "Unexpected" didn't begin to cover the emotions springing to war in her chest. Relief, astonishment, and a hint of…excitement?

What was happening?

"I'd…I would appreciate that," she said, giving Zosima a smile. "You're more than a match for any wyverns or manticores out here, I should think."

Across the fire, Mattin and Balduin exchanged an unreadable look, the hint of a smile playing at the corner of Mattin's lips. "There's only one thing that may fell Zosima, but time will tell."

Serra scrutinized the bush before her. It was the third one she'd approached on this foraging expedition; Zosima couldn't see the difference between them. They were all green. The only difference was this bush grew precariously near the edge of a rushing river and was therefore the hardest to harvest anything from.

So naturally it was the one her alchemist was evaluating with the most intense enthusiasm. At least it afforded Zo the opportunity to admire the lush expanse of her thighs and the way her trousers clung indecently to her backside. That had been the highlight of the midday foraging expedition: identifying the flowers and mosses and shrubs often necessitated bending over. And, for all that Serra might not be the quickest or the most agile, she hadn't complained once as they wended through the forest.

She also hadn't complained about walking on the road. Slow but steady. It wasn't what Zo was used to, but it was admirable.

"Are we moving on from here?" Zosima rocked back on her heels, trying to let some of her boredom seep into her tone and distract from the nascent attraction bubbling up in her.

"No, this is the one." Serra flicked a glance over her shoulder. "It's perfect—the flowers are in full bloom. They're rich in—"

"This is your field, not mine," Zo said, waving her off. "It'll go in one ear and out the other. Get what you need, but in all the gods' names—" Her fingers knotting into fists at her side as her body tensed to leap when Serra reached for a particular blossom; she resisted the urge to lunge forward.

"See?" Serra said, tucking the flower securely into her satchel. "It's fine. Cochius flowers are incredibly versatile. It's sometimes hard to find the right ones, but when you do, they're worth their weight in gold."

Zo rolled her eyes and let her tension ebb. A half dozen more yellow flowers joined the first. Serra rose, stretching her arms skyward in a way that had no reason to be as enticing as it was.

"Is that the last of them, then?" Zo cocked her head. "Or are we off for more gardening?"

"Finding these meets the most urgent need," Serra said. She twisted to adjust the satchel at her side, shifting her weight.

Her foot slipped.

Time slowed for Zo. Her body refused to move as Serra reached forward only to fall off the riverbank and down toward the rainstorm-swollen mountain river.

A loud shout of surprise rang through the trees.

The alchemist's hand vanished beneath the rushing water. There was a second shriek—this one of shock—and then abrupt quiet.

Zosima's body began to function again. She bolted for the crumbling edge of the raised riverbank, taking only a moment to glance down.

There—not far, hands clinging desperately to a rock jutting out of the river, gleaming cap of hair now dull and sodden. When Zo got her hands on that alchemist, she was going to—

She cut the thought off as she slid down along the crumbling earth and dove into the frigid water.

Serra wasn't going to escape this without consequences. Not when she'd somehow managed to wriggle herself beneath Zosima's thick skin and almost impenetrable armor. She was not going to just—vanish, not like Miquela, and she was not going to die like Pasqual had. She was going to get back on land, and then—

Once she got Serra to the shore, poured one of Serra's own healing potions down her throat, and checked her over, they were going to have words.

Letting frustration and fury course through her, Zosima clawed through the water until she made it to the rock to which Serra clung. She dug her fingers into a crevice and fisted the alchemist's tunic in her other hand, trying to help keep her head above the water.

Serra's face was frightening to behold, the usual soft pink curves gone bloodless white, the lips pale and shading to blue. But she'd not been in the water long enough to freeze—nor long enough to be lost. Serra's eyes pinched shut, her hands scrabbling at Zosima's shoulders. The panic beating at Zo's ribs slowed, water slapping at her face.

"Got you," Zo said thickly. "Take a breath and trust me. Got it?"

Keeping her mouth shut against the water, Serra nodded jerkily.

A few moments of shifting, and Zo could hook an arm around Serra's waist, angling Serra's body even as Zo held onto the rock. "Hold on," she instructed. Nervously, Serra clung to Zosima, fingers latching into her dagger bandolier. Zosima calculated: their location, the curve of the river a little farther downstream, and—

—let go.

Serra sputtered and shrieked, an arm locking around Zosima as the water carried them to the bank.

Zosima gripped Serra's shoulders tightly and dragged her onto the shore, half tangling with her. The chill soaked them both to the bone. She pressed Serra close to her, tucking the other woman's head beneath her chin. "You're safe," Zosima said, tongue heavy. "You're safe now."

Serra's breathing was ragged, her fingers clenching convulsively against Zosima's side. "Why?"

"On the shore now," Zo said through chattering teeth.

"No. Why come after me?"

Zosima made a choked sound. Wasn't it obvious? "Because," she said, roughly rubbing at Serra's shoulders to get warmth into her, into both of them, "you're ours now."

Hauling herself and Serra slowly up the riverbank and into the trees was a process. Chilled as they were, they needed to keep moving, but her body trembled from the cold and the exertion. Her breathing harsh to her own ears, Zo slumped against a tree while she worked up the willpower to continue. They needed to—but gods, she was frozen.

"No one here is ever allowed to leave unsupervised again," Balduin roared, volume and ferocity doing little to hide the concern in his voice. They heard him before they saw him, brush and saplings knocked aside as he stormed through the undergrowth, Mattin trailing him with a disapproving look.

Still cursing enough to blister ears and scorch the trees, Balduin's long-legged strides carried him to loom over them. "Give her to me," he demanded, waiting only until Zo's arms, locking up again with cold and shock, eased. He scooped their alchemist up in his arms like she was so much dandelion fluff, his brow furrowed deep with concern. Zo followed, Mattin a close shadow, all of her sodden and muddy as she scrambled to their campsite.

"I'll manage," Serra said through chattering teeth.

Balduin made a deep, almost subterranean sound. "You'll forgive us if we don't trust you on that. You're dangerously competent, but I think Zo might be getting a little protective."

Zosima swore but couldn't find it in her heart to manage any stronger denial. Her waterlogged clothing clung to her. Her heart still had not recovered from her unexpected leap into the waters, blood thundering through her veins and keeping her warm with indignation and the urgent desire to run her hands all over Serra, make sure she was intact and unblemished, desperate to drive the breath from her lungs in an entirely different way.

"Get her out of those," Zo snarled protectively as she began to strip down outside the tent, unfastening her water-logged leathers then tackling her boots. The minute she'd shed them, she slipped inside into the warmth, Mattin trailing behind her.

His fingers worked the lacings of her trousers; he cursed beneath his breath at the swollen knots. Finally, abruptly, they slithered free with a snap of his fingers and a smug laugh. Zo gave him a dirty look, easily quashed as he brought his lips to hers.

"You jumped in right after her, you idiot," he rasped. "What did you think was going to happen?"

"Mage, remember? Between you and Bal—"

Mattin worked the sodden, clinging leather and fabric off her hips and let them fall to the ground. "I can't decide if your blind, unadulterated confidence in us is arousing or terrifying." His fingers fumbled only briefly at the bandolier of daggers across her chest, unbuckling it and letting it fall beside them.

His hands were fiery brands; he slid them across the cold skin of her belly and up her sides as she worked her tunic loose. Zosima gasped, removing her breast band with a few quick motions. Mattin's hands covered the small globes of her breasts, warming them. There was a dark, hungry look in his eyes. Her eyes rested on his tousled hair and slid across the tent to find Balduin—and Serra.

Serra's teeth chattered and her hands shook. She trembled as Balduin stripped away the sodden fabric of her tunic and trousers with remarkable industriousness. She wanted to press herself against him, soak up the warmth of his body. Shame and embarrassment flared bright as she realized she stood utterly bare in the tent, but the shame was gone in an instant, washed away by a rush of gratitude. She reached with both hands toward Balduin, drawing him down for a kiss, and found herself stilled with a touch.

"As much as I want to—and believe me, little alchemist, I definitely want to," he said, mouth quirking in a grin, "you shouldn't feel obligated to do this. Or anything."

"You saved my life."

"Zo did. And I know she'd do it again."

"But she—"

"She definitely doesn't hate you," he rumbled, chafing his hands over her bare shoulders and back. "But we need to get you—and Zo—warm. If you are willing—and only if you are—I know I speak for the three of us when I say there is a particular way we could go about it."

Serra's insides quivered with hope and disbelief and delight. She cast a look over her shoulder at the copper-skinned woman—

—the exceedingly naked copper-skinned woman, bare but for the same contraceptive charm on a chain around her neck that Serra wore. Zosima was all lithe muscle and sharp angles and small-handful breasts, her eyes meeting Serra's, lambent and full of desire. Mattin pressed a kiss to the side of her neck; he was still fully clothed, and his hands glided along her body.

"Yes," Serra tried to croak. She had to wet her lips, irony of ironies that her throat was parched. "Yes," she tried again. Balduin's sound of satisfaction rippled over her skin as his fingers roamed over her shoulders and down her back with intense deliberation.

"Hands off," Zosima said thickly, her eyes dark and weighty as a caress, stepping from Mattin's embrace to swat Balduin away. "Selfish lout."

Zosima should have been cold as she pressed herself against Serra's back, should have been as chilled to the bone as Serra was, but instead Zosima's proximity sent fire along Serra's every nerve, all of them streaking to form a molten liquid pool in her core.

"Never do that again. You promised we wouldn't lose anyone," Zosima said into Serra's ear, breath tickling the soft skin there as Zo's hands wandered where Balduin's couldn't reach. "We almost lost you."

Balduin stepped away, and Serra found herself being eased inexorably to the pile of bedding that filled most of the tent. "I didn't think you cared," Serra said as her head hit a lump of something. Zosima knelt between her thighs, hands small but everywhere along Serra's skin.

"You're beautiful and competent and infuriating and wet behind the ears and nothing like I expected," Zosima retorted. "And you promised," she added with a deeper heart-sore ache, as though that mattered more than anything. She slid to stretch out beside Serra, fingers grazing her cheek and curling around it. She leaned in, skin to skin and mouth to mouth, their bodies touching to make a line of fire.

Zosima kissed like she lived, with a ferocity and passion that took no prisoners. Need washed through Serra in a wave, pushing away her worries. She wasn't a burden, wasn't dragging them down or holding them back. They wanted this—and so did she: longed to be pressed between bodies, skin against skin, in the middle of a joining that was chaotic and unpredictable and so unlike home.

It didn't make her panic or worry.

It felt right.

The broad hand covering so much of her hip could only be Balduin's, the warmth of him radiating out like she lay stretched beside a campfire. His cock pressed hard against her, hot and unyielding, a declaration of silent intent. Zosima's weight settled on her heavier, and Serra cracked open an eye to see Mattin behind Zo.

"Who's on wa—?"

"*Fuck* watch." Zosima leaned in to kiss Serra again, deep and luxurious, one hand working down Serra's body to stroke a breast. Balduin's hand wandered over her body, a blunt finger tracing the sensitive crease of skin at the top of her hip. Serra shuddered, trapped between the two mercenaries, and couldn't be happier. They were a tangle of hungry mouths and hands and cocks and cunts. Serra lost track of what belonged to whom as their four bodies crowded together. Her fingers caught in the curls of hair on Balduin's chest, cupped the back of Mattin's head as he kissed her, gasped and arched against both of them as Zosima ran her fingers along the cleft at the apex of Serra's thighs.

"You're soaked here, too," Zo said with sultry tones that turned Serra's limbs to jelly. She slid one finger inside Serra, curling it just so. Gasping, Serra bowed up, her hands digging into the meat of someone's shoulder. "Not cold, though. Not now."

Zosima withdrew her fingers; Serra chased the touch with a whine. Zo laughed, a peal of startled delight, then spread Serra's folds open with one hand and slowly, steadily pumped her fingers in and out.

Serra wanted, needed, her body willing to surrender to the hand between her thighs, the mouths that laved their way along her body and dug into the curves of her belly and hips. She closed her eyes as a pair of hands played with her breasts, rolled her nipples between their fingers, squeezed. There were hands all over her, long and narrow, broad and blunt, mouths and tongues on her clit and inside her pussy and her mouth; she could taste her own arousal, the salt-tang of pre-come, the want and worry and desire twining through the three of them as they brought her fully into their tight-knit circle. Her breath caught in her throat.

Smiling wider than she could ever remember smiling, Serra sank into the sensations enveloping her.

Whose fingers were in her cunt changed and changed again.

The sounds of skin on skin and moans.

Zo's voice was a litany of soft, surprising praise that filled the air.

When she opened her eyes again, it was Balduin's lips teasing her skin, the broad-shouldered man on his belly beside her, tongue spiraling around her nipple with obvious delight. Mattin knelt behind him, eyes closed in ecstasy, thrusting in and out of Balduin with long, languid rolls of his hips. Every stroke matched the pace of Balduin's tongue against her, soft gasps and louder groans making her sensitive skin vibrate and tremble as though in answer to Mattin's movements.

Zosima hooked her hands around Serra's thighs, tugging Serra's leg up, then sinking down to grind her pussy against Serra's. Serra slid her hand between her thighs and coated her hand with her own arousal, rubbing at her clit. Zosima made a sound of pleasure, brushed Serra's hand aside and replaced it with her own.

Hand still slick, Serra wrapped her hand around as much of Balduin's cock as she could. He swore and thrust down hard into the ring her fingers made; she could feel how deliciously taut his muscles had grown. He was hot and hard and so thick that it was impossible for Serra to touch any fingertip and her thumb together. She wondered how he'd feel buried inside her—but that was for later, some other time. It would happen, though—it was as inevitable as the alchemical reactions she had mastered.

Now she had Zosima's cunt rocking against hers, and it was overwhelming. The way Zo's pace stuttered, hand on Serra's mound and thumb a determined, steady flick against her clit, Serra thought it wouldn't be long before Zo found release. Serra wanted to push her to climax; grinding against Zo, hand stroking Balduin with a jagged, hastening rhythm, her body tensed.

A guttural cry broke from Mattin's lips, his head tipping back as his body went tense, hips driving hard one last time into Balduin. The force of his orgasm rippled through Balduin, his lips sealing around Serra's breast, cock sliding through her hand. This was nothing like the slow precision of her decoctions and extractions; this was the hungry heat of a flame, taking every touch and turning it to pleasure. The slick folds between her thighs ached, need swelled in her until her skin felt stretched, and her whole body taut like a bubble about to break.

Time slowed and stretched—the moment when a drop hung suspended, infinitesimal yet endless before it grew too heavy and plummeted.

"Come for us," someone said; it didn't matter who, only that they wanted to see her come undone, and she wanted to show them. Serra let herself fall, her last restraint gone as her body tensed, cunt tightening around the fingers filling her. A body pressed against hers, the crush of lips and fervor she recognized as Zosima's. She wrapped her arms around the other woman, sighing release into her mouth. Someone cried out a moment later; Zosima's body echoed Serra's orgasm as it trembled against Serra's. Wet heat spurted across her skin.

Serra closed her eyes, savoring the press of bodies against her as Mattin and Balduin snugged up at her sides and Zosima draped herself atop her like a proprietary wildcat. For all her fears of leaving the shop, all her worries about the wider world—this had been worth it.

Going past the bend in the road had given her this; curled up in a pile of languid bodies, she wondered what might be around the next turn in their journey.

The Seduction of Thierry Bacheler

D. A. Hernández

alcohol use (casual), bipoc, bisexual, blow job, clitoral fingering, college, cunnilingus, dimension jumping, dubious consent (mild), f/m/m, flirting, friends to lovers, fuck or die, hand job, huddling for warmth, humor, intercrural sex, interspecies relationship, magical mishaps, modern with magic, non-human character, the only solution to a love triangle is a..., past tense, penis in vagina sex, pining, puzzles and games, rivals to friends to lovers, sex pollen, student (college), third person limited point of view, trapped together

Thierry and Yuka hurried back to their cabin at the edge of campus. It was raining heavily, but they were already sopping wet from falling in the lake. This made Thierry covering Yuka's head with his coat a more gentlemanly than practical gesture, but because Yuka enjoyed being close to Thierry, she didn't say anything. When they arrived, they stood at the entrance, dripping.

Thierry pushed his long hair out of his eyes, and Yuka couldn't help but *look*: his blouse had fallen open, revealing a downy-haired chest, and wet fabric clung to his slim waist and soft belly. Thierry turned his back on her quickly, taking off his soaked boots and stumbling through the living room to retrieve towels. He slung one over Yuka's head, covering her eyes. He patted down her hair gently, from the crown of her head to her neck, his hands slow and lingering.

"You should take a bath before you get consumption, Yuka," he said, accentuating the first syllable of her name as usual. "I insist."

Only if you join me, Yuka didn't say. She peeked out from under the towel to see his warm gaze and stopped feeling the cold. She thanked him and entered the bathroom, which transformed from Thierry's luxurious space with a claw-footed bathtub into a modern Japanese bathroom outfitted with a shower toilet and compact ceramic tub—the only thing that stayed the same were Thierry's wildflowers on the sink and in the corner. It was the kind of space she'd have if she'd gone to university back home, in her own era, instead of attending the Nowhere University of Magic, located in a pocket dimension obscured from time.

Yuka looked at herself in the mirror: her wet shirt hugged the generous line of her breasts, outlining her bra. Thierry had *seen* her like that. How would he react if he saw her naked? Would he run and hide in his room? Would he come closer and run a hand down her body?

These traitorous thoughts wouldn't leave her, and perhaps they were why, while coming out of the bathroom, she let the towel slip from her fingers.

"How clumsy of you," said a sardonic voice behind her. "Next you'll be falling on all fours at my feet."

Yuka stifled a scream and snatched up her towel, covering herself as a blush spread from her face down her chest.

Sprawled on the sofa like a smug panther was Aashiq, Thierry's newest friend. His feet were bare, and he'd removed his stylish thobe, exposing a muscular, dark-haired chest over his loose pants.

"I was wondering how you guys managed to fall into the lake, but now I understand," Aashiq said, seemingly unaffected by Yuka's body.

"And why did *you* come here in this weather?" Yuka asked.

"For tea and sweets and delectable poetry, of course," Aashiq purred.

"Aashiq? Has Yuka come out of the bath? You should tell her to come take ginger tea when she can, she needs to warm up!" Thierry's voice came from the kitchen, getting closer.

"Drop the towel again," Aashiq told Yuka with a rakish wink.

Yuka fled to her room.

When she came back out, Aashiq was reciting a ghazal in Arabic, his kohl-lined eyes gazing into Thierry's as the words flowed from his mouth, and though Yuka couldn't understand a word of it, Thierry probably did—his cheeks were red, and he looked both fascinated and shocked. There was a long moment of silence after Aashiq finished, and Thierry said, with a slightly strangled voice: "Ah, that was—that was beautiful. Th-thank you."

"Anytime. Abu Nuwas was a far better poet than lover," Aashiq said, leaning back on the sofa in a deliberately sexy way.

When Thierry finally noticed her presence, he scrambled to the teapot and cups set on the table, fingers tapping on the cup as he poured a spicy concoction: "Yuka, glad you could join us! This is my own blend; it prevents consumption."

Yuka sat on the armchair in front of the sofa while Aashiq casually stretched and put his arm behind Thierry. Thierry didn't seem to notice and relaxed into Aashiq's space. Yuka felt a pang: jealousy? Envy of Aashiq's practiced flirting? Of how it seemed to be working? Was it mere embarrassment, seeing her interest so obviously reflected in Aashiq?

Flashing a bottle of his homemade liquor, Aashiq proposed, "How about we play Truth or Dare?"

"Please don't," Yuka groaned.

Aashiq grinned back.

Glancing between them, Thierry asked warily, "What is this game?"

"Will you speak the Truth, dearest Thierry, or accept a frightful Dare? Which is less terrifying for you?" Aashiq asked.

"Uh... Truth?"

"Have you ever been kissed?" Aashiq pinned Thierry with an earnest gaze. Yuka leaned toward him as well. Like a rabbit about to bolt, Thierry looked between them, red-faced.

"What? I thought this would be like a pop quiz! I—" Thierry stammered.

"You don't have to answer," Yuka said.

"You can accept a Dare instead! Take a drink!" Aashiq offered the bottle.

Thierry snapped it up and, tilting it dangerously high, drank a long swallow. He sputtered and coughed and blurted out: "Never." At his friends' wide eyes, he shrugged and scratched his chin. "Grandmother never let me out of the house by myself... I didn't know many people, aside from my tutors."

"I could—" Aashiq started, but Thierry talked over him.

"It's your turn! What about you?"

"Me? Been kissed before? Many times, by many people…on many parts of my body," Aashiq replied wickedly. Thierry got even redder and took another long sip.

"Yuka!" Thierry pointed unsteadily at her with the bottle.

"Dare," she requested.

"I dare you to do ten jumping jacks, right here, in front of us," Aashiq said before Thierry could say anything.

Yuka glared at him but complied.

Aashiq smirked while Thierry, who was moving to take another sip, dropped the bottle. He bent to retrieve it, muttering, "Sorry! I had too much already. I don't drink much; what is that liquor?"

With a *tsk*, Aashiq fetched the bottle and took a sip himself. "It's good, isn't it? I can give you the recipe. It's strong, though, so take it easy—"

Thierry snatched the bottle from his hand and drank again. "Dare!"

"I *said* take it easy!" Aashiq chided him.

Before Aashiq could offer his own awful ideas, Yuka dared, "Flap your arms like a bird."

Aashiq raised an eyebrow, and she shrugged.

Thierry stood up with a big wobble and flapped his arms, watching their reactions. He even cawed.

Yuka giggled, and Aashiq smiled with a corner of his mouth.

Thierry smiled at them, woozily, and promptly passed out.

"He was looking at your breasts," Aashiq said, sometime after they'd carried Thierry to his room to sleep it off.

Yuka, who was sipping the sweet but remarkably strong wine, choked. After a coughing fit, she managed to sputter, "Was he? It was—it was second-hand embarrassment. Like your poetry."

"He was into it. He just…doesn't know about the ways of the world. Don't tell me you don't want to be the one to teach him."

Yuka looked into the flickering flames of the hearth. "He's been my best friend at Uni since Orientation Week. I love sharing a cabin with him. He's a great cook. He's a good study partner. We even cuddle by the fire sometimes. But he's never… Maybe he's not into girls."

"What's kept you from trying to find out?"

"I don't want to ruin our friendship," she mumbled.

"You're lusting so much, it's no longer platonic," Aashiq said bluntly. "Why not go for it? If he doesn't want you, at least you'll know, and you'll be able to move on."

"But…I don't want to put him on the spot."

"You don't have to outright confess your feelings. Drop the towel. Show him what you're offering, what he could have if he says yes," Aashiq replied.

Yuka buried her face between her knees and kept quiet.

"Or you could watch while I seduce Thierry and listen to us having sex next door," Aashiq said.

Yuka glared at him from the confines of her arms. Then she sighed. "It's easy for you: you're the University's Casanova. Everyone knows of you, even if they don't know you. Never found in classes, always in parties with at least two people in your arms."

Aashiq shrugged. "Life is all the more beautiful with love around you. You need to give love an opportunity, if you ever want to find it." He emptied the liquor bottle with a long swallow. Turning to face Yuka, he extended his hand in challenge, his eyes flashing gold. "A fortnight. You give it your all, and so will I. If by the end of it he's not interested in either of us, we accept it and move on. What do you say?"

After a moment, Yuka shook his hand, and although there was no tingle of a spell or magical contract activating, she felt there was no going back.

That Sunday morning, Aashiq entered the cabin with a large cloth bag, interrupting Thierry and Yuka's study session. "Thierry, my sweet, it's a sunny day, perfect for learning how to swim!"

"I— What?" Thierry asked.

"What will you do the next time a lady falls into the lake?" Aashiq glanced meaningfully at Yuka.

Thierry turned to her anxiously.

"I can swim perfectly well," Yuka said. Then, catching Aashiq's pleading eyes, she relented. "But it's an important skill to have."

"I suppose I can try…" Thierry said.

"Excellent! I brought bathing suits," Aashiq said, emptying the cloth bag over their books and notes.

After a while, Yuka wandered outside to watch the lesson. They'd gone to the secluded cove near the cabin, where the water was colder and deeper than at the more popular parts of the lake. Thierry had chosen a 1920s-style bathing suit, the most conservative option, whereas Aashiq was wearing a flashy G-string thong that accentuated his muscular figure and left little to the imagination.

Aashiq stretched in front of Thierry before diving into the water in a graceful arc. He swam a short lap, then returned to shore and stood up, skin gleaming with water droplets. He shook water from his hair and flexed his muscles with a flirty look at Thierry, who missed a step at the edge of the water and fell into the lake face-first.

Yuka winced while Aashiq scrambled to help Thierry. "I'll drown before I start," Thierry gasped as he emerged from the water.

"Are you hurt?"

"Yes! No! The water's…cold," Thierry mumbled at Aashiq's thong. He jumped into the water and clumsily imitated Aashiq's paddling.

"Be mindful of the rhythm—it's like a dance, you need to move in sync," Aashiq suggested, swimming close to stretch Thierry's arms and lift his hips.

Thierry froze and accidentally swallowed a mouthful of water.

Patting his back, Aashiq took pity on him. "…let's get you a floatie and practice kicking."

Yuka was optimistic about her first attempt—Seven Minutes in Heaven sounded lovely—and being so close to Thierry in the dark was *thrilling*…until the contraction part of the spell kicked in.

"Why is this getting smaller?" Thierry asked inside the cramped space of what had previously been a generously sized wardrobe.

"I'm experimenting with the limits of size-modification spells," Yuka answered, distracted by the smell of Thierry's cologne.

"Is it going as planned?" Thierry pressed into her space as the wardrobe shrank again.

Yuka reveled in the feel of his thighs, belly, and chest against her.

"Yeah," she sighed out.

"Can you stop it? It's getting—tight," Thierry gasped.

"Ah. Yes. I need to go outside to do it…where did I leave the key?" Yuka patted herself down.

"You locked the door!?"

"I had to check whether the key also shrank! It must have because I can't find it. Thierry, I can't reach my own pockets, could you—?"

Thierry stuttered in response but obediently stuck a hand in her skirt pocket, rummaging around.

The wardrobe shrank with an ominous creak, pressing them against each other even more.

"Deeper, Thierry!" Yuka begged with a gasp.

Thierry groaned and put his hand as deep as it could go, finding the random papers and pieces of chalk that were always in her pockets and occasionally brushing her thighs.

"It's not here!" Thierry said as the wardrobe contracted. Suddenly he tapped her hip. "Something's glinting on the floor, beside your left foot!"

Carefully, Yuka turned around and knelt on the floor, tapping blindly until she felt the cold metal of the key against her fingers. Thierry grasped her shoulder. When she looked at him, his pupils were wide, and he was staring at her with his mouth half open. The wardrobe shrank yet more, and Yuka was pressed to Thierry's crotch, half her body between his legs.

They took a long second to react before Yuka turned to the wardrobe door: "The key hasn't shrunk!" she realized.

She banged on the door, and Thierry tried to kick it, but it didn't budge. Thierry drew a sigil in the air and whispered two syllables that brought chills to Yuka's skin and made the air around them hazy.

There was a knock on the door from outside. "Thierry?" came Aashiq's voice.

"Get us out of here!" Thierry begged.

The door opened with a bang. Yuka tumbled out into the center of a spell circle in her room. She hurried to pause the spell and didn't see why Aashiq let out a smothered giggle, nor why Thierry shushed him. When she looked up, Thierry was already half out of the door, hair messy and face red and sweaty.

"I, uh, have an essay due tomorrow, good luck with your spell!" he rambled, voice choked, before running away.

“Good job,” Aashiq winked at her.

Yuka stared at him. “That sigil—the way Thierry summoned you to help us—we studied it in *Non-Human Magics*. You’re an ifrit.”

“So?”

“You gave Thierry *your real name*.”

Aashiq crossed his arms and took a step back. “What of it? He won’t—he won’t abuse it.”

Yuka smiled. “He won’t.”

There was a butt in the middle of the forest, wiggling between low bushes. Thierry and Yuka stared, aghast, before parting the brambles to see the rabbit hole where Aashiq’s neck was buried in hard earth.

“How…?” Thierry asked.

Aashiq’s voice, muted, said, “…chasing a rabbit.”

Yuka blinked, but Thierry didn’t question it. Taking out his trusty gardening spade, he set to work digging up the rocky, packed earth around Aashiq’s neck. Yuka sighed but transfigured a nearby rock using Thierry’s spade as a model and did the same on Aashiq’s other side.

After a while, Aashiq wiggled his butt. “The earth’s loose enough, pull me out!”

Thierry and Yuka grabbed his shoulders on both sides, but Aashiq stopped them: “You need more leverage. Get behind me and pull me by the hips, Thierry!”

Yuka rolled her eyes but stepped aside. Thierry hesitated, looking down at Aashiq’s butt, and he glanced at Yuka before grabbing Aashiq’s hips and pulling.

“Harder!” Aashiq shouted.

Thierry pressed himself against Aashiq’s body and, with a mighty heave, he *pulled*—

Yuka could tell Thierry was using all his strength, but Aashiq was practically twerking in a way that was *not* helping. Thierry’s face got redder and redder, until with a groan, he lost his grip and fell backward into Yuka’s waiting arms.

As she helped him up, Thierry, with his face flustered, his neckerchief and vest askew, snapped, “Get behind me and help me pull, Yuka. And *you*”—he *slapped* Aashiq’s butt—“*pull* when I tell you to pull!”

"Sure," came Aashiq's choked voice.

Yuka positioned herself behind Thierry and grabbed his hips; on Thierry's order, they all pulled. With a *pop!* and the sound of crumbling earth, Aashiq's head came loose from the hole, and they all tumbled down into a sweaty, dusty pile.

"Is that a wand in your pocket, or—" Aashiq started, but Thierry interrupted him, placing his hands on either side of Aashiq's dirt-streaked face.

"I was worried! There are better ways to hunt rabbits!"

Aashiq was speechless.

Thierry looked at Aashiq's lips, then at Yuka. He let go of Aashiq, got up, and dusted himself with trembling hands. "Ah, my clothes are ruined, I need to take a bath, see you later!" he called as he hurried out of the clearing in the direction of the cabin.

Aashiq and Yuka exchanged a wide-eyed look, then Aashiq winced as dirt fell into his eyes.

"You're disgusting," Yuka said, helping him stand up.

Aashiq grinned at her with red-rimmed, teary eyes. He stood close to whisper in Yuka's ear, "He got *harder* when he felt you behind him."

Yuka's face was burning and her heart beating fast, but she didn't reply. She said a quick goodbye and meandered back to the cabin.

She heard water splashing in the bathtub on the other side of the bathroom door. She walked closer and imagined herself entering the bathroom, dropping her clothes in front of Thierry. Her fingers touched the cold metal of the doorknob.

After a long time, she whispered to herself, "Don't be ridiculous."

She left.

Yuka was staring at the flowers she'd put on the mantelpiece. The shiny pink-and-red petals opened shyly and exuded a mochi-sweet smell. She vaguely registered the front door opening and Thierry's voice greeting her.

There was something wrong with the way Thierry stood behind her, gripping her shoulder.

She blinked. Thierry was blocking her view of the flowers and shaking her. "That's an *Ophrys malefica*—the sex-pollen orchid! Where did you get it?"

"At the Full Moon Market. I probably shouldn't have, but I thought you'd love it," Yuka said through a foggy brain.

Thierry smiled and kissed her cheek. "Thank you for the thought. These flowers have amazing properties, though in terms of upkeep and…containment, they're…tricky." Thierry slurred the last words before drifting off, eyes half closed, and leaning into her neck.

"Are you…smelling me?" Yuka asked, reaching out for Thierry. As soon as she touched him, something sparked inside her, an electric current running down her spine, a realization spreading through her like lightning.

He wants me.

And then Thierry bit her neck, too hard, and she yowled in pain and shock. Thierry jumped away with wide eyes and a hand over his mouth. "Yuka, forgive me! It's the orchid, we need to—"

The front door banged open, and Aashiq entered with two bags of food and a loud greeting.

Thierry startled and disturbed the flowerpot on the mantelpiece, sending it tumbling down. He turned and got his hands on it, but Yuka and Aashiq, who had jumped to catch it as well, crashed into him. The pot fell to the floor, flowers and dirt spilling out.

Yuka and Aashiq knelt, transfixed by the flowers, but Thierry shakily managed to pull his neckerchief over his mouth and nose. He tried to get up, but Aashiq stopped him with a hand on his wrist: "You look delectable, my dear," he said, pulling Thierry to him.

Thierry closed his eyes and accepted the kiss Aashiq lovingly placed on his lips—currently covered by the neckerchief.

Aashiq glared at the offending garment. "Take it off."

"Oh, that's *hot*," Yuka whispered.

Thierry's ears were a deep crimson as he shook, fists clenched tight. "An antidote!" he gasped out. "I have the flowers, I can make—" He bent to retrieve as many of the blossoms as he could and ran to his room.

Aashiq watched him leave with a glum look.

Yuka reached out to pat his shoulder consolingly and somehow found herself face to face with him.

His eyes were yellow as a cat's in the afternoon light. He had long, staggeringly pretty eyelashes, the muscles under her hand were firm, and his skin was hot. His lips…

Yuka shrieked as a bucket of icy water drenched her without warning, and she jumped up—from where she had been *straddling Aashiq* on the floor??

Thierry looked between them with an awkward grimace and a complicated look in his eyes before he put the bucket down and offered two cups of something pungent and steaming.

"Drink it," he ordered.

Aashiq and Yuka complied. They retched at the disgusting taste and shivered—despite the potion being hot, it felt like a bucket of cold water inside the body.

Yuka's mind cleared, several realizations coming too quickly to process: her lips were wet and bruised and tingling, both her and Aashiq's clothes were messy, she was uncomfortably wet outside and *inside* her panties, Aashiq was watching her with a similarly baffled expression, and Thierry kept glancing between them, the bucket held protectively before his crotch.

Thierry didn't allow them time to say anything; as soon as he saw them recover, he turned around and walked stiffly to his room, muttering an excuse about finding a way to keep the orchid in containment.

The silence in the room grew.

"Let's not—" Yuka mumbled, unaccountably nervous.

"Right," said Aashiq. He stayed back, his gaze on her, as she retreated to her room.

"Are you experimenting with weather spells again?" Thierry asked, teeth chattering. The cabin was freezing, frost covering the windows from the inside.

Yuka gave him a weak grin and beckoned from the pile of blankets on the sofa. "We—we could share body heat."

Thierry approached and gently touched her cheek. "You're freezing! This is not good…wait!" He ran to the cabin door and stepped outside. "It's nicer here. Come, bring the blankets—we can camp under the stars tonight, and you can fix the spell in the morning."

The weather outside was cool enough for a couple of blankets, and the stars shone above, unlike anything Yuka had seen back home. In fact, the more she tried to find the constellations she knew, the more differences she found.

"Where's the North Star? I can't see Polaris!" Yuka said, searching for it in what she felt pretty sure was Ursa Minor.

"It's not there… That's strange, right? Does this mean the University's time bubble is in the Earth's far past?" Thierry wondered.

"Or so far in the future that the star is gone?" Yuka frowned.

"Do you know any more constellations?"

"A few…" Yuka said, searching for them.

Thierry scooched closer to her and laid his head on her shoulder. "Show me."

It was nice. For the first time in a long while, Yuka felt relaxed, beautiful, and confident. In a lull in the conversation, she caught Thierry staring at her and turned to caress his cheek. His breath caught, but he pressed closer to Yuka as she leaned in, and just like that, they were kissing, sweetly, softly. Yuka held Thierry's face with her hand, and Thierry snaked his arms around to her back, and they fell among the blankets. Thierry was a quick study: he copied every movement Yuka tried, reached for the sensitive places on Yuka's body as she did his own, and when Yuka gently bit his lower lip…he gasped, grabbed Yuka more firmly, and flipped them so Yuka was beneath him. Their kisses turned heated, and Yuka opened her legs to accommodate Thierry when she felt his hardness brush her thigh.

Too soon, Thierry pulled away, stretching his arms to look at Yuka lying beneath him.

"Thierry?"

Thierry closed his eyes and ran a hand through his hair. He stood up, and the wind that struck Yuka felt bitingly cold.

"Yuka, I'm sorry, I—I shouldn't—I— There's something I need to do," he said, his expression shadowed, a hand touching his lips. He kept that hand on his lips as he hurried away, walking toward the woods near the cabin.

Yuka spent the next twelve hours in a cloud of panic and anxiety. Thierry didn't come back until twilight the next day, and when he did, he stank of wine, he had dark circles under his eyes, and he looked so haggard that when he headed directly to his room with barely a greeting, she let him go.

Pacing her room amid a myriad of spiraling thoughts, Yuka did the only thing she could think of: she created a spell.

She went outside before dawn to draw the spell circle around the cabin, then went back in to add the finishing touches. She paused to listen to Thierry's snores from the other side of his bedroom door before going to the bathroom to wash her face and give herself a pep talk in the mirror.

"This is a big risk," she told her reflection. "School rules prohibit doing this. If anyone gets wind of it…if it fails…" Her hands curled on the cold ceramic. "I need to *know*."

She activated the spell.

Power surged through the circle, enveloping the cabin, and then reality gave a sickening *lurch*. Not a single window rattled nor plant stirred, yet she fell to the floor, knees weak.

"That wasn't supposed to happen," she muttered. She opened the curtains to the nearest window and screamed. There was nothing outside. Not a white fog, not a gray storm—just a nauseating *nothingness* that hurt the brain to contemplate.

"What have you done?" Thierry yelled; she turned to see him with his hands on his head, pale-faced and looking sick as he stared out the window.

"I—I don't know. It was supposed to keep us locked inside until we talked," Yuka said, her swollen eyes now heavy with tears.

"Ah. That's on me," said a voice behind them. They turned to find Aashiq smiling nonchalantly, though his shoulders were tense and his eyes kept drifting to the window. "Excellent spell, Mage Yuka. I added some terms and conditions. I didn't think it would do…that."

Yuka closed the curtains in fury. "What *exactly* did you add?" she asked.

"Um. We'll have to tell the truth. And. Have sex. Before we can leave the cabin," Aashiq said, not making eye contact with either of them.

"*What?*" Thierry hissed, taking a step back.

Yuka put her hands on her head and closed her eyes, mentally reviewing her spell. "Oh *no*. We turned it into a curse. It's removed us from the University's bubble. The only way out…"

"...is to fulfill the terms and conditions," Aashiq filled in.

They both turned to Thierry. He jumped like a spotted rabbit and fled to his room, slamming the door in their faces.

Aashiq knocked on the door. "Thierry, wait! Let us explain!"

"You guys do it! You're into each other. I'll, uh..."

"No, we're not—" Yuka hesitated. "*Romantically* into each other," she finished with a wince.

Thierry wasn't listening. "You want *truth*? Did you know the effects of the *Ophrys malefica* don't work on people who aren't attracted to you?"

"But you were affected too, Thierry," Aashiq pointed out.

There was no answer.

Yuka put her back against Thierry's locked door and slipped to the floor. "What have I done?"

Aashiq, with his arms crossed, shrugged. "Your locking spell was too effective."

Yuka looked up, furious. "*My* locking spell? You're the one that's forcing us to *have sex* to *survive*! How could you—!"

Aashiq closed his eyes and dropped the unaffected act. "Fine, I messed up, I *know*! I'm sorry. I did it because I was sure we could get through this. We just needed a little push. And I'm *desperate*! Yesterday at dawn, Thierry finds me at my favorite post-party resting spot, and he kisses me like—like he's *dying* for it, and then he curses and runs away! No explanation, nothing! I looked for him for the whole day, and when I found him, he didn't want to talk. What the *hell*?"

"Thierry kissed you too, huh," said Yuka, understanding dawning on her. Aashiq turned to her with a similar expression: "*Oh*, Thierry..."

They heard a soft *bonk* from the other side of the door, the sound of Thierry knocking his head against the wood. "Sorry," came his soft voice.

"No, *I'm* sorry, Thierry," Yuka said with a sigh. "I wanted us to talk without you running away again."

Thierry banged a fist against the door. "The truth is—I'm in love with you. Both of you. I didn't know it was possible! But...since I ran into Aashiq outside the library that night...you've been in my head all the time. Your poems call this 'love.' And I realized I felt something similar for Yuka. There are differences, but in the end, it feels the same, you know? I want you both in my life. I cherish your presence and your conversation. You inspire me! And I—I want kisses, and poetry, and cuddling on the sofa, and, and *sex*—but…" Thierry's voice choked up.

Pressed against the door, Yuka cradled the wood with one hand. "Thierry…will you let us see you? Can we talk face to face?"

The door opened a crack, and Thierry's red-rimmed eyes peered through. "I tried to decide. I couldn't. I don't want to lose either of you…and then I kissed you." His eyes flashed in Yuka's direction. "And it was amazing, but I felt guilty—was I choosing you over Aashiq? Would I feel different if I kissed Aashiq? So I did that, and it was awesome, but I felt guilty too. So please: don't make me choose. I'd rather you were with each other, as long as we can still be friends."

Yuka turned to Aashiq and found him already looking at her. There was a question in his tilted head and raised eyebrow, an invitation. Horribly, she realized that, despite herself, she trusted Aashiq—with her life and Thierry's.

She nodded resolutely. They turned to Thierry.

"What if you could have us both?" Yuka asked, gently.

"Romantically. Sexually. Platonically. Any way you want," Aashiq promised.

The door opened farther. Thierry faced them, eyes shining with unshed tears, a wildly hopeful expression on his face.

"Come here, you guys," Aashiq said, opening his arms. As the tallest of the three, he easily took Thierry and Yuka in a warm, fierce hug.

"Did you mean that?" Thierry asked in a trembling voice.

"Yes," Aashiq reassured, petting his hair.

"You can have us both," Yuka promised, taking Thierry's hand.

Thierry's fingers tapped hers nervously, and he buried his face in Aashiq's chest before asking, "At the same time?" He peeked at them, red-faced, something burning in his gaze that Yuka had only seen once before, that night under the stars. "We, uh, need to make sure nobody gets left behind."

"We should, shouldn't we?" Aashiq agreed with a quick look to Yuka, who bit her lip and nodded.

Aashiq pecked Thierry's lips, but Thierry caught him and kissed him, hard and passionate. When they separated, Aashiq's cheeks and ears were red, and he kept looking at Thierry like he was a revelation. When Thierry lightly pushed him toward his bedroom, Aashiq walked backward, his awed gaze still on Thierry.

Thierry was shyer when pulling Yuka toward him. They stood, holding hands. Yuka gripped his fingers tightly.

"We'll be okay," she reassured, herself or Thierry, she wasn't sure.

Thierry caressed her fingers. "It's us," he said.

When they kissed, Yuka noticed with a strange thrill that she could taste Aashiq in Thierry's mouth.

Thierry's bedroom had transformed and was now dominated by a king-sized four-poster bed where Aashiq, divested of his boots and thobe, was stretching like a cat, watching as Thierry and Yuka's kisses became more heated. Yuka did something she'd been raring to do for ages, and kissed down Thierry's neck, to nibble and suck a hickey in the soft skin between his neck and shoulder.

Thierry trembled in her arms, tried to lean on the bed, and almost slipped off. Aashiq picked him up by the armpits and pulled him to sit between his splayed legs.

Thierry drew in a sharp breath as Aashiq's strong arms hugged him from behind.

"You like being manhandled? Good to know," Aashiq whispered in his ear.

Yuka got on the bed on her hands and knees, stalking toward them. Thierry turned a heated glance on her and gasped as Aashiq kissed down his neck, licking and sucking the same place Yuka had chosen. She kissed Thierry again. She was becoming addicted to the feeling of Thierry's lips and tongue on hers. His kisses turned sloppy as Aashiq played with his nipples through his night shirt, and Yuka paused to watch Thierry's expression of dumbfounded bliss as Aashiq zeroed in on Thierry's most sensitive, pleasurable spots.

They slipped Thierry's night shirt off, and when he tried to hide his naked chest, Aashiq distracted him by wetting his finger and rubbing his nipple while Yuka swiped a broad line from his shoulder to his belly, following her hands with her tongue, exploring the places Aashiq had discovered. She licked and sucked at the nipple Aashiq wasn't touching, and Thierry made a small whimper that she'd remember forever. Even Aashiq was affected, judging by the way his breathing hitched and he pulled Thierry closer.

Yuka ventured farther down Thierry's chest, sticking her tongue into his belly button—("ah, Yuka, that's weird!")—and kissing a line down his happy trail. Aashiq's hand snuck in under her, teasing the hard line of Thierry's cock and fondling Yuka's breasts.

"Ready to take these off, Thierry?" Aashiq asked, fiddling with the band of Thierry's pajama pants. When Thierry didn't answer, Yuka mouthed Thierry's cock through the fabric, making him shudder.

"Do it," Thierry gasped.

Aashiq and Yuka slid the pants off Thierry.

"You sleep without underwear?" Yuka asked, soaking in her first glimpse of Thierry's hard cock.

"Who doesn't?" Aashiq shrugged, while Thierry nodded.

Aashiq squeezed Thierry's cock and balls, and Thierry jumped in his arms. Yuka let him settle before she caressed Thierry's thighs, kissing and sucking on the inside like she'd done to his neck.

"She's going to leave you all marked up, you'll look so good," Aashiq muttered as he watched Yuka lovingly leave a trail of hickeys up his pale thighs.

"Yuka, you're—" Thierry gasped. Aashiq was slowly pumping his cock, more teasing than serious. As Yuka got closer, Aashiq offered it to her, and she closed her mouth over the tip and sucked. Thierry held fast to Aashiq.

"One day I'll enter you while she does this," Aashiq said, pressing his hard cock against Thierry, and Thierry *moaned*—loud, filthy, without reservations. Yuka moaned, too, and sucked harder, and Thierry's breath became agitated.

Aashiq tapped her on the shoulder: "That looks so good; can I have a go?"

Yuka let Thierry's cock slide out of her mouth with a wet slurp and took a trembling Thierry in her arms as Aashiq repositioned them.

"You take this side, I'll take the other," Aashiq said, and together they licked and sucked Thierry's cock as he watched, frozen. Yuka closed her eyes as she felt the sharp taste of Thierry on her tongue, Aashiq's hot breath mingling with hers, their tongues brushing occasionally.

Aashiq was a *master.* He seemed to know instinctively what would work best, and he exploited those points ruthlessly. Yuka leaned back so she could watch Aashiq bring Thierry to the brink, rubbing her thighs together at the sight of their pleasure.

When Thierry came, he was gripping the sheets with his eyes closed, a line of drool running down the corner of his mouth.

Yuka clapped as Thierry caught his breath, half passed out on the bed.

Aashiq licked his lips, swallowed, and bowed.

"What was that with your tongue?" Yuka asked.

Aashiq took her fingers in his mouth and demonstrated. The sucking, swirling movement brought back hazy memories of her pollen-fueled kisses with Aashiq, sparking both embarrassment and arousal.

"I think I got it," Yuka said, squinting as she did when she was learning a new incantation.

Aashiq offered his own fingers for her to practice on.

Thierry turned to watch them better.

"Want to try the real thing?" Aashiq asked, teasing them with the sight of his hard, dripping cock.

"I, um." Yuka hesitated, glancing at Thierry. He nodded, eyes fixed on Aashiq's cock.

With his blessing, Yuka leaned down to practice Aashiq's technique on the man himself, receiving muttered praises and occasional tips. Aashiq was bigger than Thierry, and soon her jaw was aching. Slick pooled in her panties. *How is he still so unaffected?* she wondered, a bit annoyed, and doubled down on moving her tongue around Aashiq's cock, until he was panting and hard as a rock.

"Wait, ah, you're a fast learner." He stopped her, then sized her up. He turned to Thierry: "There's a variation of that tongue twist that works *wonderfully* with the ladies. Would you like a demonstration?" He directed the question to them both.

Thierry sat up.

"Show us those wet panties," Aashiq said, moving her so they were in Thierry's line of sight. It felt good to slowly remove her pants and panties, teasing Thierry and Aashiq with the sight of what lay beneath them. Thierry's mouth was open, and Aashiq licked his lips.

Once the panties were off, Aashiq gripped Yuka's thighs, pushed them wider apart, and got right down to business. She gasped in shock and pleasure as Aashiq's tongue lightly sucked and rubbed her hardened clit and swirled around, teasing, to come back in a steady, relentless rhythm. Yuka shook and panted helplessly, undone in a few strokes. A part of her vaguely wondered how she'd gone from wanting Aashiq out of her and Thierry's lives to bucking into his mouth in desperation, but then Aashiq began fingering her, pressing rhythmically against her sensitive places, and she stopped caring. She felt a gentle hand caressing hers and opened her eyes to Thierry's wide-eyed gaze. She gripped Thierry's hand in hers in a crushing grip as her orgasm crested and fell.

"I want to learn that too," Thierry said, approaching on all fours. Aashiq slid away, letting Thierry occupy the space over Yuka.

"I, uh. I have no idea what to do. I've fantasized about this so many times, but now…"

"You could take off her shirt," Aashiq recommended. Moving aside to give Thierry space, he stretched out beside Yuka.

Thierry's fingers trembled as he unbuttoned Yuka's shirt. Yuka raised her hands to help, but her fingers were also trembling, from her previous orgasm or nerves, she couldn't tell. They paused, giggling, then Thierry pulled the shirt over her head.

Yuka enjoyed Thierry's wide-eyed, practically drooling admiration of her breasts. "You can touch them," she said. She unclasped her bra as Thierry groped her, fumbling like a schoolboy.

"Softly, you're not kneading dough," Aashiq chided when Yuka winced.

Ever the fast learner, Thierry adjusted his touch as he sucked hickeys down her neck and licked her nipples, rolling them between his fingers like Aashiq had done for him. Yuka gasped, pleasure sparking down to her toes.

Then, Thierry started touching Yuka like he was trying to *devour* her. He slid his hands up and down her body, grabbing her hips, pinching her buttocks, leaving small bites on her shoulders, belly, and thighs. He only paused in front of her wet, messy pussy.

"What was that tongue thing again?" Thierry asked, frowning.

Impatient, Yuka grabbed his hand and guided it to her pussy, allowing Thierry to explore, caress her folds, and stick the tip of a finger inside her to collect her slick. She spread his index and middle finger to bracket her clit and move up and down around it. Thierry imitated the movement, down to the correct pressure and rhythm.

"Ah, like that," she gasped.

"You have such nimble fingers, look how quickly she's coming apart," Aashiq said, alternating between caressing Thierry's back and Yuka's arm.

"Please…" Yuka gasped out, parting her legs.

Thierry stopped, confused, looking to her and to Aashiq for guidance.

"Say it," Aashiq told Yuka.

Yuka groaned and said, "Put it in me, Thierry."

"What do I—? Oh—really? You won't—" Thierry asked, nervous again.

Yuka drew a couple of sigils on her belly, the spell lighting up with the strokes of her fingers. "Yeah, I'm good, please—"

"Hmm…I want in on this," Aashiq said. He patted Yuka's thigh and muttered, "May I have some of your—?" She opened her legs so Aashiq could rub his fingers and palm against her, coating himself in her slick. His hand was hotter than Thierry's, his touch harder. Yuka moaned and watched as Aashiq slicked up Thierry's cock and the inside of his thighs.

"What are you planning to do?" Thierry asked, a hint of panic in his voice.

Yuka sympathized with his concern but couldn't help feeling disappointed when Aashiq said, "Relax. I'm going to use your thighs. You do your work and don't worry about me, I'm good." Aashiq positioned himself behind Thierry and petted his back and shoulder encouragingly.

Thierry went back to Yuka, crawling between her spread legs. Yuka pulled him to her, letting him lay over her, and helped him line up with her entrance.

For a moment, they looked into each other's eyes. This was it: she was having sex with her best friend, and she felt no hesitation. She wanted Thierry inside her—she wanted to swallow him whole.

As one, they breathed in, and out, and with a swift movement, Thierry entered her.

They both gasped, Yuka feeling the intrusion, the stretch and fullness she had been craving for minutes, for hours, for *months*. Her aching desire was fulfilled, and she looked at Thierry, who had his eyes closed and mouth open in ecstasy. His hips moved forward by instinct, and Yuka rolled back to meet him, and they were fucking, slowly, savoring each push and pull.

"Fuck, you guys are sweet together," Aashiq breathed. He pressed behind Thierry, relying mostly on the strength of his arms, and pressed his cock between Thierry's quivering thighs.

They moved in tandem, all three of them, slowly, so as not to lose their rhythm. Yuka, already sensitive from Aashiq and Thierry's attentions, got closer and closer, and she couldn't help snaking a hand between her body and Thierry's to rub at her clit. Thierry opened his eyes to watch as she shivered and panted, tightening around his cock.

"What is—? Are you—?" He gasped and bucked harder against her. Aashiq had to hold on to keep up with Thierry's frenetic thrusts, and for a long moment, they were all a panting, sweaty, writhing mess, moving in sharp, desperate tandem, until Thierry heaved and trembled, spilling inside Yuka. Yuka felt the hot come spreading inside her and went over the edge, holding on to Thierry for dear life.

"Like that," Aashiq moaned, and pressed Thierry's thighs harder, chasing his own pleasure for one, two, three thrusts before spilling over Thierry and Yuka.

They slowly separated, falling heavily into the bed, Thierry still in the middle.

"That was delicious. I'm looking forward to doing so many things with you two," Aashiq said, stretching like the cat that got the cream—and the canary.

"I'm looking forward to you two *not* doing crazy things around me anymore," Thierry said.

Both Yuka and Aashiq looked away guiltily.

Yuka giggled, a strange, nervous kind of mirth.

Thierry and Aashiq chuckled, then laughed.

"Sorry," Aashiq said, not sounding particularly repentant.

Yuka covered her face with her hands, embarrassed by her own actions. "I can't believe I almost destroyed my own wardrobe. And spent half my savings on that *stupid* orchid. And turned the cabin into a freezer."

"Well, some of those things were bound to happen, with the way you're always experimenting with new spells," Thierry said, not sounding as annoyed as he should rightfully be.

"You knew about the bet?" Aashiq asked him.

"I knew *something* was up. Yuka's experiments were weirder than usual. And there's no way an ifrit would get his head stuck in a rabbit hole," Thierry answered.

Aashiq laughed. "One never knows, with ifrit magic."

"I'm sorry, Thierry. I had to know if you liked me back. I've been crushing on you since the day we met, and I…" Yuka said, pressing her head against Thierry's shoulder.

"It's good. In the end, I'm glad it all came out in the open," Thierry said, and kissed the top of her head.

"I *knew* we would get here," Aashiq said, getting up and stretching. Casually, he went to the window and peeked through the curtains. "We're back, by the way."

The sun was shining outside, birds chirping. Yuka relaxed on the bed, content to listen as Thierry and Aashiq made plans to go swimming in the lake.

please, may i have s'more?

Cedar D. McCafferty-Svec

bipoc, bisexual, clitoral fingering, dom/sub (subtext), established relationship, f/f/m/nb, friends to lovers, frottage, modern, non-binary, omg they were roommates, past tense, penis in vagina sex, pining (mutual), romantic getaway, sex pollen, third person limited point of view, twosome + twosome = foursome, vaginal fingering

Bailey took a deep breath of fresh forest air and promptly sneezed. She still couldn't believe they were tent camping instead of renting a cabin, but Tabitha had won the game of rock-paper-scissors. At least they had air mattresses and real bathrooms in the campground.

"Do we want to go on a hike when we're done setting up?" Bailey asked. She straightened up and stepped on the tent stake, pushing it into the soft dirt. Nice. No rocks. "I saw a few trails on our way in."

"Oh, *hell* yeah," Duke chirped. "You think the cooler will be good if we leave it in the car? The ice should hold, right?"

Mattie leaned across the top of the tent xe and Bailey were putting up, tying the tent poles in the center. "No, because the car gets warmer than the outside," xe said. Xe held out one side of the tent fly, and Bailey took it. Together, they draped it over the top of the tent, tying it down to keep any inclement weather out. "If you're worried about animals getting into it, put it in your tent. Otherwise, it'll be fine under the table."

Duke hummed. A moment later, there was a grunt and the scraping of hard plastic on wood as he, presumably, shoved it under the table.

Tabitha bounced out of the other tent, slipped her flip-flops back on, and brandished the electric air pump like a prized trophy. "Did those trails you saw look flip-flop friendly, 'cause I definitely didn't bring any tennies."

Bailey grabbed the air pump as she sighed. "Yes, they did. Also, I grabbed your tennies from the shoe rack on our way out this morning."

"Aw, you love me," Tabitha crooned. She draped her arm over Bailey's shoulder, squeezing her, and Bailey rolled her eyes fondly.

Mattie's eyes crinkled at the corners as xe took the air pump and the rolled-up air mattress. "We all know you're the one who got away from Bays, Tabi," xe joked.

Tabitha put her other hand on her chest, gasping. "As if. *Bays* is the one who got away from *me*."

Bailey playfully snapped at Tabitha's fingers when Tabitha gestured to boop her on the nose, then stepped out of Tabitha's side hug. "Go help your man with the firewood." She waved Tabitha off to the sound of laughter and turned to the task of pulling her and Mattie's belongings into their tent.

Mattie ducked in behind her, leaving xer sandals by the door. Xe shook out the air mattress and set up the air pump while Bailey put their bags in the corner opposite of the mattress. The blankets and pillows got dumped on top of the bags until the mattress was done inflating. Together, they got the bed made for that evening.

"Hey! You two lovebirds ready for that hike?" Duke called from outside the tent. A moment later, the tent shuddered and jolted, and Duke cursed, his shadow bouncing across the tent walls.

Mattie snorted and grabbed a scrunchy, quickly pulling xer curls into a loose bun. "We will be if you don't bring the tent down on us," xe said. Xe glanced back at Bailey with a smile and a tilt of xer head, as if to ask *you good?*

Bailey nodded and padded to the door of the tent, stepping back into her sneakers. She wasn't too surprised to see Duke on the ground when she unzipped the door. He was face down in the dirt as if he'd simply given up after tripping. She sighed and stepped over him. "C'mon, drama king—on your feet before your crown gets dirty."

"I like being on the ground," he responded into the dirt.

"I am *so* ready to go." Tabitha popped up behind Duke's shoulder as he stood with Bailey's help, throwing herself at his back. He didn't even flinch as he caught her thighs around his waist and held her steady. "Onwards, steed! To the trail!"

"Do you really expect me to carry you the entire way there?" Duke asked. Still, he settled her more firmly around his waist and started toward the front of the campground, where the trailheads were.

As much as Bailey hated to admit it, Tabitha had been right. Getting out of the city and returning to nature was a *good* idea. She already felt more relaxed. Mattie's arm around her waist as they walked behind Duke and Tabitha certainly didn't hurt that vibe, either.

"Oh!" Tabitha ran ahead of them suddenly, stumbling only briefly as her flip-flops caught on a dip in the trail. "Bays! Come look at these flowers!" she called over her shoulder.

Bailey laughed and caught Mattie's hand as xe drew away from her. She squeezed xer hand quickly before she jogged up the pathway. The small incline hid the flowers Tabitha was speaking about until she was at the top. Bailey sucked in a deep breath.

It was a small meadow with the trail cutting straight through it, curving out at the very end, where there was a bench. The flowers resembled larger, more vibrant buttercups. They glowed in the light of the sun; bright yellows and oranges swayed in the light breeze.

"They're beautiful," Bailey breathed.

Tabitha was practically vibrating next to her. "Bailey. *Bays*. You know what we have to do, right?"

Bailey glanced at her from the corners of her eyes, then looked back at the flowers. They were bigger than daisies but… "Are you sure they can be made into a flower crown?"

"Anything can be made into a flower crown if you aren't a coward," Tabitha quipped. She grabbed Bailey's hand and yanked her off the path, pushing into the flowers and tall meadow grass. Within moments, Bailey's arms were filled with long grass and flower stems, the flowers brushing against her chin and nose.

Bailey's nose wrinkled and she tucked her head back, her eyes watering as she held back the urge to sneeze again.

Tabitha set Mattie and Duke to the task of collecting flowers, and she gathered the other necessary supplies. As soon as they were done, she ushered them to the bench at the end of the trail.

"Mattie, you know how to braid flower crowns, right?" Tabitha asked. She folded her legs under her, sitting at the foot of the bench as Duke and Bailey sat on the bench itself.

Xe hummed with a small twist to xer expression. "I haven't done it since I was little? I only ever made daisy chains. Flower crowns were a bit beyond me when I was six, y'know."

Tabitha waved a hand. "It's easy. I'll show you. Bays, you make one for Duke, okay?"

"You sure *you* don't want to make Duke's?" Bailey asked.

"*I'm* making yours. Duke is making Mattie's, Mattie is making mine, and you're making Duke's." Tabitha grabbed a portion of the grass and started to twist them into shape in slow, even motions so that Mattie could follow what she was doing.

Duke laughed and nudged Bailey with his elbow gently. "May as well give in, Bays; you know how she gets."

In return, Bailey grabbed one of the flowers and shoved it against Duke's nose. He squawked, going cross-eyed to look at the smear of pollen left on the tip of his nose, then he sneezed loud enough that a bird startled somewhere behind them.

"Oh, it's *on*!"

"Duke, if you move, I will bite your knees," Tabitha singsonged from beside his feet.

Duke grumbled and settled back on the bench. "I'll get you later, Bays."

Bailey grinned and hooked a foot under Mattie's thigh, delighting in the pressure of it as she bent her head over the braid of grass and flowers she'd started. "You'll have to catch me first, Duke."

"I know where you sleep."

"You sleep before me, Mr. I-Pass-Out-On-The-Couch."

"Mattie will help me."

"Bold claim. Mattie knows better than to conspire against me if xe wants to sleep in my bed."

"Bailey's right, Duke. You're my best friend, but I quite enjoy cuddling my girlfriend," Mattie said. "If you want to get at her, you're gonna have to try harder." Xe fiddled with a piece of grass, furrowing xer brow in concentration before xe sighed and turned to Tabitha. "Tabi, is it *supposed* to twist like this?"

Tabitha leaned over to look, and Bailey took the chance to wink and stick her tongue out at Duke. Duke retaliated by shoving a handful of grass and petals in her face, leading to Bailey reeling sideways and spitting out a piece of grass with a groan.

"Aw, *gross*."

"That's what you *get*," Duke crowed.

"Children," Tabitha said flatly. She'd rolled her eyes hard enough to move her whole head. "Do we need to find the get-along shirt?" She turned only enough to look at them over her shoulder.

Bailey flushed. Tabitha had tucked a flower behind her ear, and the delicate petals framed the edges of her eye in just the right way to make Bailey hyperaware of how very blue they were. Was the sun getting hotter? It was really warm. She cleared her throat and shook her head, bending back over the flower crown. "Nope," she croaked, "all good. We'll behave."

"Good." Tabitha returned to helping Mattie, her voice a murmur in the background noise of the meadow. It bled into the swish of the grass and the twitter of birds around them. As long as Bailey didn't pay too much attention to the cadence of Tabitha's voice or to the low rumble of Mattie's answering laugh or to how Duke's bare arm brushed against hers, she could focus on the flower crown.

Duke's arm brushed against hers again, trailing electricity in its wake, and Bailey shivered. Heat sparked across her skin and coiled low in her belly, toes curling inside her shoes. Bailey lifted her eyes. Duke was putting his finished flower crown on Mattie's head, gently plucking pieces of xer curls out of xer bun to frame the crown and xer face.

Mattie had xer head turned toward him, xer smile soft and xer expression openly adoring.

Bailey slid a glance at Duke. He looked *just* as smitten. She blinked slowly, feeling like she was on the *brink* of figuring something out. Tabitha stretched up to kiss the bottom of Duke's jaw, her back arching, and Bailey's train of thought fled.

"Good job, baby," Tabitha said. "It looks really good!"

Duke flushed and ducked his head, laying a loud smooch on Tabitha's forehead. "Thanks, Tabi."

Bailey dropped her flower crown on top of Duke's head. More pollen shook free of the flowers, dusting his hair and glittering in the sunlight. He looked as flushed as Bailey felt.

"Bays!" Tabitha waved a hand at her, smiling brightly. "Come sit in my lap so I can put this on you." She brandished the flower crown like it was a weapon, her eyes sparkling.

With no hesitation, Bailey shifted to sit in Tabitha's lap, stretching her legs out in front of her and leaning back. For all of Tabitha's sharp angles, she made a great backrest.

Tabitha's hands were gentle in her hair, pulling it out of the ponytail and carding through her thick, pin-straight locks until she was satisfied. Bailey couldn't remember a time she'd felt this relaxed.

"Gonna fall asleep on me, Bays?" Tabitha asked in a lilting tease.

Bailey hummed and opened her eyes, unsure of when exactly she'd closed them. "I just might," she answered, "and not one of you here could blame me." She smiled, and it softened as Mattie reached over to lace their fingers together. The weight of Mattie's hand in hers, the warmth of Tabitha at her back, and the rumble of Duke's quiet laughter twisted together inside of her in a jumbled-up mess of longing. Her skin felt warm and clammy, sharp pinpricks pressing against her wherever she was touching the others.

Tabitha laughed, and it ghosted hot air across the back of her neck. Bailey shivered. "I know; I have magic fingers," Tabitha whispered.

Bailey had to take a deep breath to hide the way her entire body clenched at that.

A flower crown was placed on her head and woven into her hair. She had no idea what it looked like, but she trusted Tabitha to make it look nice. Tabitha's nails scraped over her scalp again in sweet, delicious pressure, and Bailey moaned, letting her head drop back into Tabitha's hands. The tension melted out of her shoulders, and she sagged, boneless, against her best friend. "Fuck, Tabi…"

Tabitha's fingers quivered, the motion barely noticeable, and her laugh sounded tight. "That good, huh, Bays?"

"Magic fingers—you said it yourself." She closed her eyes again with a long, satisfied sigh and melted.

Duke cleared his throat quietly behind them. "It's uh…kind of hot. Anyone else really hot?"

"A bit, yeah," Mattie said. Xe squeezed Bailey's hand and let go, but remained close enough that Bailey could feel xer warmth. "That spot with the waterfall we saw a ways back had no signs warning against swimming there. Could be worth checking out?"

"Is swimming in a strange waterfall really a good idea?" Bailey asked, cracking open one eye.

"Most ponds are safe to swim in, and that spot had a current running through it, so it's not like we're swimming in mosquito water," xe said.

"We don't have our swimsuits on us, though," Duke pointed out. He leaned forward, casting a shadow over Bailey's head.

"And?" Mattie asked. "I've seen you naked in the locker room more times than I can count, Bays and Tabi grew up together, and I *know* Bays has walked in on you changing at least three times. We can skinny dip. None of us have anything the others haven't seen already."

Bailey flushed and sucked down a breath so quickly she choked on it, sputtering and coughing. She smacked a hand against her chest and waved a hand at the concerned "Are you okay?"s that came from the others. "I'm fine," she rasped. "Just breathed wrong." She swallowed fast and hard, blinking tears from her eyes, and smiled at Mattie's concerned pout. "I mean it: I'm good. Choked on my own spit—you know how it is."

The twist of Mattie's mouth said xe didn't believe her, but at least xe let it go.

Tabitha's hands fell from Bailey's shoulders with one final squeeze. "Anyway, going for a dip sounds like a *great* idea. We aren't gonna get flagged for public indecency, are we?"

Mattie shrugged. "Don't get caught?" Xe grinned and stood in one smooth motion, reaching down to help Bailey to her feet. "Far as I know, not a lot of people actually walk the trails, and the public swimming hole is on the other side of the camp. We should be okay."

Bailey swayed into Mattie's space, heavy and warm, her thoughts more than a little muddied. She made a grabby hand at Tabitha and Duke. "C'mon, if Mattie says we'll be fine, then we'll be fine."

"Says the one who just choked at the thought," Duke quipped. Still, he nudged Tabitha forward and stood as well, stretching his arms over his head. It made his shirt ride up, showing a sliver of his stomach. Bailey couldn't stop herself from looking.

There was a joke to be made there, something about forbidden fruit being the most tempting. She leaned into Mattie and tipped her head up to steal a quick kiss.

Or it was meant to be a quick kiss anyway. Instead, Mattie's hand slid into her hair at the base of her neck, and xe pulled her in even closer. Their mouths fit together smoothly, practice and knowledge guiding their lips until Bailey's knees were shaking.

She made a small sound and grabbed at Mattie's shirt, bunching the fabric in her hand like it was a lifeline. Mattie only leaned into her more, dipping her backward, sliding xer tongue along hers and into her mouth in a slick stroke that made Bailey briefly contemplate believing in a religion. Mattie pulled away, and Bailey chased xem, her eyes fluttering. The scent of the flowers was thick and cloying.

A cough to their side made Bailey freeze. She opened her eyes completely and looked over without turning her head. Duke was flushed, his hand tight on Tabitha's waist. Tabitha was outright staring, her mouth slightly parted as she shifted her weight from side to side.

"Holy shit," she breathed.

Mattie pressed a smile against the curve of Bailey's cheek. "Told you she was looking at you, Bays," xe rumbled.

It took Bailey a moment to remember how to breathe. She swallowed hard and took a half step out of Mattie's embrace. "A-ah. Right. We, um…swimming?"

"Uh-huh. Swimming. Skinny dipping," Tabitha parroted. She gave Bailey a *very* obvious once-over, one that made Bailey squirm with a hot flush of arousal, and then grinned when she met Bailey's eyes. "Race you there?"

Bailey blinked as she switched tracks. *Less horny brain—more active brain.* Not that being horny wasn't an activity, but it certainly wasn't the one she needed to focus on. "You're wearing *flip-flops*," she protested, but only barely got the words out before Tabitha was bounding through the grass and over the gravel path.

"Tabi!" Bailey yelled after her.

"Last one there has to carry all the laundry to camp!" Tabitha cried over her shoulder.

"Oh, *hell* no," Duke responded. He took off after Tabitha, drawing a delighted shriek from her, and Bailey scrambled to follow with a laugh of her own.

Mattie outpaced every one of them, stopping on the mossy shore of the swimming hole. Xe turned with xer hands on xer hips, grinning widely as everyone trailed in behind xem. Last to arrive, Bailey wheezed, one hand on her side, and let herself bend over her knees.

"God, I am *not* a runner," she panted. "I wasn't built for this life. Duke...Duke, you can have my mug collection. Tabitha, burn my laptop. Mattie, I love you." Bailey put her other hand on the ground and lay down, groaning. Her lungs were on fire, and she hadn't even run that fast nor far.

Maybe she *was* having an allergic reaction to the flowers.

Her friends were laughing at her, but that was fine. She was good on the ground. The moss was cool to touch, and the ground wouldn't betray her.

"Now who's the drama queen?" Tabitha quipped. She stood over Bailey, blocking the sun, and Bailey squinted up at her.

"Still you," Bailey answered.

Tabitha huffed a laugh and shrugged before leaning down and grabbing Bailey's hands. "Come on, then, drama *princess*; let's get in the water, yeah? If you're gonna die, you may as well die comfortably cool and wet instead of hot and bothered."

Mattie and Duke both broke into laughter as Bailey pulled her hands free from Tabitha's hold, smacking at Tabitha's hands clumsily and ineffectually. "You!" She also laughed and batted at Tabitha again as she rolled up to her knees. "Incorrigible!"

Tabitha wiggled both brows with a broad grin. "I'm not *wrong*."

Bailey got back to her feet and, in a fit of daring, pulled her shirt off in a smooth motion. "If I have to carry all of this back to camp, then you better put everything in a neat pile. I might forget to bring something back otherwise. You know—on purpose." She folded her shirt in half and draped it over a nearby fallen tree trunk. It was as mossy as the rocks underfoot but safely away from the spray of the waterfall.

She kept her back to her friends as she stripped off her shorts and underwear in one smooth motion. It was best to keep her underwear tucked out of sight because she'd certainly made a mess out of them. She put them under her shirt and topped the whole pile with her bra.

A splash behind her was her first clue that someone was in the water, and the husky yelp of "Fuck, that's cold!" told her it was Duke.

"Of course it's cold; we're in snow run-off territory, dumbass," Mattie said, trying to hold in a laugh. Xe had a pinched quality to xer voice. "But I bet it feels *fantastic* because of how hot out it is. What temperature is it, anyway?"

"No clue," Bailey said. "I left my phone at camp. I think the high today was only supposed to be mid-seventies, though."

"The weatherman lied." Tabitha dropped her pile of clothing off next to Bailey's, and her hand fluttered across Bailey's side as she moved toward the water.

Bailey had to take a moment to remember how to breathe. She followed after Tabitha's touch, her stomach clenching, and paused at the sight of her three best friends heading into the water. She *had* seen them naked before, but the sight took her breath away. Mattie's dark skin contrasted against Duke's surfer tan, Tabitha's freckles on full display…

Bailey swallowed hard and kicked off her shoes, picking her way over the shoreline until she waded in up to her hips. Duke was right. It was *fucking cold*. Goosebumps raced up her spine and over her shoulders. She crossed her arms over her chest and hissed. "*God*. Are we sure Duke still has balls?"

"I mean, you can check for yourself," Duke said. He turned in the water to face her, grinning. His flower crown sat askew on his head, but it lent him some boyish charm. "Or Tabi can." He waggled his brows at Tabitha salaciously, and Tabitha splashed him.

"Trust me, Bays, it takes more than a little cold water to make those disappear," she said.

"Get him in a locker room full of naked men and the threat of cold showers if he's not fast enough to get out of his uniform, though, and they'll disappear." Mattie waded up to Bailey and wrapped xer arms around her, lifting her effortlessly—despite Bailey's squeak of protest—and wading farther into the water. "Never seen Duke move so fast."

"A cold shower is *very* different from wading in a cold pond," Duke pouted. He sank into the water until it covered him to the base of his neck. "I can adjust to this. Cold showers are like…tiny hailstorms, and they hurt."

Bailey looped an arm over Mattie's shoulders, using the other to idly splash water up Tabitha's back. She didn't get to see Tabitha's reaction, though, as Mattie turned and dunked her into the deeper water. Bailey came up sputtering, her bangs limp and plastered over her eyes and forehead. Somehow the flower crown hadn't come out, but it did sit awkwardly enough that she could feel it pulling on her scalp.

Mattie howled in laughter, xer voice catching breathlessly. Bailey managed to get her hair out of her eyes in time to see Duke lift Mattie like xe weighed nothing and throw xem a few feet into the water.

A moment later, Duke yelped before going under as Mattie presumably yanked him down.

Bailey laughed and reached up to fix her flower crown, only to jump when warm hands slid over her stomach. A line of heat pressed up against her back, broken only by the drastic chill of what could only be nipples. Tabitha's chin rested on her shoulder, and Tabitha hummed low in her throat.

"They're cute together, aren't they?" Tabitha asked. Her voice was no louder than a whisper; her breath was as soft as butterfly kisses over Bailey's skin. "Sometimes I forget how much history they have together." She shifted, and her nose trailed up Bailey's neck, nudging under the cut of her jaw and pressing into the soft dip. "Tell me, Bays—have you ever thought about Mattie and *Duke*?"

Bailey dropped a hand to cover Tabitha's on her stomach, her breath stuttering out of her in a nervous laugh. "I—"

"I have," Tabitha murmured. "When I'm sitting around, letting my mind wander, I think about watching them touch each other, love each other. I think about them just as much as I think about you."

Bailey froze. Alarm bells clamored in her head only to be silenced by that single admission spiraling around and around. Tabitha thought about her. Tabitha thought about her *intimately*. "Tabi…"

"You know, I think the four of us could be something *beautiful*," Tabitha continued. She slowly moved her hand, bringing Bailey's with her, to caress over the dip between her rib cage below her sternum. "God, Bays, you have no idea how much we want you—"

Bailey turned sharply, putting a hand over Tabitha's mouth. Her lower lip quivered as she drew in ragged breaths, desperate to steady herself amidst the muddle of her thoughts and the flood of emotions she couldn't parse. " 'We'?"

Tabitha smiled, her cheeks pulling up under Bailey's hand. Bailey wanted desperately to kiss the mole beside her chin. "Duke and I," she clarified. "We've talked about it, talked about you, about Mattie, about the bigger 'us.' " Her smile became all the brighter when Bailey's hand slipped off of her face, landing instead on Tabitha's chest.

Bailey could feel how fast her heart was racing.

Tabitha's palms were *warm* as they landed on Bailey's waist. Her fingers dug into Bailey's sides, and Bailey shivered. Warmth pooled in her stomach, her fingertips tingled, and her toes curled into the silt of the pond bed. "What do you say, Bays? Want a little test run?" Tabitha asked. She licked her lip. Bailey traced the motion with her eyes, her fingers curling against Tabitha's chest.

"Wait! Shit! *Tabi*, you didn't ask her without me, did you?"

Duke's voice was enough to break the spell Tabitha's mouth had placed on her, and Bailey jerked, making a quiet sound. She was warm and flushed, and *God*, she wanted someone—anyone—to touch her. It felt like peak puberty, when her hormones had been at their worst and she hadn't been able to get enough of her hand or the edge of her bed. How many times had she finished with Tabitha's name clenched behind her teeth?

"Tabi's finally making a move?" Mattie said, voice close. Xe pressed a hand into the small of Bailey's back. "Took her long enough."

Duke drew up close, one hand settling on Tabitha's waist and the other resting on Bailey's upper back. "We were *going* to talk to you *both* about it this evening while we had s'mores. We had a plan." He pouted and leaned in, nuzzling at Tabitha's cheek almost petulantly. "Tabi, we had a *plan*."

"Yep." Tabitha popped the "P," and her hand trailed sideways. Her fingertips pushed through the neatly trimmed hair between Bailey's legs—Bailey had to grab onto her with both hands to stop her legs from buckling—as she leaned in and smiled. "Had it all worked out. Big seduction plan. Was gonna pour my heart out to you. And then your date-mate said 'Let's go skinny dipping' after we got covered in this pollen and *God*. Bailey. *Bays*."

Her fingers quirked through Bailey's curls, tugging gently, and she *whimpered.*

"You're so *fucking* hot and so naked, and I don't want to wait till this evening." Tabitha ducked her head just enough to brush her nose against Bailey's. Her eyes crinkled at the corners as she smiled. Bailey crossed her eyes to try to keep her in focus. "Duke and I may *also* have picked this particular campsite because of these flowers. A lot easier to spill your guts when you're horny out of your mind."

Bailey blinked slowly, her mouth parting slightly. "I thought I was having an allergic reaction," she admitted.

Duke snorted and dropped a kiss to the top of her head. "Nope. Or, well, yes? There's some science behind it; Tabi knows it better than I do. Don't worry; it wears off, but boy, it sure does boost the sex drive while you're affected."

"And when did *you two* find time to come out here and research that?" Mattie asked. Xe slid xer hand down, petting over the swell of Bailey's ass slowly. Bailey didn't hear the answer because Tabitha chose that moment to slide her hand between Bailey's legs, and all of Bailey's attention narrowed in on that heated touch.

"Oh *fuck*," Bailey gasped. "Yes, yes, yes. Just—fuck." She rolled her hips between Mattie and Tabitha, closing her eyes as she gave in to the inferno rolling inside of her. "We—God—we're going to have a fucking talk later, but right now if you don't *touch* me, I'm—"

Tabitha laughed and curled her fingers, dragging her nails over Bailey's lips. "What's to talk about, Bays?" Tabitha asked. Her voice dropped to a growl as she leaned in. Her breasts slid over Bailey's skin, and Mattie caught Bailey's weight when Bailey's knees went weak. "You want me, and I want you—*we* want you. We're all consenting adults. The flower doesn't compel you to do anything, just makes you more open to things you already *want* to do. It just…lowers your inhibitions a bit."

"You're—" Bailey hissed and twitched her hips as Tabitha pressed a finger slowly between her lips—"you're treading a *real* fine line, Ta—ah—Tabi."

"Yeah, but you like a bad girl." Tabitha laughed and curled her finger again, running the pad over the bud of Bailey's clit. "Mattie, you should kiss her again."

"Mm, best idea you've had all weekend, Tabi," Mattie murmured. Xe kept one hand on Bailey's ass and used the other to turn Bailey's head and fit their mouths together. Like in the clearing, the kiss was all-consuming. It blew the thoughts right out of Bailey's head, and she went boneless, moaning helplessly into Mattie's mouth as xe pressed xer tongue past her lips. Xer tongue slid over her teeth, flicking along the top of her mouth, and Bailey's thighs quaked.

Tabitha's mouth found Bailey's neck. She scraped her teeth over the sensitive hollow between her shoulder and her neck, then latched on and sucked.

Bailey tangled a hand in Tabitha's hair to hold her there, breaking the kiss with Mattie momentarily as she moaned and gasped for air. Now she was *really* burning up. Mattie caught her mouth again, dominating her, and between xer and Tabitha's finger working a small circle against the tip of her clit, Bailey was losing it.

"Let me lighten the load for you, Mattie," Duke said behind her. His voice had dropped, rough and growly with arousal. "Bays, I'm gonna pick you up." He put his hands on her thighs, and Bailey bounced on her toes to help as he lifted.

She ended up with her back pressed up against his chest, the head of his quickly growing cock pressing against her inner thigh as he spread her legs with his hands. It gave Tabitha and Mattie all the more room to work. Bailey could scarcely get a breath in before Mattie's mouth descended on her breast, latching onto a nipple and sucking.

Tabitha renewed her effort to mark up the side of her neck and pressed two fingers against Bailey's clit. She spread her fingers, pushing the folds aside so that the rock of Bailey's hips made the water rush over her exposed core, and Bailey threw her head back with an overwhelmed moan. The flower crown dug into her, the flowers crushed between her head and Duke's jaw. Bailey tossed her arms up and behind her, looping around Duke's neck, and writhed.

"*Fuck*, that's hot," Duke gasped. He tightened his hold on her thighs, his fingers digging in, and Bailey squirmed and gasped. He adjusted slightly and pulled her legs even farther apart. She hissed, her thighs tensing. He murmured an apology and loosened his hold, letting her fall back into a natural position.

Her reprieve didn't last long, though, because Tabitha's fingers slid down, gliding over Bailey's slick heat, and sunk one finger inside her. It was no more than a brief dip to test the waters—Bailey laughed breathlessly at the thought—but it was more than enough to make Bailey roll her entire body to chase the sensation.

Mattie let go of her nipple with a soft *pop* and dug xer fingers into Bailey's side. Xe dragged xer nails over her stomach, and Bailey arched into it with a long, drawn-out groan. "You can be rough with her," Mattie said. "She likes it. Mark her up; use your nails."

Bailey whimpered again as Mattie did exactly that, circling her other breast with xer nails just hard enough to leave red trails. Bailey didn't need to see them to know—she always marked up easily.

"She likes to be fucked hard and fast." Mattie's hair tickled Bailey's nose as xe leaned up past her. Duke made a quiet sound, nearly a moan, and Bailey opened her eyes to see Mattie kissing him as firmly as xe'd kissed her. Mattie's hand slid down from her breast to cover Tabitha's hand, and xe guided the motion of her fingers on Bailey's clit in large, rough circles.

Bailey clamped down on nothing, tightening her hold on Duke's neck as she cried out. She pushed her legs farther apart, bearing her hips down to meet the rougher treatment. Three matching swears hit her ears. She whimpered and whined, digging her fingers in. They slipped down to Duke's shoulders, and he groaned as he bounced her higher up. The head of his length pushed against her folds, sliding between them and bumping against Tabitha and Mattie's fingers.

Tabitha laughed against Bailey's neck, breathless and thready. "Yeah, Bays? You like that?"

Bailey realized abruptly that she'd been babbling, begging, *praying* for more to quell the heat inside her veins. Despite the water, she was wet and slick, and she was certain that if they took her on shore right now she'd be a leaking mess.

Instead of answering Tabitha, she tipped her hips back and let the roll of her body pull Duke to where she wanted him. "Please." She rolled her hips forward into Tabitha's and Mattie's hands and back into Duke's cock again, and again, and again.

"God, I never thought she'd be this needy," Tabitha said.

"Should see her when we've been edging for three days," Mattie said. Xe slid xer fingers back, spreading Bailey even farther open, and the head of Duke's cock got caught on her entrance for one brief moment before sliding free to bump against Tabitha's fingers. "Relax, baby girl. We'll take good care of you."

"Jesus fuckin' Christ," Duke breathed.

Bailey groaned and let herself go lax; only her toes curled and uncurled with the compounding waves of pleasure. "Mattie," she slurred. She dropped a hand from Duke's shoulder and reached for her partner. "Ma—ah—Mattie, please. Want—" She groped blindly at Mattie's waist as xe stepped closer to her searching hand. But there was Mattie's clit, firm and stiff between xer legs as Bailey spread xer lips with her fingers. She could feel it bumping against the base of her fingers.

The first press of Bailey's questing fingers drew a moan from Mattie, a low swear that made heat flush through her from her toes to the tip of her ears.

"That's it. Good girl," Mattie said. Xe rocked xer hips slowly, and Bailey followed the motion with her fingers. Years of practice went a long way toward enabling her to please her partner. "That's it, baby, just like that. You want Duke, darling? You want Duke to fuck you?"

Bailey whined and opened her eyes again, unsure when she'd closed them, and tried to focus on Mattie. Xe was a wobbling blur above her head, but xer hooded eyes and soft smile stood out all too clearly. Her heart hammered in her chest. "Yeah," she gasped. "Yes, please. Tabi, harder?"

"Good girl, using your words." Mattie brushed a lock of hair out of Bailey's eyes and came back with a crushed flower. Xe dragged it over her cheek, across her neck and chest, circling the swell of her breasts and nipples. Heat followed in the petal's wake, and Bailey slammed her eyes shut as another moan was wrenched from her.

"Full disclosure: those are way more potent when they're broken like that," Tabitha said in a rush.

"What have you been *testing* in that lab you work at?" Mattie asked.

"Government projects. Mostly. And some fun biochemical shit like this."

Bailey lost track of the conversation. Her head was spinning, her blood pumping, and Tabitha had switched to a beautiful, rough, tight back-and-forth rub just under her clit that made her see stars. Bailey couldn't do much beyond hold her partners tight and let the tide sweep her away.

Partners. Plural...Who would have thought?

Her orgasm crested, fell, then crested again so swiftly that she could only give a strangled yell. Multiple climaxes weren't out of reach for her, but two so quickly? She writhed, panting and shaking and overwhelmed. Gentle hands ran over her stomach and legs, grounding her even with heat still coursing through her.

"Please," she gasped. She twitched her hips again and let her head fall back against Duke's chest. "*Please.*"

"Yeah, baby? You still not satisfied?" Duke rumbled in her ear. He sank a little—the water was blessedly cool against her heated skin—and used the water to help hold her up as he edged his fingers along her legs and up to the core of her. He pet gently over her lips; his fingers were rougher than she'd expected.

Bailey whined and dug her nails into his shoulder. "Jus' fuck me, *please.*"

Mattie laughed, and Tabitha groaned. Bailey worked her eyes open with effort to see Mattie holding onto Tabitha with one hand around her waist, guiding her into grinding against xer leg—xer thick, muscular leg that flexed underneath her and always felt *so good*—

Duke pressed two fingers into her, and Bailey's thoughts scattered before focusing in on the sweet, delicious sensation of *fullness*.

"Oh, *fuck*," she moaned, "Duke!"

"Fucking…shit. You sound so good saying my name," he said. He curled his fingers and twisted them just right, and Bailey dragged her nails down his shoulders.

She dropped a hand between her thighs and made tight circles over her clit. She pulled back the hood, flicked over the stiff bead, and rolled her hips all in one motion. The pleasure was electric, sweeping through her and whiting out her senses. It was fire and fullness and good and not *enough*. She clenched down on his fingers, a broken noise escaping her. If she was saying words, she didn't know what any of them were.

Another set of hands joined hers, taking over rubbing her the way she liked. A body slid along her side, and someone ground against her thigh, gasping moans into her ear as they did. Then finally, *finally*, Duke's fingers pulled away and his cock replaced them. He dragged the head of it over the length of her, imitating fucking her once, twice, three times. Frustration made her twist and cry out, her toes curling as she brought her knees up farther.

The first push into her made her sob, choking on air she didn't have nearly enough of. He was hot and firm and pulsing just as much as she was. Hands were on her clit, on her breast, in her hair, holding her waist and lifting her and lowering her back down—

Bailey rode the firestorm that brewed within her. She rolled her hips and tossed her head, and she lost count of the number of times her thighs quaked from the crest of an orgasm that flowed into another and another. Someone was talking to her. Maybe all of them. She didn't know. She couldn't hear them over her pulse in her ears and the roar of whatever those flowers had done to her.

It was only when Duke, Mattie, and Tabitha cry out, spasming around her, in her, rocking their bodies in tandem with hers, that she slammed back into her physical body. She arched off of Duke's chest with a scream, and if it weren't for the waterfall behind them, she thought she'd have heard an echo.

Bailey couldn't stop shaking in the aftermath. Her body felt sensitive and wired in ways she'd never felt before. She blinked unseeing eyes up at what she thought was the sky and waited for the ringing in her ears to subside. Even with the cool water surrounding her, she was hot, sweaty, and sticky. It was a *lot*.

"Fuck." She blinked again and got her eyes to focus on the wavering picture of Tabitha. Tabitha gently combed her hair out of her face, and the flower crown gave up holding onto Bailey's hair. "Fuck?" Bailey repeated.

"Yeah, baby?" Mattie asked. Xe nuzzled at her ear, xer breath hot and moist.

Bailey giggled and managed to unclench her hands from Duke's shoulders. "Yeah." She patted her shaking fingers on Tabitha's head and shuddered as an aftershock made her clench down on Duke, who, even when softening, was still very much a solid girth inside her.

"Ugh, fuck." She dropped her head back against his chest again and arched slowly. "That's not—mmm—fair. God. I'm too tired, but you're—"

Duke rolled his hips, and she hiccupped as she spasmed.

"Don't worry, Bays; we've got all weekend," he said softly. He pressed an obnoxiously loud kiss to the crown of her head, and she could feel his smile. "Need me to carry you back to camp, princess?"

The name was a tease. It didn't stop Bailey from flexing and rolling her hips down as a reward. Was it a reward for him or her? Hard to tell.

"Please," she said. "I don't think I have legs right now, and I'm *starving.*"

"Hot dogs and s'mores time," Tabitha said in agreement. She blew her bangs out of her face and smiled at Bailey. "And then we can have *s'more.*"

Bailey blinked slowly and then groaned. "I'm moving out. I can't with you. You're horrible. Terrible. *Tabitha, stop laughing*!"

But Tabitha didn't. She kept laughing, clinging to them until all four of them were laughing.

It ended with them red in the face and aching for other reasons, but Bailey had never been so happy in her life. She'd even take the shitty puns. She let herself be cradled in Duke's arms, piled with the clothes they couldn't get back on, and relaxed for the trip back to camp.

It was lovely right up until she looked past a pair of jeans to see that only *one* of their tents was still standing. Tabitha and Duke's tent looked like it had spontaneously developed a mind of its own and started snapping its limbs for fun.

"So... which one of you put in the wrong tension rod?" Bailey asked.

"Oh, gee, look at the time. I'm gonna start the fire!" Tabitha bailed toward their wood supply.

Bailey broke into laughter again, Duke and Mattie both joining her.

"You can sleep with us," Mattie offered. "We sleep pretty solid, and the air mattress is big enough for all four of us."

Bailey smothered her giggles with her hands and nodded quickly. "Mhmm!"

"Thank you," Duke said. He shifted his hold on Bailey and grinned down at her. "And now, I think I'll have dessert before dinner."

Bailey shuddered as she met the hungry gleam in his eyes. Something told her she wasn't getting off that air mattress any time soon. Guess the s'mores were going to wait longer, after all.

Shadow Dealings

Mina Kramek

alcohol use (casual), bar, bipoc, bondage (rope), cunnilingus, demon, dom/sub (subtext), enemies to lovers, f/f/nb, face sitting, fighting to fucking, flirting, friends to lovers, immortal, love declaration, modern with magic, monster hunting, non-binary, the only solution to a love triangle is a…, past tense, pining (mutual), shape changing, teleportation, third person limited point of view, vaginal fingering, violence (non-graphic descriptions)

They always tried to run. Even the ones who should've known better.

Niya watched the bargainer race down the dingy alley at full tilt. She could have caught him by giving chase, but why ruin her heels?

With a wave of her hand, her corporeal form dissolved into smoke, leaving a lingering scent of burning pine to strike the next passerby with unease. Niya popped back into existence on the opposite end of the alley and leaned against the grimy brick wall in the shadow of a fire escape. The bargainer, one Gerald Fitzgibbon, had spent the twenty-year count-down to the lien on his soul coming due behind a desk at his Fortune 500 company or on a beach in the Caymans, not training to make a break for it. It was easy to reach out from the darkness, manicured nails lengthening into blood-red claws, and grab him by the neck.

Disappointing, considering Gerry had been among the foremost sorcerers of his generation before he became another corporate clone, down to the slicked-back salt-and-pepper hair and orange complexion of a tanning salon regular.

Niya slammed him into the wall, relishing his screams. The fear bleeding from him tasted like popcorn.

Gerry was her last call of the night after a full fourteen hours of collecting souls for Hell, and there was a bubble bath and the possibility of a booty call waiting for her back in the fiery pits. She had the right to a bit of manhandling.

"Gerald Fitzgibbons, your debt has come due." She manifested gum in her mouth for the express purpose of blowing a bubble in his face, a pointed expression of boredom. It popped, and he whimpered. "Twenty years of wealth and debauchery for an eternity in Hell. There is no escape. Hope it was worth it."

They always found, in the end, that it had not been.

"Wait, wait!" Gerry squeaked, followed by a garbled name that would've been unintelligible if Niya hadn't found its owner infuriating yet intriguing: "Temerity Jones."

Niya loosened her grip just enough to allow Gerry to speak clearly. "You have thirty seconds to make this worth my while. Twenty-nine. Twenty-eight…"

"Jones has been haunting a cocktail bar that opened a few months ago, the uh, The Lipstick something, sticking real close to the owner. Cutting her hunting hours short for it."

It had been an unusually long time since Temerity last tried to interfere with one of Niya's bargains. At least two months by the mortal calendar.

No wonder the job had been so boring recently.

Temerity, with her bleeding, idealistic heart, thought that Hell tricked its bargainers into giving up their souls in exchange for fool's gold. As if there wasn't a thirteen-step process that took months to earn a meeting with a demon—circumventable in life-or-death situations—with nothing set in stone until a contract was signed in blood. Temerity was also the bane of code-breaking vampires, werewolves, and sorcerers everywhere, but that was none of Niya's business. Whoever named Temerity must have been a prophet, for she was a one-woman whack-a-mole to creatures of the night, the most dauntless demon hunter of her generation. Even if she was cute when she blushed.

If Temerity was skipping out on hunting to hang out at a bar, its owner must be prophesized to free all souls from Hell, or something equally ridiculous.

"Hmm. Interesting. Enjoy the lava."

Gerry burst into flames, his mortal flesh consumed in an instant but his suffering just beginning. Niya breathed in his soul, a yellow flame with a core like an oil slick, and it nestled in her lungs with the day's two other souls.

Fitzgibbons, Inc. would be missing a CEO and under federal investigation come Monday. Hell had never promised Gerry a legacy.

As for Niya, the bubble bath could wait. Yanking Temerity's chain would make tonight far more interesting.

The Lip Print, as the bar turned out to be called, announced its presence with a hand-painted sign depicting a lipstick stain on a wine glass under a magnifying glass with a rainbow arcing off as if refracting light. To open a bar in this neighborhood, packed with long-lasting-yet-failing mainstays, the owner either had a gimmick they thought was a sure thing, was exceptionally foolhardy, or had preternatural forces on their side.

Niya was banking on the latter. As she pushed open the door, she was struck by how clean it was, though she could taste the memory of the hedonism of a profitable Friday in the air. The interior had a speakeasy theme, with Art Deco wood paneling carpeted in a plush teal fabric. Atop the bar, a miniature non-binary pride flag peeked out from an aluminum container that overflowed with pencils. At this time of night, closer to dawn than dusk, the only clientele was a quartet of college students drooping over the dregs of far too many drinks.

Any of them might have been up for making a bargain in exchange for an end to finals and a smooth career path, if Niya were the sort of demon to go around dropping copies of *The Summoner's Primer for Fools and Tyrants* in mortals' paths to boost their numbers in hopes of a promotion (and why go to the trouble when climbing the demonic ladder only meant fewer vacation days?).

The bartender looked up from wiping down the bar when the door shut behind Niya with an unearthly squeal on rusting hinges. They were dressed like a detective from an old noir film, save that the trench coat—sleeves rolled back out of the way of bartending flourishes—suspenders, and slacks over an appealingly half-unbuttoned white shirt were all an eye-popping pink that complemented the cool undertones of their brown skin. Round cheeks, glistening from hours at work, and warm brown eyes that held a thousand in-jokes were framed by chin-length twists. A silver-and-iron pendant with garlic flower embedded in resin hung around their neck, an all-in-one charm for warding off werewolves lost to the transformation, fae, and vampires.

They were the reason Niya was here, but there was no realignment of the Earthly planes shouting that the end was nigh, not even the slightest hint of recognition of what Niya was in their eyes. In fact, the mortal barely noticed her inspection, too busy taking Niya in in return.

"What has someone who looks like the center of attention at a billionaires' gala walking into my cocktail bar at 4 a.m.?" asked the bartender. In a perfectly pressed and fitted suit—made by a designer who had secured eight decades before her soul came due by promising to keep Niya appropriately outfitted—Niya was decidedly out of place. Still, the bartender's words held interest. "In search of better company, perhaps?"

Demons tended to go one of two ways in human guises: so off-putting a single glance would fill the toughest fighter with the uncontrollable urge to cross the street, or dangerously alluring. Niya liked to be admired and had long favored the form of a beautiful Phoenician queen she had once known.

Niya slid onto a barstool. There was a newspaper-like sheet laid out at each place. Not a menu, but an elaborate mystery surrounding the murder of a prohibition-era police commissioner who had been cracking down on speakeasies. It was composed of crosswords, cyphers, and other puzzles; customers could get hints from the bartender by buying drinks.

At a glance, Niya knew the answer.

"What can I say? I keep my own schedule." Her claws retracted to a more human length, just long enough to make a satisfying *clack* on the lacquered wood of the bar. "The widow did it so she could run off with her lover, the notorious lesbian bootlegger. Tell me, do they live happily ever after or does it all go down in flames?"

"I usually let my customers decide, but between you and me, I like my fictional romances fucked up, not tragic. Although"—the bartender set the rag aside and quickly washed their hands—"usually it takes around ten visits to solve, and I've never seen you here before. How *did* you manage it?"

"Maybe I'm just good at noticing what people want." Niya let her teeth drag slowly over her lower lip and watched their gaze fixate on her mouth. "Does solving the mystery mean I win access to the menu?"

"There isn't one. Usually, I ask customers to give me a flavor profile, but I like to guess the tastes of beautiful—"

A pause, for Niya to fill in the blank. "Women." This century, at least. "I know it's in poor taste to hit on bartenders, so let me ask outright—are you flirting with me, or should I buy a drink and sip it quietly in the corner?"

Niya knew the answer, but humans liked to be asked.

"Definitely flirting, but I haven't decided how seriously yet."

"In that case, I'm Niya, and it's very *nice* to meet you." She held out a hand, and when the bartender took it, raised it so a ghost of a kiss brushed against their knuckles. They shivered, staring at Niya's lips. "Could I get a name, and a recommendation for a drink?"

"Rae," they started, belatedly reclaiming their hand to unnecessarily smooth their coat. "About that drink, let me surprise you. On the house if you don't like it. Any allergies?"

"None, but nothing too sweet. I'll melt like a wicked witch under a bucketful of water." The one time she'd tried a pumpkin spice latte, it quite literally sent her right back to Hell.

"No peeking; you have to guess the ingredients."

Niya held a hand over her eyes, humoring them, listening to the splash of pouring liquids and clink of a spoon against glass until Rae slid the glass toward her.

Rum of course, and ginger strong enough to burn. And was that a hint of cayenne? But the base, the flavor that stirred her interest was… "Pineapple?"

"Not too sweet, but you said nothing about sweetening *you* up."

A very un-demon-like giggle bubbled up from Niya's gut. If not for that foreign, unexpected reaction, she might have replied, *you're welcome to try, where the passing millennia have failed.* "That was terrible."

"But you liked it."

Niya was surprised to find that she had, though maybe she shouldn't have been. Straightforwardness was a rare thing, rarer still in Hell. But she wasn't here to let herself be charmed into bed with someone who might still be destined to free the damned, despite all-too-ordinary appearances.

"Say I did. Maybe I'd like to get to know a prospective lover before allowing *myself* to be seduced. What drew you here?" Niya hoped asking would prompt Rae to tell her more about their association with Temerity.

"You first."

"I'm in sales, unfortunately. It's about as interesting as it sounds." An oversimplification, yes, but not technically a lie. Humans thought every soul bartered away was scandalous, profane, but even the most rewarding of callings could become dreary monotony when it spanned centuries.

"I graduated with a degree in accounting and only then realized I couldn't imagine picking through other peoples' finances for the rest of my life. I got a job at a hotel bar and moved here once I'd saved enough to open this place, to be closer to—it doesn't matter." They shrugged. "The rest is history."

Oh, it most certainly did matter. "For a partner?"

A parade of conflicting emotions crossed their face. Promising.

"Ah, someone you wish was yours. Tell me about them."

"She's never witnessed an injustice she didn't want to fight, from cuts in school arts funding to reverting anti-homeless benches to usable spaces. She isn't afraid no matter how terrible her opposition. And she's gorgeous. She could crush my head with her thi—" They cut off mid-sentence, squinting at her doubtfully. "Asking me about a woman I love? And here I thought you were trying to get into my pants."

"It got you talking, didn't it? And I learned you have the cutest dimple on the left side of your mouth when you smile." Niya came to The Lip Print with a goal, a curiosity she still meant to solve, but she wouldn't say no if Rae offered a bonus. "Although, do you always try to keep people out of trouble?"

"My *friend* is a special case. On my own, I *am* trouble."

"Oh?" Niya rested her chin on her hand.

"That hotel where I used to work hosted terrible conferences under a manager who scheduled too few people for too many shifts in a row and never counted overtime. When I was near ready to leave, the manager assigned me to a rocket science conference. If you put a thousand scientists in one room with unlimited drinks, they'll regress to their youth within the hour. Creaky old professors start dancing and throwing back drinks like they're a fresh-faced eighteen. Grad students either try to impress anyone who might be a good connection or they act like they've been left unsupervised at summer camp."

Niya's only dealings with scientists had been the rare few with enough supernatural knowledge to summon her to advance their careers. They tend toward madness and whimsy, often seeking an escape from an endless cycle of failed grant applications as much as recognition. "Did someone etch the schematics for a manned rocket to Jupiter into a table?"

"Someone had a half-full pack of Mentos and held a spontaneous competition for the most impressive volcano made only of materials in the hotel ballroom."

"I see. Summer camp."

"Summer camp." Rae agreed. "I requested tarps from my manager, Tony, and he pretended not to hear me. So I let them use the tablecloths—which did nothing to stop the foaming soda from sinking into the carpet." Their eyes went wide for the space of a sentence as they feigned innocence. "I *tried* to stop them, but they just wouldn't listen. Tony ignored my warning, so he was demoted. Malicious compliance."

"Perhaps I should take a page out of your book and campaign for *my* manager to stop dropping from the rafters to give me assignments." The Manager of Deals and Acquisitions was a tougher case to crack than some capitalism-brainwashed human, but Niya was stubborn.

Rae, of course, could not know the middle management literally hung bat-like from the ceiling. They leaned a little farther across the bar, their smile open and honest. "Maybe you should."

Niya matched her, Temerity forgotten in favor of listening to the rise and fall of Rae's voice, experiencing the ordinary mortal world coming to life around her.

"—and he tumbled head-first off the stage, only to somersault onto his feet and stumble right into his crush's lap."

Niya should have kept one eye on the window, but it was only when the door pushed opened and Rae turned with a smile full of worry that Niya caught sight of a familiar mass of blonde curls escaping their bun.

Niya rushed to wrap herself in shadow, slinking toward the dark corner that held the restroom to eavesdrop.

At some point, the undergrads had left, and Niya *hadn't noticed.* She'd been down to the dregs of her drink, leaning halfway across the bar, and *entirely* off topic. What was it about this mortal that so captivated not only Temerity, but Niya herself?

For Rae was entirely human. Not the faintest whiff of the supernatural around them save the pendant that Niya would bet was a gift from Temerity.

"I thought you might not be coming tonight," Rae was saying.

"And leave you to close by your lonesome?"

Temerity was flirting. Badly, the rhythm of her words stumbling and uncertain. But flirting nonetheless, when Niya had been convinced violence was her only love language. Temerity never tried to flirt with *her.*

The toned muscles of Temerity's thighs flexing as she approached the bar were more than enough compensation. Temerity was nearly as addicted to the leg-press machine as stalking the night, and distractingly fond of miniskirts. This one was pink, little white hearts around the hem, with a matching sweater.

"Well, someone was keeping me company— Huh, where did she go?"

The Temerity Jones Niya knew would have gone on red alert. This one made calf eyes and stole Niya's seat. "If she dined and dashed, I'll chase her down for you."

"The only way out was past you. Unless people who can turn invisible secretly walk the Earth, she's probably in the bathroom."

Despite Rae's joking tone, Temerity grimaced. Temerity was many things, but an actress was not one of them.

With a sigh at the lack of response, Rae continued, "When will you tell me what has you keeping such odd hours? And *don't* say it's night shift at a hospital. You would have told me up front."

Niya held in a snicker. Only Temerity wouldn't even *try* to come up with an excuse.

"Rae…I would tell you if it was *safe*—"

"Don't. Silly me for thinking this would be any different than high school. But, no. Canceling on the movies last minute and showing up at school half asleep covered in bruises just became forgetting to text when you're over an hour late. How was work, can you at least tell me that much?"

"Some success, but I missed someone I've been looking for by minutes. I'm better now that I'm here with you."

Rae slid a glass of soda water across the bar, and Temerity reached to grasp it, covering their fingers with hers, only for Rae to pull back. "Don't."

"I meant your bartending skills, obviously." Temerity's smile was brittle as she knocked back a gulp of her water.

"Sure." Rae said, their tone flat and expression shuttered. "You don't have to check in on me every night, you know. I live upstairs, and you have to walk halfway across the city."

"Maybe I want to see for myself that no ruffians are fucking with my friend."

Rae's brow quirked up. "Uh huh. Why don't you make sure of it by taking me out to do something normal? Monday evening, let's go play mini golf and try that new Moroccan place Elise was raving about."

Temerity shifted on her stool, radiating conflict. "I'd love to."

Rae deflated. The taste of her momentary hope dissipating was mouthwatering. "I know that look. Let me guess, you're going to say 'but—' "

"—I can't," they said in unison.

"I *can't* take any time off, not until I find her, and..." Temerity trailed off. "I really haven't made time for you, have I? I *do* have to work, but I can squeeze in dinner."

Rae let Temerity take their hand this time, a fond, familiar smile playing across their lips.

They were so deep in each other's eyes it was like all of reality was trapped between them, and Niya was left on the outside. Not her favorite feeling, and as a demon, she didn't have to stand for it.

"Until you find who?" Niya perched on a table with one leg crossed over the other, perfectly posed for when Temerity whirled around, planting herself in front of Rae, instantly on defense. Niya waved, her claws extended. "Looking for me?"

A growl a werewolf would have been proud of rose in Temerity's throat as she threw herself at Niya, flicking knives into her hands from her sleeves.

Niya disincorporated into smoke before she could make impact, forcing Temerity to turn her momentum into a handspring over the table. She reappeared behind Temerity and leaned casually against a wall before drawling, "Awww, darling, you missed me."

"Like a hole in my head." Temerity spun as she lashed out with a knife.

Niya ducked and grabbed hold of Temerity's wrist, pulling her flush against her. "A lobotomy could be arranged; I'm sure your old friend Dr. Moreau would love to get her hands on the brain of a hunter"—Dr. Moreau, a vampiric mad scientist who had named herself after the literary figure due to their shared interest in human-animal hybrids, had recently returned to town, and was likely the "her" who Temerity was hunting—"but your replacement wouldn't have your sparkling personality, or be quite so cute."

A flush spread under Temerity's freckles. Her breath hitched; her eyes widened. For the barest second, she leaned into Niya. Then, she bashed their foreheads together, hurting herself more than Niya. There was a prick at Niya's throat, and a burning chill spread from the point of a razor-sharp silver knife. One of Temerity's thighs slotted between hers, pressing her hard into the wall, though Niya still held her other arm captive.

Temerity had managed to surprise her. That was new. Clearly she'd been training hard, fighting *other* monsters in the months since Niya last gave in to the urge to pop by and annoy her.

With the flat of the blade, Temerity tilted Niya's chin up. That same blade had killed lesser demons, but it couldn't kill her, and Temerity knew it. But being cut with silver *would* hurt; it was one of the few mortal things capable of sapping her powers and sending white-hot cold running through her veins for the next week. Niya would have to hide in the mortal world until it wore off, lest an opportunistic colleague take advantage of her weakness.

Temerity didn't press down farther, her gaze fixing instead just above Niya's shoulders, where blood-red roses dangled from Niya's ears on a chain of thorns. "You're wearing my earrings. I thought I lost those."

"Nope, I stole them." And for her pains, Niya had been forced to listen to Mephisto ranting about her "obsession with that obnoxious hunter" for an hour. "They're more my style, don't you think?"

She dug a claw into the tender backside of Temerity's knee, just hard enough to make her flinch and her pupils dilate, covering all but a sliver of the golden-brown of her irises. Temerity went beet red, deliciously furious. Attraction to Niya had no place in Temerity's black-and-white image of the world. The chill of silver eased as she lost focus.

It was enough of a distraction for Niya to shove her back, sending her crashing into the bar. Temerity was trained in how to fall and managed to cushion her spine from the full force of impact. But her knives dropped from her grasp.

Temerity looked like she spent every spare moment at the gym. Niya would not have looked out of place on a runway in Milan. Appearances did not stop Niya from pinning Temerity against the bar by the throat and holding her there.

The imprint of lips, Niya's lips, nestled below Temerity's collar bone. Left there over a year ago as a parting gift, the day Temerity persuaded a young woman not to give up her own soul to bring her boyfriend back from the dead. The day that had ended with Niya pushing Temerity against the railing of a bridge and, scarcely knowing what she was doing, pressing a curse into her skin.

"The fearsome demon hunter falls at the hands of a demon yet again. I could be excused for thinking you enjoyed being at my mercy. Unless you were simply too ashamed to have my little present removed?"

The salt of Temerity's skin had lingered on Niya's lips after she returned to Hell, more pungent than the acrid scent of the lava pool that decorated the lawn of the bargainer's offices. She had assumed Temerity had the curse removed soon after. It hadn't been meant as more than an annoyance, a reminder that Niya had put it there, sending an electric spark through her when touched.

Temerity bit her lip, refusing to answer, her eyes defiant.

Niya reached up to graze over the mark with the back of a claw and watched with giddy glee as Temerity fought to keep a sound from slipping through her lips. "You *did* keep it on purpose. Never even reported it, did you, naughty girl?"

"Shut up," Temerity snapped, starting to roll her hips to buck Niya off her, ready to start their fight again.

"It's cute that you can't even think of a—"

"Why are you making a mess of my bar when you so obviously want to fuck?"

As Niya turned to look at the source of the voice, she pressed her finger harder into the mark. A startled, horrified moan slipped through Temerity's lips as Niya locked eyes with Rae, who was seated in one of the booths, nibbling on a pretzel.

For reasons Niya could not fathom, they hadn't run. Only flipped the "Open" sign in the window to "Closed" and settled in to watch.

"Let me see if I have this right. You"—they pointed to Niya—"aren't human. Vampire?"

"Nothing so pedestrian. I'm a demon. Don't worry, I won't steal your soul unless you ask me to." She let her tongue flick out, delicately forked at the end, her canines sharpening into fangs. Demons didn't have a true form, not really, but playing into mortal misconceptions was fun, especially when it sparked a dilation of pupils, the swallowing of a rush of saliva.

Rae crossed and uncrossed their legs, then forced their attention back to the issue at hand. "You called my friend a hunter. Why?"

"Because she is one. Eighty-nine confirmed kills." Niya leaned down so her breath teased across Temerity's ear. "Isn't that right?"

"How did you know—?" Temerity clamped her lips shut and swallowed, her pulse rabbit-quick under Niya's fingers. She obviously didn't want to show how flustered she was, yet she couldn't hide it.

"Of demons specifically?" Rae asked after a pause.

"Anything that goes bump in the night."

Rae nodded, but they couldn't know the extent of the world their friend and would-be lover had been hiding, not yet.

"Anyone hurting innocents," Temerity hissed through gritted teeth.

"When did you figure out the difference?" Niya's tone was condescending, but if Temerity truly *had* begun to see the world around her for what it was, her stubborn crusader had just gotten that much more fascinating. "Does your family know that you have?"

Her silence was answer enough.

"So," Rae said, "tonight, you—Ritz—thought Niya was here to hurt me, and decided to have a homoerotic fight with her while I sat here having my worldview upended."

Temerity stammered out a weak denial, but Niya spoke over her, thinking Rae's deductive work deserved praise. "You're taking this very well."

"I'm not, really. I'll probably freak out later. I don't like being lied to." Rae shrugged and then, pointedly, bit their lip. "Helps that that was hot."

Oh, they were taking this *very* well indeed.

"What are you talking about? This is a fight. She's *dangerous*," Temerity protested, as if this hadn't long progressed past a fight and into a negotiation of favors.

"Somewhere in that stubborn, gorgeous head of yours, you know the danger is the point." Niya twirled a lock of Temerity's hair around a claw. "Or you would have taken advantage of the distraction to stab me by now."

"Please admit you want to fuck the hot demon." Rae managed to sound amused over undercurrents of heartbreak and fear.

"No. Rae, I—" Temerity shook her head violently enough that Niya had to ease up her grip to avoid drawing blood. Temerity didn't try to break free, didn't even seem to notice, too focused on denying her attraction to seize the chance she had ostensibly been waiting for. "I can't want her."

"Why not?" Rae asked.

"I'm in love with *you*." Temerity yelled her confession with an intensity that nearly made Niya let go. Nearly.

Rae stood, taking a few careful, disbelieving steps forward. And stopped, their stance firming. "You are not doing this to me right now. Not when I've just found out what you've been hiding from me. So try again."

"I can't let a demon seduce me. It's wrong," Temerity insisted, but her argument was feeble. After all, what was there now to hold her in place but her own hidden desires?

"Darling"—Niya skimmed a finger over her mark on Temerity's collarbone and felt her shiver—"this says I seduced you ages ago."

"It's perfectly normal to fantasize about the supernatural from time to time," Rae said. "I'd say yes in a heartbeat."

Niya threw a smirk over her shoulder at them. "The offer's still open."

Rae closed the rest of the distance between them and pressed their lips to Niya's. They requested entry with a delicate swipe of their tongue along the seam of Niya's lips, and she allowed it, letting Rae show her what they wanted, how they might please her.

The stamp of a boot heel on Niya's instep forced them apart too soon.

"Stop that." Temerity's expression was a pout forced into a semblance of horror. Niya suspected she felt left out. "You don't understand, Rae, she steals people's souls."

It was too much to hope that Temerity had seen more sides to *her*, part of Hell's infernal legions, so easily as she might creatures closer to human. Rae seemed more open-minded, intrigued enough they might want her to come back assuming Temerity's people didn't wipe their memory. Niya didn't think Temerity would report this to her superiors, not when doing so would risk her losing Rae forever, but she couldn't be certain. Temerity didn't think things through when she thought she was protecting someone.

"I let people sell me their souls," Niya corrected. "It's not *my* fault if they don't consider the consequences of their actions."

Rae glanced at Temerity, a considering look in their eye. They asked Niya, "Do they have reason to regret it?"

Always, but never because Niya hadn't given them what they asked for. "Only when accounts come due."

Rae hummed; Niya could feel the weight of their consideration, see their conflicted feelings in how they looked from Niya to Temerity. Presumably, they were considering what they wanted, and whether Niya alone would do. Niya wouldn't blame them when the answer was no—she felt the same, teetering on the edge of months and years of tension, finally ready to break.

"I'm good at sharing," Rae said at length. "Are you?"

Monogamy and demonhood rarely went hand in hand. "Why don't we ask her?"

Niya expected resistance, continued denials, perhaps leading to her ending the night alone after all.

But all it took was Rae leaning down to whisper in Temerity's ear. "Do you want me? Do you want us?"

"Yes," Temerity said, the admission torn from her throat.

"That's my girl." Smiling, Rae patted Temerity on the cheek, earning a quiet whimper. "Have you thought about this before? Touched yourself, thinking about us?"

Temerity's head snapped to the side, avoiding the question. That suited Niya well enough, for she had no desire to dissect the vibrant energy that flooded through her whenever they fought, when the entire force of Temerity's attention was focused on her. She especially didn't want to examine the creeping possessiveness she'd felt when she realized Temerity was in love with someone else. Not even the way her stomach swooped when Temerity shivered at the scrape of Niya's nails trailing up her thigh.

But she did want to find out what Temerity sounded like when she begged.

Niya released Temerity's throat to slide her hand between the V of her tits, along the length of her belly, and over the sensitive expanse of her inner thigh, her claws gently scraping all the while—never hard enough to draw blood, just enough to make Temerity twitch and squirm, and to slice through her panties in two quick strikes. Reaching the apex of Temerity's thighs, Niya retracted her claws and circled a finger through her folds.

"You're so wet for us." Niya removed her hand, showing her glistening fingers to Rae. "Look how desperate she is."

Rae took two of Niya's fingers into her mouth, swirling their tongue to lick off the evidence of Temerity's desire before sliding off with a *pop*. "Mmm. I think she's thought about this."

"I'm right here," Temerity complained. She was flushed across her freckles, her breathing shallow, like she was trying to stop herself from panting and only half succeeding.

"And you're being very stubborn. It's cute." Rae kissed Temerity on the tip of her nose. She glared up at them, unbearably fond.

"Shall I put these in you now, and leave traces of them inside you?" Niya slid her hand back between Temerity's thighs, lightly tracing at her entrance while she waited for an answer. "Use your words, darling, yes or no."

"Please." Temerity's tongue darted out to wet her lips. "Yes."

Niya didn't keep her waiting any longer, two fingers slipping inside as easily as if Temerity's pussy was welcoming them home. She found a rhythm, crooking her fingers against the rough, sensitive spot that made Temerity's walls contract, made her try to grind against the heel of Niya's hand—with little success, until Niya took pity on her and brought her thumb to her clit.

Rae had a hand up Temerity's shirt, playing with her tits and swallowing the swears and sighs that poured from Temerity's mouth as she unraveled.

Niya hadn't decided whether to let Temerity reach her peak yet, but the sounds she made—muffled by Rae's mouth—were everything she'd wanted across dozens of altercations. She'd never believed Temerity would give them to her willingly.

"Wait." Rae grabbed a hold of Niya's wrist, stilling her as Temerity whined in protest. "We're not having sex on my bar."

Niya arched a brow. "Pretty sure we are."

"We're not going any further here; I have sanitary standards to uphold."

"Is that it then? I *could* leave her wanting for you." Disappointing, but absence and fondness and all that.

Rae shook their head. "That's not exactly what I have in mind. I live upstairs."

"Hold your breath," Niya warned, and kissed them, keeping hold of Temerity's collar as she transported them all through the shadows of eternity and up precisely one floor. They landed on a bed with a bounce, Niya and Rae on their knees, Temerity collapsing into the sheets.

Rae coughed, waving their hand in an effort to rid the air of the sulfurous scent.

There were too many pillows, piled so high Niya assumed at least half must end up on the floor every night.

"That should have killed the mood," Rae said.

Niya lay on her side alongside Temerity, propping her head up to look at them from under her lashes. "Did it?"

"No," Rae said after a beat. "The question is, whatever shall we do with her?"

They bent to brush a lock of Temerity's hair out of her face. Niya had never seen Temerity look so soft or so vulnerable, longing for something that was right in front of her. Rae, on the other hand, was obviously conflicted. Wanting this, and wanting to make the woman they loved feel the same betrayal that coursed through their veins.

Niya might be a demon, but she knew there were more constructive ways to work out those feelings. "You want to punish her for her transgressions against you. Perhaps…bondage?"

Rae's eyes, wide and transparent, met Niya's.

She laughed. "No, I can't read your mind, just your feelings. I can tell what people want, and I can tell she wants you too."

"Do you? Want that?" Rae asked.

Temerity nodded, enthusiastic against the pillows. "I'm sorry. I've always wished I could tell you."

There were a thousand reasons to keep the supernatural hidden from ordinary humans, and a thousand reasons more why the rules the hunters lived by, raising their children with one foot in two worlds, never fully a part of either, were restrictive and cruel.

None of that mattered in this moment. This was only a negotiation that would change two lives forever, and that would hand Niya what she wanted on a silver platter.

Rae cupped Temerity's jaw in their hand, gently tipping her face upward. "You've been keeping secrets from me, Ritz. How will you make up for it?"

Temerity's breath rushed out of her lungs, the one word she spoke barely a whisper. "Anything."

"Good girl." Rae stroked their thumb over Temerity's lips, then pulled away. "Take off your shirt and put your hands over your head."

Temerity hurried to obey.

"Leave the skirt on," Niya ordered when Temerity's fingers dipped beneath her waistband.

Temerity looked to Rae for approval. At their nod, she hurriedly lay back down, grabbing hold of the bars of the wooden headboard, knocking a few pillows off the bed in the process.

Rae rose and grabbed a bundle of rope from the closet, the same shade of pink as Temerity's skirt, like they'd had it waiting for her. They undid the figure-eight knot and extended a length taut between their hands as the bed creaked under their renewed weight. "Remember, 'no' means 'no' until you give me a safe word."

Temerity's gaze caught on one of the pillows, this one in the shape of a winged, cartoonish yellow-and-black insect. "Bumblebee."

"Bumblebee," Rae repeated, as if it meant something. One among a myriad of memories shared between them that Niya was not privy to—never should be *privy* to, because Temerity was a flirtation and Rae a dalliance, as humans were meant to be. They would work things out between them, and Niya might battle Temerity again in the future with the added relish of knowing that she, a hunter, had succumbed to Niya's infernal charms.

That was all.

"Very good choice. That's my girl," Rae was saying as they tied Temerity's wrists together with a double column and secured them to the headboard. They moved back to strip off their suit, piece by piece, revealing small tits with hardened nipples, top surgery scars, a softness around their middle, and an ass that would have inspired sculptors in times gone by.

Every one of Rae's motions was practiced, showing them at ease with the languages of kink and sex, but the hesitant way Temerity tested her bonds made Niya wonder if she was new to many aspects of tonight. Niya hadn't expected that.

Niya placed a hand on Temerity's thigh and played with the hem of her skirt. "Have you done this before?"

"Not—this, exactly," Temerity admitted. The flush under her freckles was Niya's little secret, invisible to humans in the dim light of the bedroom. "But I've imagined it, so many times. I can please you, Rae. Please let me please you."

"Hush, Ritz, I've got you, you will. Look at me, that's it," Rae whispered in a gentle litany.

"But what will I do with you, darling? Do you know how long I've wanted to eat you up?" Niya shrugged off her jacket and undid her buttons with a gesture and a thin thread of power, but stopped there, leaving her pants on and her shirt to hang open. She tilted her head, showing a hint of fangs and inhuman red eyes, her pupils narrowed to slits.

Temerity was too far gone; Niya could feel the strength of her desires, and Temerity didn't pretend to deny them. She swallowed and asked. "How long?"

"Years. I've imagined you under me since the first time you lectured me on right and wrong with my claws at your throat," she said. "Are you finally going to let me?"

Temerity nodded feverishly.

They were ready to begin.

Rae straddled Temerity's face, holding onto the headboard behind them for balance. Temerity dove in with more enthusiasm than skill, until Rae muttered instructions and she settled into a rhythm of broad, firm strokes across their clit pausing, occasionally, to fuck into them with her tongue. Having seen her fill, Niya began mapping Temerity's legs with her fingers; Temerity's mouth faltered when Niya found a sensitive spot on the planes of Temerity's muscular thighs, the sharp peaks of her pelvis. The softness of her relaxed abdomen contracted to firm strength under Niya's touch.

"You're distracting her," Rae complained.

That was kind of the point. "I can do worse."

With that, Niya settled between Temerity's thighs and put her mind to driving her incoherent. She sucked marks into the skin of Temerity's thighs until Temerity tried to wrap her legs around Niya's head to force her closer. Niya pushed her legs apart and turned her attention to Temerity's clit just as Rae cried out, arching their back and shaking apart all over Temerity's face.

Niya gave a quick, playful lick, and Temerity bucked into her, whimpering, stopping her ministrations to Rae entirely.

Rae grabbed Temerity's jaw, guiding her back to their pussy. "Did I say you could stop? Keep going."

Temerity did her best to obey, even when Niya slid two fingers inside her and interspersed teasing licks with suction, never quite letting her reach her peak. Only when Rae came down from a second peak, climbing off of Temerity to nestle, panting, among the remaining cushions, did Niya raise her head.

"What do you think? Has she been good enough?"

"I'd say that was an acceptable performance," they pronounced.

Temerity was not too far gone to protest. "Acceptable?"

Rae laughed, and Niya sensed that the shadow of the lies between them were not gone, but had diminished. A tear that could be mended with a needle and thread and a bit of careful, dedicated time. "You know you were good."

"*Just* good? I—"

Temerity's face was shiny with Rae's juices, but Rae didn't seem to care when they leaned in and kissed her on the lips for the very first time. They didn't come up for air no matter how Niya made Temerity gasp into their mouth, as she fucked her harder with her fingers, redoubling the pressure on her clit.

It was with Rae's fingers on the mark Niya's had left on Temerity's neck that Temerity finally came.

Niya eased Temerity through her orgasm, slowing and gentling until she stopped twitching with the aftershocks. She slipped her hand free to rest in the slickness coating Temerity's thigh, relishing the warmth of her. Time passed before Rae unbound Temerity and rose, returning with a damp washcloth, to clean up the lover they intended to keep.

Niya took that as her cue, rising from the bed to redo the buttons of her shirt and to sling her discarded jacket over her shoulder.

"You're leaving?" Temerity asked.

Niya might have heard hurt in her voice, or maybe it was wishful thinking. There was a limit to how long she could stay in the mortal realm without it becoming an excess of indulgence, the sort that would make her more ambitious colleagues take notice.

"Things to do," she said, keeping her voice light with affected boredom. "Souls to steal, lives to ruin. All the things you always accuse me of."

"I don't believe you anymore," Temerity said. Of course she chose now to see the truth of what Niya had long been telling her. "What if I—what if *we* want you to stay? You didn't even let me kiss you."

Niya couldn't let Temerity kiss her. Not now, at least. Maybe never.

But Temerity's sincerity was enough to make Niya pause and say a proper goodbye, to spark a flutter of hope in the hollow of her chest where a human heart would have lived.

"Maybe it would be best if you did believe me. But"—Niya trailed her fingers over her mark on Temerity's collarbone one final time—"next time. You can touch me next time. If you get the better of me." And to Rae, she added, "Good luck with her. She's a handful."

They grinned. "Oh, I'm looking forward to it. Will I see you around?"

Niya tilted up Rae's chin and kissed them thoroughly, a promise of what was in store when next they met. "Count on it."

She did them the courtesy of walking out the front door of the flat and out into the dawn.

Her phone rang.

If she didn't answer, Niya would be treated to increasingly powerful electrical shocks until the Manager grew bored or she groveled, whichever came first. She swiped to accept the call but didn't bother to hide her irritation. "My shift doesn't start for another five mortal hours."

The Manager's voice came through the speaker tinny and high-pitched, designed to grate on the eardrums. "We have a *violinist* with *star potential* wanting to make a deal. If you're not there in the next five minutes, I'll give this one to Amy."

"No you won't." Niya hung up and incinerated the phone. Another would be in her pocket by the time negotiations concluded with the violinist. But at times, it served her well to remind the Manager that she was the best Hell had to offer.

Double Take

Eliot Lovell

alcohol use (casual), anal fingering, bipoc, bisexual, clitoral fingering, established relationship, f/m, f/m/m, flirting, getting drunk, modern, omg they were neighbors, penis in anus sex, present tense, smoking (casual), third person limited point of view, twosome to threesome, vaginal fingering, voyeurism

Any praise George deserves for arranging his bed frame—*and* mattress—to be delivered the same day he moves in is undermined by him accidentally leaving his phone charger in his old shared flat. George should be upstairs unpacking his few possessions, but instead he's waiting outside because he has no idea when his bed will arrive, and *they* have no idea which apartment he lives in.

His weather app never mentioned *rain.* How was George supposed to know?

George smacks his dead phone against his palm, trying not to annoy the other person sheltering beneath the building's overhang.

Somehow his silent companion is bone dry, his exquisite grey suite immune to the sideways-falling rain, but George is damp almost to his knees. The stranger lights another cigarette, face pinching every time he glances over. He looks good, leaning at an effortless lounge, and so handsome George has to turn away to avoid outright staring.

"Do you live here?"

George whirls around to face the smoker so abruptly his elbow cracks against the wall.

"I just moved in," George blurts, belatedly realising how *stupid* it is to tell a stranger where he lives. At least he didn't say which apartment, though give George eleven seconds and he's sure he can slip it into the conversation.

"Waiting for someone?" the man asks. He stubs out his cigarette on the wall. "Nathan—I live here too."

"I'm waiting for a delivery," George admits.

Nathan tilts his head, looking so effortlessly confident that George's stomach rolls with jealousy not solely for Nathan's sharp jawline. Wordlessly, Nathan glances up at the building, pulling one eyebrow up in a silent question.

"No, I— My phone is dead, so I don't know when they're coming," George says. "They can't call me when they arrive."

"And they're an anti-lift delivery company?"

George sighs. "I didn't know my flat number when I paid. I am living a curse of my own making."

Nathan's mouth briefly quirks with amusement, just on one side. It softens his face a little, enough that George doesn't feel laughed at.

"What kind of phone?" Nathan asks.

George doesn't know why it matters, but he spins the device over in his hand. Nathan makes no response; he pushes out of his lounge and stoops to grab the briefcase hiding behind his legs. To George's surprise he's not getting up to leave, only to rifle through his briefcase. Almost immediately Nathan retrieves a cable, holding it out.

"Get out of the rain." Nathan says.

"What about *your* phone?" George asks, hesitating with his hand an inch away.

"This is my spare," Nathan says, insisting again, "go on."

"I—"

"See you around," Nathan says, and he pats his pocket, retrieving his cigarettes again.

The desire to watch Nathan smoke another is not non-existent, and George remains frozen until Nathan has his hand cupped around the flame of his lighter to protect it from the still-drifting rain.

"Thank you," George says before he can forget, and Nathan *winks* at him.

George darts through the glass doors and races through the lobby with his head down. The moment he's in front of a lift, George slams his palm against the call button and allows himself a glance back outside.

Nathan is right there, hovering behind the clear panels and watching George. The lift doors open with a too-loud *ding*, and George realises he never introduced himself.

When George accepted his new job, he was too enamoured with a future devoid of customer service that he failed to appreciate the 7 a.m. starts. George isn't designed for mornings.

The apartment building is quiet enough when he stumbles from his apartment that George manages to pick up a faint alarm going off a few doors down. George makes no effort to hide his yawn as he presses the call button to head downstairs; it's not like he's going to run into anyone else.

The elevator slides open while George is rubbing his palm against one tired eye, ringing its already-familiar chime and, sounding from its depths a bright, "Good morning."

George chokes on *air*, so stupefied by this woman's sudden appearance that he barely remembers to cover his mouth as he coughs through it. She proves herself to have a beautiful laugh, beckoning George into the elevator with a wave that sets the bracelets on her wrist clinking together.

"I'm not used to seeing people awake this early," she says. Her smile implies she's happy about it, like she's been desperate for early morning conversations.

"Hi," George says thickly, blinking. She's distractingly pretty—warm dark skin and something shiny spread across full lips. George wishes he was more awake to appreciate her. "I mean—good morning."

She keeps smiling, head tilted to one side and sparing no subtlety while raking her eyes along the length of George's body. The warmth in her expression transfers over to him, unfurls pleasantly in his stomach.

"George," he introduces himself, desperate to avoid making the same mistake he had with Nathan.

Almost a week after moving in, George had run into Nathan by pure chance, returning the cable he's been carrying around since and making sure to introduce himself.

"Mia—I live a few floors up," she says, touching his arm. "And *you* must be why I saw all those boxes in the recycling."

Again she looks him over, and George cannot fathom what she finds so interesting. His job has no dress code, and he looks scruffy, hair barely brushed, and hoodie pulled on to cover the worst of the creases in his button-up shirt. Mia looks *phenomenal*; slim jeans and sleeveless turtleneck really work for her.

"Sorry," George says honestly, struggling to think of something interesting to say. "I'm not good with mornings."

Coffee might be good, but true to form, he slept through all his alarms and left himself no time to grab something on the way to the office.

"Maybe I should set four alarms," George mumbles, rubbing his eye again.

Mia laughs as beautifully as last time. Being the cause of it fills him with enough pride to see him through the rest of the day. Even when his foot catches on a divot in the pavement as they step out of the building together. At least he doesn't fall all the way to the ground.

The slam of the taxi door is loud on the quiet streets, and George wobbles as he leans down to speak through the rolled-down back window.

"Text me when you're home," George insists.

Martha nods, waving him away. "Go to bed—you got drunker since we left, I swear."

"I'm fine," George tells her. He *feels* fine. The unsteady legs could be because Martha insisted on so much *dancing*. "Congrats again!"

Quite seriously and over the annoyed sigh of the driver, Martha presses her hands together and intones, "May neither of us ever work retail again."

George laughs, lightly tapping the roof of the taxi as he steps back, and Martha is whisked away into the night. Martha will be fine. She'll message him in a few minutes, and if she doesn't, he'll come right back downstairs and—

"George?"

Mia's voice makes him whirl around, too abruptly for how much wine he drank, and he barely manages to avoid falling on his ass. Mia seems to have that effect on him.

"Hello, handsome," Mia drawls, shuffling over to him.

Nervously, George drags his hand through his hair, long since flattened out of its style by sweat and humidity. Earlier he felt confident, but the once-bolstering cling of his jeans now feels uncomfortable, highlighting the parts of him he prefers hidden. George saw Mia this morning—he runs into Mia *most* mornings—and somehow, she looks even *better* now. Dressed down in faded jeans and an oversized shirt unbuttoned over a tank top. There's paint on her arms and cheek, even up into her hair, a pale smear over one little space bun.

George still doesn't know what she does for money—she *must* be an artist, right?

"How are you awake?" George blurts.

Mia just shrugs, the most subdued he's ever seen her. She swings forward an almost-sheer plastic bag that George is certain wasn't there before. It's gone three in the morning; presumably Mia has been to the outrageously expensive convenience store at the end of the street.

"I keep odd hours," Mia explains. "Hungry?"

George isn't, but when Mia offers him an individually wrapped ice cream cone from the plastic bag, he takes it.

A few seconds late he says, "Thanks."

Gently, Mia touches his arm, encouraging him to follow her inside. The lobby lights are turned low, but not off, the brightest glow coming from the strip light inlaid into the recess above the mailboxes. It lights up the clock in such an *off* way, George thinks it's creepier than if they had the lights off completely.

"Third floor?" Mia asks, tapping for both this and the round, silver six.

George didn't notice them entering the elevator at all; he might be a little worse off than he thought.

"Did you have a nice night?"

George nods, takes some of the ice cream on his tongue, and the shock of cold is enough to clear some fog from his brain.

"She got a new job," George explains. "Martha—" He pauses, looking at Mia to catch her nod. He's mentioned Martha before. "We're celebrating."

"You deserve a night out," Mia says, her hand on his arm again. "You always seem to be working."

"It's not so bad," George argues with no real effort.

They're about the same height, but sometimes Mia wears little wedge heels and George has to look *up* to meet her eye. He can't say he minds it either way.

The noise of the lift opening makes George jump, but he doesn't think to leave it until Mia laughs. She does it so easily, but George can't get enough, thinks he could listen to her amusement forever without getting bored.

"Need a hand?"

George shakes his head. "I think I better get to bed."

"Not going to see you today, am I?" Mia asks, giving him a little push to get him moving. Again, George shakes his head, looking at her once he's in the hallway. Something cool drips over his fingers, reminding him of Mia's gift. The way she looks at him when he takes another bite is fonder that he's any right to.

Mia waves as the doors slide shut, her voice so sweet she almost sings her parting words.

"I'll miss you!"

Generally, George tries not to waste too much money on takeaway coffee, only indulges on days when he's absolutely struggling at work. After his night out with Martha, however, he makes an exception. The walk down the block feels less horrifying than filling up his own kettle.

The bell above the door tinkles, and it's a surprise, but not a disappointment, when he spots *Nathan* at the counter, talking to the young girl setting pastries into a box on his behalf.

Nathan cuts an impressive figure even out of his fine suits; dark jeans and a leather jacket highlight the breadth of his shoulders. Nathan is too preoccupied to notice George, which is fine by him because it gives him a chance to just *look* at Nathan without embarrassing himself.

Since when has he been so *tall*?

"Good morning," calls a second employee, approaching the counter.

Nathan turns on reflex, barely sparing George a glance then twisting back so fast that George worries about his neck. Nathan never really *grins*, but this comes close, his gaze *intense* enough to make George almost squirm where he's standing.

"George," Nathan says, almost *breathless*. "I didn't expect— What are you getting?"

"Oh, I—just my usual I guess," George stammers.

Nathan beckons him with a single flick of his green eyes, and George drifts closer as though pulled by a string.

"And whatever George's usual is," Nathan tells the employee. "Please."

"What? No—it's okay."

"Don't worry about it," Nathan dismisses, settling his hand softly on George's back. "My treat."

George attempts another protest, but Nathan cuts him off. Sensing the creeping discomfort of the server, George rattles off his milk-heavy coffee preference and points out his favourite pastry.

"Good week?" Nathan asks, clutching his box of pastries while they stand to one side for their drinks to be made.

"I guess," George says, shrugging one shoulder. "Living alone is different than I expected."

"Too quiet?" Nathan guesses.

Again, George shrugs, wishing he wasn't so hopelessly tongue-tied. Nathan is always so attentive, asking how he is and if he's getting on okay. Like he has some kind of vested interest in George's wellbeing.

"Martha was pretty quiet," George explains. He's talked about her with Nathan, too. Nathan's smile is always more obvious in his face than in the shape of his mouth, and George feels special every time he spots it.

Stupid. George never learns, never gets *attached* to the appropriate people. A crush on Nathan—*and* Mia, for god's sake—falls somewhere on his shit-scale between dating Martha's sister and falling head over heels for the guy in the bedroom next to him at university. The wall between their bedrooms had been roughly three sheets of paper thick and it was immediately apparent when he moved on, even though he neglected to tell George.

"Living alone is a big change—you're doing great," Nathan says, because he doesn't know George fell asleep with a pizza in the oven last week.

At least the smell is mostly gone.

Their coffee arrives before George can do anything overly embarrassing.

Nathan hand lingers on George's when he hands it over; it makes a lead *brick* fall into George's stomach when Nathan turns to pick up the *two* drinks.

It makes sense that Nathan isn't single. George should have expected that.

"I'll walk you back," Nathan offers, and George shakes his head, trying to draw on his limited good sense.

"I'm heading out," George lies. "But thanks—I appreciate it."

The disappointed set of Nathan's mouth must be George's imagination.

"—you're exaggerating."

"I'm not," George insists, tucking the phone between his cheek and his shoulder while he unlocks his mailbox. "Everyone in this building is stupidly hot."

"There are *worse* things to deal with," Martha says.

George acknowledges her with a vague noise, blindly searching his mailbox. Impossible for him to see in there properly without employing some kind of step.

Martha keeps talking, but judging from the way she barely takes a breath, it's okay that he's not paying attention. George has received a delivery notice, but clearly the package isn't in here. It takes a few seconds of fumbling before his finger catches on the edge of a sharp card.

In alcove is scrawled sideways across the card.

George rocks back onto his heels with such a rough sigh that Martha cuts off her monologue.

"*What*?"

"Denied delivery on grounds of height," George mumbles. "I don't *need* new shoes."

"Why don't you get one of your hot neighbours to help," Martha laughs.

"Oh sure," George deadpans. "I'll go find one of the hottest people I've ever met and—" George cuts off with an unfortunate sound when a hand brushes against the base of his spine.

"Easy, short stuff," says a steady, familiar voice.

"I'll call you back," George blurts into his phone, cutting off Martha's *squeal.*

Nathan crowds against his back, easily grasping the edge of the package. He steps back the moment he has the parcel in hand, and George feels suddenly cold.

"I'm not short," George says, turning to face him.

Apparently saying *thank you* is overrated.

"Or course not."

"I'm *not*," George insists. He's not *tall* but saying short is *rude*. If one cares about that kind of thing—which George unfortunately does.

"It's not a bad thing," Nathan cajoles. He reaches out with his empty hand like he's going to tuck the hair hanging in front of George's face behind his ear. Nathan lets his fingertips brush against the mussed strands, then reaches over George's shoulder to slam his mailbox shut.

"Thank you," George says, finally.

Nathan shakes his head, pushing the parcel awkwardly into George's hands. His lips press into a flat line, leeching all the colour out of them.

"Are you—?"

"You should come over for dinner," Nathan interrupts.

"Dinner?" George repeats. He remembers the second coffee cup in Nathan's hand.

Nathan's expression eases into a smile. "I'll make food, you'll come up to the apartment and eat it," Nathan says. "I assume you eat."

"I eat," George confirms.

"Well, that's a relief," Nathan says. Being teased doesn't sting like it normally does. "Thursday?"

"Thursday works," George says. "It's a date?"

The intention is to sound confident, to state rather than ask, but Nathan smiles so broadly his eyes actually crinkle a little at the corners.

"It's a date," he confirms.

George nods, goes to make a break for it with a wave, so convinced he's done something embarrassing his cheeks *burn*. Anxiety turns over his stomach, and George makes it to the doors before Nathan calls him back.

"I live in 608, okay?" Nathan says, watching as George back through the doors. "Come by about seven."

"Seven," George repeats. "Okay—see you."

It's a shame George is too *confused* the first time he hears Nathan laughing outright to really enjoy it. The safety of the elevator beckons him, but Mia is revealed on the other side, pretty as ever and moving towards him in a single breath. Seeing her doesn't fill George with regret, exactly, nor anything quite like it, but there is something not altogether pleasant unfurling in his chest.

"Hi," Mia greets, usual brightness dimming the moment she takes him in. "Are you okay?"

"I'm fine," George says, forcing his legs to work and take him inside. "I'm just—um."

"Get some rest," Mia suggests kindly, brushing his arm as they pass each other. George manages a smile, and she adds, "We'll see you soon."

It takes George so long to decide what to wear that he skips right over being too early and barely avoids being late. He tugs at his shirt, utterly unconvinced by his choice, while he waits for Nathan to answer his door. His near-meltdown the other day is starting to feel a little embarrassing. George is more than happy to be here, embarrassingly eager for this to go well.

The door opens before George can dwell on it too long.

"Mia?"

"Hey, handsome," she says, smiling. For once her long legs are exposed; she's wearing an embroidered black dress.

"Sorry," George blurts. "I must be in the wrong place."

But he's so sure he has the right apartment number, had double-, triple-checked it before he knocked on the door.

Mia simply laughs, grabbing him by the wrist to drag him into the apartment in a way he's powerless to resist.

"I'm meant to be…" George starts to explain, but his eyes catch on a picture hanging in the entryway and he immediately forgets his train of thought.

Nathan and Mia. Together. Nathan facing the camera, in a suit even fancier than his workwear, with Mia on his arm, angled to display her nearly backless wedding dress.

George feels nauseated. How oblivious is he? How did he never realise?

Mia tugs him farther inside, not giving him time to catch his breath. It's remarkably similar to his own flat, a little larger and with an extra door for the second bedroom. The living space *smells* incredible, savoury steam drifting towards him and Mia from the kitchen on the other side of the space.

Mia says something, but George can barely hear her over the weird *hum* in his ears. They go straight into the kitchenette where *Nathan* is cooking with his shirt sleeves rolled to his elbows.

"Here he is," Mia sings. "Right on time."

Nathan wipes his hands off on the *apron* he's wearing, rounding the kitchen island to close the space between them in a few strides.

There's a *wedding* ring on Nathan's finger. George has got to pay better attention to what's going on around him.

"You made it," Nathan says, kind of breathless, *relieved,* as though George's journey was farther than three floors.

Nathan wraps an arm around him for a brief hug, nosing into his hair in something *like* a kiss before pushing it behind George's ear with a gentle hand. When Nathan pulls back, George blinks up at him. He wonders what his face is doing to make Nathan's brows notch together like that.

"You're married," George blurts.

Mia squeezes his wrist, and Nathan smooths back George's hair again, glancing briefly at his *wife*.

George is too confused to think of a good lie and lands somewhere in the realm of embarrassing honesty without second guessing himself. "I thought you were asking me on a date."

Nathan's cheek twitches, but Mia completely fails to hide her amusement, snickering at his side.

"I was," Nathan says.

"But—you're married," George reiterates.

"Uh, yeah," Mia says.

"I don't—"

"*We* asked you out on a date," Mia says.

George swings his gaze back and forth between them, both of them looking at *him,* intent and a little nervous, if he's learnt to read them correctly.

"Both of you?"

Nathan lets himself *grin* for once, brushes the backs of his fingers over George's cheek. "Both of us," Nathan confirms.

"Oh," George says. "That's—*huh*. Wow."

Mia lets go of his wrist but doesn't go far, just presses herself against George's back and wraps her arms around him. She sets her forehead on his shoulder, and for the first time her voice is low, almost guarded.

"Oh darling, we adore you."

George tries to speak and comes up short. He manages to pet across Mia's bare arm, and she squeezes him so tight a little of the air leaves his lungs.

"Stay for dinner?" Nathan asks. "And we can talk about it."

"It smells good," George says.

"I do all the cooking," Nathan says proudly, and he starts to back away, gesturing into the kitchen.

"I just burn things," Mia admits.

"Oh, same," George breathes.

They insist on taking him *out* for a second date, and it's *fine*—fancy—but George only really enjoys *them* and the way they end up tangled against his apartment door.

Mia kisses with the same enthusiasm she brings to everything, and George does his best to return everything she gives. It's hard, though, with Nathan tall at his back, hands almost *chaste* where they rest at George's hips.

George is on the cusp of inviting them inside, wondering how much of a *mess* he left everything, when Nathan gives a sharp tug on his hips, and he's dragged out of Mia's grasp.

"Hey," she complains, adorably petulant.

"If I'm not allowed to kiss George after our first date, you're not allowed to debase him against his front door after our second," Nathan says, and he steps to the side, keeping his hand on George's arm. It's probably obvious how unsteady George's legs have gotten.

"You're just jealous," Mia says.

"A little," Nathan admits, and George's heart *thumps*.

"You can have a turn," Mia teases. "I'll allow it."

Nathan's expression closes off, completely unreadable for a few heartbeats, then she shakes his head, offers George a smile that's only a little strained.

"We should take it slow," Nathan suggests.

"Slow," George echoes.

He's okay with slow. He's also *not* okay with slow.

This whole situation is a little confusing, honestly; the only thing he's sure of is that he likes them both. So, so much.

Nathan kisses his forehead, almost platonic.

"Goodnight, handsome," Mia says, and George is ushered inside.

Nathan might have been the one to suggest they *slow down*, but he's also the one to push him onto their bed before the dinner he spent so long crafting has even been eaten. It's the most natural thing for George to allow Nathan the space he needs to crawl between his thighs and peel George out of his hastily ironed shirt.

A waste of effort, it turns out.

George attempts to speak and his words muffle against Nathan's mouth. When Nathan tries to pull back, though, George clinging tight, fingers digging into the muscle of Nathan's back, what George was planning to say is suddenly unimportant.

When Nathan manages to drag himself away, he's a little wide-eyed.

"Are you okay?"

"I'm—yeah," George stammers.

Colour stains Nathan's cheeks and embarrassment forces colour into George's own face, but he manages to stay resolute against the desire to turn away. Almost trembling, George drags one of his palms from Nathan's shoulder, broad and strong under his crisp shirt, down to the taper of his waist.

With a smile, Nathan shifts his weight to one hand, pecks a dry kiss against George's mouth. A hand settles against George's chest; there's no pressure, just fingers against his collarbones, but George's breath hitches unevenly.

"Yeah?" Nathan drawls. "All good?"

George nods dumbly, and Nathan takes it as permission to explore George's chest. The weight of Nathan's gaze is heavy but not unpleasant, his focus on George's reaction to each touch. Nathan notices George's sharp inhale at the first brush against his nipples, watches intensely when he brings his hand back with more purpose, rolling and pressing until George fails to hold back a shaky moan.

Nathan hums, settling his weight back down. "No need to be shy."

George doesn't have time to pretend he's not before Nathan kisses him again, nibbling the corner of his mouth and slipping his hands down his torso to grip *his* waist and press fingers to the soft part of George's hips that has always made George a little self-conscious. Nathan *groans*, a rough noise that makes George's toes curl against the mattress and wipes every thought from George's mind. He's clumsy with his affections, grasping and stuttering with every new press of Nathan's fingers and teeth.

George wants him *naked.* Now. Twenty minutes ago. He gives Nathan's shirt a rough tug, fabric bunched in his fist, and Nathan chuckles, a vibration in his chest that George feels against his palm.

"Easy now," Nathan says, barely brushing their noses together. "Whatever you want, baby, just use your words."

Baby.

The pet name pulses inside George's head, makes him feel dumb with joy, affection swelling so fast he thinks he might burst with it. Using words feels *beyond* George right now, his entire focus on the feel of Nathan's hands on his body, his cock thickening in his jeans.

Nathan lets his hand drift lower, burrowing under the tight waistband of George's jeans. George trembles, lifting his hips to Nathan's silent urging, holding as steady as his excitement allows while Nathan peels open his fly.

The loud *smack* startles George, and Nathan *moans*, biting down on George's lip with force that feels accidental. Nathan kneels back between George's legs, and Mia comes into view, climbing onto the bed in nothing but her underclothes and unbothered by Nathan's glare. Her lingerie isn't anything special, just black cotton trimmed with cute lace.

"Hi babe," Mia teases, flexing her hand. "Getting carried away?"

Nathan *huffs*, tilting his head towards where he has George supine before him.

"Completely understandable," Mia laughs. "Off—you're no good to us like this."

Nathan pecks her on the mouth then turns to leave three parting kisses down the centre of George's torso as he backs off the bed.

"Get him naked," Nathan calls over the rustling of his own shirt.

"Oh *gladly*," Mia drawls, and then she's right *there*. Straddling George's thigh and leaning down over him.

"Hi," George blurts, and she smiles softly, pressing closer.

She's less careful about how she pins George down, but so, *so* soft under George's hands.

"You're beautiful," George says honestly, and Mia freezes with her head tilted ready for a kiss.

"Thank you," Mia mumbles, like the compliment surprises her.

George gently grips her shoulders, pulling her closer so they can kiss at an easy angle. Mia sighs, relaxing into it, her thighs gripping tightly around George, more of her weight pressing him down. Petting across her back, George tucks his fingers under the straps of her bra until she arches into him. Hoping eagerness means more to her than finesse, he works the clasp open and drags the straps down her arms. Mia doesn't stop kissing him to pull her bra free, just drops it off the edge of the bed.

Mia flattens herself over him, grinding softly against George's thigh. Her skin is cool, almost cold, and George shivers a little when her bare breasts crush into his chest. He chafes his hands against her arms, feeling her smile against his mouth, and tastes a laugh that's almost a *giggle* with her contentment. The sound relaxes him, her joy infectious and calming.

"I can't wait to watch Nathan take you apart," Mia mumbles, dropping a kiss to his chin.

"What?"

"Nathan's been talking about it for *weeks*," Mia stresses.

"About—me?"

"Uh huh," Mia says.

"Who else?" Nathan calls.

"Has it all planned out in his head," Mia explains. "Might make him kind of intense. That okay?"

It's *more* than okay. More confident now, George runs his hands over her, clutching and groping as he goes. His palm curves perfectly around where her ass meets thigh, and she makes the prettiest little noise when he digs his thumb into the thickest part of her. George gently plays with the hem of her underwear, and after a slow grind, she eases off, twists about to kick them all the way off when George pushes them to the top of her thighs. She settles back naturally between his thighs, and George drags her up by the arms so he can kiss down from her mouth to her neck and across the top of her chest. She's warmer now, and he nuzzles into her, working his way down the slope of her breast.

"*Now* who's distracted?" Nathan cuts in.

The bed dips.

Mia retreats with a laugh before George can mouth at her nipple. "Oops," Mia says, utterly unapologetic.

Nathan towers behind her, pushing George's hands off Mia's body so he can grab her hips himself and roll her almost carelessly to George's side. She settles with another laugh, scooting herself towards the pillow to prop up on her arm, curling towards George's body but not touching him.

Nathan slips back between George's legs before he can start to feel awkward, dropping lube and foil packets onto the bed so he can settle atop him again. He kisses a return path identical to how he left, under and beneath George's belly button, then directly in the centre of his chest. Nathan's hands curl into the waistband of his unbuttoned jeans, and George raises his hips, but Nathan hesitates, looking up at George with his chin propped on his chest.

"Okay?"

George bobs his head eagerly, and Nathan smiles, eyes crinkling, but doesn't yank George's jeans and underwear down like he's expecting.

"He needs actual words, handsome," Mia says.

George swallows. "Please," he blurts, trying and failing at the first hurdle to avoid *begging*. "Yes, please."

Nathan strips him bare in what feels like three efficient jerks of his arms, denim, and underwear thudding to the floor a second after George's cock slaps down against his belly, heavy and tacky at the tip from being long ignored. Now it's only Nathan wearing anything, but George quickly loses the breath to complain when a delicate hand wraps around his cock.

"Fuck," he gasps.

It's Mia's hand, but Nathan is the one *staring* at him, breaths heavy and slightly uneven. George has thought about Nathan being intense before, but it's altogether something different to be the sole focus of it, to have that layered on top of something that is already almost too much. Two sets of hands and eyes, two people that obviously *desire* him in a palpable way.

George has never felt like this before.

Mia rubs her thumb over his cock head, uses that slickness to ease her movements as she strokes him back and forth, grip a little loose and movements slow. Still staring, Nathan pushes George's thighs farther apart, pressing his fingers to the sensitive skin behind his knees and dragging them slowly towards his groin. George's breath comes embarrassingly loud, moans building in the back of his throat as pleasure unfurls low in his belly.

"You want a taste?" Mia says, and George can't quite make sense of it, not at first, not until the heat of Nathan's mouth is suddenly right there, tongue sweeping over the head of his cock, lapping up the dampness with a high, needy noise.

"Oh fuck, oh fuck, oh fuck," George babbles.

Mia laughs.

Nathan's mouth bumps Mia's hand, and she lets him go. George is desperate for something to hold on to, some way to transfer a little of this *tension* elsewhere. He thinks about burying a hand in Nathan's hair as he steadily descends over George's dick, but Mia beats him to it, fine fingers tangling amongst dark strands with such an obvious *grip* that George loses more breath. His hands scramble at the sheets, eventually bumping Mia's soft thigh. George tries to grip her softly, but his fingers tense with every intense pulse of pleasure.

Nathan's mouth is hot and very wet, the noise obscene in the quiet bedroom. Mia coos, at which of them George can't be sure, shushing George specifically with a pet name and a glancing kiss to his shoulder when the noise that leaves his mouth is entirely *whine*. Nathan's hands clench on the back of George's thighs, and that punches yet another noise out of him.

George wants this to last forever, wants to be rolled over onto his belly so Nathan can *fuck* him, wants to get his own mouth on Nathan and then Mia, wants to do everything and anything with them all at once. Thinking about everything else is too much, too fast, makes his belly clench and his balls draw up even though it's only been a *minute*. Restlessly, George's heels scrape against their fine bed sheets, and Nathan's mouth pulls off of him in one go. Both of them are panting, George's eyes squeezing shut, head digging back against the pillow as he tries to remember what it's like to breathe without cognitive thought.

Mia's mouth brushes George's ear when she asks, "Can Nathan fuck you?"

"Um."

"Please," Nathan whispers, still so close to George's cock, held back only by Mia's grip in his hair. His breath falls over George like a caress.

George nods, then tries to find his voice. "Yes."

Nathan rears back in a heartbeat, settling on his heels and digging amongst the sheets for the items he discarded earlier. The *snap* of the lube bottle lid seems to echo in the room.

"Should I roll over?" George asks. He always has before, but Nathan shakes his head so vehemently that George almost bites his tongue.

"He wants to watch you," Mia explains, kissing his shoulder again.

Nathan makes no verbal response.

George turns his head and catches Mia's mouth with his own.

"What about you?" George asks her. "I should—I *want*…"

Mia grins, explaining, "I want to *watch*."

"But—"

Mia takes George's hand from her thigh and drags it up, presses his fingers against where she's hot and wet. George does his best, despite the awkward angle, to seek out her clit, to try and give her *something*, lightly rolling his fingertips over her sex until she gasps.

"See," Mia says, immediately breathless. "I'm having oodles of fun."

Any grand plan George might have to keep his movements up are quickly shot when Nathan starts touching him again. He cups over George's cock with a dry hand at the same moment slick fingers press between his cheeks. George tilts his hips up, presses into the touch, and Nathan *grunts*.

George tries to breathe, to *relax*, to make Nathan's job easier, but it doesn't seem to matter when he can't manage. Nathan's gaze flits between George's entrance and his face, lingering between his thighs each time George feels the extra pressure of his body giving way for more of Nathan's fingers.

There's not so much *confidence* in Nathan's fingers as eagerness, working him up inside and out, thorough in a way George has never experienced. George trembles through each stroke, clenching his jaw and trying not to lose it over and over again every time he's stretched wider.

"Beautiful," Nathan mutters, three fingers deep and thumb pressing against George's taint. "Perfect. You're—fuck, George." The noise from between George's thighs is *wet*, the slickness of it obscene, even when Nathan slows down, even when he leaves George briefly empty then feeds his fingers back in one at a time.

"Nathan," George blurts. "I'm— Please Nathan." George feels like he's been ready for hours—weeks.

Nathan laughs, but it sounds hollow, a little raw, like the noise is being dragged out of him over gravel. George tries to offer comfort even as he's holding on by a thread himself, strokes his calf up Nathan's thigh and over his hip.

"You're not even *naked*," George complains, rubbing his ankle against the soft cotton of his clinging boxers.

This time, Nathan's laugh is more genuine. He grabs George's leg, raises it up to kiss his ankle at the exact moment he *crooks* his fingers. George's vision temporarily whites out, and when he blinks back to reality, he's achingly empty, dick drooling against his stomach.

Mia shifts closer, pressing against the side of his body. Slowly she drags his hand from between her thighs, wrapping his own damp fingers around his cock and starting to move them back and forth at an aching pace. She hooks her leg over one of his, pulls it towards her so he's splayed wider than before. As George turns to kiss her, to thank her, to let her know he *wants* her, there's a telltale crinkle of foil.

"Easy, handsome," Mia says, squeezing his hand into a firm grip around the base of his cock.

Nathan pushes back on George's thigh, tilting his hips up and back. He wraps his free leg around Nathan as best he can, noting that still Nathan hasn't pulled off his underwear. George would huff about it, complain all over again, but Nathan is at his entrance again, cock pressing against but not into him.

"Nathan," Mia says, sounding as desperate as George feels. "Babe—come on."

George is eternally grateful to her for voicing what he is currently unable to. And for clenching her hand around his again, helping him fight back the almost overwhelming feel of Nathan pressing inside him.

The noise George makes is loud, lasts longer than it takes for Nathan to work his full length into George's body. Mia mouths over his jaw, nips gently at his skin, and murmurs something he can't work out. Nathan breathes heavily, not quite groaning but making *some* kind of noise, a low rumble that warms George from the inside out. Allows him to relax enough to accept Nathan into his body.

Nathan's brow is furrowed, staring down at where they're coming together, his hair in disarray, sweat dampened at the root. He looks *beautiful* like this, red with exertion, eyes dark and unwavering from George's face.

"Kiss me?" George begs, desperate for more, even as Nathan fills him perfectly, as his cock drags over his prostate and his thighs *smack* against George's skin with the force of his thrusts.

Mia moves, levering up on one arm, grip going slack around his cock as she seals their mouths together. She all but *licks* into him, and it's not necessarily what he was asking for but it's *good*, it's better, Mia's soft body pressed against his, weighing him down onto the mattress as Nathan continues to move inside him. Absentmindedly, George resumes stroking himself, trying to relieve some of the mounting pressure. Pleasure surrounds him from all angles. It's so much—not quite too much, but more than he had been anticipating.

Mia pets across his chest, scratches her nails against his collarbones, and moans softly.

"I—shit," George blurts. The pit in his stomach *burns*, his muscles almost painful with how tightly he's clenched.

For a second Nathan stops, pushes again on George's knee until he's folded almost in half. George hiccups, almost sobbing with relief when Nathan starts up again, rolling his hips strong and steady.

"George," Nathan grits out, words sounding like they're half trapped behind his teeth. "Are you—?"

"Yeah, yeah, yeah," George chants. His hand is slick with pre-come. The sound of him jerking off is muffled by Nathan's thrusts, by the creak of the bed moving beneath him, by Mia panting into his ear. "Nathan—I need…"

"What is it, baby?" Nathan insists. "Tell me—tell me."

"Don't stop," George cries, his eyes watering with the intensity of everything.

It's the only thing he really needs, for this to last a *little* longer. Everything is perfect, everything is too much, George is tense and strung out, he's teetering on the edge, a hair away from—

"Please," Mia whispers. "Come on—show us how much you like it."

Wetness creeps from the corner of his eye as he comes; the noise he makes cuts off halfway with no air in his lungs to see it through. There's only a half second for him to catch his breath, to try and slam himself down to Earth, before Nathan is pulling out of his body with a rough curse.

"Fu-*uck*," Nathan groans.

Mia collapses onto her back beside him, and George blinks, focuses on Nathan between his thighs, hand moving fast over his freshly bare cock.

Nathan doesn't cry out when he comes. He just mumbles something under his breath and *gasps*, eyes fluttering closed as he adds a hot splatter of his own mess to George's stomach. Mia moans softly, whimpering in a way that throws Nathan into action before George can even *blink*.

A hand hooks under Mia's knee, yanking her down the bed. Her leg drapes over George's again, and it gives him the presence of mind necessary to caress the silk soft skin of her inner thigh as Nathan slips fingers inside her and her own hand goes to her clit.

"Jesus, Mia," Nathan groans.

"Just—yeah," she groans. "Like that, Nath. Yeah—oh my *god*."

"Kiss her," Nathan demands.

George twists over to do so, clumsily bumping their mouths together. A little too much teeth, probably, but Mia whines prettily against his mouth, arching to let him kiss her as deeply as he could ever need.

Mia trembles, the muscles in her thigh twitching and shivering as she goes clumsy too, almost stops kissing him back, pants against his mouth as Nathan fills her up with his fingers and she works herself over the edge.

Mia moans through her release, and it's the sweetest thing George has ever tasted against his tongue. Nathan collapses on his other side, pressing a kiss to his sweat-damp shoulder.

"All good?"

"I—*fuck*," George chokes. "Yeah. Yeah—all good."

George is definitely going to be late for work, but it's actually not his fault for once. Not *entirely* his fault, anyway.

The elevator ride downstairs seems to take *forever*, but he's rewarded for his efforts by coming across Mia clutching coffee and Danishes in the lobby.

"You start so *early*," Mia pouts, blocking his path.

"Agreed," George says around a yawn.

"At least you'll have breakfast for once," Mia says, an actual *angel* when she passes him a large coffee out of her tray.

"A lifesaver," George tells her.

"Nathan still asleep?"

George's cheeks burn, still flustered after several *months* of this happening.

"He's asleep *now*," George says carefully.

Mia laughs. "Conked right out after you were done, huh?"

"Yeah," George says. "He's already showered, though."

"Go to buy my boys a treat and I miss all the fun," Mia says, pouting again.

George drops a kiss to her full bottom lip, lingering as long as he dares when they could be interrupted at any moment.

"I'll make it up to you later," George promises.

"You better."

Wintersong

Alex Bauer

aftercare, alcohol use (casual), aromantic, artist, blow job, christmas, cunnilingus, dom drop (minor), dom/sub (background), established relationship, f/m/m/nb, f/nb, friends to lovers, hair pulling (minor), huddling for warmth, kissing, m/m, modern, non-binary, omg they were roommates, open relationship, pain play (mentions of), pining (mutual), present tense, third person limited point of view, trans male, twosome + twosome = foursome, united states of america, vaginal fingering

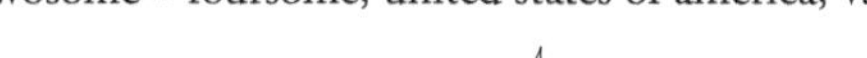

Late November nights are made for silence. Snow dances gently down to the Duluth backstreets, swaddling the world in white while frost nips at the windows and does its best to steal through the poorly angled second-story porch door. The sky is gray, city lights reflecting from the clouds and falling back to Earth. Wind rattles the siding—soon, the old house will need new clothes.

Cam Woods stares blankly out across the small backyard and curls their fingers in the blanket draped over their lap. The blue TV light shimmers across the ball Skylar has made of herself next to them; it's a beautiful contrast to the fresh welts and bruises blooming on her thighs. Her breath flutters the hair that's fallen into her face as her fingers twitch against her stomach. She's curled up in one of Cam's old sweatshirts, clutching at the cuffs like a lifeline as she stirs briefly, and they slide a hand up the heated outer curve of her thigh to tease at the hem. It earns them a disgruntled "Fuck off" before Skylar cracks an eye.

"It's *cold*, you ass," she grumbles. Her gaze is bleary but not unkind as she laces her fingers with theirs and brings them to her lips. When she glances at the TV, she snorts. "The Grinch? We haven't even hit December yet."

"You're sitting on the remote and I refuse to get up and change the channel myself," Cam says. They quirk their lips in a lopsided smile. "Don't like watching your old family videos?"

"Yeah, just call me Cindy Lou."

"We both know green's more your color."

Skylar dumps their hand unceremoniously, but they catch a smile as she yanks the hood over her face and shifts to rest her head on their thigh. Her hair spills out of her shelter like an oil slick: thick and dark and impossible to maneuver in without causing an accident. When she looks up, she's pasted on the world's most unconvincing pout. "You're a mean one, Cam."

"Mm, but you like it when I'm mean." Cam tugs gently on her hair before inching their fingers inside of the hood to massage her scalp. Her sigh is a beautiful sound, satisfied and still rasping from Cam's earlier abuse of her throat. The contentment settles easily throughout them, soothing the burrs prickling at the back of their mind about being too much, too hard, too violent.

The wind kicks up in the minutes before Skylar speaks again. When she does, she props herself up on one elbow planted dangerously close to their balls. "Have you asked Parker to do a shoot for you yet?"

Cam purses their lips, sucks in a breath through their teeth. "Thought about it."

It's not a lie. They *did* consider it while staring at Parker grading papers across the dinner table, got too into the fantasy of him haloed in silver light and snow, and immediately discarded the idea upon realizing that the fluttering in their stomach was not, in fact, the two-day expired hamburger they'd risked for lunch. Parker would make a beautiful subject, and Cam knows he'd make a fine addition to their portfolio.

The feelings that have cropped up around the whole idea of alone time with Parker make the prospect much less appealing—*want* is not something they're prepared to pick at right now, in the middle of their busy season.

Skylar tuts and pokes their forehead, then mashes her thumb into the furrow between their brow. "Ask," she drawls, drawing out the word until it's nearly uncomfortable. "He can't say yes to Cam Time if you don't offer it."

"How was asking Adrian on a date, like you said you would last weekend?"

She had not asked; Cam has pointedly saved that little prod for a rainy—or snowy, tonight—day.

"That's—"

"—absolutely no different." Cam pokes her back and bends down so they're forehead to forehead, then squashes her cheeks with both hands, ignoring her huff. "You are a coward, I am a coward, and here we are, whining together while they're out at the bar."

"We're killing it," Skylar says, though it comes out muffled and warped. When Cam lets go of her face, she rubs it against their chest and adjusts so she's sitting in their lap, both arms around their shoulders as she makes a face at the TV. "He's been complaining about being single for *ages*, Cam—just go for it."

"Yeah, but the"—Cam winds their hands in a vague gesture—"roommate weirdness."

"You've done far weirder to me."

"*You* are different. We have history," Cam says. They nuzzle into the hollow below her jaw and press a kiss to her pulse. "And I don't have to explain to you that hey, I love you and I want you, but please allow five to ten business days for romantic reciprocation. You just…get it."

"He is kind of a sap, isn't he?"

Cam snorts. "*Kind* of like Adrian's kind of a nerd. Ah—" They hold a finger to her lips when she makes to protest. "You've seen his merch collections; you can't deny it's true."

"Pent-up nerd. He upped his testosterone recently and he is, in his words, 'stupid horny.'"

Sticking their hands into Skylar's sweatshirt pocket and pulling her close, Cam says, "Babe, if he was complaining to you about it, that was your chance. Should've gotten in there."

"God, I just want him to get into *me*." Skylar slumps against them, legs falling ever so slightly open in offering before the back door opens and booted footsteps stumble into the entry hall. They both freeze but relax when Parker's familiar tenor shushes Adrian's whining about the cold. Winter gear hits the ground in a thudding clamor. Cam is seconds away from saying fuck it and suggesting they actually do get to bed when the rustling stops and Adrian moans.

Skylar snaps to attention so fast she nearly nails Cam's chin with her head, and it is only through several years of dealing with her ability to cause them bodily harm via excitement that they avoid it. "Are they—?"

Parker murmurs something; Cam doesn't strain to hear exactly what. They do, however, very clearly hear the "Yeah" and the "Right there" Adrian lets out from somewhere in the vicinity of the kitchen.

"Oh my God," Skylar whispers, clapping a hand over her mouth, eyes widening in delight. "Since when have they been fooling around?"

"News to me," Cam says. They hook their chin over her shoulder and drag a finger lightly up the inside of her thigh, relishing the shiver the action draws out. "'S the thought gettin' you all hot and bothered?"

"Like it's *just* me." Skylar grinds down against their filling cock before pulling their hand between her legs and cupping it against her. "I think," she sighs, canting her hips into their palm, "maybe we should ask them if they want to share."

"Yeah?"

"Parker stares at you sometimes. Just caught him the other day." She winds a hand back into their hair, and bright sparks of pleasure skitter through them when she tugs. The heat of her cunt rocks back against their cock. "You'd gotten home from the gym all gross, and Christ, he looked like he wanted to lick the sweat off you. Kind of a turn-on, actually."

Cam teases her underwear to the side and slides two fingers into her folds, teasing along the edges of her hole until her breath hitches. "You're a needy little slut today, aren't you? Three orgasms wasn't enough?" they say. "Maybe we should go join 'em. Show off how well you took your punishment today." They squeeze the underside of her thigh with their free hand, and she hisses at the pressure against the crop marks. "Show 'em how good I make you feel."

"Cam, please," she gasps just as a loud cry from downstairs is followed by a drunkenly dramatic hush.

With a huff of laughter, Cam buries their face in her neck and teases no further. Skylar is easy to pick apart, especially on the tail end of extended aftercare: hook your fingers deep, let her ride your palm, rake your nails across her skin, and she falls to pieces.

They swallow down her cries when she comes, kissing her deep until she breaks away with a sharp groan and squirm of overstimulation. When she reaches back to stick a hand down their sweatpants, they shake their head and adjust themself. Skylar is easy; they are not. "'M good for tonight," they say. "Is—? Would you like that? All of us?"

"I think it could be fun," Skylar murmurs against their cheek. Then, she leans back and sticks a hand out between them. "Solemnly swear to tease the hell out of them before bringing it up, but we *will* see if they're game."

Cam swallows their nerves, takes her hand, and shakes. "Let's do it."

Dawn creeps slowly across the city the next morning. Cam sits alone in the kitchen with their coffee, savoring the quiet creaking of the house in the moments before chatter fills the halls. They've got no plans—work they *could* do, but nothing pressing—save for catching up on the sleep they missed last night. After bundling Skylar into her bed, they'd lain awake for hours, staring up at the ceiling and mulling over the pros and cons of following through with the bargain.

Pros: everyone already gets along well, they've all got their roles in the house sorted, and everyone seems to have some shade of interest in one another…plus, it's not like all four haven't brought a string of outsiders home during the years they've been living together; the only rule is "no fucking in public spaces."

Cons: the whole situation feels like a Goddamned sitcom episode.

They prop their feet up on the empty chair across from them and mutter as much into their mug before registering movement in the hallway. Adrian slips out of Parker's room and clicks the door shut behind him, padding into the kitchen and looking every bit like a mauling victim when Cam turns around to look at him. They arch a brow as they take in the dark marks littering his neck and chest, some accompanied by what look to be actual bites, but Adrian bears them without shame as he putters around, making his coffee in silence.

Cam does not speak until he's settled across from them. "Rough night?"

"Satisfying." Adrian's eyes crinkle over the rim of his mug.

"Good."

"I, ah…" Adrian leans back in his chair, a small smile playing across his lips, and takes a deep breath. "Were we loud?"

Cam shrugs and hums noncommittally. "Happy you had a good night, but we did hear you."

"Sorry."

"Don't be." Cam sets their mug on the table, then purses their lips. "Skylar was quite interested."

Eyes snapping up, Adrian says, "Really?"

"Ask her about it."

"Yeah, maybe," Adrian sighs. He rubs the back of his neck sheepishly. "I've actually been meaning to talk to you about her. Would you mind if I—" He bites the rest of the sentence off and freezes.

Cam looks back to see Skylar leaning against the wall, still wearing Cam's sweatshirt and what appears to be the world's shortest pair of athletic shorts. Purple has blossomed across her thighs, in sharp contrast to her milk-white skin. Baring her teeth in a wolfish grin, she whistles and gives several slow claps as she ambles stiffly forward. "Damn, did you come home with a fucking badger last night?"

Adrian flushes crimson all the way down to the scars on his chest before gesturing wildly at her legs. "Depends. Were you…shit—riding? Jockey?"

"*Impressive* fumble," Cam says.

"I thought we were having a friendship moment," Adrian hisses. "Back me up."

"Friendship means I get free rein to tease you when you flop." Cam leans back in their chair and crosses their arms, grinning when Adrian rolls his eyes with a muttered curse.

Skylar ruffles his bedhead before bending low, lips brushing his ear. "Who knew Parker had it in him?"

Adrian turns impossibly redder. "*Skylar.*"

"Oh, was it in you instead?"

"Cheeky shit," Cam says. They grab Skylar's arm and wrangle her into the chair next to them, nudging at her ankle with theirs until she lets them slide a foot between hers. She steals a sip of their coffee and grimaces at the bitterness. When she complains, they say, "Get your own, then; you're a big girl."

"I'll get it," Adrian offers.

Skylar grins. "My hero."

"Don't fall for the doe eyes—she'll have you at her beck and call soon enough," Cam says, prodding. It pays off: Adrian inhales sharply and turns away, and as hard as he tries to hide the flush riding his cheeks, it sticks.

"It's okay, I don't mind," he mumbles, stumbling backward over his chair in his haste. He busies himself with the pot and Skylar's favorite mug—*Good Morning, Assholes* in nice gold lettering on white ceramic—and only looks back an impressive two times, shifting on his feet as he does so.

Skylar's fingers linger on his when he passes the mug to her. Cam knows the glint in her eyes well enough: the thrill of possibility, of the hunt. She asks, "So what's the deal with you two now?"

"I dunno, we didn't really talk about it." Adrian rests his chin on a fist and slumps sideways, staring off into the distance as Cam watches fondness fall across his face by degrees. "Wouldn't mind doing it again, though, he's just…"

"Dreamy?" Skylar suggests. "A bit neurotic? Lonely? Excitable?"

Cam gently swats the outside of her thigh with the back of their hand. "That's enough. Be nice."

She looks about to argue, but apparently thinks better of it as Adrian says, "Passionate."

With a soft hum of acknowledgement, Cam lets themself drift away as the conversation resolves into the usual weekend catch-up about work, the book Adrian and Skylar are co-reading, winter's approach, the upcoming week's dinners. Everyday mundanities. Outside, two cardinals flit around the birdfeeder Parker had insisted would brighten the yard, vibrant splashes of crimson against the fresh white backdrop. Cam's eyes follow lazily, allowing the birds and the background hum of familiar voices to lull them into a quiet peace broken only when Skylar snickers and says, "Morning, Badger."

Parker stands in the hallway, all loose limbs and wild brown curls backlit by the stark light of the rising winter sun. He glances at Adrian, then Adrian's chest, and blushes. "Morning?"

"Coffee's already on," Cam says, tipping their head toward the machine.

"Have you eaten yet?" When Cam shakes their head, Parker breezes by the table and begins pulling out what appears to be half the fridge: eggs, cheese, enough vegetables to feed the city, a pack of strawberries, then bread from the cabinet. He whisks and dices and deftly avoids the conversation Skylar is *itching* to drag him into and, before long, sets an omelet with buttered toast and a bowl of strawberries in front of Cam. For Skylar, sauteed mushrooms and peppers. For Adrian, French toast.

"Thanks," Cam murmurs under Adrian's rambling breakdown of what exactly constitutes an acceptable plot hole—not, apparently, the one he and Skylar have recently discovered in their reading material.

"You good?" Parker asks, nudging his foot against Cam's briefly under the table.

Cam pokes at the omelet and avoids his questioning look. There's too many answers to the question, too many permutations and accidents waiting to happen when they try to say "I like the way you moan" or "I didn't anticipate wanting you" or "Do you know how special that makes you?"

They shake their head. "Long night."

Parker grimaces. "Sorry."

Cam waves the concern away, pasting on a small smile around a mouthful. "Don't be. Sounded like you had fun, and you've needed it."

"Yeah. Speaking of fun, though—" Parker clears his throat, drawing Adrian and Skylar's attention. "Is anyone doing anything over Christmas? My parents aren't going up to the cabin and wanted me to go check that everything's good. I thought maybe we could go and…I dunno. Chill? It's up by Lutsen, so you could get some skiing in, Skylar."

She nudges Cam. "You haven't gone in ages."

"I think it'd be fun!" Adrian claps his hands, beaming, and warmth blooms in Cam's chest at the way Skylar melts at the excitement.

They say, "I'm game. Most of my shoots are booked in the next couple of weeks anyway; I can block some time off."

"Really? *Sweet.* Okay, all right, I need—" Parker breaks off with a little groan as he searches for one of the ten million notepads he keeps scattered around the house. "We should plan."

"Relax," Skylar drawls. "It's early, Parker, and we never have mornings together like this anymore. Sit your ass down and let me hassle you."

The first weeks of December fly by. Cam's days are packed with families stressing about their last-minute Christmas photoshoots, and their nights are spent under a weighted blanket praying the tension squeezing their head will dissipate before the next volley of screaming children and frazzled caretakers. Skylar does not pester them about getting Parker in front of the lens again but *does* natter about her and Adrian's grand plans for hitting the slopes when they all leave the city behind for Christmas weekend.

"Are you coming out with us?" she asks one night, kneading Cam's shoulders.

Cam grunts into their pillow. "'S gonna just take a break," they say. "Stay in and not think about anything."

Skylar smooths one hand down Cam's spine, then the other, and again and again until the rhythm has nearly put them to sleep. "That's Parker's plan, too," she says softly, leaning down to kiss their temple. She doesn't prod further.

That night, Cam dreams of relaxing into Parker's warmth.

The nagging want for more tugs consistently at them, pushes and pokes like a puppy just discovering the joy of playing fetch. It's *infuriating*—they much prefer the casual indifference of acquaintanceship, not the stomach-twisting nerves of a crush. Despite their distaste for the whole situation, by the time the four of them pile into Adrian's truck to make their way up the coast early Friday morning, Cam itches with the need to take Parker's face in their hands and kiss him breathless.

They're smashed together in the back seat with Parker's laptop and one of his favorite movies—some animated thing about gangs and guns in a desert—when he says, "Any grand plans for the afternoon? The other two are gonna be out until late, they said."

"Taking a nap."

"Oh." Parker frowns, just slightly. "Is that, like… it? I was going to ask if you wanted to play word games or something while we have the place to ourselves."

Cam shifts their leg closer to his, their knees knocking as Adrian flies over a bump. "Ask nicely."

"Spend some time with me," Parker says, and it's the closest Cam's ever heard him come to begging. "Please? You've been so busy recently, and I miss you."

"Well..." Cam feigns indecision, staring off into space until Parker elbows their side. "Okay, damn!"

Parker leans close, dropping his voice. "Did Adrian tell you he's gonna ask Skylar on a date?"

"Yeah." Cam glances at him out of the corner of their eye. "And?"

"I think they're good for one another." Parker shrugs, crossing his arms, and even Cam can recognize the forced nonchalance. "Have you *ever* thought about, you know...adding someone else?"

Choosing their next words carefully, Cam says, "I'm not opposed." Their gaze drops briefly to Parker's lips before they wrench their head to the side. "For the right person."

"Mm."

"I'm not interested in pursuing a relationship with Adrian, if that's what you're asking." Cam keeps their voice low, barely audible over Skylar's valiant, if failed, attempt at channeling Mariah Carey in the passenger seat. "I like him just fine, but he's not really my type."

To their surprise, Parker scoots a few inches closer and asks, "What *is* your type?"

You, Cam manages to bite back. "Skylar," they say, then wince. "Um, I don't— If I want someone, I just...want them."

"Oh." Cam does their best not to let the disappointment coloring Parker's voice take root and bloom into shame. "That's nice."

"Yeah," Cam says, and it feels like anything but.

The rest of the ride passes quietly. Though it's only noon when they arrive, the sky is dark with heavy clouds, and the forest surrounding the two-story log cabin is eerily still. It begins to snow as they're finishing unloading the truck, thick white flakes of almost impossible size that accumulate quickly. Cam watches through the massive windows lining the porch as Adrian and Parker chase each other around, attempting to shove one another into the fluffy snowbanks.

"You have a look, Cam." Skylar winds an arm around their waist and leans her head against their shoulder, then shoves her hand down the back pocket of their jeans. "*Now* who's the Grinch?"

"Fuck off," Cam says, though it's fond, and they ruffle her hair even though she squawks in indignation. "Your man's going to be too cold for skiing if he keeps that shit up."

Skylar grins. "I know plenty of ways to warm him up." Glancing up at Cam, she continues. "What were you and Parker muttering about in the car? I heard my name."

"Oh my God." Cam rubs a hand down their face, turning away from the window and flopping back on the overstuffed, blanket-laden couch. "He surprised me."

"Oh, no."

"I told him you were my type when he asked who *was* after I told him Adrian is not."

"Cameron Woods!"

Cam throws their hands in the air before letting them fall dramatically into their lap and groaning. "I panicked!"

"You're going to use your alone time to make a fucking move." She punctuates the last few words with sharp jabs of her finger, protesting half-heartedly when they pin both wrists to her chest. "You," she says, pressing their foreheads together, "will tell him your type is teachers who wear their old-man slippers out to the mailbox."

"Will I?"

"I'll let you fuck my ass later if you do."

"*Manipulation*," Cam accuses. They let her go to smack a hand against their chest in mock indignation, the familiarity of the banter eating away at the sourness encroaching on their mind. "Underhanded, conniving, sneaky—"

"Loving," Skylar adds.

"—*loving* little bitch," they finish, and her laugh rings from the log walls as Parker and Adrian stomp through the door and beeline for the kitchen, dragging snow all across the carpet.

It's not home, but they settle in easily nonetheless. Cam tosses their and Skylar's bags onto the massive bed in the main bedroom, decorated with kitschy forest wallpaper and bear-themed decorations. The rest of the cabin is plastered in more of the same; Parker wastes no time in complaining about it when Cam pokes fun.

By the time Skylar and Adrian are ready to head out for an afternoon of skiing, the storm has picked up enough steam to merit a travel advisory. Cam pulls back the curtains a few inches and winces at how high the drifts are already, then pads back to the hand-hewn dinner table where Parker's set up a board game called Munchkin. "I didn't think it would get this bad," Parker apologizes as Skylar and Adrian discard their winter gear and slump dejectedly in the chairs across from him. "But I guess there's always tomorrow for going?" He gestures outside as he sits on the bench seat next to Cam. "And some nice fresh snow for you both."

Cam pulls their shoulders in and shoves both hands between their knees, but they loosen up when Skylar gently kicks at their shin with a pointed look at Parker. They relax ever so slightly as the game draws on, more so when Adrian suggests wine to usher in the second round. The alcohol settles gently into their veins, dulling the spike of anxious desire when Parker brushes his knuckles against their thigh.

They lean into his side, and Skylar's soft smile—her approval—when they pillow their cheek on Parker's shoulder is a welcome warmth.

They've all migrated to the living room floor with a massive pile of pillows and blankets to watch Die Hard—there's more arguing about its validity as a Christmas movie than actual attention being paid—when a loud *snap* sounds from the side of the cabin.

Adrian glances nervously at the wall. "What was that?"

"Probably a tree going down. It's still going strong," Skylar says. On cue, a sharp gust of wind sends snow, which sounds more like hail, flying against the windows, and she pulls her blanket tighter around her shoulders. "Though if trees are going down from the ice…"

There's louder, closer *snap* just as Adrian says "Fuck, the power—"

And then, darkness. The electricity cuts out with a dull whine, the sudden silence nearly deafening before Parker breaks it with a muttered "Fuck" as he fumbles for his phone. He turns on the flashlight, searing Cam's retinas, and stumbles his way into the kitchen to rummage through the drawers for tea lights and a lighter. "Stellar," he says. "Just *fucking*—"

Cam sheds their blankets and pads over to him, wordlessly asking for the lighter when they notice the tremor in Parker's fingers. "It's fine," they murmur. "Not the first power outage we've been through. We'll live."

"Yeah, but I should've checked the weather again before we left. *Shit.*"

"It's fine," Cam assures quietly.

Adrian comes up behind them and puts a hand on each of their shoulders, leaning his head between them. "You know what this means, right?"

"That the weekend's ruined," Parker snips.

"Well, I was gonna suggest sleeping," Adrian says, "but maybe out here, together, unless you've got a backup generator somewhere for the heat."

"You just jump right into it, don't you?" Skylar calls.

Adrian shrugs, his candlelit grin a wicked thing.

Cam ducks out from below him and turns to face Parker, who's chewing on his lip. On instinct, they reach out and tug it from between his teeth, allowing their thumb to linger on the torn flesh. It isn't until Parker's breath hitches that they realize and snatch their hand back, face heating. "Sorry."

"No need."

"Okay." Cam teases their fingers between Parker's, inching closer until the tension begins to bleed out of Parker's shoulders. They rub a small circle on the back of his hand with their thumb. Distantly, they register Adrian pulling away and settling back next to Skylar, and the soft buzz of their conversation. "We'll handle it, all right?"

Parker lets out his breath in a long rush. "Right."

"Do you want to sleep together?"

"It *will* get cold."

Cam tugs gently on his hand, stepping backward through the kitchen until their feet hit the soft living-room carpet. "Come on," they say. "It'll be okay for a few hours; we can tell stories or some shit. No campfire, but…"

"Camping sucks anyway."

"You take that back," Skylar gasps, but pats the floor beside her before bundling Parker in a thick fleece blanket and gently tipping him toward Cam, who rests a steadying hand on his knee.

Parker's breath evens out after a minute, and his fingers no longer shake when he unabashedly grabs the hand and laces his fingers with Cam's. To their left, Adrian flops down with a loud *oof*, pulling Skylar down along with him. She goes willingly, and Cam has never seen her fall asleep so quickly.

They'd bet money she's faking; however, they couldn't care less.

"Hey," they say softly, turning to Parker. His face is barely visible, but by the faint shine of the candles on the table, they make out a small smile.

"Cam," Parker says, "you have me, you know—if you want. If I'm not reading you *wildly* wrong."

The wind howls, and the pelting snow drowns out the shuffle as Cam pulls a pillow close and lies down, staring up at him. They huff a laugh. "You're not."

Parker tucks his lip into his teeth again but does not bite, only lets it fall back into place with a soft noise as he looms over Cam. "Can I kiss you?"

"Yeah." Cam reaches up to cradle his cheek. "I'd really like that."

They wake up warm. Consciousness is a slow, oozing thing, creeping through them by degrees as they wonder at the unfamiliar weight of the arm thrown across their stomach. Breath puffs softly against the back of their neck, and it takes several seconds longer than it should to realize it is not, in fact, the usual culprit—Skylar is currently starfished across most of the floor in front of them. They scrunch their nose before rubbing the back of their hand across bleary eyes, waiting none too patiently for their mind to settle somewhere near the realm of functional.

The air outside of their blanket cocoon is still freezing, but the power's come back on at some point. The living room lights are too bright in addition to the bright white glow of the outdoors, and Cam does their best to avoid it by burying their face in the corner of one of Skylar's blankets. They attempt to pull their pillow over their head, too, but are foiled by the dead weight of what must be Parker's head.

"Cam?" he croaks.

Words have never come easy upon waking; today is no different. Cam just grunts.

"You 'wake?"

"No," Cam groans. They roll onto their back and tip their face toward him anyway.

The light hits Parker's eyes in a way that turns their beautiful brown into molten amber, and Cam—without thinking—reaches up to brush the hair out of them. Parker presses briefly into the touch before shuffling forward, shoving one leg between Cam's and resting half his weight against their side. His mouth is inches from Cam's ear when he says their name again.

"Hm."

With the honesty quiet mornings tend to bring, Parker says, "I didn't wanna stop kissing you last night." A pleased sigh eases out from deep in his chest when Cam rests a hand low on his stomach. "Can I?"

Cam does not answer with a yes, a please, a needy whine—only a hum of assent before leaning up to press their lips to Parker's. It is a fleeting, chaste thing, and when Parker pulls back, he's wearing a smile Cam's never seen on him before. It makes him look unbearably charming. They say, "Again."

Parker slides one hand down the length of their torso and cards the other through their hair, and only when Cam is wound tight with anticipation does he kiss them again. He's *good*, too, all tenderly filthy as he licks at the seam of Cam's mouth, then slips his tongue in. Cam gasps when Parker pulls back to nibble at their bottom lip, sucking gently before letting it go with a very satisfied noise. "You have *no* idea how long I've wanted to do this," he murmurs.

"You could've asked." Cam registers the sound of Skylar shifting behind them, but reaches up to cradle Parker's jaw as they avert their eyes. "I'm not good at…signals. Gestures, the whole…" They wriggle their other hand out from under the press of Parker's shoulder and wave it back and forth above their heads. "I didn't know how to bring it up."

From behind, Skylar's icy fingers brush against their nape. "Just like this, Cam."

"How's this for a signal?" Parker takes Cam's face in both hands and stares into their eyes, thumbs brushing against their cheeks as he says, "I want you, if you're comfortable with it." With a sheepish smile, he cants his hips forward, pressing his stirring cock into the plane of Cam's thigh. "I mean, like, to *be* with you, but also… If you want! I know you're not really into—*mmph*."

Cam surges up and rolls Parker onto his back, leaning their full weight onto him as they kiss him breathless. They plant one elbow above his shoulder and grind into him, and his high whine when Cam's cock slides against his own is loud enough to rouse Adrian, who startles.

"Oh, damn! Good morning to me," he mumbles when he gets his wits about him, and is quickly shushed by Skylar.

Parker wastes no time in teasing his fingers under the elastic of Cam's sweats and grabbing their ass to pull them even closer, breaking the kiss only to shoot Adrian and Skylar a curt "Sorry."

"I don't care if they see," Cam says.

"Yeah?"

"*Please*," Skylar says. "Fuck, it's hot watching them get all bothered, for once."

"Skylar," Cam groans.

She sits up and ignores Adrian's hiss at the sudden loss of warmth as the blankets go with her, then spreads her legs, dangling one hand between them in anticipation. "I mean, if Parker and Adrian don't mind..."

"Only if you get back *down* here." Adrian yanks Skylar flush against him, and Cam twitches against Parker at the sight of Adrian's hand snaking down the front of Skylar's pajamas. Adrian closes his eyes and inhales sharply. "Christ, you really *do* like it," he says. When he pulls his fingers out, they glisten. "I wanna see—take these off."

Cam turns their full attention back to Parker, whose eyes flutter shut when they hike his leg up with their knee. "Okay?" they ask.

"God, I want to suck your dick," Parker blurts, immediately covering his reddening face with both hands. Then, peeking through his fingers, he says, "Please?"

Skylar snorts. "You won't have to ask them twice, they love getting head."

Flipping her off with one hand, Cam presses two fingers of the other to Parker's lips. "Show me what your mouth can do," they say. "Suck."

Parker drops his jaw and lets his tongue loll, staring up with heavy-lidded eyes as Cam deftly pets across it. He's fully hard now, straining against the shorts he wore to bed, and Cam shifts forward to kneel above him, rocking back against his cock. When he wraps his lips around Cam's fingers and does as he's bid, Cam realizes there's not a snowball's chance in hell they're going to last long when they stick their cock down his throat.

"Shit," they murmur, looking up at the ceiling and grinding against the soft give of Parker's stomach. They close their eyes and roll their hips, pressing their fingers deeper into the wet heat of Parker's mouth, and smile at Skylar's breathy whimper, the slick sound of Adrian's tongue against her folds. When they crack an eye, Skylar meets their gaze and arches her back proudly, putting on a show.

Parker's grip is tight against the curve of Cam's waist, hands flexing with each particularly deep thrust of Cam's fingers until he pulls off and says, "I want it."

"This?" Cam draws Parker's hand to their cock, curls his fingers around the bulge, and grinds against his palm. "You're cute when you're gagging for it, you know. Look at that blush." They nuzzle into Parker's cheek as he works to shove their pants down, and they suck in a breath as the cool air hits their leaking head. Parker's mouth opens, his eyes slipping shut in rapture as Cam feeds their cock between his lips.

They rock forward, bracing themself with one hand and fisting the other in Parker's unruly hair. Their brow knits when Parker hollows his cheeks and sucks hard and fast, urging Cam's hips forward with a firm grip. Next to them, Skylar's broken moans and aborted whines are a familiar foothold in this unfamiliar territory, and Cam blindly fumbles for her hand to squeeze as Parker swallows them all the way down.

The clutch of his throat sears around them, wet and warm and *loud* as he swallows again and again, and his moan sends desire lancing in a sharp curve up their spine. When Parker rakes his fingers down their thighs, they shiver. When he looks up with teary, hazy eyes, they coo "Good boy" and revel in the way his whole body goes slack with the praise.

Cam lets go of Skylar's hand to reach backward for Parker's cock, idly wondering as their hand wraps around him if he'd ever let them tie him up and tease him until he cries. The resulting mental image is *stunning*, and their breathy whine is loud enough that Skylar's quip of "*Nice*, man," makes Parker choke as he laughs around Cam's cock.

He pulls off with a rough cough, eyes watering, and rasps "Thanks?"

Skylar shoves a fist out for him to bump.

"You are a horror, babe," Cam chides.

Parker bumps it anyway.

Adrian shimmies up from between Skylar's legs, the entire bottom half of his face wet with her arousal as he runs a hand through his hair and grins. "He's good, isn't he?" he says. "Could spend days with him between my thighs."

"Yeah." Cam thrusts forward into Parker's throat once more, holding him down for several long seconds before allowing him a gasping breath. When they tug his head back, he looks up with bleary eyes and a dazed smile. "You're doing so well for me," they praise. "Again."

Skylar sucks in a tremulous breath at the sight, rolling Adrian over and pausing briefly before Adrian says, "Touch me." He arches into her with a low whine when she runs two fingers through his glistening folds, and Cam nearly falls apart at the sight of her knuckles-deep in pussy, steely determination in her eyes.

They *do* come, unexpectedly and down Parker's throat, when Parker presses his thumb against their perineum and rubs firmly. Their cock kicks against his palate, and Parker swallows without complaint, letting his head flop back to the pillow when Cam untangles their hand from his hair.

"God," they wheeze as they shuffle back to wrap a hand around him, looking up through their lashes at his fucked-out face. "You're *so* good, Parker. Who knew you had a mouth like that?"

Parker's answer is a hitched breath when Cam laps at his dripping head, and it's all too easy to draw out an orgasm from there. He comes with a hoarse cry, bitter on Cam's tongue, and yanks Cam gracelessly on top of him before sticking his tongue back in their mouth, heedless of the taste. "Wanted that so bad," he mumbles. "God, if you knew how bad—"

"*Fuck*, Skylar, right there," Adrian whines, interrupting Parker and drawing his attention. Cam watches pride steal across Skylar's face as she leans in and fucks into him relentlessly, feral grin fully in place as tension spirals through him. When it breaks, his belly heaving with the force of it, she drinks down every whimper and groan with a messy kiss until he gently pushes her away. "That's— Mmph, enough, please."

With a pleased hum, Skylar swings her leg off him and sprawls in the space between him and Parker, reaching to pet at Cam's shoulder as the four of them come down. When Parker begins to shift his legs under Cam's weight, they climb off and shove themself into the remaining space at Skylar's side. Parker grumbles as he attempts to pull the blanket back over them, struggling until Adrian takes pity on him and helps.

"I," Skylar says, "cannot believe this took so fucking long to happen." She wiggles her clean hand up to skim cool fingers across Cam's jaw, then kisses the tip of their nose. "Thank you."

Parker sighs, slinging his arm around Cam's middle and nestling closer, face buried in the curve of their neck. "That was... perfect."

Craning their head back, Cam says, “The fist bumping was a first.”

“I thought it was funny.” Parker shrugs, jostling Cam’s shoulders.

“It was.” Adrian reaches across Skylar and tangles his fingers with Parker’s atop Cam’s hip, and Cam does not shy away from the touch. “*Nice* wake-up call, though; I wouldn’t mind doing that again. Maybe, you know, planned next time, so I can bring a strap.”

Skylar guides Cam’s face back toward her, then draws them into a lingering kiss before asking, “Thoughts?”

Cam looks from her to Adrian, embraces the flutter in their stomach at the suggestion, and relaxes fully into the warmth of Parker’s embrace. “Yeah,” they say. “I think we could make that work.”

Getting the Band Together

enchantedsleeper

anal fingering, bipoc, bisexual, blow job, clitoral fingering, cunnilingus, established relationship, f/m/nb/nb, f/nb, face fucking, friends to lovers, friends with benefits, great britain, the grumpy one(s) are soft for the sunshine one(s), idiots to lovers, love declaration, m/nb, musician, non-binary, omg they were roommates, past tense, penis in vagina sex, performer, pining (mutual), sex toy, third person limited (multiple) point of view, twosome + twosome = foursome, voyeurism, walking in on sex

"So, I'll be round at 7 tonight?" Don checked as he and Vincent swept and tidied the music shop floor after closing.

Vincent winced, and Don felt a sense of foreboding.

"I'm so sorry. I was going to mention it earlier and I completely forgot," Vincent said, his eyes huge and apologetic. "Natalie had a family thing come up, so we had to move date night to tonight—"

"Oh. Right. Yeah, of course," Don was already saying with a forced laugh.

"You know I would never cancel on you otherwise," Vincent finished.

"It's fine, really," Don said, louder than necessary. "It's just one week."

This would be true for most people, but for Don and Vincent, film night had been sacred ever since it started with an impromptu sleepover at Vincent's when they were eight. They kept the tradition up without fail as they got older, even as they became adults with jobs and dating lives. It wasn't even necessarily about *watching* anything; the time together was what mattered.

Vincent gave Don this stricken look, and Don looked away; he'd never been able to resist Vincent's puppy-dog eyes.

"You don't have to act like it's no big deal," Vincent said quietly. "I can tell when you're lying."

And okay, he was, but Don was aware his reaction was excessive. Natalie wasn't just anyone; he'd watched the two of them dance around each other for long enough before Vincent asked her out, and he'd been cheering for them. It became obvious over time that they were great together. Don needed to be okay with this, because there was always going to be someone, eventually, who Vincent put ahead of him.

"I just wasn't expecting it," he said honestly, but he went over to lock the back door so that they (Vincent had recently started using they/them alongside he/him pronouns) couldn't see his face. "We can find another day—I know spending time with Natalie comes first. Are things still...good?"

"They're *amazing*," Vincent enthused, and Don pasted on a smile before turning around. "We never run out of things to talk about, and even when it's not something we have in common, it's still really fun. The three of us should hang out—I know you'd get along really well."

"I mean, we've met," Don pointed out. "At the café."

"Sure, but—different context."

Don wasn't dying to be Vincent and Natalie's third wheel, but he nodded anyway as Vincent finished tallying up the cash register. "Well, at least you're ditching me for something important," he remarked. When Vincent's brow creased again, he added, "Relax. I'm joking."

After they'd closed up, they both lingered outside, and Vincent said, "You could set up a jam session." At Don's blank look, he elaborated, "With Alec. You *are* still jamming, right? You weren't just saying that?"

Don had a flash of his and Alec's last "jam session" in a rented garage space. Alec had stepped inside, set their bass down, and said, "Are we going to pretend to play this time, or are we going to cut to the chase?" In response, Don pulled them in and kissed them roughly.

Matching his intensity, Alec had yanked apart the buttons on his shirt. "Cut to the chase it is, then."

A few minutes later had found Don up against the wall, his hands bound tightly with a guitar strap to prevent him from touching Alec or urging them on as they sucked him off with methodical, relentless thoroughness.

"We are," Don told Vincent, shaking off the memory. "But it's not like we're friends or anything. It's just"—*sex*—"music."

"I know, but it means a lot that you're doing it," Vincent said earnestly, his dimples, which Don had decided years ago were the universe being cruel, showing. "Considering what happened at the audition—"

"You mean the part where they called me an arsehole and stormed out?"

"—you two playing together is a big deal. I know we can make this band thing work, Don. I'm excited for it."

"I know." Don gave Vincent's shoulder a little push. "Go on, or you'll be late. I'll see you tomorrow."

Don waited until Vincent was out of sight before running his hands over his face. He had to get better at dealing with this, because Vincent was happy, and Don should be happy for them.

It wasn't Vincent's fault Don was in love with him, after all.

"I am so *fucking* done with today," Alec declared to the flat as they walked in.

They paused, waiting for a response of some kind, but all the spaces Alec could see into were empty. "Nat?" Alec called, slinging their bag onto the living room armchair.

"In my room," came the faint, distracted reply.

Alec nudged open Natalie's door to find their flatmate sitting on the edge of her bed, carefully doing her eye makeup. Right—Natalie had a hot date with Mr. Perfect, Vincent Chang, tonight. That meant she wouldn't be available for Alec to whinge at about their terrible day and then coerce into getting drunk and putting a terrible romcom on. Damn it.

Alec did a dramatic flop onto the bed, making sure to land far enough away that they wouldn't jostle Nat. "Today was crap," they said, muffled by the duvet.

"So, Joy's party was…not good?" Nat asked, putting the eyeliner back in her makeup bag and picking up the mascara.

"Total fucking chaos," Alec grumbled. "And none of the little psychos were at all grateful for the effort I put into setting up the music for them. They just screeched demands in my ears all day." Alec theatrically rubbed at one ear. "Forget playing bass—*this* might have made me deaf."

"Ouch," Natalie winced sympathetically, angling her pocket mirror as she ran the brush over her eyelashes. "At least it's over and done?"

Alec just groaned and rolled over onto their back.

Nat shut the mirror and leaned over them, smiling slightly, a tendril of blonde hair dangling just above their face. "I've got a bit of time before I need to head out," she said. "Do you want a backrub?"

Alec scrambled to sit up. "Oh, God, *please*."

Nat snorted with laughter and shuffled into position behind Alec, flicking her long beaded skirt to one side. Alec closed their eyes as Nat leaned in. The softness of her breasts pressed against their back as her hands worked the muscles lower down.

Alec knew exactly how those breasts felt in their hands, how to roll the nipples in the way that Nat liked, that made her gasp and moan into their mouth. They wondered if Vincent knew that about Nat yet. Unfortunately, thinking about Nat with someone else didn't do anything to kill Alec's libido, it just produced a spike of irritation followed by a mental image of broad hands cupping Nat's breasts instead of Alec's. *God fucking damn it.*

"How's that?" Nat murmured, pressing in a little more firmly, and Alec was rattled enough to flinch away, jumping up off the bed.

"Great! Amazing. That really helped," they babbled while Nat stared at them in confusion. "I shouldn't stop you getting ready, though."

Alec should know better than to fall into old habits. Just because they'd been friends with benefits for years, that didn't trump Nat being in a serious romantic relationship.

And sure, Nat was polyam, but Alec had no indication that Vincent was interested in sharing. Nat was so happy with Vincent—that much, Alec knew from multiple gushing conversations—and there was no indication she wanted anything else. So, why rock the boat?

It was Alec's own fault they'd never said anything about making it permanent.

Nat had finished gathering her things and now stood by the bedroom door, chewing on her lip. "I'll be back late, probably," she said. "But, if you're up, can we talk?"

Oh, great. Alec could guess what *that* would be about. "'Course," they said, fiddling with their phone and not looking at Nat. "Have a fun evening."

After Nat had gone, Alec stood in the silent flat for a few minutes and then thought *Fuck it* and opened up a new message.

Me
busy tonight?
got the flat to myself

Arsehole
Sure
text me the address?

Forty minutes later, the bell for the ground-floor entrance sounded, and Alec went over to answer the intercom. "It's me," said Don, and Alec buzzed him up.

Alec couldn't really say how those initial, tentative jam sessions had turned into hooking up every few weeks. After the clusterfuck that was their audition for Don and Vincent's "band," they hadn't wanted to set foot in the same room as those guys ever again. But the little, run-down independent music shop where they worked kept having things that Alec needed, and so Alec kept running into them.

And, okay, maybe it turned out that Don could be funny sometimes and not just an arsehole (though he still *was* an arsehole) and that the two of them had some things in common, like coming from single-parent Caribbean families and having too many annoying siblings.

But the main thing uniting them was that they were both stupid over people they couldn't have.

Alec opened the door to Don mid-knock. As Don stepped inside, he gave the room an approving look. "Nice flat," he said.

"We got lucky—for London—but the rent's a bitch," Alec said. "Still, place to ourselves this evening."

They crowded Don up against a clear stretch of wall, leaning in to kiss him and bite at his lip. Don kissed them back with equal force, their teeth clacking together, and slid his hands into Alec's jeans to squeeze their arse. Alec groaned and ground up against Don, feeling how hard he was already.

Instead of touching him, they broke the kiss and moved to tug at Don's earlobe with their teeth in the way that always drove him crazy. Don made a little punched-out noise and went still, panting, as Alec teased and sucked at his ear. Pressing their advantage, Alec moved to mark up Don's neck and then suck at the bite mark.

"What's the matter?" they asked Don, whose eyes were closed, his head tilted back against the wall. "Too much for you?"

One eye opened, and that was all the warning Alec got before they were lifted up, spun, and pinned to the wall, their back slamming into it none too gently. Reflexively, they clamped their legs around Don's waist.

Don skimmed his hands down their sides, hot through the gauze of Alec's silver blouse. Alec didn't like their chest being touched, and Don faithfully respected that boundary. He flicked open the button on their jeans, sliding them down, and then slipping a finger under the lace of their thong. Alec made a guttural noise as Don grazed their clit, massaging it in torturous, slow circles.

"You were saying?" he said, smirking and pressing in with intent.

Alec threw their head back, the silver beads threaded through their locs clinking against the wall. "Not bad," they said breathlessly.

In response, Don added a second finger, drawing the two fingers along their folds and back again, spreading their slickness around. He slid both fingers into their entrance, and Alec swore, trying to buck their hips up against Don's hand.

"Yeah?" Don asked. "Still 'not bad'?"

"God, this is so good," Natalie said, deftly wielding her chopsticks as she devoured a bowl of beef bulgogi with glass noodles. "I'm so glad we came here. I'm really sorry for hijacking your film night, though."

Vincent made a bit of a face, reminded of how bad they still felt over not telling Don about the changed plans. "It's okay. Don and I will work it out. It was my fault for not giving him a heads-up, but our friendship can withstand one missed film night."

"Hmm," said Natalie with a knowing smile.

"What?"

"No, nothing. I love that you've always made time for each other," Natalie said. "But I don't think it's the film night he's upset over. Are you completely sure he doesn't have feelings for you, too?"

Vincent sighed at the resumption of a well-worn topic between them. Their dates were half a commiseration club for two people pining after their closest friends. "Don's not… He likes women," Vincent said—yet again. "I don't want to read too much into things just because I wish there could be more. Now, you and *Alec*—"

"Oh, hang on," Natalie said with her mouth full, shaking her chopsticks at him. "Don't turn the subject around; we're talking about *you*."

"No, but…you said that you and Alec had a weird moment before you left?"

Nat sighed, accepting the change of subject. "I was giving them a backrub, but they got skittish all of a sudden and pulled away. I just wish we could *talk*, so I can find out what's bothering them. We've always been upfront with each other, but I think Alec's made some wrong assumptions, and…they pull away every time I try to bring it up."

Vincent considered this, leaning his head on his hand. "Would it help if I was there?" they asked carefully.

"What?"

"For support," Vincent said, warming to the idea. "Or to convince Alec that we're serious about making space for them in our relationship. We could do it tonight."

Nat stared at him, a little stunned. "I can't ask you to—"

Vincent smiled, reaching across the table to take her hand. "I'm *offering*. Would it help?"

"I… It might," Nat said with cautious excitement. "If you're really sure… Did I mention you're amazing? And brilliant? And sexy?"

Vincent snorted with laughter, their cheeks heating up. "A couple of times," they said. "Let's see if this works, first, though."

"*Fuck*," Alec swore as they ground down on Don's cock. The two of them had progressed to the middle of the living room floor, couch shoved aside to make room. "*Ah*—God—" They'd been enjoying watching Don's expressions as he got close, feeling the gradual build of their own climax, but now it became more insistent.

They leaned down to pant a warning into Don's ear and registered a sound at the edge of their hearing: a jingle of keys that meant *Nat was home*. But Nat wasn't due back for—

"Alec? Are you—? *Oh*, my god!"

Alec got a brief glimpse of Nat and Vincent frozen in the doorway before they buried their face in Don's neck, but the image of Nat's flushed face seared itself into their mind's eye, tipping them over the edge. They couldn't suppress a tiny moan as their orgasm rippled through them.

Don met their gaze for a knowing two seconds as they pulled away. Then he looked over at Nat and Vincent. "Oh, this makes way too much sense."

Right, so Alec hadn't actually told Don that their flatmate was the same woman who happened to be dating his best friend. Maybe they should have mentioned that.

"Uh," Alec panted, their heart still racing, "what are you guys doing back so early?" They reached for the nearest item of clothing, which turned out to be Don's shirt, and hastily knotted it around their waist as they dismounted. It was too little, too late, but Alec didn't want to be naked from the waist down while whatever was about to happen happened. "Is everything okay?" They managed to find Don's boxers and threw those to him.

"No, yes, it's— I'm so sorry; I didn't know that you guys were…busy," Nat said, her face scarlet. "I texted, but I guess now I know why you didn't reply. I just— *We* were hoping we could talk."

Vincent was still behind Nat, watching Don with a stunned expression, but they roused themself and put a supportive hand on Natalie's back, nodding.

Now? Alec thought in disbelief. "You guys cut your date short to come and have this conversation?" They glanced at Don, who shrugged, looking as baffled as they felt.

"I didn't know we'd be interrupting," Natalie said, agonised. "We can come back later, it's just…I really wanted to talk about things between the three of us."

"Sure, why not?" Alec said, resigned. "Might as well get it over with."

Nat looked lost. "Get what over with?"

Alec sighed. They hadn't wanted to do this in front of Vincent—or Don, although at least Don could relate to what was happening—but they guessed it was his business, too. "I know you're in a serious relationship now, and I get that it means we can't keep doing…well, what we were doing before—"

"Wait, Alec, I think you've got the wrong idea," Nat said, starting towards them, which immediately activated Alec's fight-or-flight response. They jumped to their feet, but there was nowhere to actually *go*.

"I know it's awkward having your ex-friend-with-benefits hanging around, and I don't expect anything, but if you need me out of your ha-*mph*—"

That was as far as Alec got before Nat pulled them down to her level and kissed them. Alec was more than happy to kiss back, but…what?

Nat pulled away and smiled, holding their face in her hands. "Like I said, I think you've got the wrong idea about what I wanted to say."

Alec stared at her and touched a hand to their mouth. Their brain was in overdrive. Nat coming here, cutting her date short to talk to them, Vincent standing there looking *approving*…

"So…you don't want me to go," they ventured.

"No," Nat said, still smiling and flushed pink. "I'd actually like for you to be more involved, if you're interested."

"…does that mean I can kiss you again?"

In response, Natalie pulled them back in for another, much more thorough, kiss.

Don took a moment to enjoy the sight of Alec and Natalie working things out before casting around for the rest of his clothes. Alec had stolen his shirt, the thief, but he could at least put some trousers on before making his exit.

He was happy for them, but he wasn't needed for whatever was coming next.

He sidled towards the door, but, of course, he couldn't sneak past Vincent. "You're going?" his best friend asked.

Don laughed a bit in disbelief. "I think I'd just be in the way. Congrats on the, er…trio, though."

Vincent shrugged, but smiled. "It's not conventional, but I knew how happy this would make Nat, and that's what matters. We both understand…" He trailed off and coughed. Before Don could ask exactly *what* they both understood, Vincent continued. "So, you and Alec."

"I wasn't lying about the jam sessions," Don said quickly, because he knew how it looked. "It started off that way, but then it became something…else."

"Something else?" Vincent repeated, their eyebrow raised.

"We both needed an outlet," Don said, because fuck it; he might as well be honest. "For…wanting people we couldn't have."

Vincent stepped closer, looking at Don. "I need you to spell this out for me," he said, softly. "Because I think I know what you're saying, but I need to be sure. Who was it you couldn't—thought you couldn't—have?"

Don swallowed, and it shouldn't have been so hard to get this one word out, but suddenly his heart was beating quadruple-time. "You," he said. "It's you."

A giddy smile spread across Vincent's face, the dimples that Don had always secretly wanted to rest his thumb in appearing once more. "I've got some good news," they said. "You can have me. Uh, what I mean is, I'm really into you. Too."

Don clutched Vincent's upper arms, barely able to process what was happening. "So…can I kiss you?"

"Please," Vincent said, already leaning in, and Don met him in the middle with a gentle, almost tentative kiss. Vincent responded by pressing in and deepening the kiss, sweeping his tongue across Don's lower lip and making him groan.

Dimly, Don thought that he heard Alec say, "Fucking *finally*," and he aimed a middle finger in their rough direction. He heard Natalie laugh as he and Vincent broke apart, and he brought that hand up to cup Vincent's face instead.

"So," Vincent said, seemingly unable to stop smiling. If Don was honest, neither could he. "I think we've both been idiots. How long have you…?"

God, Don didn't even know at this point. "Years. But I didn't think you would…I mean, I didn't want to mess up what we had."

"Same here," Vincent said with a little, self-deprecating huff.

"So…what now?" Don asked. He glanced over at Alec and Natalie, but they were happily wrapped up in each other; Natalie's top was on the floor, and Alec had pulled the cups of her lacy, sky-blue bra down to expose her breasts, massaging them and thumbing the nipples. As he watched, they bent down to take one into their mouth.

He looked back at Vincent, who was smirking. "Well, I'd like to kiss you more," he said. "And actually, if we're sharing confessions…" He leaned up to put his mouth to Don's ear. "Seeing you with Alec was fucking hot."

Vincent's words and their voice rumbling against Don's ear went straight to his cock. He groaned, and Vincent's expression turned devious.

"Does that get you going? Or is it…" They tugged experimentally at Don's earlobe with their teeth, then ran their tongue around the shell of Don's ear. Don turned his head and caught Vincent's mouth, kissing them harder and more hungrily than before.

"I was close when you both walked in," Don told him. "If you keep that up, I might not last."

"Ah," said Vincent. He gave Don an almost bashful smile, and then smoothly got down onto his knees, running his hands over the outline of Don's cock under his jeans. "I know a way to help with that."

Don gaped.

"Is that a yes?" Vincent asked with a hint of laughter in their voice.

"Fuck. Christ," Don said, unable to find any other words. "If you want, then yes. Fuck, yes."

Vincent thumbed open the button on Don's jeans, pushing them and Don's boxers down and out of the way before taking his hard-on gently in one hand. Don had the brief, nonsensical thought that he could have skipped putting those back on before every thought he'd ever had fizzled out as Vincent wrapped his lips around the head of Don's cock.

"*Shit,*" Don breathed. "You're going to kill me."

Vincent pulled back off to say "I'll try to avoid it," and then took Don fully into their mouth.

Don made a sound he didn't know he was capable of.

Vincent's approach to giving head was slow and languid, almost like he was savouring the experience. They would take Don into their mouth and then draw back, following the motion with their hand, before swirling their tongue around the tip of Don's cock. For Don's part, he couldn't do more than utter a series of inarticulate noises and the occasional bitten-off swearword, curling his hands carefully in Vincent's hair.

After what felt like an age, Vincent started to build up more of a rhythm, and Don's legs were actually shaking slightly. "Vince," he said. "I'm close, I—"

At that moment, Vincent took him all the way in and *hummed*, and that was all it took to tip Don over the edge, emptying himself down Vincent's throat. Vincent, the sly fucker, swallowed it down easily and then pulled gently off Don's cock, licking away a few more beads of come as Don stared at him, lost for words.

"Marks out of ten?" they asked, and damn if they didn't sound a little bit hoarse after having Don's cock down their throat.

"Fuck. Twenty," Don said, and Vincent looked even more pleased.

"You shouldn't start too high, or how will I improve?" he joked.

Don's response was to pull him up to his feet and kiss him. Tasting himself on Vincent's tongue was strange but kind of hot. Don gave them what he hoped was an inviting look and brushed a hand over Vincent's own hard-on.

"Can I…return the favour?" he asked.

Weirdly, Vincent suddenly looked a little shy. "Don't feel like you have to," they said in a bit of a rush. "I mean, I'd love it, but we can just—"

Vincent's bashfulness made Don bolder, and he undid the button on Vincent's dark, formal trousers and dipped his hand beneath the waistband of their boxers. Hearing Vincent's breath hitch as Don closed a hand around them was extremely satisfying.

Don slowly stroked his hand along the length of Vincent's cock, feeling the shape and the weight of it, fully intending to take his time just as Vincent had done to him. Just then, however, a shuddering moan coming from their left made both of them look over.

Natalie had clapped a hand over her mouth, flushing pink. She was wearing only her bra, still pushed up above her breasts, and was lying on some strategically placed cushions on the floor. Alec knelt between her spread legs, both hands cupping Natalie's arse to raise her hips slightly and gain easier access to her pussy.

"Sorry," Natalie said, her voice thready. "I was trying to be qui—*ahh*," she gasped again in response to something that Alec was doing. "Al, come on."

Alec raised their head and smirked. "Sorry," they said without sounding it in the slightest. "Want to come and take over?"

This was directed at Vincent, whose gaze had gone dark as he took in Alec and Natalie, his breathing coming quicker. His erection was hot and heavy in Don's hand, and Don felt a stab of regret that he wouldn't get to follow through on what he'd promised. At the same time, he knew that if he wanted whatever this was with Vincent (and at some point, they would need to have an actual conversation about it, probably), that picture would also include Natalie. And Alec, too, it seemed.

Vincent glanced guiltily at Don, who smirked and gave Vincent's cock another squeeze before letting it go. "We can pick this back up later."

"Really?" Vincent asked, and when Don nodded, they gave Don a fast, hard kiss. "You're so fucking good," they breathed into Don's ear before walking over to where Alec knelt.

Natalie propped herself up on her elbows, a blush spreading down her pale skin, as Alec shuffled backwards to let Vincent kneel between his girlfriend's legs. "How did I get this lucky," Natalie joked, looking between both Vincent and Alec.

"I was thinking the same," Vincent said, running their hands down Natalie's legs to cup her arse in the same way that Alec had been doing. They massaged her cheeks for a few moments, causing Natalie to groan and hitch her hips up towards Vincent's mouth, her head falling back against the cushions.

"God, babe, please," she begged, and Vincent gave her a look of sheer affection as he bent down. Alec, meanwhile, moved towards Natalie's torso and ducked their head to mouth at Natalie's breast. Natalie moaned, short and high-pitched. So much for trying to muffle the sound.

Don felt out of place as the only person not involved in the tableau. But then Alec looked up at him, their expression wicked, and quirked an eyebrow as if to say *What are you waiting for?*

Don kicked his jeans and boxers off and got down behind Alec, who was still wearing his shirt around their waist. "I think you'll find that's mine," he said, reaching forward to untie it.

Alec let the shirt fall to the floor. "What do I get, instead?" they asked.

Don traced a finger down the crack of Alec's arse, drawing a strangled noise from them. "I have some ideas," he replied. He nudged Alec's legs apart and found their slick clit, beginning to massage it in circles while simultaneously sliding a finger from the other hand into their waiting entrance. Alec raised their head from Natalie's nipple to gasp as they clenched around Don's finger.

Natalie watched them with a smile. "I love the way you look when you're getting off," she told Alec.

Alec stretched over to kiss her, moaning as Don pulled his finger out and thrust it back in. A second later, Natalie broke the kiss to gasp at something Vincent was doing, causing them to look up and grin. Don felt like he and Vincent were connected as they each worked to pleasure Alec and Natalie, who met in the middle as Alec trailed kisses down Natalie's body and sucked and massaged her breasts. As Alec moved around, Don repositioned himself behind them, sliding in a second finger alongside the first as he pinched and stroked their clit.

Natalie's gasps, which had faded into background noise for Don, suddenly began to increase in volume and urgency. Don watched as she threw her head back against the cushions, pushing her hips towards Vincent's mouth. Vincent adjusted his grip and sucked her clit, causing her to emit a high-pitched whine.

"That's it," Alec coaxed, also watching her. "Come for us."

Natalie moaned, her hips jerking against Vincent's mouth, and then went completely silent, as if holding her breath. Alec bent down and sucked at Natalie's neck, pulling away from Don's fingers, leaving Don to continue watching. After a suspended moment, Natalie gave a tiny cry and then gasped as she came, pressing up against Vincent before going limp and boneless.

Vincent gently lowered her down onto the cushions, dropping a kiss on each of her calves. "You okay, babe?" they asked, and Natalie gave a dopey grin.

"That was amazing," she said. She sat up, and she and Vincent exchanged a long kiss, Natalie holding their face in both hands.

Eventually, they broke apart, and Natalie held a hand out to Alec, who leaned over to kiss her. "You both were fucking hot," Natalie said to Alec and Don. "Don't stop for my sake."

Don shrugged. "I'm not in a rush," he said honestly. "Are you?"

Natalie laughed. "I'm not exactly working to a plan here. But whatever it is we're doing, I'm having fun. I want to keep going." From where he was still knelt on the cushions, Vincent nodded.

"I was actually thinking about something we could do next," Alec told Natalie, who tilted her head in inquiry. "Have you still got Veronica?"

This meant nothing to Don, but Natalie's face lit up. "Oh, my God, of course. Shall I go and get her?"

"Yeah, why not?" Alec said, and Natalie jumped up. Still wearing only her bra, which she adjusted back down over her breasts, she walked over to what Don could only assume was one of the bedrooms and disappeared inside.

Vincent climbed to their feet and gave Don a hand up. "I don't know who or what Veronica is, before you ask," they said. Don shrugged and leaned in to kiss him. Vincent returned the kiss a little hesitantly, maybe worried about kissing Don right after going down on their girlfriend, but Don was way beyond caring about that. It was heady and fantastic to be kissing Vincent, inhaling the scent of the aftershave he'd put on for his date. Although…

"You're still far too dressed," Don told Vincent. "Like, I love this"—he tweaked the collar of Vincent's dark-red dress shirt—"but I'd like it even better on the floor."

Vincent rolled his eyes. "Cheesy, but I'll allow it."

He let Don unbutton the shirt and push it off his shoulders, then strip off the undershirt underneath. Don ran his hands over smooth, tan skin with a smattering of chest hair, and Vincent shivered as Don grazed his nipples. "Like that?" Don asked, his voice coming out as a low rumble. He gently thumbed over Vincent's right nipple and then, experimentally, pinched it lightly and rolled it between his fingers. Vincent moaned, and Don felt like he'd won the universe.

They kissed again, Don continuing to see how many different sounds he could draw out of Vincent by stroking and playing with their nipples, which were highly sensitive. In retaliation, Vincent slid his hands down to grab Don's arse and ran their tongue around the rim of Don's ear, making him shudder and swear.

"I found her!" came Natalie's triumphant announcement, and Don turned to see her bearing aloft a strap-on with a large purple dildo attached.

Oh, so that was Veronica.

Vincent snorted with amusement.

Natalie slipped into the harness and adjusted the dildo (Don was *not* going to call it Veronica) against her pelvis. "How do you want to do this?" Natalie asked Alec as she slicked the dildo with lube from a little bottle.

Alec considered, then turned so that they were on their hands and knees. "Like this?"

"Oh, yeah," Natalie said as she positioned herself behind Alec, giving their arse an appreciative stroke. "I love seeing you take me in."

She coated her fingers in the lube and used them to penetrate Alec first, although Don was willing to bet that they were still wet and open from his fingering earlier, not to mention when they'd ridden his cock. After a few slow strokes in and out, Natalie positioned the head of her strap-on against Alec's entrance and pushed smoothly in.

Alec's breath punched out of them as Natalie filled them up, staying fully seated for a few minutes to let them adjust to the sensation before pulling back. A few more slow, methodical thrusts, and Alec craned around to glare at their flatmate.

"Nat, if you don't get on with it and *fuck me*—"

That was asking for it, and Natalie snapped her hips forward, thrusting into Alec.

Alec made a little, winded noise but looked extremely self-satisfied.

"Your girlfriend's a tease," Don couldn't help commenting to Vincent, who nodded their agreement.

"She's good."

An idea struck Don, and he reached down to gently palm Vincent's cock through the fabric of his trousers. "Keep watching them," he told Vincent, and got down so that his head was level with Vincent's navel. His trousers were still unbuttoned, making it easy for Don to push down the two layers of fabric and free Vincent's cock.

He'd never actually given head before, but he'd been on the receiving end, and he knew what felt good. Vincent was watching him with a kind of awe, their cheeks flushed, and Don reiterated his instruction. "Watch them. Not me."

"Don't I even get to enjoy the view?" Vincent mock complained, but he obeyed, looking over at Natalie and Alec. Natalie was building up a rhythm of thrusts, drawing little gasps and whines out of Alec. She looked over at Don, and Vincent and winked.

Don took just the tip of Vincent's cock into his mouth to test the waters, and Vincent made a choked noise. Hoping that was a good sign, Don took them in a little farther, swirling his tongue around Vincent's cock as he did.

"Jesus, Don," Vincent murmured, resting a hand lightly on top of his head. "Is this payback for earlier?"

Don snorted lightly, pulling back to say, "You'll just have to find out."

Vincent gave him a brief, amused glance, and whatever he saw made his eyes widen before he looked away again. Don applied himself with renewed confidence, taking Vincent's cock all the way in. He couldn't see Vincent's face clearly (a drawback, but it was easier to fumble his way around this without being watched), but he heard Vincent make another strangled noise as he gripped Don's head harder.

Don teased them, drawing them in slowly before pulling back, occasionally breaking off to run his tongue around the head of Vincent's cock or along the length of their shaft. He enjoyed listening to the bitten-off noises that Vincent couldn't hold back and encouraged them as much as he could. When he experimented with lightly pressing a thumb to Vincent's balls, Vincent moaned outright, and their hips stuttered forward, like they were barely restraining themself from fucking Don's mouth.

The thought was unexpectedly hot.

Don pulled away and said, "Do it."

"What?" Vincent stared down at him, his gaze a little glassy.

"Fuck my mouth. You want to," Don asserted. "Don't hold back."

"Are you s—?"

Don grabbed hold of their hips, steering Vincent's cock into his mouth, and looked up at them with raised eyebrows.

Vincent got the message. Putting both hands on Don's head, he thrust into Don's mouth, gently at first, then with more conviction.

Don let his mouth go slack to allow Vincent in more easily, then started moving to match the thrusts, encouraging him to fuck that little bit deeper. Vincent's thrusting became quicker and more erratic, and Don could tell he was getting close. To help him over the edge, Don hollowed out his cheeks, adding some suction, while reaching under his cock again to gently massage his balls.

Vincent cried out, which was the only warning Don got as Vincent came in his mouth.

Don hadn't given any thought to swallowing or not swallowing, but luckily, Vincent made that decision for him. After he pulled off, he pressed a kiss to the tip of Vincent's cock.

Vincent stared down at him. "Jesus Christ," they said, fervently.

Natalie and Alec had paused what they were doing to watch, Natalie still wearing the strap-on, shiny with Alec's slick. Alec leaned up against Natalie, blouse open to show glimpses of their binder. He was really glad he hadn't known they were watching.

Alec gave him a nod, seeming almost impressed, and Natalie was flushed in a way that he didn't just think was from the fucking.

Suddenly, he was hauled up to his feet by Vincent and kissed very thoroughly. "Not bad for a first go?" Don couldn't help asking.

"First..." Vincent looked as though that hadn't occurred to them before that moment, and they gently leaned their head against Don's collarbone. "First go. Christ. Yeah, it was good. It was very good."

They exchanged a few more lingering kisses before Vincent confided, "I think I need to sit and chill for a bit." He was still dimpling contentedly, so Don didn't feel too worried.

"Sure, go for it." Don still had a fair bit of energy, and Vincent fucking his face with abandon had got him half-hard again, but he was happy to let Vincent wander over to the cushions and drop down with a small sigh.

Alec turned and gave Natalie's shoulder a light push. "Go and cuddle with Vincent," they instructed.

"Oh, but you didn't— Do you not want to—?" Natalie began.

"It's fine. Donny boy, here, is going to take over," Alec said, standing up.

"Don't ever call me that again," Don told them, but he went over and pulled them in for a kiss. It was weird, switching partners so quickly, adjusting to Alec's height and remembering how it felt to tilt his head back to kiss them. But it was easy to slip back into the groove with Alec—it had always been easy.

"Did you enjoy the show?" Don said into their ear.

"Not half bad," Alec replied.

"Want to put on another one?"

In reply, Alec kissed him again, this time more slowly, and then guided his hand down to feel the wetness between their legs. Don played with their folds for a few minutes, spreading the slickness around, then said, "I have an idea, if you're up for it."

Alec arched a brow at him. Normally, their dynamic was a lot of wordless fucking and occasionally some sarcastic banter; requests were new.

"Bend over and touch the ground," Don directed them.

Alec snorted. "Is that all?" they asked, putting their bare arse temptingly on display as they did so.

Don palmed the lube that Natalie had left and coated his fingers in it, then circled Alec's arsehole with one fingertip. He heard them catch their breath as they realised what he had in mind. "Okay?" he asked quietly.

"Keep going," Alec told him.

Don crooked his finger, slipping the tip into their hole and drawing a gasp from Alec. He moved the finger in a brief circle before sliding it back out, then did the same again, penetrating a little deeper. Out of the corner of his eye, he caught sight of Natalie moving, drawing up her knees to her chest and reaching down to circle her clit as she watched them. Vincent, noticing this, moved behind her to undo her bra and free her breasts. He cupped them in both hands, pinching and rolling the nipples.

To the soundtrack of Natalie's quiet gasps and Alec's low moans, Don worked Alec's arse, sometimes pausing to massage the cheeks and pull them apart before sliding a different finger in. With his other hand, he slid one finger into Alec's soaking-wet cunt, then a second, stimulating both holes at once. Alec's breathing grew ragged, and their legs began trembling, but they managed to hold their position.

Finally, Don reached down to touch Alec's clit, stroking it and tracing it with one finger until they were pushing back against his hand, desperate for release. He leaned down and said in a low voice, "Natalie's watching you. She loves seeing you getting fingered by me." Alec groaned. "She's touching herself, watching you get off. Can you hear her? She's looking at you with your arse in the air, getting turned on seeing you get close, watching you come apart, coming right in front of her for the second time—"

Alec made a desperate noise, and a second later was gasping out their release. Don held their hips as they shook through their orgasm, massaging Alec's clit until it became obvious the stimulation was too much, then taking his hand away.

Alec spent a few moments catching their breath before straightening up. "That was good," they told him, actually smiling a little. "Genuinely."

"Glad you liked it," Don replied, making sure he sounded sincere and not just smug. He *was* smug, but that had also been a lot of fun.

They joined Natalie and Vincent on the cushions, and from there, things unfolded slower, more languidly. Vincent and Natalie made out with Natalie's leg hooked over Alec's shoulder as Alec ate her out, bringing her to a gentle climax. Afterwards, Don and Natalie tag teamed Vincent, taking turns stimulating different areas of their cock. It could have been weird, but Don was surprised by how easily they worked together with the goal of pleasuring the person they were both into.

Finally, all four of them lay there, somewhere between basking in the afterglow and processing what had just taken place.

It was Alec who finally said, "Can anyone be arsed to move?"

"No" and "Nope" came from Don and Vincent, respectively, and Natalie made a non-committal noise.

"Me neither." Alec reached up and tugged on a throw that covered the sofa, and with a bit of effort, brought it down on the group.

"G'night," Natalie said vaguely.

It was surprisingly easy for Don to drift off, his head pillowed on Vincent's arm, his feet tangled up with Alec's.

Don didn't expect to be woken up the next morning by someone singing. Even stranger was the fact that he couldn't identify who it was.

He sat up slowly, the sight of Natalie and Alec's flat filtering in along with memories of exactly what had taken place the previous night. The melodic singing layered over sizzling noises as Natalie turned something in a pan.

"You're awake!" she said as Don padded towards the kitchen. Behind him, Alec and Vincent were stirring into consciousness. "Sorry about the weird wake-up. I got a bit carried away."

"You can sing," Don said carefully, shooting a look back at Vincent, who raised their eyebrows. Vincent played drums, Don guitar, and with

Alec, he supposed they had a bassist. But they still needed a singer.

"Oh, well," said Natalie. "I learned a while ago, and it's classical, not—you guys mostly play rock music, right?"

"We've got a wide repertoire," Vincent said, walking over and kissing Natalie on the cheek. "We'd love to have you, honey."

"Ugh, nauseating," said Alec from the cushion pile, but they looked amused. "I didn't agree to join any band, you know."

"You literally tried out for it," Don pointed out.

"I retracted that."

Vincent pouted at Alec. "What incentives can we offer you? What about naming rights?"

Don didn't think that Alec would go for it, but they hummed thoughtfully, stretching their arms over their head.

"Deal."

Soul Splinters

E. K. Victor

alcohol use (casual), anal fingering, bipoc, blow job, car accident (past), character injury (permanent), established relationship, first kiss, first person point of view, friends to lovers, gay, has a disability, illness (serious), jealousy, m/m/m, masturbation, modern, penis in anus sex, pining (mutual), present tense, puzzles and games, second chances, twosome to threesome, united states of america, walking in on sex

I.

I've had this dream more times than I can count.

The setting varies. Sometimes it's an airport, other times a train station or a bridge I must cross alone. Often I remember nothing but the kiss. The kiss is always the same. We hold one another, chest to chest, hip to hip, and kiss slowly, deeply, every motion loaded with longing. My heart overflows. My eyes brim with tears. I'm aroused, but on waking I rarely find evidence of an erection and never anything more. I invariably awaken—not with a start, but with a whimper. The tears are mostly real.

Usually I dream about Warren. Sometimes, it's Steve. After, I lie wide-eyed in the dark, listening to the thumping of my heart, and think of the only true friends I've ever had, whom I abandoned. I promise myself I'll call them tomorrow, then remember: with an ocean between us, the time to call would be *now*—and turn over with a groan.

Time is ruthless. I used to think about them whenever I wasn't busy. Then only occasionally. Almost never, nowadays. But the less they occupy my conscious mind, the more the dream visits, and the heavier it weighs with the love aging in me like wine in the cellars of a vacant house, never to be tasted.

So it's no surprise when I have the same dream while dying on the operating table. We stand at the entrance to the LHC tunnel, pitch black inside. Both my friends are there, for once, but only I may pass. I fear death only because of everything I haven't said to them, though it's really just one thing. That I love them—that I never stopped. There's no kiss. I suppose my brain is too caught up with the desperate reboot attempts to solve the three-body problem just now. But I take their hands, and they lead me away.

Eventually, I wake.

The first thing I do when they clear me for sitting up and holding small objects is call Steve. Steve, not Warren, because I can count on Steve to talk if my tongue gets tied. Which is exactly what happens, but I manage the essentials. I tell him I almost died. That he and Warren were who I saw when "my life flashed before my eyes." That I'm coming home and I want to see them. And at last, "How are you doing? How's Warren? You two are still together, right?"

It's the first time I've managed to render Steve speechless.

But not for long. "If by 'home' you mean that nest of vipers—"

"Well—"

"You can stay with us. As long as you want. We'll arrange for everything you need, medical stuff, whatever. You know money's not a problem."

"I know, but—"

"Dee." He pauses, as if he knows that saying it will drive tears to my eyes. No one else calls me Dee. "C'mon, Dee," he whispers. "Say yes."

It takes a lot more than my acquiescence to make it happen, and it doesn't happen for another four months, what with the surgery to fix the issue that caused the stroke. But at last I'm cleared for light exercise: walking, stretching, and the nine-hour intercontinental flight to the West Coast.

2.

Warren and I play chess on the veranda. He could never beat me, back in the day. I'd let him win once, but he figured me out and held a grudge for a week. It looks like now he'll be able to return that dubious favor. Unlike me, he hasn't stopped practicing.

I feel his gaze on me. He won the first game today after I'd made an incredibly stupid mistake, distracted by dappled light in his golden hair. I'm not letting that happen again. I won't look at him. I won't—

I look at him. His eyes darken as his pupils dilate, but there's no trace of mockery in them. Only tenderness.

"To hell with it," I mutter under my breath, blushing, and take his queen.

He shakes his head. "Your mind is elsewhere. I've got checkmate in three."

"I don't see it," I say. "Another gambit?"

With a sigh, Warren starts to move the pieces. "Knight takes bishop, pawn to D3—"

Ah. "Rook takes D3 and—"

"Game over."

"Damn."

He starts putting away the pieces using his good hand, then shakes his head as if admonished by some inner voice and switches to the other. The missing one. He wears a handsome bionic prosthesis, but from what I've seen, it's less of a preference and more of a chore. He misses the pawn three times in a row and finally topples it.

Steve told me that Warren had flat-out refused to use a prosthesis for several years after the crash. He hadn't believed it could be useful and wouldn't wear one just for appearances. He'd only agreed to have the required electronics implanted recently, on Steve's increasingly desperate insistence. But he's uncharacteristically lazy when it comes to actually using the prosthesis, and he takes it off whenever he can find a half-feasible excuse for doing so. He won't hear of further surgery, never mind the potential benefits.

My heart aches as I watch him struggle.

"This is worse than doing one-arm push-ups, I swear," he says, brow glazed with sweat. It's no joke. I saw him at it one morning. Then Steve rose and gave Warren the evil eye till he put on the prosthesis and resumed his exercise with it. His left arm is visibly thinner than his right. Used to be the other way around. He also used to have an impressive six-pack. Now he has a beer belly and his muscles only show through on the chest and shoulders.

He finally picks up the pawn but drops it an inch shy of the box with an annoyed *tsk*. It rolls under my chair, and I bend to catch it, brushing tiles hot enough to burn where the sun has crept over them.

It's pleasantly cool and dark in the house. I hadn't noticed the exhaustion encroaching on me but now it's like a weighted vest. I almost slam into Warren when he makes an abrupt stop.

"Should've known," he mutters, gazing down at a cluster of grocery bags abandoned halfway to the kitchen. Steve's been out shopping.

Warren looks at me, lifts a finger to his lips, then stalks toward the living room. We find Steve there, snoring on the sofa, his long limbs strewn over the cushions and drool glistening from the corner of his mouth. Westering sun glows on his dark skin, turning the hair on his arms into amber fairy lights.

It was his turn to make dinner.

I smile at Warren, and he smiles back, shaking his head. He pulls the drape over the window, and we backtrack quietly to the foyer.

"I'll cook," he says in a hushed voice. "You go rest."

"Do I have to?" I ask playfully, but my reluctance is real. An insatiable craving for his company tugs on me. "I can help."

"You're tired," he says. "It's the heat. Have a glass of water and lie down. I'll call you when the food's ready."

His concern breaks my feeble determination and I sigh. "Fine."

My bedroom upstairs has a bathroom of its own. I splash my face over the basin and drink from the tap, then throw myself on the bed. The aggrieved creak it gives reminds me.

My balcony door was open last night. The matching door in the master bedroom must've been open too, because, for the first time, I *heard* them.

At first, I'd taken the rhythmic thudding for Warren's footsteps, but it lasted too long, and moved nowhere, and after a while I made out the plaintive squeaking of the springs in their mattress. My eyes grew wide, my mouth agape, as their rhythm gradually built up to a frenzy. And then it stopped so suddenly my breath hitched, and in the silence,

I heard Steve moan something unintelligible that, in hindsight, must've been a plea. Because the pounding resumed then, in all its bestial vigor, and ended with a muffled cry.

I covered my face and laughed. My heart was racing, and lust coiled in me like hunger, making my cock painfully stiff. I hadn't had an erection in ages, nor any interest in sex. Perhaps coming back from the brink of death had restored that part of me too?

I'm hard again now, thinking of it. I rub myself experimentally over my clothes. Oh, yes. Sensitive too. I recall how the drumbeat of their lovemaking had stopped, and the begging, and I worm my hand inside my underwear. For a while, it feels good to stroke.

Only…I don't want this, I realize with a pang of sorrow. I want someone else to touch me and be pleased by me. I want some other hand to stroke.

Warren's?

Steve's?

I try to picture them: hovering over me, kissing, licking, biting, their hands gripping my flesh. Warren would have to be on my right side so he could use his good arm. Steve would pull on my sack while sucking my nipple. And my hands would be on them too, pumping them frantically, out of sync, as we all three get closer and closer—

No. No, no, no. It feels wrong to daydream about them, let alone while holding my dick. Like abusing their hospitality. They'd chosen each other and I was left out and nothing has changed.

With a groan, I turn and press my burning face into the cool linen of a cushion, unwilling and undone.

3.

Entering the kitchen, I witness Warren grab Steve in a mock chokehold while Steve squeals. When he sees me, he laughs and elbows Warren's side. Mortification replaces Warren's unguarded cheer as he meets my eyes, and he pushes Steve away as if he's been caught doing something criminal.

As a new couple, they'd taken care to avoid all displays of any but the most chaste, friendly affection in my company. Back then, I'd been quietly grateful for that. I had no wish to see them touch or hug or kiss or whatever it was I'd imagined couples did. Just *seeing* them had been difficult enough. They haven't been doing anything overtly couple-ish in my presence now, either, slipping into the old pattern.

"You don't have to do that, you know." I flip a chair around and straddle it. "It's nothing to be ashamed of. And I don't mind."

Warren turns his back to me without a word, busying himself over a huge bowl of salad. Seeing me wilt, Steve winks at me as if to say, *it's ok: that's just his way.*

With the food on the table—grilled pork chops, oven-heated buns, and a mountain of fresh vegetables—they take their seats on each side of me. But just as Warren and I are about to lean in, Steve theatrically props his feet on Warren's knee. Warren freezes, looking first at Steve with annoyance, then at me, apologetically.

"What?" Steve says. "He said he doesn't mind."

Warren grunts and stuffs his mouth full.

"What?" Steve repeats, looking at me, and I realize I'm grinning.

"Nothing," I mutter. Oh, god. Now I'm blushing too.

When we've all pushed our plates away, Steve serves us the white dessert wine they've stocked just for me. The talk is light and silly, and I'm reminded of how safe I used to feel in college, enveloped by the protective aura of my friends: Steve with his irresistible charm, and Warren with the quiet confidence of a man who'd never been beaten in a fair fight.

"I hear you've forgotten how to play chess, Big Dee," Steve jabs, looking me in the eye and grinning.

The "Big" thing had been odd enough in college, but it's even stranger now, since both he and Warren continued growing through their twenties, while I'm the same size I was at eighteen. The other night we drove to town for drinks and the bartender asked for my ID because freshly shaved, with my hair let out, and dressed in black, I still look like a brooding teenager. Steve's five inches taller than me, and Warren has another few on Steve. Not to mention I'm half Warren's weight. Sometimes his lips curl when Steve calls me Big Dee, like he's thinking, *Little Dee*. But he'd never say it out loud, in fear of offending me. As quick as we've regained the casual intimacy of old friends, he's still handling me with the same caution as the delicate wine glass in his prosthetic hand.

I grin back. "True."

"He makes no effort," Warren rumbles.

"*Not* true. I'm rusty, and you've gotten way ahead of me. That's all there is to it."

Steve turns to Warren. "You should give yourself more credit, man. You're smarter than you look."

Warren looks at us with a deadpan expression.

"Hey, it's a compliment," Steve says. "Sure beats 'you look smarter than you are,' which is what I usually get."

That cracks us up.

Warren rises from the table first. He makes to walk past Steve, but Steve grabs his good hand and kisses it. After a moment's hesitation, Warren sighs and squeezes Steve's hand, and when Steve looks up, Warren kisses his forehead. He then looks at me, calmly, his hand resting on Steve's shoulder. Steve is looking at me too.

I freeze as something—not quite fear and not quite excitement—twists in my chest. Warren steps around the table and stands behind me for a second before I feel his hand on my shoulder. On impulse, I copy Steve's motion, craning my neck to look up, and sure enough, Warren bends down and presses his lips to my forehead. The kiss is slow, solid, and heavy, like all the unspoken things between us. I inhale his scent, smoke from the grill and the warm musk of sweat under it.

Then he's gone.

The world rushes back in. From the adjacent seat, Steve watches me. I can't begin to guess what he's thinking behind his carefully arranged, neutral expression.

He up-ends his glass. "It's not shame, by the way. Or shyness, or any shit like that."

"Huh?"

"The reason he pushes me away when you're around."

"Oh." I feel like I should be able to follow, but my mind is blank. "What, then?"

Steve gets up and stretches, arching his spine in a graceful curve. "He doesn't want you to feel excluded," he explains, all casual, like it's something we discuss over dinner every day and not a decade-old open wound. "You know?"

I don't, but I say nothing.

4.

The sounds of an approaching vehicle are the first intrusion from the Outside World I've experienced in my three weeks here. Warren tosses the controller on the seat beside him and rushes out, while Steve, usually the one to jump at an opportunity to socialize, throws his head back and lets his own controller slowly slip from his hands as if someone has unplugged him.

"Who is it?" I ask, walking to the window. A green SUV has stopped in the driveway and produced a tall, tanned woman in a sporty outfit. She and Warren shake hands—he offers his left, prosthesis and all—and she gives his shoulder a solid slap. They laugh like old friends.

The padding of bare feet over the hardwood floor tells me Steve has elected to rejoin the living. He stands beside me and sighs. "Helen Watson. She's his"—he gestures and shakes his head—"coach-slash-physical therapist, I guess."

His *coach*? From Steve's hesitation, I expected no less than *masseuse*. Outside, the woman—Helen—points at her car, and again, Warren laughs.

Steve lets out a pained groan.

"Between the two of you," I tease, "I'd have taken *him* for the jealous one."

"I'm not." Steve crosses his arms over his chest. "Normally. What triggers me is how he changes around her."

They walk to the car, where Helen reveals something in the trunk that makes Warren laugh once more. That's more sightings of his laughter in these two minutes than in all my time here so far, and I can see what Steve means. It's embarrassing for sure. But try as I might, I can't relate to jealousy. Even back in the day, after I'd first learned that Warren and Steve were having sex, and perhaps more importantly, that I wasn't indifferent about it like a friend should be, I hadn't been *jealous*. I'd been...hurt, I'm able to confess now, a decade later. I had thought we were a trio and then suddenly I was excluded, as Steve put it the other night. What about me, I'd kept asking moments before the crash, or so I remember it. What about me?

And then the pickup that had been only a distant beam in the rear-view mirror seconds before crossed into my lane, and I swerved away wildly, and there was the sense of terrible inevitability. The next thing I remember was Steve's eyes, huge and brilliant with tears, as he stood by my hospital bed with a mesh bandage over his head, saying, *it wasn't your fault, Dee. He'll be all right. He'll be all right.*

As "all right" as one can be after losing a limb.

"I don't get it." I turn to discover Steve much closer than I can account for. Have I inched toward him, or he toward me? I clear my throat. "I thought he wasn't interested in women."

"Eh, you know how it is. Every rule finds an exception after you're thirty."

I know no such thing. And besides, "You don't seriously think he'd...?"

Steve sighs. "No. And I'm an ass for casting shade on her. She's...good for him. She can get him to do a lot more than I can—you know, with the arm. But she can also fix his mood in ways I can't. I guess that's why I'm bothered."

A note of genuine self-deprecation laces his voice. His throat works, up and down, and my eyes follow. Such a finely sculpted throat. His bare chest is close enough to touch, and I find myself imagining what it would be like to feel the soft ridges of his muscles with my fingertips.

Prying my eyes away, I look through the window, where Helen has loaded Warren up with a bunch of props from her car.

Steve shifts his weight, and now I can feel his breath in my hair. "I wouldn't be bothered if it was you," he says.

Like a punch in the chest, it leaves me breathless. I double my efforts to appear absorbed in watching Helen and Warren walk down the path to the tennis court. "If I was what?"

"C'mon, Dee," Steve whispers. "You know what I mean. I've seen how you look at him. He's seen it too. We talked about it."

Panic rises in me like a towering wave. "Talked about what?"

"Leaving the door open."

Steve's voice has gone soft and velveteen. He moves closer still, so my shoulder is a breath away from brushing against his chest and I feel his heat like prickling electricity. I stare stubbornly through the window, pretending I understand what Steve just said, pretending I don't, ignoring his closeness, praying he'll close the gap.

"You two will have to work it out between yourselves," he says after a long silence. "I know it's a lot to ask. You're like Kirk and Spock: everyone knows you want to fuck but neither of you is capable of saying *sex*, let alone asking the other to have some."

A startled giggle bubbles out of my throat. "I can say *sex*," I protest, absurdly, while heat spreads through me like a stain.

Steve licks his lips and leaves them ajar, glistening. They quiver under my sideways scrutiny, which I'm sure he's aware of, though he too pretends there's still something to look at outside. "I wouldn't mind, is what I'm saying," he concludes, and his throat goes up and down and up again while I gape, dazed.

My breath hitches as he drapes an arm over my shoulders. Feeling me start, he pulls back, but I clasp his hand and press it where it first landed. He squeezes gently and, a moment later, kisses my temple. I close my eyes, trembling.

"You know we love you, right?" Steve whispers.

I love you too, I want to say. And a dozen other things, but just like in my dreams, I can't.

Steve retreats and leaves me alone.

I go on staring through the window till Warren busts into the room, bearing a tennis ball in his prosthetic hand like a trophy.

"Look, Dee! I caught it!"

Blinking in confusion, I realize the light has changed completely and Helen's SUV is no longer in the driveway.

5.

Steve excuses himself from dinner, claiming he needs to attend to something urgent in his office downtown. But I suspect he's trying to give Warren and me an opportunity to "work it out"—whatever "it" may be.

Oh, who am I trying to fool. "It" is an offer to join them in their bed. Not even I am enough of a Spock to pretend I don't understand.

The idea makes me dizzy. In the past, my daydreams were mostly about Warren, with Steve magically removed from the position to interfere. But it's not like I've never thought about him that way. His sex appeal resonates with something raw inside me, but I've put so much effort into ignoring it that now it's almost as if I'm exposed to it for the first time. I try to imagine it. Having the license to touch him. Taste him. Both him *and* Warren?

"Dee?" Warren says. "You okay?"

"I don't think I can eat," I blurt out. We're in the kitchen, and he's about to put leftover seafood pasta on the stove. He freezes. "I'm fine," I hurry to assure him, terrified he'll send me to my room to hydrate and rest. "Just…" I lean on the counter and laugh, letting my hair fall around my face.

Warren puts away the pan. "Did Steve say something to upset you?" When I don't answer, he steps closer. "Damn it, I told him to leave you be. You didn't have a fight, did you?"

"No, nothing like that. He said…he said you and I are like Kirk and Spock."

"Who?"

"From Star Trek. They're…very close friends who are…unable to talk about their…feelings for each other."

Glancing up, I see Warren arch his brows. "Two gay men?"

"Oh, no. Well, not in canon. But they were the first slash ship. In fact, the term 'slash' for gay fic originates from them. Kirk-slash-Spock." I try to grin, blushing wildly.

Warren licks his lips. "We're not *unable* to talk—"

"Yeah. I mean—"

We both laugh. But then he comes closer still, and a hot lump rolls into my stomach. He says, "Do you, uh…want to? Talk?"

"God, no." More tense laughter. "I want…" *…to kiss you.* I puff out a breath, hot like I'm running a fever.

He approaches. Ridiculous to think a guy so big and confident would tiptoe before me, but that's what his halting steps look like. "Dee," he says, in a voice so deep it vibrates through me. "I'm here."

I snort. "Yeah."

"Dee."

With peculiar perception, he's positioned himself so I can let go of the counter and lean onto him without raising my head and risking exposure. Even so, it's the hardest thing I've done since leaving for CERN. As my forehead touches his chest, a gasp tears out of mine, and I press my face between his breasts to stifle it.

For a second, he's still. Then he carefully folds his arms around me. "Is this okay?"

I nod, fresh out of words. My heart bangs hard enough to shake my ribs. But after a minute, as he rocks me to and fro, a calm descends on me as deep as the ocean: a blissful absence of all thoughts and wants, and I feel I could stay like this forever.

6.

The next day I rise late to an empty house. There's a note from Warren letting me know they'll both be out till the evening, running some errands in town. It's sizzling outside. I stay in my room, browsing the websites of nearby universities, updating my CV, and writing emails with tentative inquiries for several people in the state who I've collaborated with in the past. Nothing better than a bit of work to prevent my thoughts from running circles around yesterday's events.

But my peace of mind is an illusion that shatters as soon as I hear Steve's car coming up the driveway. I almost drop my comb into the toilet trying to get my hair in order, and I change in and out of three identical black shirts before I settle on a crumpled loose top, sweating already.

I steel myself for awkwardness, but we go through the motions of preparing for dinner like any other day, and once we're seated, Steve expertly draws Warren and me into a lively discussion of the pros and cons of the mass-commercialization of video games. It's a subject we never tire of, and the titles we've sampled during my stay fuel endless theories and arguments.

Flushed with drink and loud conversation, I laugh while Steve caricatures the speech of some game studio CEO, bragging about billions of sales while claiming in the same breath that every player can have a fully customized experience. We're well into the second bottle of mead. When Warren squeezes my knee, the pleasant arousal that's been building inside me turns into fizzling euphoria.

He searches my face while sliding his hand to the middle of my thigh. "Shall we… retire?"

Heat rushes between my legs. I nod.

"Should I bring the bottle?" Steve asks as we push away from the table.

"Depends on how much you want to remember tomorrow," Warren says.

Everything, I think. I want to remember everything.

In the silence that follows, I realize I said it out loud.

Warren's hand slips into mine. He guides me to the living room, where just a day ago I stood shivering in anticipation of Steve's touch, and pulls me closer till my chest is flush against his. His heart is pounding, same as mine. As he circles my waist with his maimed arm, his eyes smolder with the unspoken question.

"Please," I breathe, and he leans down.

My world shrinks till there's nothing in it but the kiss I've coveted, oh, likely since the day we met. Neither of us close our eyes at first, but then his fingers sink into the hair at the back of my head, and the tip of his tongue parts my lips, and I cling around his neck, moaning.

His kiss is slow. Thorough. Like with everything else he does, he savors the moment: the gentle slide and brush of our tongues, the perfect fit of our lips, as if we've been doing this for years. His breathing grows heavy as he puts his weight in it, filling my mouth. I melt into a boneless mush and only realize he's picked me up when my feet touch the ground again.

Across the way, a dark, catlike figure with glimmering eyes crouches at the edge of the sofa. Little by little, my world enlarges enough to understand it's Steve, who's been sitting there, watching us, unblinking. The curl of his expressive brow betrays…vulnerability. And for once, it's easy for me to understand him. He has just witnessed the love of his life passionately kiss another man.

"Come," Warren rumbles, extending his hand.

Steve puffs out a breath he might've been holding this entire time. "You sure? I could just…go upstairs or something."

It's not clear who the question is directed at, and Warren and I answer at the same time. "No," Warren says, and I say, "Don't go."

He rubs his face, stands up, and takes our hands. Warren draws him into a kiss: shallow, nibbling, and so tender it makes my heart ache. I watch, entranced, while they touch and taste and reaffirm their love, bracing myself for the old hurt, but it never comes. All I feel is the rising burn of arousal.

I twine my fingers with Steve's, and he lets his head roll on Warren's shoulder so that we stand in his embrace in perfect symmetry. *See what it costs me to trust you again*, Steve's eyes say when he looks at me.

No one knows it better.

The moment passes, and the raw emotion in his gaze gives way to the more familiar mercurial glint. "Up for another one?"

"Hm?"

"Another first kiss, dummy."

My eyes must be comically wide because he laughs. "Come on. I won't bite. Unless you ask for it."

I nod enthusiastically, and he draws closer. His proximity is intoxicating. Here's that same expanse of velvety skin I longed to touch yesterday, the mild slopes of his chest and abs and the valleys between them. My hand shakes, hovering between us. He takes it and presses it against his breast, then deftly moves my thumb over his nipple, small and stiff like a pebble. And then he sighs, leaning his forehead against mine.

I kiss him with a needy whimper. His lips are every bit as soft and lush as I dreamed they would be. A painful flash of desire courses through me when his tongue darts out to meet mine, and I groan into his smiling mouth. Breaking off sooner than I'd like, he hooks an arm around my neck and hugs me, kissing my forehead. Then Warren's arms close around us.

"I love you both," he whispers.

The air between us is dense and moist with our breathing, almost completely devoid of oxygen. I open my mouth to try and get the words out; say, *I love you too*, but Warren kisses me again before I have the chance, and in another moment Steve joins in as well. It's a mess, and we laugh at the clumsy crossings of tongues and anglings of noses, but then the air grows thick again with sighs. The nerves in my skin wake into tingling alertness. My cock twitches when Steve's hand worms inside my back pocket and squeezes my butt. Then another hand—Warren's—cups my crotch, and the sensation is so intense that for a second I think I'll come from that alone like the touch-starved near-virgin I am.

"Guys," I breathe, but they pay me no heed. By some silent agreement, they manhandle me in concert, and before I know it, I'm sandwiched between them. Warren holds me from behind, his prosthetic arm draped over my chest in a light but sure grip, while his good hand slides under my top. I shudder at the contact, throwing my head back against his shoulder. I've never been this sensitive. Every touch sends live current to my groin. He presses into me with an appreciative grunt and his erection prods at my lower back.

And then Steve's hands are under my shirt too, all over my stomach and ribs and chest. His fingers find my nipples, pinch them into hardness, and I squirm, gasping, till he quiets me with his tongue. My hips jerk forward when his hard cock rubs against mine through our clothes. In response, Warren grinds against my ass.

Lightheaded, I clutch Warren's prosthesis with the desperation of a drowning man while the fingers of my other hand dig into Steve's shoulder.

"Oh, god," I manage when he lets me breathe. He gives me a diabolical smile as he unbuttons my pants. "Oh, god," I repeat. "Guys. I can't…I won't…"

Steve pauses, searching my eyes. "Too much? Too fast?"

From behind, Warren nuzzles my ear. "It's okay," he whispers. "We can go on another time."

Looking down, I see my cock straining up from under the waistband of my shorts, red and glistening with pre-come. Stopping is the last thing on my mind. "It's just…" I laugh, then press Steve's warm palm to my twitching stomach. "I'm like…edged already."

I feel Warren's smile on my neck. "Me too," he says in a deep, raw voice that sends a pulse down the live wire inside me.

Steve bites his lip trying to suppress giggles, but his gaze is soft and tender. I guide his hand back down till it closes gently around me. He kisses me, rubbing my cock slowly with the heel of his palm, then kneels and lowers my pants. My legs shake when he caresses my inner thighs, and Warren's grip on me tightens. His hips move against my butt in uneven thrusts.

I didn't know it was possible to be this aroused. I grab the back of Steve's head and pull his face between my legs. He looks up with drunken eyes, cups my balls, and draws his tongue from the base to the tip of my cock—over my underwear—then closes his lips around the wet stain on it.

Warren rumbles, turning my chin so he can fill my mouth with his tongue again. Below, Steve peels off my shorts, grips my shaft, and sucks in the rest.

It's overwhelming. Their hands and mouths are everywhere, their touches and kisses are everything, and I'm a helpless tangle of sensation, with excitement and pleasure swelling so huge inside me I fear I'll come apart at the seams. Steve's tongue circles me relentlessly, and I don't know if the obscene smacking noises come from him or from Warren's kisses, gone messy and urgent.

I've never felt this good, and I want it to last. But it doesn't.

"I'm gonna..." I manage on a stolen breath. "Fuck, I'm gonnnngh..."

The orgasm shatters me. Every nerve in my body ignites and dark stars explode in front of my eyes as I spurt into Steve's throat. I cry out, and next I hear a groan from deep inside Warren's chest as he comes, spilling with such force I feel it even through his pants.

I'm shaking. I feel like I might cry. Like I'm breaking asunder.

But they hold me together. Warren's arms are wrapped around me, his breath warm on my neck, while Steve rests his cheek on my trembling stomach, and for a long time we stay like that, absorbing the enormity of what just happened.

I taste salt as the tears of some unfathomable emotion trickle to my mouth from the corners of my eyes.

Steve looks up at us, and for a moment, his beautiful eyes shine with devotion. Then he grins. "You owe me one," he says. "Each!"

7.

I wake up in my room, alone, and it takes me minutes to convince myself it wasn't all a dream.

Warren had to half carry me to bed after I'd almost fainted bending down to scoop my clothes from the floor. I had thought I'd be too excited to fall asleep, that I'd rise after half an hour and rejoin them, but instead I slept like a baby.

Thinking of how good it felt to be with them, to be touched and kissed and handled, how simple and natural it was, like everything we do together, leads by some inconceivable Dee-logic to thinking of how many days we've wasted dancing around it. In a few weeks Steve will have to get back to work, and Warren too, when the school year starts. They'll move back to town, and if I want to stay close to them, I'll have to come up with some long-term arrangement that doesn't involve living off their charity.

Tears prick my eyes as I imagine parting with my friends. Going back to my old life, now that I've had a taste of...this, whatever it is, would be like returning to prison. A joyless, loveless existence hanging by the fingernails onto my dwindling passion for science, forever haunted by regrets.

A familiar creak stops that train of thought. I hold my breath. After a moment, I hear a stifled moan.

My body reacts, sending sweet, hot pressure between my legs even before my mind settles on whether or not I'm making it up. The door of my room is open—they must've left it like that. I slide out of bed to peek out. And true to Steve's word, their door is open too.

Another groan reaches my ears, and I tiptoe forward, enduring the indignity of my half-hard cock bobbing up and down. But then it goes all the way hard as I take in the scene.

Warren lies on his back in the middle of their king-sized bed, propped on pillows, his hair a magnificent mess, and Steve straddles his hips, facing him, oiled up and stretched out around Warren's erection.

"You're tight today," Warren murmurs.

"Nhhh," says Steve. "Because you two…left me blue-balled." His cock strains toward his belly as if to prove his point.

I swallow.

"Poor baby," Warren teases, stroking Steve with his good hand.

"Keep that up and I'll come."

Warren laughs. "You both need some serious stamina training."

"You were pretty quick yourself last night. Hands-free too."

During this banter, Steve has managed to lower himself another half inch. My heart races so fast I fear I'll faint. There's no way I can— They seem fine on their own— I should probably just—

"Wish he was here," Steve says softly.

"Me too."

"Actually—" I say, or try to, mouth too dry for anything but a whisper. But they hear me. Warren moves nothing but his eyes, as if he knew I'd been lurking there, while Steve twists elegantly, muscles flowing under his dark skin like water.

He breaks into a surprised smile. "Dee!"

"Come on in," Warren says, a pink blush spilling over his handsome features. He taps the bed beside him.

I hesitate in the doorway, hiding my ridiculous cock, which feels ready to burst. But as I step in, their expectant scrutiny excites me even further. Trembling, I climb onto the bed.

Steve is the first to kiss me, while Warren strokes me gently. He thumbs the bead of pre-come over my slit, and I thrust into his palm, one hand on his bare chest, the other touching Steve's cock. We sigh into each other's mouths. When I bend over Warren to kiss him as well, Steve palms my butt and his fingers slide over my hole.

"God, you're hot," Steve whispers.

"No, you are." I look in Warren's eyes. "And you."

Steve chuckles, dripping some lube on Warren's fingers. "Dee. Have you, uh…done this before?"

"No. But I want to." I start to kiss and lick down Steve's gorgeous chest and stomach.

"We'll go easy," Warren says. His touch is wet and cold as he spreads the lube between my butt cheeks. My balls tighten. Breathing hard, I take Steve's cock in my mouth just as Warren's finger enters me.

This feels…insanely good. Steve has started to rock slowly, riding Warren while thrusting into my mouth. His cock is heavy and warm, in delightful contrast to the lingering cold of Warren's light probing. I wriggle, ready for more, and he adds another finger. His breaths come in bursts now that Steve's fucking him in earnest. The head of Steve's cock rubs against my throat, driving tears from my closed eyes.

"Ease up," Steve breathes.

I lift my head, a thick rope of drool hanging between us, and mouth, "More."

"God." He grips my butt-cheek, tangling his fingers with Warren's to coat them, and then it's three fingers inside me. Leaning my forehead on Warren's, I steal the hot breath from his mouth as I sink my tongue into it, but then I almost seize when a finger brushes my prostate. I arch my back and push into their hands. "Fuck!"

Steve chuckles breathlessly. "I knew you had it in you, Spock."

"Shut up, McCoy."

"What? No! Uhura, please."

"Now I'll *have to* see this show," Warren rumbles, and we all laugh.

They pull out as I shift forward, nearly edged. Fleetingly I wonder how the girth and length of three fingers compares to having a fat cock inside. My own cock drips over Warren's belly. "Let's do this," I breathe.

I straddle Warren, chest to chest, and Steve pulls on my hips till his hot erection glides between my butt cheeks. He roams my back with one hand as he guides himself in with the other, and all the while Warren rocks us both up and down from beneath, undeterred by our combined weight, eyes locked with mine. No more laughs, now. Excitement blooms in my chest and rolls into my gut, making me gasp for air.

"You move at your own pace, yeah?" says Steve. He presses forward, and then he's in, and it feels so good to have him inside me I think I might weep again. With a deep breath, I prop myself up, bracing on Warren's firm breasts, and slowly push back.

"Oh, god," I mutter, my spine arching. The stretch is phenomenal, but almost disappointingly painless. I can feel it all the way up between my ribs, I swear, and all the way down the length of my cock, and when Warren's hand closes around it, the pleasure spikes in me so violently I cry out.

My grip on what's happening goes loose. Steve utters one tender obscenity after another. Warren's sighs turn to grunts. His chest is slippery with sweat, and my fingers bury in his flesh deep enough to bruise. Our movements are out of tune at first but grow steady as the two of them fall into the familiar rhythm of long-time lovers. All I have to do is close my eyes and let them carry me.

I feel the stretch anew as Steve grows even harder inside me. One of his arms is wound around my waist, and he squeezes me closer, biting my shoulder as he comes. The teeth alone are enough to end me, but then Warren's grip on me tightens almost painfully as he groans, making the final, jerky thrusts. I yelp, convulsing. My release throbs out of me in rope after rope, spilling all over Warren's chest.

My arms trembling, I fall on top of him. His heart pounds and his breaths stutter just the same as mine. Sweat breaks out all over my body as the strange notion I had last night, that I'm too small to contain these feelings, washes over me again. *Little Dee*. I hide my face between Warren's breasts.

Eventually we recover enough to untangle. Steve pulls out, lifts himself up from Warren gingerly, and wraps the condoms in a tissue. I use another to wipe myself and Warren, who watches us with a big, sleepy smile. At last we settle one next to another, with me in between, staring contentedly at the ceiling.

"I'm not going back to Europe," I say before I know I'll say it. "I'm not going back to my family, either. I want to stay here. Not *here* here, but close enough to keep in touch. I have enough saved to stay afloat for a couple months, and if all else fails, there's always teaching. I—" I grope for their hands. "I love you. I don't want to lose you again."

Relief floods me, and I laugh, though my eyes sting.

My friends rise on their elbows in perfect sync and hover over me.

"This might not be the best moment to make big decisions," Steve says. "You should think about it when you're not high on mind-blowing sex. That said…" He presses his lips to my hand. "Thank fucking god you're considering it. I was afraid you'd be like, 'thanks for the tumble, but *real* life awaits.'"

I take a breath to reply, but Warren beats me to it with a soft chuckle. "Telling Dee to think is like telling water to be wet." He takes me by the chin till I face him. "You've been at it for weeks. Haven't you?"

"Months," I confess. "Ever since the stroke."

"What a coincidence," Steve cries, affecting wide-eyed shock. "We've been thinking about it for months too!"

"Years," Warren rumbles, settling down again with his head over my heart. "You never 'lost us', you know. You never stopped being a part of our lives. So you're not *welcome*. You're welcome *back*."

I look at Steve helplessly through a gush of tears. He smiles, kisses Warren's temple, then my cheek, and all the pent-up tenderness in me explodes in a single, silent sob.

Then I'm suddenly all right. I squeeze Warren as best I can, my arm puny compared to the vast expanse of his sweaty back.

We'll be all right.

Steve nuzzles into the crook of my shoulder. "So…ready for another round?"

A Communion and Other Rituals

Alec J. Marsh

aftercare, age difference, bipoc, bisexual, blood drinking, blow job, bondage, demisexual, dirty talk, dragon, established relationship, exhibitionism, f/m/m/m/nb, f/nb, face fucking, hand job, m/m/m, masochist, modern with magic, multiple orgasms, non-binary, open relationship, orgasm control, orgy, past tense, penis in anus sex, politics, public sex, religion, sex furniture, spit roasting, strip club, telepathic communication, third person limited point of view, united states of america, vampire, voyeurism

The king of the Portland Underground held court in a club called Sticks and Stones, tucked between a bar advertising three-dollar well drinks and a neon sign of a woman with her tits out. Isaac couldn't say why he was shocked, but he was.

"This is a strip club," he said.

"It's Portland," Holly answered, as if that explained it. "And he's a succubus. Where else would he live?"

Isaac grimaced.

"You aren't turning prude on me, are you?"

Isaac raised an eyebrow. "People can take their clothes off as often as they like, for as much money as they can make doing it," he said stiffly.

"I'm not the target audience."

"I'm teasing," Holly said, and leaned into him. "You'll be okay?"

"Of course I'll be okay," he said, and leaned down to kiss her. She responded enthusiastically, grabbing a fistful of his hair, her fangs pressing against his lower lip, and Isaac forgot they were on a public street. Holly's kisses always did that to him. Holly herself, gorgeous and graceful and funny, was the gravitational center of any room she was in. He thought he'd understood desire before he met her, but there was no one who affected him the way Holly did. She could turn off his brain with a raised eyebrow and a smirk, and now, she was doing a lot more than that. She grabbed his ass and ground her belly into his cock, eliciting a broken gasp from him.

"Work—" he mumbled against her lips, grabbing for the fragments of his focus.

"Work," she agreed smugly and stepped back. She wiggled, pulling her dress down and her boobs up. "We'll parlay with Sebastian, you'll tip generously, and then we'll be back to the hotel, and I'll make it up to you."

"I don't mind," he promised. He glanced back at the sign. "I've been to plenty of drag shows. This is basically the same thing."

"Exactly the same thing," Holly said. "Sebastian's been doing drag longer than drag's been gay." She squeezed his hand and led him inside.

It was what Isaac expected: dark and loud, with sex and alcohol assaulting his senses. It was also clean, with plenty of small booths and a long hallway in the back leading to God-knew-where. Lori's court in Seattle was much the same, although that had more of an industrial hipster bar feel, even with the dance floor. Vampires didn't have many places that were just for them, which left the few clubs they eked out needing to provide for everyone.

A stage ran along the back of the room, a hundred tiny disco balls following the line of the curtains. A woman spun on the pole, but the front row was a mix of genders. There was no sign of Sebastian, but in this lighting and with the amount of makeup everyone was wearing, he could have been anyone.

Holly leaned on the bar. A man with a pink mullet, long feather earrings, and a cropped sequin top nodded at her, mixed several bright-blue drinks, and then gave them his full attention.

"What can I do for you, love?" he asked.

"We're here to meet Sebastian," Holly said. "Professional business, unfortunately."

His gaze flicked to the stage, then back to them. "Do you have an appointment?"

"If I did, I would have said."

The man raised an eyebrow with two rings in it.

"I'm here representing the Seattle coven," she said. "It's, uh. Delicate business."

"I'm sure it is." He sighed. "Sebastian's busy tonight. Should I pull him off stage?"

Isaac looked back at the woman upside down on the pole, head thrown back, hair flying, and couldn't tell if she was Sebastian or not. It made him feel much more at home.

"I can wait," Holly said.

The man nodded. "Great. Let me get you drinks."

He pulled several bottles out from under the bar and proceeded to mix without asking their orders. He wore rings on every finger and two on some of them, and his leather bracelets glinted under the neons. "You should enjoy the show," he said. "We've got a good lineup tonight. All types. I'll let Sebastian know you're here. Anything I should add?"

"We're not here to start trouble," Holly said.

"Oh, I know." The bartender grinned, flashing teeth, and Isaac saw the danger. "I wouldn't have let you in if you were."

Anyone who worked here would be part of the underground, and the man smelled like vampire. But it was easy to forget that, sometimes, when everyone Isaac spent time with these days smelled like magic of some kind. There was a predator under the earrings and nail polish. He'd missed it completely until the mask dropped.

He took his drink with a nod of thanks. He wasn't going to protest whatever he was handed, as long as that man stayed hospitable.

Holly tilted her head. "You're security here," she said.

The man blinked once in acknowledgement.

"Cedro sends his regards."

The predator was gone as soon as it had appeared. "He's good?"

Holly nodded. "He likes being a kept man."

The bartender's next smile was boyish. "It's a good life. There's an empty booth on the second floor. I'll come get you when we're ready for you."

"Kisses," Holly answered. Just as Isaac was about to follow her toward the stairs, the bartender reached out and grabbed his wrist. Their eyes met, and Isaac couldn't move. The man's eyes were very blue. He could have commanded Isaac to do anything, and Isaac would have obeyed. It wasn't often he brushed up against power like that. The only time he'd seen it before was from Holly, and she directed her power inward.

The bartender whistled. "You should have warned me, Holly," he said. "You've got a firecracker on your hands."

Holly's answering smile was wicked, sharp as a blade. Isaac's blood heated as the two predators stared each other down. "He'll be good," Holly said, sickly sweet.

The bartender let go, his fingers tracing Isaac's palm. "I'm sure he will."

The booth was cozy and private and smelled of lemons. The woman on stage had finished her act in the time it had taken them to climb the stairs, and a man with perfect abs was now shaking his ass.

"Who was that?" Isaac asked.

Holly drained half her glass. "Security," she said. Then, "Bradford Greenway. He's—well, no one's sure how old he is, because he's very good at slipping out of the historical record, but creeping on toward a millennium, I think. Old friend of Cedro's."

"Those are strange thoughts to reconcile." Cedro was one of the only vampires Isaac had met who had neither ego nor ambition. He would never have been involved in politics at all except for his unfortunate attachment to the queen of Seattle and longtime friendship with Holly. He didn't collect enemies like Isaac did. "Then again," he said, "Bradford seems to like being a kept man." Isaac reconsidered. "He's fucking Sebastian."

"Almost certainly," Holly said. "Rumor has it the king of Portland has two consorts: the oldest vampire in North America and a literal fucking dragon."

Isaac gulped down his martini. "You might have warned me."

"Didn't want you in your head about it," Holly said. "We aren't here to start a war anyway."

"Great," Isaac said. "So the dragon will be on our side." He was already ready for another drink. The music picked up; the man danced faster. He watched without seeing. He was a bad person to bring along on a diplomatic mission. He served the queen of Seattle, and everyone liked her, but if people knew anything about him, they knew he had slippery loyalties and had been involved in a shitshow of a power grab that had resulted in several public deaths. If he didn't have the queen's forgiveness or Holly's patronage, he would be dead.

"Please tell me I'm not here to threaten the dragon."

"'Course not," Holly said. "You're here to be sweet and earnest and awkward. I'll threaten the dragon."

"That makes me feel so much better."

Holly leaned her pointed chin on his shoulder and ran her nails up his chest. "Need me to take your mind off it?"

He pressed a kiss to her temple. "I'd like nothing better, but I'm a distracted mess as it is."

Holly still kissed him, slow and deep, before she pulled away. "I love what I do to you," she said.

Isaac wanted to lie down in her lap. He wasn't good at these sorts of political negotiations. He scrubbed his face with his hands. He was here for Queen Lori, and that was a good enough reason to try. Demons were creeping through cracks around Seattle, and someone had to stop them before they revealed the underground to humans. Lori had said he'd be useful. He would do a good job for her. He'd do whatever she said.

A low moan cut through the music. He looked around, but the booths were high and curved inward.

The noise came again.

Holly rolled her eyes. "Brad put us on the sex floor," she said, and flicked her gaze at the curtains hanging open at the entrance to their booth.

The moans were picking up speed, combining with the unmistakable slap of flesh on flesh. Isaac rubbed the plush velvet of the curtains between his fingers, and it sparked at the touch. Soundproofing spells, he guessed; if only their neighbors had thought to close their curtains properly.

Holly giggled as the person in the next booth let out a particularly theatrical scream. She pulled Isaac back to the corner and hooked a leg over his.

"I need you to focus," she said. "You're Lilith's vessel, even if you don't act like it. That's power."

He twined his fingers between hers and kissed her knuckles. In dim light like this, her tawny eyes glimmered golden. She was his high priestess, and she was the one who could shoot lightning from her fingers. She was the one who could level a room with a sword before anyone had time to draw on her. He had questionable visions of the future and a direct line to the Great Goddess, Lilith. Power, maybe. Predator, he was not.

"I'm focused," he said. "I'm here to work." He exhaled. Sebastian Xie had the most extensive magic library in North America and two ancient beings on his side. If he couldn't help, no one could.

As if on cue, footsteps sounded on the tile floor. Isaac ripped his gaze from Holly's. Two men stood at their booth. One was tall and broad, his black T-shirt clinging to his muscled chest and his powerful thighs wrapped in motorcycle chaps. His long, dark curls hung loose, and his eyes glowed green in the half-light. He smelled of brimstone and salt.

The other man was slight and wore nothing but a frothy pink bathrobe, his face still made up in drag. He'd taken off his wig, and his hair was revealed to be jet black, held back with a pearl headband. He slid into the booth across from them. The other man remained standing, leaning against the booth with his arms crossed.

"I'm the king of Portland," Sebastian said unnecessarily. "It has been a while."

"An age." Holly didn't feign obeisance, but Isaac bowed his head.

"This is Kyril," he said. "My second." Kyril was hard to look away from, and the thing was, Isaac could picture him with wings, could nearly see smoke curling from his nostrils. He swallowed dryly. Kyril met his gaze, and his lips twitched up in a smirk.

"And here is your little protégé," Sebastian purred, and Isaac looked back with effort. "He's cute." Sebastian's gaze was sharp, sizing Isaac up, no doubt seeing his weaknesses.

"Lori came down to see me when she became queen," Sebastian said to him. "I was expecting you to come along."

"Isaac was too young to be left alone," Holly said.

Sebastian hummed. "A baby," he said. "You don't smell like a baby."

His five years were nothing compared to centuries. He swallowed. "There's some…" He waved his hand vaguely.

Sebastian clicked his tongue. "Don't be coy. Tell me what you are, darling."

"I don't know," Isaac said. "A chosen of Lilith. I can see into the future and across space. I speak to her in my dreams, or I did. She's gone quiet lately." He wasn't here to be a threat.

Sebastian leaned forward, robe gaping to show a sliver of marble-smooth chest. "You can speak to the Great Goddess?"

"We used to," Holly said. "I'm her priestess, and Isaac's her anchor. And even so, we can't seem to contact her."

"And you think I can help?"

Holly raised an eyebrow that said otherwise she wouldn't be here.

Sebastian pressed his forefinger to his lower lip. "What's the hurry?"

"There's lilins in the Cascades," Holly said. "They're starting to hunt people. That's bad enough, but the park rangers think it's rabid bears, and they're about to start clearing out innocent animals. I need to know if Lilith sent them, or if they've gone rogue, and if I have permission to kill them."

"And where do I come in?"

"You're an energy worker. I need a power-up."

Sebastian sucked his teeth. "What's in it for me?"

Isaac didn't need to look at Holly to know she was rolling her eyes. "Besides the long-term ecological health of the Cascades? If lilins break containment and start killing people in the cities, you'll be next."

"Altruism, then," Sebastian said.

Holly huffed. "Don't waste my time. I'm asking a favor."

"I don't know why," Sebastian said. "You have a nine-volt battery in your pocket already."

It took Isaac a beat to realize Sebastian was talking about him. "I'm useless," he said quickly.

"I doubt that." Sebastian looked him over with a critical eye. "You might be still coming into your power, but there's a lot of it there. If you're as sworn to Holly as I think you are, she should be able to draw on you whenever she needs it."

They were mates, it was true. They had a psychic connection that came and went at inconvenient times and a compass in Isaac's heart that led him home to her.

"If he was enough, I wouldn't be here," Holly said. "Now, will you help me or not?"

"Careful," Kyril rumbled, and even his voice spoke of age. "You know who you're talking to."

Holly lifted her chin. Neon reflected off the brown of her cheek, and her eyes flashed. "Don't waste my time. We both know if I was here to attack, my organs would be in neat little boxes on their way to my queen already."

Sebastian chuckled. "I'll help you for a chance at seeing the Goddess for myself. It's no skin off my nose to do a little energy working, and you haven't leveled any threats at me. But I'm a succubus. I've got one skill set, and you'll have to work with it."

"You're an energy worker," Holly said. "There's more energy than lust."

"Perhaps." Sebastian shrugged. "But I have a specialty, and it sounds like you're in a hurry."

"I don't fuck for power," Holly said. She had, once—Isaac had picked up snatches from her—the desperation of being poor and Black in the 17th century, the need to keep men happy. She'd come out of it dripping in jewels and blood, teeth and claws secured so no one could ever touch her again.

"Don't worry, you're not my type." Sebastian's eyes locked with Isaac's. "Do you think your mate will share you?"

Isaac's stomach flipped.

Sebastian's dark brown eyes glittered, and his lips parted. He wanted Isaac.

Isaac glanced at Kyril hopefully.

Kyril grinned, and Isaac understood that he wasn't just a pretty face and thick muscles.

"I'll do it," he said. "For the sake of the poor little bears."

Holly grabbed Isaac by the neck and pressed her cheek against his. "You don't have to do this." She spoke into his mind, the words more an impression than language.

"I'm willing," Isaac replied, and kissed her.

Holly drew away first. "So, what—he sucks your cock, and you give me what I want?"

"He's the one who has to come," Sebastian said. "As many times as we can manage it. The more people watching him, the better. Get him all charged up, and then you and I will feast."

Isaac's heart jumped to his throat. His cock twitched at the promise in Sebastian's voice. He glanced at the stage, where two topless women shimmied. Once, he'd gone to a goth club in Belltown, and he'd been followed to the bathroom by a man in leathers who outweighed him by easily a hundred pounds. The man had pressed Isaac up against the stall door and fucked him until he couldn't walk straight for a week. All through the experience, voices had filtered in from the club.

Until Holly had fang-fucked him in front of the Seattle court, it had been the most erotic experience of his life.

"No," Holly said.

"Yes," Isaac argued quickly. "I'll do it."

Sebastian laughed again. "That's my boy."

"Not a boy," Isaac said, too preoccupied with the thought of going to his knees on the stage to hold his tongue.

"I'm sorry," Sebastian said seriously. "I shouldn't have assumed. Well, darling, I'll need to go tell people the show is ending early tonight. Unless they want to stay for yours. Any limits?"

Isaac didn't want to give any. He wanted to surrender his body and his mind to the people in the club, to Sebastian, to Bradford with his heavy rings and leather cuffs. He wanted them to treat him like the desperate slut he was. But no limits was a red flag in any cruising situation, because it meant he hadn't considered the consequences, and he very much had.

He resisted the urge to trace the scars that no longer existed on his arms. "No knives." They brought a release it would take him weeks to recover from, one he couldn't trust.

"We can work with that," Sebastian said. "Show time at midnight."

Holly twitched the curtains shut. All sound from the outside cut off abruptly, and it was only the two of them, lit by a single flickering electric candle.

"I don't need this that bad," Holly said. "We can just kill the lilins and our Goddess can deal with the consequences. It's not your fault she's gone silent."

Isaac said, "It takes energy to come to this plane. If she's tapped out, that might be our fault." They had certainly called on her plenty when they fought to secure the Seattle Coven. "Even if it isn't, we swore to help her. But also…" He shrugged as if trying to brush off his excitement. "I want to."

"Want to help Lilith, or want to get fucked in front a crowd?"

Isaac's face must have given him away because Holly's smile quirked up, amazed.

"You never told me you wanted group sex. You know I wouldn't have minded."

Their relationship was business partners as much as lovers. They spent too long in each other's minds and pockets. Sometimes, the thrill of a new partner was a breath of fresh air. Holly had old lovers, including one casual girlfriend who came back periodically, once she'd gotten over the fact that Holly would be twenty forever and she would continue to age. But Isaac had been so busy trying to come to grips with being a vampire that he hadn't had time to do something as pedestrian as date. But then, even when he had been human, he'd never dated. He'd hurtled from painful, anonymous release to codependent abuse and back again.

"It's not the group sex," he said. "It's—uh—the public part of it, I guess."

Her eyebrows went up and her grin got wider. "You nasty little harlot. I never would have guessed."

"It's not really your thing."

Holly, for all that she turned every head in every room and dressed to accentuate it, was deeply private. All the more private because she tricked everyone into thinking she was an open book. It was only after the fact that he understood what she had sacrificed to claim him publicly as her mate. She didn't enjoy anything that might show people a weakness, even a weakness like him.

"It's not," Holly agreed. "Can I watch, though?"

He'd known she would be watching, but all the blood still flowed to his cock at her words. "I wouldn't do it if you weren't," he said.

Her grin turned sly. "I'll be watching," she promised. "I'll let all those men ruin you, fuck you open again and again and again until you're actually at your limit. I hope you cry."

He squirmed now, and Holly leaned forward. Her teeth grazed his neck and her nails scraped against his jeans, tracing the pulsing outline of his cock. "You think you're begging after I'm done with you?" she whispered. "Just imagine what a whole crowd can do. Think I can give them tips? I want to see two of them take your ass at once."

Isaac moaned. Holly squeezed his cock. He was already dizzy.

Holly drew her hand back. "Not tonight," she said into his ear. "Tonight you're Sebastian's property, and you'll only come when he lets you. Understand?"

Isaac swallowed. "And if I don't?"

"If you fuck this up for me?" Her lips were back at his throat. Her teeth pierced the hollow at his shoulder, a place where she could leave a livid, bloody mark without taking too much blood. "I'll have you locked up so tight you can't come for a month."

The spinning disco lights had been turned off, but the overhead lights were just bright enough that Isaac couldn't judge how many people were in the crowd, and he couldn't hear heartbeats over the soft techno beat. The pole had been taken off the stage, replaced with a leather bench and a rack of toys.

Sebastian approached. His dressing gown dripped off one shoulder, revealing an expanse of milky skin. He took Isaac's hand and led him to center stage.

"Fellow degenerates," Sebastian said. "Thank you for staying for tonight's show. We hope our willing sacrifice for the night will entertain."

Isaac was aware of every stitch of clothing that rubbed against his skin. If a match dragged down his chest, it would be put to flame just from contact with the heat pounding through his veins. He reached for his shirt buttons, already hazy with the beat of the music and the press of people's eyes, and Sebastian laid two fingers on his wrist.

Not yet.

Sebastian beckoned. Holly slithered onstage, a sway in her step and a gleam in her eye. This was the Holly he had first fallen to his knees for, the one he would serve until the last drop of blood fell from her body. She wore the clothes she had come in, a slinky gold shirt and black jeans, a sliver of the warm brown skin of her stomach visible. In her right hand, she held a leather whip. She took a seat on a raised dais behind them, and the braid of the whip trickled over her knee and hung between her legs.

"For tonight, we have our representative from Seattle," Sebastian introduced her. He had a presence that brought the crowd to silence, lent anything he said gravitas. "She has graciously lent us her plaything." He cupped Isaac's chin with his hands.

Isaac wasn't used to looking up, but Sebastian wore stilettos that lifted him above everyone else. He pressed a thumb to Isaac's lower lip.

"Our rules," he said. "From this moment forth, you make no decisions. You may beg, but we do not promise to please you. We will hurt you, if it gives us pleasure to hear you cry. We will chain you, if it gives us pleasure to see you bound. Your queen may stop the proceedings at any time, but she will not stop us on your behalf. You belong to us until dawn. Do you consent?"

Isaac nodded. Then, "Yes," he managed, past dry lips.

"Very good. Now, may I kiss you, my lamb?"

Isaac shivered at the nickname. His goddess called him that.

Sebastian's nails bit into his skin. "I asked you a question."

"You may do whatever you want to me," he replied.

Sebastian smiled glittery lips and pressed his open mouth to Isaac's. It was as thorough as a fucking, tongue and lips, deep into Isaac's soul, Sebastian's touch pulling far more from Isaac than physical pleasure. Sebastian's mind caressed his, stroking Isaac nearly to climax within moments.

He pulled away, and Isaac whined.

"You're very easy," Sebastian cooed. He unbuttoned Isaac's shirt, nipped at exposed skin with the flat of his teeth, and slowly pushed it off Isaac's shoulders.

Sebastian undid Isaac's belt and slipped it out of his belt loops. Brad and Kyril circled Isaac. He turned his head to follow them, and Sebastian grabbed his face so tight his nails pieced skin. Blood trickled down his chin. Sebastian considered it for a moment, then wiped his bloody fingertip down Isaac's sternum.

Warm hands pulled Isaac's wrists behind his back; cuffs clicked into place. He shuddered.

Sebastian peeled Isaac's pants off, his hands on Isaac's hips just enough direction to tell him to step backward, out of his pants. He was fully naked, surrounded by a triangle of men who watched him with predatory intent. His cock bobbed in the cool air, and his stomach quivered with anticipation.

Sebastian licked his lips. "Down," he commanded.

Isaac dropped, his knees slamming into the slick black stage. Sebastian trailed his nails through Isaac's hair, then looped Isaac's belt around his throat and pulled it tight. The stiff leather pressed against his Adam's apple, nudging his chin up.

Those same warm hands adjusted his ankles and snapped cuffs around them, too, forcing his knees as far apart as they could go without pain. The anticipation of aches throbbed in his hips.

He tugged Isaac toward his hips and the neat, tight bulge of his cock in his pink briefs. His robe and Isaac's mouth fell open.

"Do you want this?" Sebastian asked.

Isaac nodded. He didn't deserve this attention, to have another vampire as powerful as Sebastian letting him pay homage.

Sebastian raised an eyebrow.

"Please," Isaac whispered, then louder, "Please, Majesty, let me taste you."

He guided Isaac forward with his belt again, and Isaac pressed an open-mouthed kiss to the fabric of Sebastian's underwear. The chain between his wrists pulled taut, bending his shoulders back. Isaac licked up, sucked his lips around the damp spot where the tip of Sebastian's cock lay.

"Keep talking."

"Thank you," Isaac mumbled, lips brushing against fabric. "I want more; please, fill me up."

Sebastian rolled his hips against Isaac's mouth. He tightened Isaac's collar until he couldn't draw breath or swallow. Arousal shot through him, and his hips bucked as he strained for Sebastian's cock.

Sebastian pushed down the waistband of his underwear and slipped his cock between Isaac's desperate, drooling lips. He cupped Isaac's jaw and ran his thumb over the hollow of Isaac's cheek.

It wasn't enough. Isaac tried to move his head, to fuck his mouth on Sebastian's cock as he should have, but Sebastian controlled the pace—slow—the tip of his cock meeting the tip of Isaac's tongue.

"Look at you," Sebastian crooned. "You're so eager. You're being so good, aren't you? I could play with you for hours." He tugged the belt and gave Isaac another inch of cock. "This is where you belong," he continued. "You're a desperate little slut, and all you're good for is pleasing us." He kept stroking Isaac's jaw slowly, maddeningly. Isaac was hollow all through, his cock aching, his balls tight. He tried to beg, but all he could manage was a whine deep in his chest.

"All of Portland will know you're nothing but a set of holes for any man to use."

Isaac's muscles tensed, his hips bucked frantically. He tried to get his mouth free to speak, his hands free to grab his cock, but he was at the coven's mercy. He climaxed, gasping for control, shaking against his bonds.

Sebastian stepped back and pulled his robe tight. He clicked his tongue. "Oh, honey," he said softly. "What a mess you've made. Who gave you permission to do that?"

"I'm sorry," Isaac gasped.

"You'll have to be punished," Sebastian pouted. "Luckily, you have two good holes worth using until you're ready again. But I see no reason to be gentle now that you've wasted my time."

Isaac trembled. Kyril's massive hands, burning hot, lifted him to his feet and slung him on the bench. It was just big enough to hold his torso, his hips bent over one end, his head hanging off the other.

The snap of leather cracked through the air, and then the pain hit, searing up from his thighs. He gasped, but as fast as the pain crashed through him, so did the resultant pleasure.

Another crack and another wave of pleasure. Isaac's eyes slipped shut. There was nothing but the throbbing in his thighs, the trembling in the pit of his stomach. He was nothing but flesh, electric sensation.

And another crack. Isaac moaned. Cool hands gripped his ass and dug fingers into the blooming bruises.

"You're enjoying this," Brad accused.

Isaac whimpered and squirmed under the pressure, grinding against the leather under him.

"Want something stronger?"

Isaac shook his head into the bench.

Brad's nails dug in. "I didn't hear you."

"No," Isaac said.

"Too bad." Brad pulled Isaac up by his handcuffs, bending his back into a painful arc, and Kyril loomed over him. "Show him your trick."

Kyril's eyes kindled brighter, and his smile took on a sharp edge. Red-hot coals glowed under the darker swirl of fingerprints. "How many will it be?"

"Until he begs you to stop," Brad said. He pulled Isaac against him and locked his arm just under Isaac's ribs.

Kyril pressed a finger to his sternum. Isaac's flesh sizzled, and he yelled obligingly. It hurt far worse than the flogging had.

"Do you like that?" Kyril growled.

"No," he lied.

"Want me to stop?"

"Punish me," Isaac gasped, "I deserve it."

Kyril pressed another finger a few inches down. The pain was unbelievable, shorting out any resistance Isaac might have given. He panted and snarled, trying to get some clarity back. The air around him was hot. Was Kyril smoldering too? He could smell burned flesh, and smoke curled around his face.

A third finger pushed into the soft flesh at the top of his belly.

"Ask me to stop," Kyril said.

Isaac heaved for breath. He would take this. He could take this. His cock jumped.

Sebastian's chest pressed against his shoulder, his hand lazily stroked Isaac's cock. "That's right, baby," he said in Isaac's ear. "You know when you need to be taught better. But oh, dear, you like this, don't you?"

"I didn't ask permission," Isaac said, "and I'm sorry."

"So very sorry," Sebastian said, and pressed his fingers to Isaac's open wound. Isaac's groan was ripped from him, desperate. "Next time you come before I say so, the burns will be lower. Let him go, Brad."

Brad pushed Isaac down to the bench again, his tender, burned flesh sticking against the leather. He squirmed, trying to get comfortable. The head of his cock dragged through the hair on his stomach, as if willing to take whatever touch it could get. Brad pressed him the rest of the way down, so he had no room to grind.

Kyril took a fistful of Isaac's hair, bending his neck up so Isaac's eyes were level with the bulge of his arousal against his fly. His belt buckle was an enormous flower, petals sharp enough to wound. He flicked his belt open and freed his cock. It was so heavy it hung down between the zipper of his jeans. Isaac opened his mouth without being told, and Kyril held Isaac's jaw as he guided his cock in. If Isaac still had to breathe, he wouldn't have been able to take his entire length, but Kyril fucked to the back of his throat and then farther. He rolled his hips, filling Isaac so completely he couldn't tease or caress or swallow, only take what he was given.

Cool fingers slicked his ass and delved inside him. It was the most cursory of preparations before the familiar slippery thickness of a cock spread him open. When Sebastian began to thrust, Isaac's mouth moved around Kyril.

Then Kyril started fucking properly too, pistoning into his mouth, sliding pre-come across his tongue. He lifted Isaac by his hair, and Isaac could do nothing but hang limply, his arms still cuffed behind his back.

Kyril pulled out and came all over his face, spurt after spurt of boiling-hot seed dripping down his cheeks and spattering his mouth. He dropped Isaac back to the bench with a crash.

Isaac's thighs shook as Sebastian pressed a hand to the small of his back and kept moving inside him.

"How did he taste, darling?"

"Like salt," Isaac panted. "Like stone." Come slid down his cheek and between his lips. He shoved back against Sebastian's cock, trying to urge him deeper.

"You're so tight," Sebastian murmured. "Been a while since you've been fucked properly—that feels good—"

"You feel so good," Isaac answered. "Please, I'm close—"

"Not yet," Sebastian told him.

Isaac bit his cheek and clenched his fists as Sebastian went deeper, rolling his hips in time with the thumping of the music. Every twitch was agony, but he focused on the taste of blood in his mouth, the ache of his shoulders—anything but the drag of flesh against his pleasure center.

Sebastian dug his thumbs into the bruises on his ass and leaned forward. "That's right," he whispered. "Come for me."

Isaac shuddered, spending against the leather, limbs shaking. The noises behind him faded and warped; the music was still playing, but he couldn't parse it. Sebastian was whispering something to him that sounded only like the susurration of fabric against skin.

Soft hands undid his cuffs and turned him over. The ceiling was strung with tiny, soft lights.

His arms were spread, dropped down over the edge of the table, and cuffed to the legs. His knees were bent, his ankles cuffed. He inhaled, Sebastian's peculiar musk and brimstone and lilies, and many hands were massaging his over-sensitive skin.

His head rolled, and he saw Holly on her throne. She was sprawled, limp, eyes heavy, but she was still fully clothed. The whip was tight in her hands.

She licked her lips, and her mind brushed against Isaac's. There weren't any words but, instead, a flood of her arousal, her desire for him. She was contained, but Isaac knew if he knelt at her feet, he would be able to smell her, and if he bent his head between her legs, she would be dripping for him. His mouth watered, and a thread of desire curled in his stomach, though his body was too exhausted to respond.

Fingers dipped into his burns, and he dropped back into his body with a jolt. Sebastian leaned over him, eyes black in the dimness, and he smiled. "That's my lamb," he murmured, and pressed two fingers into Isaac's mouth.

Isaac wrapped his tongue and lips around them obediently, swallowed, and tasted blood. Heat shot through him, and he was half-hard again, thrashing against his restraints.

Brad leaned over Isaac to kiss Sebastian, and the head of his cock rubbed against Isaac's cheek. Sebastian met the kiss, but his hands stayed on Isaac's chest, toying with his burns. Hands so hot they could only be Kyril's stroked his cock, grip punishingly tight, twisting the delicate skin. Every stroke was like sandpaper, and yet he responded, straining for more touch, seeking another release. Lube was added, its slick coolness easing the torturous friction.

Sebastian's hands lifted, his stilettos clicked against the stage, and then he lifted one long leg and stepped across the table where Isaac was chained, straddling him in one smooth movement. He trapped Isaac's aching cock under the crease of his thigh and wriggled into place.

"I never thought I would have the lamb of the Goddess between my legs," he observed. "Do you want to fuck me, my lamb?"

Isaac nodded.

Sebastian's nails bit into his skin.

"Yes," Isaac amended, and then, "no, please, I'm not sure I can take it." Any more sensation might send him into fits; spots swam before his eyes.

"That's too bad," Sebastian purred. "You don't actually get a choice."

He rose up, then sank onto Isaac's cock. He was slick and smooth, tight enough that Isaac sobbed. Sebastian lowered himself to his elbows so they were pressed chest to chest, lips inches apart. He kissed the corner of Isaac's mouth, and then the pulse point of his jaw.

Holly's whip cracked through the air.

"A pity," Sebastian whispered. "I'd risk anyone else's wrath, if it meant I got to taste you. You smell like the desert." He kissed again.

Holly's rage broke through Isaac's fogged mind.

"Please," he whined. "Don't."

Sebastian pressed himself up and beckoned for one of his lovers. Brad's light-wash jeans stepped into view at the head of the table. He pressed his erection to Isaac's cheek and kissed Sebastian, loud and messy.

The kiss above Isaac broke just long enough for Sebastian to say, "I want you to come down his throat." Then the noises of kissing resumed, even as Brad fumbled at his button fly, shoving his underwear aside. He grabbed a fistful of Isaac's hair, pulled Isaac's mouth toward his cock. The kissing kept going. Brad moved with shallow, short thrusts, already coating the back of Isaac's tongue in pre-come.

Kyril's massive cock breached Isaac's entrance, and even having already been fucked, even with a fistful of lube, he was nearly torn open. He cried out around Brad's cock, and Brad's thumb brushed his cheekbone. Sebastian wrapped his hand around Isaac's throat, providing resistance every time Isaac swallowed.

Kyril's hands were on either side of his belly, between Sebatian's thighs. He fucked into Isaac brutally, stretching him open, dragging along his prostate with such depth that the pressure never stopped. Sebastian rolled around his cock, clenching and fluttering. Brad kept thrusting, going deeper, pressing against the back of his throat.

"I'm hungry," Sebastian whispered, and Brad answered something soft Isaac couldn't hear. They came closer together, so all Isaac could see was the pale lines of Brad's hips, the drape of his long necklaces brushing Isaac's face.

Brad cried out with pleasure as Sebastian's fangs sliced into his neck. Blood dripped down his stomach. His cock jumped against Isaac's tongue. Isaac opened his throat just as Brad climaxed, whimpering and bucking.

Brad pulled out, and Isaac gasped for breath. The smell of blood overtook everything, rich and sweet and heady. Kyril kept fucking, his hand around Sebastian's cock, and Sebastian was riding, too, up and down on Isaac, shouting his pleasure. He grabbed Isaac's jaw and pushed two bloody fingers into his mouth. Brad's blood was dark, powerful. Isaac tried to suck, but he couldn't get his mouth to close.

"I'm so close," Sebastian said. "Come in me, lamb." He clenched down around Isaac, but every inch of Isaac's skin was burning. It was too much. Kyril was still inside him, deeper and harder, and even when Isaac closed his eyes, there was nothing but the overwhelming tsunami of sensations.

Kyril spent inside Isaac, burning hot.

Sebastian clenched down around him, coming into Kyril's hand.

Heels clicked against the tile. Holly's coconut and cinnamon scent reached him, clean and clear, his guiding light. She hovered, shimmering and golden above him.

She kissed him gently.

"It's time to finish, my sweet," she said, and Isaac obeyed with such force the room went white with light.

Isaac was shaking too much to move. Sebastian's hands dug into his chest as he levered himself off. His and Isaac's mingled come cooled against his belly, and when he tried to sit, he remembered that he was still manacled to the table.

Sebastian pressed a kiss to the corner of Isaac's mouth, and he cringed away. Every nerve had been sanded raw, and now he was aware of the ache in his shoulder, the smell of blood in the room, the chafe of leather against his jaw.

Holly said something.

He gathered himself and tried to listen.

"Did you get what you needed?"

"More than enough," Sebastian was saying. "Let's go into my office."

Fabric rustled.

Isaac rolled his head to watch Sebastian pulling his frothy robe around himself.

Holly met Isaac's eyes. There was blood on her face, her fangs obvious between her parted lips. Even her touch would be too much, but he wanted it anyway.

Brad moved between them, forcing them to break their eye contact, and bent.

Isaac's manacles dropped.

"Easy, bud," Kyril said softly. He loomed over Isaac and scooped him up in his arms. He was burning hot. Isaac didn't get to feel warm very often. He couldn't remember ever being carried like this, cradled in strong arms.

They left the stage for a back hallway. Holly didn't follow them.

They came to a private room with a huge bed. Kyril put him down on the comforter, and Isaac let out an involuntary whimper at the loss of body heat.

"You want us to stay?" Brad asked.

"Please," Isaac mumbled. Even the single word came out oddly garbled.

The two men stripped each other out of the remnants of their clothing, then rolled Isaac into the blankets. They lay down on either side of him, a firm pressure rather than skin on skin. Isaac's eyes slipped shut. He was hollowed out, his thighs still throbbing with the aftershocks of orgasm.

Kyril was a solid furnace beside him. There was something irreplaceable about the warmth of a person, the pumping of blood. When Brad shifted, his hair brushed against the pillow, but his breathing was so low Isaac had to strain to hear it over Kyril's heartbeat. It settled Isaac's frayed nerves, brought him to some level of comfort a dead body couldn't bring itself.

Kyril put a heavy hand just over his heart. "Go to sleep," he rumbled.

Isaac must have obeyed because he woke to the sound of Holly's heels on the carpet. She stood in the doorway, and the two men slid from the bed and grabbed for their clothes. Her eyes were glowing.

"I found her," she said. "Are you ready for another road trip?"

Good, Evil, Ex

Taliesin Owens

5 + 1 things fic, body modification, break-up (past), breast play, clitoral fingering, cunnilingus, dimension jumping, enemies to lovers, f/f/nb, face sitting, fantasy with technology, first kiss, hand job, immortal, magic use, non-binary, pining (mutual), present tense, second chances, third person (alternating) point of view, vaginal fingering, veteran

I.

Luce hasn't even made it to the front door when they feel the blade at their back. It's a nasty, slim, serrated thing—a field knife from the Qasti Republic, if Luce isn't mistaken. The edge pressing through their silk shirt feels like it's in impeccable condition despite being sixteen hundred years old. They give a wry, humorless smile over their shoulder.

"Will it matter if I say I don't want a fight?" Luce feels the hand on the knife tighten, feels the shift of direction and preparedness, but it doesn't press any farther into their skin.

"Give me a single reason I should believe you." Jana's voice is low, furious, and exhausted. The reflex to tease and goad her tickles Luce's throat, but they didn't come here to rehash centuries-old battles.

They raise their hands in surrender. "I want to help you get Ari back."

The silence is deafening. Luce counts it instinctively as it ticks on. Ten seconds. Twenty. Thirty. Rabbits rustle in the bushes of the garden two houses down. Fifty seconds. A television in the house across the street broadcasts the news. Ninety seconds.

At the two-minute mark, Jana finally grits out an answer: "In. Side."

Luce nods and steps, slowly, letting Jana anticipate the movement. The room they enter is clean but barren. Luce gets only a moment's view of it before Jana grabs their arm, spins them around, and slams them against the wall. The knife lands on their throat. Luce lets it happen. Jana's face fills their vision, olive skin and thick brown hair and eyes Luce memorized millennia ago.

"Ari," Jana says shortly.

"Ari."

"You need two knights of the Bytherean Empire to unlock the gate to the Other."

"Well." Luce withdraws a ring from their pocket and holds it up for Jana's inspection. "Good thing I came, then."

Jana's eyes flick from Luce, to the ring, then back to Luce. The knife wavers. *I could disarm her now*. The thought is instinctual. *Irrelevant*.

"You weren't…stripped, somehow?"

Luce expected the question, which is the only reason they manage not to laugh. "*How*?" they say. "They must have told you—when you bind yourself to the Exalted Emperor, it's permanent. Nothing can undo it, not even when the Exalted Ass himself has been dead for three thousand years." They turn the ring in their hands, rubbing over the sharp, blazing white gem at its center. "It doesn't matter that we spent centuries trying to kill each other. Neither of us could undo that binding. Why do you think I hated him so much?"

Jana's knife lowers at last. Her face is doing something complicated as she processes that information. She never has been good at hiding her emotions.

"Why would you want to help me do anything?" she asks. "Why now?"

Luce purses their lips. "It's not for you, it's for Ari. I'm just not fool enough to think it's me she'd be coming back for." Their hand darts down, seizes Jana's, and drags the knife's point back to their throat. "So what's it gonna be, butterfly?"

Jana yanks the knife away and holds out an empty hand. "Give me your ring," Jana demands.

Luce blinks at her. "*What*?"

"Your soulring. Give it to me."

Luce recoils. "That's— You can't just—"

"You say you want to help Ari. Fine. I guess I believe that. I know we have"—Jana winces—"similar histories, there. But." She glares. "I have no guarantee you won't stab me in the back as soon as we pull her over. You have my word that I won't use it unless you try to kill me. And you know I keep my promises."

Luce swallows the fury trying to claw out of them in lightning and hungry shadow. With bone-deep reluctance, they hold out their hand.

Jana plucks the ring out of it and drops it in a pocket. "So. Truce?"

Luce grits their teeth and takes Jana's hand. "Truce. Let's get Ari back."

2.

There's something insurmountably bizarre, Jana thinks, about seeing the erstwhile Lord of the Wastes scrunched into the blue-gray, musty seat of a cross-country bus. Their legs are too long to fit comfortably, knees pressing into the seat in front of them and slowly gaining the criss-cross imprint of the netted seat-back pocket. Jana watches their mouth—their lips are so Wastes-damned red; people used to whisper that the Dark Lord smeared blood on his mouth for lipstick—for a heartbeat too long. Luce doesn't seem to notice, their eyes fixed on the landscape passing outside. They'd left the city an hour ago; now there's nothing but thin lines of trees interrupted by gas stations and fast-food restaurants.

"Was this necessary?" Luce doesn't turn, only hisses the question out between their teeth as if they're incapable of holding it back.

Jana lets herself smirk. "What?" she asks innocently.

Luce *does* turn their head at that, green eyes flaring with restrained magic. "You're *enjoying* this," they accuse.

"It's the path to the gate," Jana protests.

"Shitballs it is." Luce's shoulders hunch inward. "We couldn't have flown?"

"There's a ritual. The gate can only be reached if you approach by 'the pilgrim's path,' " Jana says. "Nothing more pilgrim-like than a public bus."

Luce knocks their head into the back of the seat. "The Emperor and his *stupid* rituals."

"Don't like rubbing elbows with the peasants, *Highness*?"

"No, I'm just going to die of boredom before we get there." They stretch dramatically in the chair. "Eight millennia of existence, crumbled to dust because I only had an Empire soldier to talk to for five days. Tragic, really."

Jana feels offended despite herself. "I can be interesting!"

"Oh?" Luce raises their eyebrows. "You're gonna entertain me?"

Jana feels as if all the blood in her body has rushed to her cheeks. She glares, more out of reflex than anger. Luce smirks, and Jana can't stop her eyes from straying to Luce's *fucking lips* again. Worse, Luce *notices*—their smirk widens.

"I can think of a few ways we could pass the time," they say, their voice soft and husky.

"Shut up," she says eloquently.

Luce snorts but subsides.

The bus rumbles on, leaving Jana to spin around in her own thoughts. She spends too much time in those these days, and she's never liked being left alone there. "Hey, Luce?" Jana's voice is quiet. Luce grunts a disinterested acknowledgment. "What if…?"

" 'What if' what, butterfly?"

Jana flinches at the old taunt. *The Emperor's favorite butterfly*. She takes a deep breath and plows on before Luce can notice. "What if she's not…Ari, anymore? It's been almost a thousand years. Should we even try to bring her back?"

Luce purses their lips. "It's not like she got locked shadeside. The Other isn't a torture dimension, it's just…other. A series of mirror worlds. They're strange and not always safe, but…" Luce shrugs. "If I know anyone who could take a millennia-long dip into the shifting threads of unrealized timelines and consider it a neat vacation, it's Ari. I was lucky she stayed with me for a whole year."

"A year?" Jana's voice is louder than she means it to be. "*One* year? I thought she was with you for a decade."

Luce looks away. "You know how she was. Is. Never sits still for long. Except with you, I guess."

Jana presses her eyes closed for a count of three and then snaps them open again. "You abandoned your last haven in the Wastes, nearly took my knife in your throat, offered me a truce, and handed me your *soul-ring*, all for a person you spent *one year* with?"

Luce pointedly looks out the window. Neon billboards advertising Isafall City's profusion of casinos flash by, the lights playing over their face. "Some people change you," Luce says. "Doesn't matter how long they have to do it."

They spend the rest of the bus ride in silence.

3.

Because Jana never outgrew her mother's frugality, she gets them a single room. The motel smells like industrial cleaner and instant coffee. The paint is peeling and the carpet is tired, but it's serviceable. They've both slept in worse conditions.

Luce casts a glance upward. "I'll take the bed with the mysterious ceiling stain above it."

Jana snorts. "Aren't you accommodating, sweetheart?"

The pain is instant, shocking, and familiar. It's hardly the first time Luce has punched Jana in the chest hard enough to crush a ribcage. It *is* the first time Jana has been so unprepared for it. Battle instincts flare up with a vengeance. Her ring springs to white-hot life on her hand, spreading spectral golden armor over her like a second skin as she goes through the wall in a crash of dust and bricks.

Luce emerges from the smashed wall in flickering shadow. Their eyes are full of lightning.

A battle that would take out half the city crackles in the air between them.

Jana makes a decision and, with immense effort, retracts the armor. With a forced, slow breath, she raises her hands. "*Truce*," she grits out.

It's a long moment before Luce blinks. The lightning flickers and dies. The shadows settle. They take the exact same forced breath. "Truce," they say furiously. "Don't ever. *Ever*. Call me that."

Something cold and nauseous trickles through Jana's veins. She nods slowly and lowers her hands. "I'm sorry."

Luce shuts their eyes. "*He* used to— I was his *good girl* for so *fucking* long. The Exalted Emperor's *good sweet girl.* Docile and obedient and flawless." They open their eyes. "After I left, I found a mage who could grow me a dick *just* to spite him."

Jana's eyebrows jump. Her eyes can't help the downward glance. "Did you keep it?" The words tumble out of her mouth ahead of any thought of saying them. She claps a hand to her mouth, heat rising in her cheeks. "Don't answer that, I didn't—" She stops, because Luce is *laughing.*

They step in close—too close—backing Jana up against the opposite wall of the alley. They lean in until Jana can feel their body heat. She's hyper aware of her own skin, of the slick of summer humidity, of the cool press of uneven bricks at her back, of Luce's breath ghosting over her forehead.

"Wanna find out?" they ask.

Jana's swallowed by heat, by the press of muscle, by the tantalizing ease of sliding her fingers down until—

"What the fuck?" The bewildered voice comes from the motel.

Jana jerks her hand away; Luce jumps back.

A woman wearing a shirt with the motel's logo peers through the hole in the wall. "*Hey*!"

Jana and Luce glance at each other.

"Run?" Luce asks.

"Run."

They flee the alley at speeds no human could match, sprinting down the maze of city streets until Jana can't contain herself any longer. She snorts, giggles, laughs and laughs until she has to stop running, leaning against the wall of a deserted corner and gasping.

Luce skids to a halt beside her. They look at Jana and dissolve into their own inelegant, snorting laughs.

It's nearly ten minutes before they both manage to hiccup their way to quiet.

Jana wipes her eyes. "We're a mess, huh?"

"Just figuring that out, butterfly?"

Jana shakes her head. "I really am sorry," she says, quieter. "You were… No one wanted to talk about…before."

" 'Any man who speaks of the Lord of the Waste's time as a knight shall lose his tongue,' " Luce quotes. "I know. I'm sorry for overreacting. For a second, I…forgot." The sun slips a fraction lower, forcing them to turn their face. "The bastard's dead and he still fucking haunts me."

"I..." Jana licks her lips. "You probably don't want to hear me say I understand."

"Do you?"

"I can still feel it if someone's standing on the ground where his throne once was. It's a deli now. Drives me nuts every afternoon."

"Yikes."

They're quiet for a moment. The city is dusty and dry with summer heat. The low murmur of crowds spills out of shops and restaurants, thrumming in Jana's ears. She presses her temple against the cool brick of the wall. "He really was an ass, huh?"

Luce makes a strangled noise, violent agreement choked by surprise. "That's a word for it," they manage.

"Why are we still fighting?"

Luce is sitting on the edge of the sidewalk, staring at their open hands.

With abrupt and terrifying certainty, Jana reaches into her pocket to retrieve Luce's soulring. She sits down on the curb next to them and presses it into their hand.

Luce startles and looks down, and their eyes widen.

"I trust you," Jana says.

Luce sucks in a breath. "Thought you learned not to."

"Yet here I am." She lets go but doesn't move away. Luce is so close that Jana can smell them, sharp and clean like the air just after lightning. She inhales. She wants to grasp that scent and hold it close, a reminder that being alive is supposed to be electric and interesting rather than a gray march of never-ending existence.

"Because of Ari?" Jana can hear trepidation in their voice, read the anxiety in the set of their shoulders.

"Because I'm tired of being enemies."

Luce turns their head, and suddenly their faces are much too close together. Jana can feel their breath, a brush of breeze in the warm air. "You're too damn nice for your own good."

"Maybe." Jana should pull away. She doesn't want to. "Maybe I'm just ready to let you kill me."

"Careful what you wish for." Luce sounds breathless. "I might...get ideas..."

Jana doesn't know how the gap between them closes. Luce's lips are chapped, and they taste like cheap coffee, and for the first time in millennia, Jana feels like she's soaring. Her hands catch Luce's blouse and crush it in her grip, dragging her closer. Luce's hand, hesitant at first, then bold, then eager, slides up the back of Jana's neck and tangles in her hair. The kiss is wild, desperate, delicious. It's the best fucking thing Jana's felt since Ari walked out on her.

Then Luce reels back and claps a hand over their mouth.

Jana blinks, her brain muddled.

They stare at one another for a heartbeat.

Luce scrambles to their feet. "I shouldn't've—I'm so sorry."

"No, I—"

"*Don't.*"

The air has turned stifling, choking the air out of Jana's lungs. "We need to find somewhere else to stay for the night," she says stiffly. "Let's just— Let's go."

At their next motel, they get separate rooms.

4.

"This is it?"

Luce can't blame Jana for sounding dubious; this little urban park with its browning grass and vague omnipresent stench of urine hardly seems like a doorway into the Other. The single bench is missing a slat and spattered white with bird shit. A sign declares the park to be closed after sundown, but the weeds and vines entwined through the wrought iron gates make it clear no one bothers locking up. The only nice thing is the fountain with a stone statue of a cheerfully coiled dragon spouting water from its mouth.

"It's not like anyone besides us knows it's important." Luce shrugs. "The Exalted Emperor's throne room is a deli. My dread fortress is in the middle of a fracking field. The gateway to the Other is, apparently, where every dog in the neighborhood comes to pee."

"There's supposed to be a guardian," Jana says, eyes bright with cautious magic-sight. "Defeating it is part of the ritual."

Luce glances around. Their eyes land on the fountain. It's a surprisingly accurate rendition of a juvenile Greenback acid-spitter. They climb onto the edge and stick out a finger, letting the water run over it.

"What are you doing?" Jana asks.

Ignoring her, they take another glance around the park. No one else is in sight. They grimace and reach for the magic in their ring, ignoring the nauseous burning in their throat. They can stand a trickle of it, and if Jana is right that this is part of a ritual, they don't want to fuck things up by using shade magic.

Then they roundhouse kick the dragon in the head.

It shatters beneath Luce's foot in a shower of rock dust and rusty pipe.

Jana yelps.

Water sprays wildly.

Luce lets it rain down on them; it cools rapidly as the faint, ancient magic dissipates. They hop off the fountain, grinning at Jana. "I defeated the guardian."

"You can't go around destroying public property!" Jana hisses.

Luce rolls their eyes. "I'll anonymously donate the funds to repair it. You ready?"

Jana bites her lip and looks shockingly young, so much like the fresh-faced soldier, armor unblemished by blood or battle, that Luce once faced. They reach out and take Jana's hand without thinking. Her touch burns. Luce can't tell if it's literal magical burning, or just their excruciating awareness of the warmth of Jana's hand in theirs, of what it means to stand here and hold her hand and look into her eyes and say, softly, *fondly*, "It's gonna be okay, you know," of what it means that Jana nods, a small, trusting movement. She squeezes Luce's hand, and Luce *burns* and says nothing.

They step to the gate. Luce reaches into their pocket and slips the ring onto their finger with a wince and a hiss. It pulses, turning her hand so cold it hurts.

"Let's do this fast, before Empire magic makes me lose my breakfast," they say.

Jana nods again. Each of them sets a hand on the gate and pulls, wrenching it free from a decade of weeds and vines. It groans, resists, and then, with a shriek of rust, it swings open. As one, they reach into the flood of magic and light.

5.

Even before Ari got trapped in the Other, she let the world carry her where it would. Her arrival in this endlessly shifting dimension, sliding between realities anytime someone sneezed, had only reinforced her natural inclinations. She hadn't come here on purpose, but it had felt serendipitous at first: a world that could never stand still, never bore her, never pin her down. Surely she had been made for this place.

After a couple centuries, Ari learned to be tired of movement.

She's hoped often enough that Jana or Luce might find a way to pry the gate open and drag her out. When she sees a familiar light split the air, awe and relief swell inside her with such a vengeance that, for a moment, she can't breathe. Then she sees two hands reaching toward her and wonders if she's finally gone mad. That Jana and Luce might work together to retrieve her was a fantasy she'd nursed only in the dark and quiet of 3 a.m. bedrooms.

She almost doesn't grab their hands in time.

She's hauled forward, through a head-swimming shift in gravity, and then her feet land on solid stone and both of them are in front of her. Different—Luce has changed their hair color again, and Jana isn't standing like a soldier—but unmistakably her Jana, her Luce, holding hands with each other, holding hands with Ari. A complete circle. The three of them stare at one another. The silence seems to quiver, stinging like the dissipating magic leaving sparks on Ari's skin. Weakly, she manages, "Well, I wasn't expecting this to be my welcoming party."

It's the wrong thing to say. It sends Luce tearing their hands free and stumbling back. Ari reaches out, calls "Wait!", and belatedly realizes that Jana has done the same. They glance at each other, then back at Luce.

Luce's feet have stalled. Their expression is perfectly blank.

"Let's…go back to the motel, at least?" Jana asks tentatively.

To Ari's astonishment, Luce nods.

It's an awkward, stilted walk to the motel where Jana and Luce spent the previous night. Because that was a thing they had done. Apparently.

When they reach the building, Luce splits off from them, muttering about grabbing food. Jana looks reluctant to let them go but tugs Ari into one of the motel rooms, and suddenly they're alone.

It's easy to fall back into Jana's arms. Later, there will have to be conversations, disclosures, confessions. For tonight, though, it's easy to be happy that she's home, that they are together, that there will be a later.

It's easy to clasp each other in a hug that Ari could have stayed in for a century, to tilt her head and meet Jana's lips in a kiss so achingly familiar that tears escape down her cheeks. It's easy, and comforting, and Ari wants to ascribe any hesitancy to the strangeness of their reunion. Except they're startled apart by the door opening. They turn to see Luce standing in the doorway, looking at the two of them, expression perfectly blank.

Violent potential lives in the air. For the length of Jana's sharp, startled inhale, Ari feels the hairs on the backs of her arms stand up with the crackle of anger and hurt and jealousy. Then Luce steps back and closes the door. Before Ari can turn to Jana, before she can say anything, Jana's fingers dig into her arm.

"Ari," she says, "can you—would you ask them to stay?" She swallows, nervous. "I don't…know if they'll listen to me."

Something fragile and hopeful blooms in Ari's chest. She leans in and kisses Jana's cheek.

"I'll be right back," she promises. "We both will."

+I.

"Luce?"

Ari's voice arrests Luce's progress. They stand in the hallway, frozen. The smell of industrial cleaner and cheap coffee fills their nostrils.

The touch on their elbow startles them even though it shouldn't. Adrenaline surges in their veins. They could send Ari flying through a wall. They could take down this entire hotel and everyone inside it, bury Jana and Ari in ten feet of rubble.

They don't want to do that.

They want to run away, but their feet won't fucking move.

"Are you leaving?"

Luce bites their tongue until they taste blood. The flavor is almost calming. They force a smile and tilt their head back for Ari to see it.

"Best I leave before Jana and I remember we want to kill each other. I'd hate to spoil the reunion."

Ari is quiet for a heart-aching moment. Her fingers curl more securely around Luce's elbow. Luce imagines them sliding, pressing along their bicep until the fabric of their sleeve bunches beneath the touch, imagines the heat of her breath on Luce's face as she says—nothing. She would say nothing.

Luce blinks hard.

"Come to bed with us."

The world tilts beneath Luce's feet. They stare, forced smile faltering, finally meeting Ari's gaze. Her eyes are deep and gentle and as serious as Luce has ever seen them.

"With you, sunflower?" Luce manages, voice high and thready. "Anytime. Anywhere. Call me and I'll come. But—" Their eyes flick toward the room where Jana is surely waiting. The wooden door with its pockmarked green paint looms, insurmountable. Luce shakes their head. "I—can't."

Ari's fingers do move then, not up Luce's arm but down. They slip into their hand, and Luce can't stop themselves from interlacing their fingers when Ari presses the suggestion into their palm.

"She wants you to," Ari whispers.

Luce has to shut their eyes, has to turn their face away, has to breathe sharply through their nose to hold back tears. Their hand squeezes Ari's reflexively, seeking comfort they have no right to take.

Ari squeezes back.

"I'm so tired of hurting people," Luce says. They want to say more, to explain or excuse or argue for Ari to let them go, but their throat closes.

There's a touch on their cheek.

Their eyes spring open as Ari leans in. For a panicked moment, they think she's going for a kiss, but all Ari does is press her forehead against Luce's. Their breath mingles, hot against Luce's cheeks.

"Hey, love. What if we don't want to hurt you either?"

Something in Luce melts. They lean into Ari as if her touch is the last thing in the world keeping them upright.

"Help me. Please?"

Ari snorts. She releases Luce's hand, but it's just so she can cup Luce's cheeks. "Took you Wastes-damned long enough to ask," she says, and she kisses them. Luce wants to dissolve into it: wants to steal that kiss, keep it for themselves forever, grab Ari's hand, and run away with her.

Running away never works, though, and it sounds exhausting. So when Ari breaks the kiss and tugs them back down the hall, they go.

Jana is sitting curled up on bed, knees half bent, picking at the sheets. Luce gets a glimpse of her mostly relaxed pose before Jana looks at the door and jolts upright at the sight of them. Luce wants to bolt again, but Ari is tugging them over the threshold. She pauses at the edge of the bed and looks sternly between the two of them.

"Both of you want the other to be here," she says. "I've been back for five minutes and that's already obvious. And I want you both here." She pauses. "You should know, I always thought you two would get along if you weren't so busy being stuck on opposite sides of an endless war."

"You're a hopeless optimist," Jana says.

Ari raises an eyebrow. "That's you, actually. I'm just the only one here with any perspective."

"We've gotten at least a few centuries of perspective by now, surely," Luce mutters.

Ari shoves their shoulder, pushing them forward until their knees hit the edge of the bed. Luce hesitates, and Ari's expression softens. "This doesn't have to be anything but tonight," Ari says. "No one's swearing any vows or making anyone promise to stay. But"—she glances between them—"I've missed *both* of you, and what's between you two now has been a long time coming. So why don't we just—take a night together?"

"You say that like it's easy," Jana groans. She glances up at Luce, hesitating. "But I—want that, if both of you do."

It's a cheap motel. Their surroundings should feel grander, stranger, more momentous. They shouldn't be having this conversation on over-bleached bed sheets with a bucket labeled "FREE ICE" in the corner. But maybe they can only have this conversation here, stripped of everything that once made them grand and strange. They're just three people who are tired, and lonely, and want so badly to touch.

They give a single, sharp nod. Then, with another long breath to steel themselves, they crawl onto the bed.

Jana's lips part just enough for Luce to see pink and white between them.

"May I—?" Luce's voice catches. They clear their throat. "May I kiss you?"

Jana nods.

Luce leans forward.

The kiss is quiet this time, missing the terror of their first. Jana's lips are soft against Luce's, welcoming. They come apart gently after a few seconds. Jana's eyes are still closed.

"Can I confess something?" she asks.

"Go ahead," Luce invites cautiously.

A flush creeps up Jana's neck and into her cheeks. "I used to have fantasies about losing battles to you and being, um, taken captive." Jana opens her eyes but keeps them downcast. "I imagined you…seducing me. Pinning me down and forcing me to want it. You. Making me beg. I guess it was—the only way I could imagine leaving, maybe? Even when I didn't think I wanted to. But also—" Their eyes dart up, dark and hungry. "I guess I'm saying I've always wanted to—you know. Oh, gods." She breaks off, covering her face with both hands. "Is that too weird?"

The world hangs suspended.

Luce is intimately aware of Ari holding her breath behind them. They grab Jana's wrists and pull her hands away from her face, pressing her down into the pillows. Jana goes, eyes widening.

"Has Ari told you that you're adorable when you're nervous?" Luce asks. "I'll gladly pin you down, butterfly."

Jana makes a sound, involuntary and breathy. Luce leans down and skims their mouth over Jana's again, more teeth than lips. The mattress dips as Ari slides onto the bed behind them, and her heat slides along Luce's back as she presses a featherlight kiss to their shoulder.

"And you?" Ari asks. "What do you want?"

Luce's breath hitches.

Ari goes still against their back. She always was too good at reading them.

"Most people assume the Lord of the Wastes simply takes whatever he wants," they say lightly.

Ari pinches their arm. "Don't be stupid."

Jana is frowning at both of them.

Luce tugs their arm free. "Look," they say, "we have time, right? So let me—let me make you both feel good, and then you can—" They inhale through their nose and force the words out. "Just, don't leave me alone afterward?"

Jana and Ari exchange a glance, and then Ari presses another kiss to the back of their neck.

"Well I, for once, have no plans to go anywhere," Ari says. Luce can feel her smile against their skin and, despite themselves, their lips quirk up. Jana's eyes still look doubtful. They flicker over Luce's face, searching.

"Don't do anything to be—accommodating," Jana says.

Luce shakes their head, brushing Jana's hair back from her temple. "I've spent a lot of time hurting you. Let me—do something else, for once?"

"All right," Jana says softly. She looks over Luce's shoulder at Ari, and a smile grows on her face, slow and mischievous and promising. "Hey, Ari. Want to tell them what I want?"

Luce feels Ari's shiver against their back, and it sends a thrill down their spine and to their groin. "I'd love to," Ari purrs, and then her lips are against Luce's ear, teeth brushing along the shell of cartilage as she speaks. "You all right with taking some pointers?"

Luce doesn't trust themselves to speak. They just nod.

Ari presses closer against their back and whispers, "Get her shirt off."

Luce's fingers feel clumsy as they find the hem of Jana's shirt. They tug upward, sliding it up the gentle curve of her belly and over her ribs.

Jana wiggles, helping, letting the shirt slide up her back. She has to sit halfway up to let Luce pull the cotton T-shirt—amazing invention, Luce's brain offers, distracted and desperate, thinking of all the buttons and ties they used to have to undo—over her head and off her arms. Then she's on the bed half bare, in only denim shorts, her arms flung on the pillows over her head and her breasts rising and falling with each breath.

It's all Luce can do not to immediately yank her pants off too.

"She likes teeth as much as you do," Ari says in their ear, and Luce doesn't need more prompting. They reposition themselves, swinging a leg over to straddle Jana's hips, and then they lean down. They take one of Jana's nipples in their mouth and run their tongue lovingly around her areola, reveling in the taste of her, soft and warm and growing harder by the second. They press their teeth into the skin—gently, so gently, the barest reminder of their existence—and Jana gasps so loud that Luce's crotch seizes with heat.

"Fuck—no, don't stop—don't you *dare* stop—"

Luce shifts, lifting their mouth off Jana's breast to kiss their way up her sternum. Jana arches in response. Luce's hand finds the nipple they had been sucking and massages it, twisting it gently between their fingertips until Jana keens. They suck a bruise into the skin above Jana's collarbone as Jana's hands twist in the pillowcase. They bury their teeth into the skin, biting down, not hard enough to draw blood but hard enough to leave a mark, and Jana shouts.

Luce lifts their head. "Something you wanted to say to me, butterfly?"

Jana's eyes are hazy with desire. "Please." She squirms, legs kicking out. "Please touch me, I want—I want you to touch me."

"Not yet," Ari says. She sounds breathier than before. Luce glances over their shoulder; Ari has undone the zipper at the front of her pants and has one hand in her underwear. She tilts her head at Luce and smiles faintly. "This all right?" she asks.

"More than all right," Luce says. They can't tear their eyes away from the motion of Ari's hand, from the growing wet spot shadowing the bottom of the fabric, but a harsh inhale from Jana draws their attention back. They run a finger around the edge of one of Jana's nipples. "What should I do with you now?" they ask. Jana whines, and Luce grins. "How far can you get with just touch to these?"

They lean down again, a hand massaging one of Jana's breasts and their mouth on the other. They kiss a circle around her nipple, sometimes teasing with teeth, sometimes pressing nothing but soft lips to her skin. Luce can hear Ari's breaths getting heavier, can almost hear the slide of her folds parting, of the wet stretch as she fits another knuckle inside. They keep their focus on Jana's chest, on the way it's heaving beneath them, on the increasingly incoherent pleas not to stop. It fills Luce's head, chases everything else away. Their hand squeezes Jana's breast. It fits perfectly, like it was made for their hand, warm and eager under their touch. Then Ari's voice comes, ragged with need.

"Wait," she says. "Don't let her come yet."

Luce pulls off Jana. She's flushed and panting, her eyes hooded, and she sends a glare toward Ari.

"You're not allowed—to still know me this well—when we haven't slept together—in centuries," Jana pants. Luce glances at Ari, sees her flick the bottom of Jana's foot, which makes her yelp.

Ari gives her a wicked grin. "You invited me to coach," she says innocently. "I'm just doing my best." She sets a hand on Luce's shoulder and guides them backward, sitting on Jana's legs. "Let's get those pants off now."

Luce is too eager to do a properly seductive job of it. They tug the zipper down impatiently. Jana, fortunately, is just as eager, kicking the pants and soaked underwear the rest of the way off as soon as Luce has tugged them past her thighs. Meanwhile, Ari slides off the bed and strips her own clothes, efficient and eager, until she's standing naked beside the bed.

Luce's eyes are fixed between Jana's legs, on the wiry curls of hair and the pink skin peeking out like a promise.

Ari crouches down and kisses the corner of Jana's mouth. Jana turns to meet the kiss open-mouthed, sloppy and hungry, and Luce—isn't jealous. They'd spent so many nights imagining Jana and Ari together, angry without outlet or direction, not sure which of them they were envying, that it knocks them sideways to realize nothing about this hurts. Jana and Ari break apart, and Ari traces the corner of Jana's mouth with a finger. She looks up at Luce.

"If you don't mind if I join in," she says slowly, "Jana is good at multitasking." Her eyes flick down to Jana's open legs. "I know she'd appreciate your mouth."

The groan of desire that Jana makes is all the assurance Luce needs. They shift farther back, tucking their arms beneath Jana's legs, lifting them to get a better angle. Ari climbs back onto the bed, swings a leg over Jana's head, and lowers herself onto her face.

Luce can't see Jana's face, but they can see Jana's hands grip the stretch-marked skin of Ari's legs, fingers digging in until the skin pinks and pales beneath her grip. They can see the arch of her throat as she finds the best angle. They can hear the wet noises as Jana's tongue explores the already dripping folds and Ari's answering groan. Their gaze travels up to find Ari's gaze fixed, hot and heavy, not on Jana, but on Luce.

"Go on," Ari whispers. "Please?" The last word breaks from a command into a whine, and Luce would have hurled themselves into the Emperor's eternal fires if Ari had asked.

They lower their gaze back to Jana's cunt, pink and wet and so inviting. They go slowly, only pressing the gentlest, most teasing of kisses along the inside of her thighs, using a thumb to stroke away the tangles of hair and kiss up one edge and then the other. Jana's thighs tense, rock-hard on either side of them. Luce remembers, vividly, those same thighs pinning her in battlefield mud, the strength behind them. They move their lips up, finding the painfully hard nub of her clit with their tongue, and give it a tiny, gentle suck. Ari's weight barely muffles the filthy noise Jana makes. Her body spasms on the bed. Luce sucks harder, grazing her teeth over Jana's skin.

They feel her orgasm in the pulsing of her cunt, in the spilling slick that soaks over Jana's thighs and Luce's chin, in the way Jana's legs cross and lock behind Luce's head. Adrenaline and instinct drive a single spike of panic through Luce before they realize Jana is shaking with the effort of holding back her strength. In a rush of tenderness, they press a hand to the outside of Jana's leg, stroking.

Jana groans. Her legs lock tighter, then she relaxes. Her cunt is still pulsing with aftershocks. Luce looks up and sees Ari was right about her skill at multitasking: her movements are more languid now, but she's clearly still working over Ari's cunt. Ari's pupils are blown so wide that Luce can see no brown in her gaze. Her hips rock back and forth gently, grinding down on Jana's mouth. Luce tears their gaze away, shifting themselves up and forward enough to press soothing kisses along Jana's happy trail, up to her bellybutton. They mouth softly at her stomach, feeling the shuddering muscles.

"Fuck," Ari's voice says above them. "Fuck I— I didn't— Oh *fuck*." She moans. Luce raises their eyes to stare as she orgasms, enraptured at the mingling sweat and escaped tears sliding down her cheeks. When the height of it is over, she shifts back, sitting on the pillows and letting Jana pull her head free.

For a moment, there is only the sound of heavy breathing.

Ari takes a deep breath and speaks again, voice ragged. "I knew that I'd enjoy—this, with both of you. But I didn't realize…" Her fingers trail through Jana's hair. Jana leans into the touch. "I've missed you both so much. I'm glad I didn't have to choose who I came home to."

Luce shrinks away. That sense of invasion they'd had when they saw Jana and Ari kissing returns, twisting in the pit of their stomach. The two of them sitting together on the bed look so peaceful. Before they can spiral further, though, Jana leans forward and snatches their hand.

"I'm starting to know that look." Her voice is hoarse but no less fierce for it. "She *just said* both of us, you idiot." Jana's hand is so tight around Luce's that Luce is worried she'll break fingers. They twist the grip, forcing Jana's hold to loosen, and interlaces their fingers with hers.

"I know," they make themselves say. Maybe it's a lie, but they meet Ari's gaze again and tension bleeds out of their shoulders. "I know," they repeat.

Jana squeezes their hand in response. "So now," Jana says, "what do *you* want?"

Luce considers, eyes drifting to their clasped hands. They bite their lip and look down at the bedsheet.

"Would you…hold me? Just hold onto me while Ari— You know what I like." They raise their eyes and find the softest expression they've ever seen on Jana's face.

"Of course," she says.

There's a couple moments of repositioning. Luce unbuttons, shimmies out of their pants, and discards their underwear.

Jana's eyes dart downward and then back up with a sly smile. "So you *did* keep the dick."

Ari's eyebrows raise. "Did you tell her the story with the mermaid or the one where you won it in a card game?"

"I told her the truth," they mutter, ears burning.

"I want to hear the mermaid one, though," Jana says, and Luce entertains the idea of collapsing the motel after all. Jana pokes them. "I'm kidding. Get up here."

Jana settles herself against the headboard. After a moment of hesitation, Luce turns around and leans their back against Jana's chest. She's warm, still sweaty. Her arms hover, uncertain. Luce takes Jana's hands and guides them to rest on their stomach. They look up to see Ari sitting at the end of the bed, waiting for them to get settled.

"Keep it simple," they say.

Ari nods. She rubs her thumb and two fingers together, and Luce catches the spark of a minor spell. Ari's hand, when she brings it to Luce's cock, is slippery with oil.

There's silence as Ari coaxes Luce's erection to full hardness with patient movements. Luce leans back into the reassurance of Jana's heat behind them, the feeling of her chest rising and falling with each breath, the steady beat of her heart. They let their eyes drift to half-mast.

"This is…peaceful."

The words slip out, murmured into the quiet in a moment of unaccustomed laxity.

Jana's laugh is breathy and surprising in their ear. "Isn't that ironic?"

Luce nods, the motion slow. Ari's hand runs up and down their cock, long, slow strokes, tugging just to the edge of pressure and then sliding her hand back down with the barest tickle. Their breath staggers on the next inhale. Jana's hands press against their stomach.

"Ari," Luce says. Ari's hand pauses. Luce's hand wanders down the bed and fists in the sheet. "You said you came *home*."

Ari's lips part slightly. Her eyes drop. "Even I got tired of wandering eventually."

"I can't offer you— I abandoned my keep," Luce says. "I'm homeless."

"Is this really the conversation you want to have with your dick that hard?" Jana's voice is an amused rumble against Luce's back. "We can if you want, but—"

Luce lets out a weak laugh and releases the bedsheet to press a hand over their eyes. "You're right, I'm…thinking too far ahead." They hesitantly reach for Jana's wrist. Jana doesn't flinch, so they leave their hand there. "Just tonight, right?"

"One thing at a time," Ari says. "Tonight first." Her hand returns to Luce's cock. She gives the head a gentle, playful pinch, just enough to make Luce squirm. "This first."

Luce nods.

Ari returns to stroking, up and down, up and down, *squeeze*, pause, and up and down again. They sigh, their head dropping into the crook of Jana's shoulder. Jana gently, hesitantly, nuzzles against Luce's temple.

"You'll have to teach me what to say," Jana whispers, just to them. Ari's rhythm is picking up. Luce's hips buck, canting upward, chasing the friction. "You'll have to tell me what you like and what's got bad memories attached to it. But I want you to know—" She's harder to hear as the roar of blood builds in Luce's ear in tandem with the strain in their cock, as Ari shifts forward and presses a knee into Luce's crotch, adding to the building pressure, but they cling to Jana's words with all their might. "—I want you to know that you've made me feel more alive than I have for centuries, and I don't want tonight to be the last time."

The orgasm is so sudden it almost hurts. They cry out, scrabbling desperately at Jana's arms. Ari recovers from her surprise in time to stroke them through the aftermath, her hand gentle as it soothes the twitches of Luce's softening cock, as she moves from there to their hip bone, as she leans forward and presses the softest kiss Luce has ever tasted to their lips. She stays there, breath mingling with Luce's, all three of their heads close enough to touch.

"Don't go," Ari pleads. "Either of you. I'm sure it will be messy, but—don't go."

Luce lets go of Jana's arms to reach up and circle their arms around Ari. They pull her down against their chest and hold her tight.

"I don't want to," they say. "I'm—tired of running away."

"And I'm tired of being lonely," Jana says.

"So, are we all going back to that sad, empty house Jana has?" Luce asks.

Ari shakes her head. "Somewhere new," she suggests.

"New sounds good," Jana agrees.

Luce runs a hand up Ari's back, learning the shape of her afresh. "I'd like that," they say.

Ari hums, pleased, and nuzzles into Luce's chest. "Tomorrow, then. Tomorrow we all start over."

Index

About the Authors

Alex Bauer

Born and raised in the Wisconsin northwoods, Alex Bauer is a part-time author and full-time menace. When he's not writing, he can be found communing with his animals via prolonged eye contact and inhuman chittering. Summoning him is as easy as leaving a cup of coffee unattended (or rolling a shiny object past his hidey-hole).

He developed a passion for books and writing in early childhood, concerning librarians and classmates alike with the number of books he could devour in any given week. Ever since, he's endeavored to channel that passion (and his queer experience) into his own creative work.

He is a proud multi-fandom multi-shipper. His favorite characters are mostly powerful, wet-cat-energy protagonists who would rather be anywhere else but their current story. While he started out as a *Naruto* fiend, his current favorite fandoms include *Trigun*, *Bungou Stray Dogs*, *Voltron: Legendary Defender*, and *Boku no Hero Academia*.

enchantedsleeper

enchantedsleeper is a writer and general fandom enthusiast from the UK who has been knocking around the internet and fandom since 2004-ish. She came to fandom through anime and manga and reading second-person quizzes on Quizilla before discovering Fanfiction.net and, later, AO3. She mainly creates fanfic but has also dabbled in fanart, cosplay, fancrafts, fanvids, and meta throughout her time in fandom.

She previously published an essay in Ofic Magazine, "From Anime to (Quiz)Zilla: A fandom origin story," about her history with fandom and how it has shaped her life. This is her first published original fiction.

D. A. Hernández

An author who works as a teacher, reads fanfiction compulsively, gets inspiration from her weird dreams, lives for long naps, and once in a while writes a story or two. Find her original stories in the Duck Prints Press anthologies *She Wears the Midnight Crown* and *Aim for the Heart*.

ilgaksu

Full-time fandom cryptid, Furby enthusiast, and the human embodiment of that one gif of Elmo on fire, ilgaksu was born and raised in an undisclosed location, living in several others, and now currently residing in [REDACTED]. Their interests include collecting haunted toys, using their artistic practice as an excuse to forget to do their laundry, and playing with fictional men like Bratz dolls. They have not unclenched their jaw yet today, but they do remember to drink lots of water.

Mina Kramek

Mina has been looking through archways and in tree hollows for a portal to another world since she was six years old, and discovered along the way that she loves exploring this world almost as much. The first stories she ever told were fairy-tale retellings, and she still has a soft spot for them. She's been writing fanfiction since long before she knew what it was but finished a story for the first time in 2020 after watching *The Untamed* three times in a row. Since then, she's posted about 750k worth of stories on AO3 and modded a Big Bang. She would always rather be sipping wine by a river and learning the history of somewhere she's never been before, but staying home with her cats, a book, or the occasional crochet project is pretty good too.

Eliot Lovell

Eliot (they/them) is a queer author from the UK who has been obsessed with writing stories for as long as they can remember. Even though they can't swim, they love living close to the sea and, on the rare instance they're not actually writing, they can invariably be found thinking about bees.

Lyonel Loy

Lifelong maladaptive daydreamer, finally working up the courage to write those daydreams down. Spends time cosplaying as a Responsible Adult With A Job.

Alec J. Marsh

Alec lives in the Pacific Northwest, where they write romantic adult fantasy and self-indulgent fanfiction. They make candles inspired by their favorite characters.

K. Martin

K. Martin is a queer disabled writer from Canada. She has a degree in English & Contemporary Studies and a gold medal in Faculty of Arts from WLU. Previously, she's had poetry published in ImageOutWrite Vol. 5, short fiction in Torquere's *Harvest Moon* anthology, and erotic flash fiction in NSP's *Erato* anthology. When not writing fanfiction or the final draft of her novel, she's on Tumblr as @queerfictionwriter or talking about writing over on Patreon.com/K'sCorner.

Cedar D. McCafferty-Svec

Cedar D. McCafferty-Svec has over two decades of writing experience, a bachelor's degree focusing in English and Theater, and a passionate love for telling stories. He is fascinated by fantasy and sci-fi and grew up adamantly wanting to be a dragon. Cedar enjoys experimental writing, attempting shorter works, and has an unfortunate knack for stumbling on stories that could be entire sagas. He lives happily with his life partners and menagerie of animals in the Midwest and hopes to share his writing far and wide.

YF Ollwell

YF Ollwell (he/him and she/her) is a queer transmasculine writer, artist, and graduate student currently located in sunny California. He has been writing both original work and fanfiction for over a decade, posting predominantly in horror and anime fandoms but has only recently began publishing his original work as well. She's a sucker for historical settings and loves to read and write strange interactions between complicated queer characters, especially in or about the horror genre she's devoted most of her life and study to. When not writing for work or play, YF can be found experimenting with new art modes, watching grindhouse movies, or re-reading *The Stand* for the seventh time.

Taliesin Owens

Taliesin is a queer author who grew up bouncing around Europe and the US and currently calls Chicago home. They've been writing stories since they had to pester their mom to help them transcribe their words on the family desktop computer. After half a million words of posted fanfiction and a lot of kind encouragement from friends and strangers, they are delighted to be making their publishing debut with Duck Prints Press. They work as a stage manager, dog walker, bartender, and hold a Master's degree in humanities with a focus in literature. No amount of school or chaotic array of part-time jobs has yet managed to stop them from reading and writing voraciously. They can also occasionally be found doing calligraphy, baking, getting really excited about Shakespeare, or walking out to look at the lake because everything seems a little better when you can stand at the edge of the water for a while.

E. K. Victor

E. K. Victor, aka Smehur (they/them), is a queer writer, artist, and stargazer. They have been writing fanfiction for fifteen years (mostly for *Mass Effect*, but also *The Elder Scrolls* and, recently, *Darksiders*), and original fiction for about half as long. Working with Duck Prints Press is their first foray into traditional publishing.

In one way or another, Smehur's fiction is always about troubled m/m relationships where deception, jealousy, mental illness, and/or the barriers in understanding between neurotypical and neurodivergent characters are balanced by love, loyalty, or, sometimes, obsession. Their favorite trope is second chances.

Outside their creative pursuits, Smehur is a low-energy creature who shies from company and enjoys reading, gardening, and gaming. Increasingly, they worry that the world will end before they get to tell it all their tales.

Dei Walker

Dei Walker (she/her) is a queer New Englander abroad, having spent almost half her life overseas. She currently lives with her family in Beijing, China. When she isn't writing, she can be found knitting, scuba diving, or playing games (video or tabletop).

Terra P. Waters

Terra is a scientist by day who lives in the Pacific Northwest with her family. She has been writing fiction as long as she can remember, and has always told her partner of 17 years that if she wasn't a scientist, she would be an author. During grad school, she discovered fanfiction and immediately began writing her own. After many years and several fandoms (including *Teen Wolf*, *Hawaii Five-0*, and *Stranger Things*), she returned to writing original fiction. To date, she has self-published two novellas in a '90s-nostalgia polyamory comedy series and has drafted two YA/NA sci-fi novels. When not doing science or writing, you can find Terra indulging her yarn addiction and knitting.

Premium Backers List

Our Top-Tier Patreon Backers

Anonymous
A Taylor
Sam Brown
Tina Houck
jumblejen
Aria L
Karen Welborn

Our Premium Kickstarter Supporters

Anonymous
Caelan and Reili
JujYFru1T (aka Julia)
Bryn Green-Lowe
Marina H
Kimberly M. Lowe
Leo Otherland
Gary Phillips
Nova/Lilith Vollmers
Rachael L. Young
Babak Zarin

About Duck Prints Press LLC

Duck Prints Press LLC is an independent publisher based in New York State. Our founding vision is to help fanfiction authors navigate the complex process of bringing their original works from first draft to print, culminating in publishing their work under our imprint. We are particularly dedicated to working with queer authors and publishing stories featuring characters from across the LGBTQIA+ spectrum.

Become a Duck Prints Press Patron by backing us on Patreon!

Find us online at our website, **duckprintspress.com**, or on social media:
Bluesky: duckprintspress
Dreamwidth: duckprintspress.dreamwidth.org
Facebook: duckprintspress
Instagram: duckprintspress
Mastodon: @dppunforth
Patreon: duckprintspress
Pillowfort: duckprintspress
Pinterest: duckprintspress
TikTok: @duckprintspress
Tumblr: duckprintspress

Goodreads: https://www.goodreads.com/user/show/129902473-duck-prints-press-llc
Storygraph: https://app.thestorygraph.com/profile/unforth

www.ingramcontent.com/pod-product-compliance
Lightning Source LLC
Chambersburg PA
CBHW060942030726
47503CB00003B/691

* 9 7 8 1 9 6 2 4 8 8 1 5 0 *